LAUREL'S QUEST

By Nancy M Bell

Amazon print ISBN 978-1-77299-287-8

BWL
Books We Love
A quality publisher of genre fiction.
Airdrie Alberta

Cover Art Michelle Lee

Dedication

For Hamish Miller, whose inspirational work, *The Sun and The Serpent*, helped me show Laurel the way. Last, but certainly not least, my husband, Doug.

* * *

The May Day song sung at Padstow is an old traditional folk song. The story of St. Tues and Uther is my retelling of a Cornish myth. All other verse and the tin mine story are the original work of the author

For Ella
I hope you enjoy the journey
Nancy M Bell.

Chapter One

It's a Long Way From Home

Laurel curled up tighter on the train seat and pressed her face against the window. The passing countryside unfolding before her was a blur, as was the blue shine of the sea to the west. She swallowed hard and hoped she wouldn't embarrass herself by hurling. *What if Mom gets worse or dies while I'm in Penzance?* Two fat tears crawled down her cheeks, and she squeezed her eyes shut to stop more from falling.

It sucked being on a train in a strange country going farther away from home with each annoying clack of the wheels. A huge wave of desolation swept through her and threatened to break the slim hold she kept on her emotions.

Worms of anxiety twisted through her stomach and she struggled to breathe normally. Why did she ever agree to visit her mother's friend in England? It seemed like such a great adventure when Mom suggested it. Everything was already arranged when the doctors discovered the cancer. Dad insisted she take the trip as planned. He just kept saying Mom would be better soon. But, what if she wasn't? Laurel smacked her fist on her blue jean clad thigh. *I should be with her!*

A boy with sandy blond hair dropped a backpack onto the seat opposite her. "This one's free, inni't?" He indicated the window seat.

She shook her head, not trusting herself to speak.

"Excellent!" he exclaimed. With an easy motion he flung the backpack into the overhead rack before he hurled himself into the seat, looking out the window with obvious delight.

"Nothing like heading home!" he said with a grin that revealed uneven white teeth.

Laurel studied him through the curtain of her hair. He was about her age, she guessed, maybe a little older. His eyes were a vivid blue above prominent cheekbones.

Without taking his eyes from the window, he said, "Name's Coll. What's yours?"

The way he pronounced the name made it sound like *kawl. Coll, what kind of a name is Coll?* She would never get used to the odd-sounding British names. No one she knew in Canada was named Cedric, or Sebastian, or *Coll.* She put her feet back on the floor before she answered Coll, who was clearly waiting for her to speak.

"Hi, I'm Laurel. I'm headed to Penzance. Are you from around there?"

"Born and bred, lived in Penzance all my life."

"Is there much to do there? I'm visiting a friend of my mother's for a little while."

Suddenly very aware of the scuffed boots on her feet and her long legs encased in faded, worn blue jeans, she realized it was painfully obvious she was not from Britain.

"Where ya from?" he asked, his brow wrinkled in thought. "You don't sound quite like a Yank, but I don't know."

She sat up straighter and looked sternly at the boy across from her. Her smoky grey eyes met his levelly.

"I'm Canadian." Laurel spoke with more heat than she intended.

On the long plane ride, the couple seated beside her assumed she was an American. When they learned she was from Canada, they wanted to know if she knew anyone in Toronto. As if! Alberta was a long way from Ontario.

"North of the forty-ninth parallel," she continued, "and no, I don't know anyone from Toronto!"

"Okay, sorry." Coll held up his hands in surrender. "Who are you staying with in Penzance? Bet I know them. I know everyone in Penzance."

"Sarie Waters, she's an old friend of my family. I've never met her before."

"Oh, Sarie, you'll get on fine with her." He paused. "You do like horses, don't you?"

"Are you kidding me?" Laurel smiled for the first time. "I love them! Does Sarie live on a farm or in town? How many horses does she have?"

"She lives off the road out toward Marazion; she has Fell ponies and keeps a couple of old work horses."

"Do you live near her?" Coll wasn't half bad to look at once she got talking to him, and he seemed nice enough.

"Not far, 'course nothing's that far in Penzance. Handy like."

"Maybe I can come and visit you while I'm here? I don't know anyone in Cornwall."

"How do you know Sarie then?"

"She's an old friend of my Gramma Bella's. Her and my Gramma went to school together or something, I think. I've only talked to her on the phone a couple of times. Is she easy to get along with?"

"She likes her horses better'n most people. Sarie's all right when you get used to her, though. Talks to her horses like they understand her." Coll shook his head and grinned.

If Sarie liked horses and was kind to them, hopefully she wouldn't be too hard get along with. Laurel released a tiny sigh of relief and shrugged the tension from her shoulders.

"I can help her out with the animals. I have a horse back home, but I haven't ridden him much since my mom got so sick. I miss him."

"Ya have your own horse?" Coll exclaimed enviously. "Your parents must be rich."

"Not hardly. Lots of people have horses in Alberta, some for fun and some for ranch work. I rode Sam in 4H, and I belonged to Pony Club, too."

"Did you ever punch cows, like in the movies?"

"Punch cows? You've been watching too many old western movies; nobody uses that term much anymore. I help my folks move the cows from the home quarter to summer pasture and back in the fall. Sam is so good. He just pushes the cows back into the herd when they try to stop and wander. It's fun to chase them when they try to run off"

"You said your mom was sick. What's wrong with her?"

Holding her breath and willing away the tears she could feel burning at the backs of her eyes, she bit her lip and looked out at the sky and the sea.

She spoke without turning her gaze from the window. "She has cancer. I don't know if she's going to get better."

There it was out, she had said it. The fear she hadn't been able to acknowledge until now.

"Wow, I'm sorry.. That must be hard. I live with my Gramma. I don't even remember my mom and dad. I was too young when they died."

It felt natural to share her worries with Coll after he told her about his parents.

"My dad doesn't have time to look after me or the ranch right now. He spends all his time in Calgary with Mom. They thought it would be better for me to be somewhere new and have other things to think about. This trip was already planned, so both of them really wanted me to go. Nobody asked what I think. They just keep saying everything's going to okay. I want to be home with my mom!"

The last sentence came out mixed with quiet sobs, abandonment and loss breaking the tenuous hold on her emotions.

Through her tears, Laurel saw Coll's look of dismay, crying girls were apparently not his area of expertise.

"Don't cry," he stammered. "We can have lots of fun while you're here. We can go pony-trekking and swim and sail. Do you sail? And maybe go out to St. Michael's Mount." Coll trailed off.

Laurel wiped her eyes on her sleeve and dug in her pocket for a tissue. Finally giving up the search, she wiped her nose on her sleeve as well. "What's pony-trekking?" she asked in a steady voice with no trace of the tears from a minute ago.

"You take the horses and just go for a ride, wherever the track takes you," Coll explained.

"You mean like trail riding?"

"What's trail riding?"

"You take your horse and bedroll, pack some stuff to eat and just ride. We stop, cook lunch or supper, and swim if we're near the river. Sometimes, we put the horses on the trailer and go to ride in the mountains. There are horse campgrounds with trails leading in all different directions. You can ride one trail for a while, come back to camp, and ride a different trail the next day, or that afternoon. Lots of them start and end back in the campsite. There are maps and everything, so you can't get lost, even if you don't ride there all the time."

Coll's blue eyes widened. "What mountains do you ride in? Are they really high?"

Laurel wrinkled her nose at him and named the two places she knew most people associated with the Canadian Rockies. *How can he not know about the Canadian Rockies?* "The Rocky Mountains in Alberta, where Banff is, and Lake Louise."

Laurel really preferred to ride in the Kananaskis country near Bragg Creek, but the National Parks were beautiful, too.

"Can you ride by the lake?" he asked disbelievingly.

"You rent horses from the outfitters at the corral behind the hotel. They take you on a guided tour along the lake trail, up into the mountains to the Lake Agnes Teahouse. It's pretty cool, but not as much fun as riding your own horse."

"I don't think pony trekking is that exciting," Coll said doubtfully, "but it is fun, and we can gallop along the ocean. If we go as far as the moor, it's a great place to race. We can visit the Dancing Maidens and Men An Tol."

"Who are the Dancing Maidens and the Men An…what?" *This might be an adventure after all.*

"The Dancing Maidens are a ring of standing stones, sort of like Stonehenge, but smaller. Legend says they were mermaids who were dancing on the moor in the full moon and were caught by the sunrise and turned into stone. There are two other stones a little ways from them called The Pipers. They're supposed to be the musicians who supplied the music for the maidens to dance to, so they were also turned to stone as punishment. Other old stories say they were fairies who angered some sorcerer who turned them into stone. There are lots of old tales and folks who keep the old ways in Cornwall. The 'Obby 'Oss festival is coming up. It's been celebrated for centuries. You're gonna love that!" Coll ran out of breath.

"What's the Men An…whatever you said?" She refused to be distracted by guessing what a Hobby Horse festival was, picturing dozens of people on stick horses parading down the road. *It couldn't be that could it?*

"The Men An Tol is a standing stone all by itself. I think it's called a dolmen stone or maybe a menhir. Sarie will know. Anyway, it has a hole in it large enough to crawl through. Legend says if you pass through the hole nine times at the full moon you can enter the otherworld of the fairies. Other tales say if you do the same thing, especially on one of the old fire festivals, it will heal sickness. Sarie knows more of the legends than I do. That's where I heard them," Coll finished.

"Do you think it's true?" she asked, "It can heal sickness, like cancer?" Hope leaped in her chest. "I wonder if I crawled through thinking about Mom really hard, if it would work, even just a little bit. I could keep doing it over and over until it all kind of built up, and then she would be okay."

"I don't think it works like that," Coll said warily. "Sarie says you have to be careful dealing with the Good Folk, or you can end up promising things you really don't want to. Or they give you exactly what you ask but not what you think you're asking for. You need to talk to Sarie or my Gramma before you try anything like that."

"Do you think Sarie will take me there? You'll come too won't you, just to see it with me?"

"We'll ask her after you get settled in. You'll have to convince Sarie you ride well enough and can take care of her pony before she'll even consider letting you go that far," Coll cautioned.

Laurel settled back in her seat feeling more hopeful than she had since leaving home.

"What's the 'Obby 'Oss Festival?" Laurel could never let anything go undiscovered once it tweaked her curiosity, and a town full of people parading along on stick horses was certainly worthy of further exploration.

"Big party, sort of, in Padstow," Coll answered. "It starts early in the morning on May Day, that's May first," he elaborated at her puzzled look. "People go out into the woods and fields and bring back green things, flowers, or leaves, and such. Then they go through town dancing and singing to show summer has arrived."

"Doesn't summer begin on June twenty-first?" Laurel asked.

"Nope, by the old reckoning May first is the start of summer and June twenty-first is actually mid-summer. Like Shakespeare's A Mid-Summer Night's Dream," Coll replied. "Anyway, a man dresses up in the 'Obby 'Oss costume. It's all white, with black and red, the parade winds all through town. Everybody lining the streets sings. The horse chases and catches girls and young women, the tales say if the girl isn't married, she will be soon, or if she is married, that she'll have a kid within the year. Every so often the horse does this weird dying thing. He falls down, and all the singers change their song to really sad one. Then the horse leaps back up, alive again, and the song changes back to the happy one. They repeat the whole thing all over town. It's fun though with lots of good fair food."

"What do they sing?"

"It's a crazy, old song. It goes:

"Unite and unite and let us all unite
For summer is i-cumen today
And whither we are going, we all will unite
In the merry morning of May."

Laurel giggled, the song sounded funny coming from the boy sitting across from her kicking his heels against the seat.

Coll grinned back at her. "Just wait till you hear the whole town singing it. It's like there's no other sound in the world."

"Where's Padstow? Is it far from Sarie's?"

"It's up the coast a ways, toward Arthur's Castle. Sarie goes every year, so I think she'll take you with her this year."

"What's Arthur's castle? You mean like King Arthur and his knights and all that?"

"That's him. It's actually called Tintagel, and it's where King Arthur was supposed to have been born according to the old stories. Sarie might take you there if you really want to see it. It's just a bunch of old stones and ruins," he finished doubtfully.

"I'd rather see the Hobby Horse Parade if I had the choice."

"You say it 'Obby 'Oss," corrected Coll.

"Whatever, a horse is a horse." Then she giggled. "Or 'Oss in this case, I guess."

He grinned and lapsed into silence. Laurel watched Coll out of the corner of her eye, while she pretended to read the book she picked up from beside her. He was so different from the kids she knew at home. From what he said, he seemed to hang out with adults more than kids his age. He hadn't mentioned anybody their age. Not so different from her in that regard. She preferred her horse and the barn cats and didn't have a lot of close friends.

But she did miss Carlene and her brother, Chance. They always met up on the range road half way between their home quarters. Most times they would spend the day riding the wide prairie. They liked to picnic by the Old Man River which wound through the coulee, sheltering behind the big rocks if the Chinooks were blowing hard. Laurel could almost smell the hot dry dusty scent of prairie grass and wind with an edge of sage mixed in. And horse, she missed that most of all. The scent of prairie dust, clean horse, and sweat mingled with dried manure. It was just *horse* to her nose.

Coll's voice brought her back to the present; she noticed he rushed his words. There was a panicky look in his eyes. She guessed he was hoping she wasn't going to start crying again.

"Did you know Sarie doesn't live right in Penzance? She lives out toward Marazion. Her place is about halfway between. She says that's why she likes it so much, 'cause it's a *between* place."

"A *between* place." There was something appealing about the idea. "Between what?" she wondered out loud.

"Don't think it matters," replied Coll. "It's like in between places are openings to new possibilities. Like doors, I think, without them you can't come in or go out."

The sun was setting on the Cornish countryside, its light slanting across the interior of the rail car. Outside the glass pane, wind bent the grass and low shrubs against a backdrop of strong sunlight and blue sky with clouds piling up in the west. Unnoticed, the blue of day faded to the iridescent royal blue of early evening, as the light leaked away with the setting sun. White stars shone in the night, and the moon etched the moors with silver light.

Coll stretched up to reach his backpack down from the baggage rack. He rummaged around for a bit, muttering under his breath. Finally, he produced a bag of somewhat crumpled sandwiches, along with a couple of bags of potato chips.

"Want some?" Coll offered her a sandwich and a bag of chips.

"Sure." She accepted the food gratefully, not having realized just how long the train ride was and neglecting to bring any snacks. The British money was too confusing still and she was reluctant to purchase anything from the canteen in the next car.

"The crisps might be a bit mashed." Coll regarded the flattened bag ruefully.

"What did you call them? Aren't they chips?"

Coll laughed. "Only to Yanks, and I guess Canadians," he added at the look on her face. "Chips are what we get with fried fish at the chip shop."

Laurel grimaced in frustration. It was going to be harder to fit in than she thought. How was she supposed to know chips were called crisps and French fries were chips?

"We call those French fries, although we do call fish and chips, fish and chips. Oh, it's all too confusing," she exclaimed in disgust. "Let's just eat the damn things!"

Her dad would be furious with her, her face flushed hot with guilt at the cuss word. She turned her gaze resolutely to the dark window. *Well, he doesn't know, does he?* If he didn't send me all this way on my own, he *would* know. *So,* she reasoned, *it's actually his fault.*

Feelings of rebellious freedom swept through her. As long as no one ratted her out to her parents, she pretty much had a free rein to do as she pleased. *Within reason,* she amended silently. Laurel was pretty sure this Sarie would be lenient with her; she could always say she didn't want to worry her parents if she did get in real trouble and beg Sarie not to tell.

Sneaking a look at Coll's reflection in the dark glass, she saw he was too involved in making short work of the sandwich in his hand to take any notice of her silence. She took a bite of her own sandwich.

The quiet of the car was broken as a group of older kids trouped by. Coll glanced up at the sound of their approach; dislike flooded his good-natured features as he recognized them. Some of the group stopped by their seats and seeing Coll, made rude gestures at him. Coll pointedly ignored them, until one boy dropped his knapsack on the table and glared at him.

"You have to go to school on Monday," he said nastily. "You can't hide forever."

"Sod off!" Coll snarled at him.

What the heck is going on? That guy is threatening him! Without thinking, Laurel pulled her booted foot back and kicked the tall, rangy stranger hard in the knee. He spun around on one leg, swearing.

"Who the hell's your little friend?" he growled at Coll.

He looked at her with his face twisted in anger. "You should be more careful about who you pick as friends and who you kick. You never learned you dawn't shuv your granny when she's shevin?"

Temper ran away with her, and she slid out of her seat. She could not stand bullies. Laurel ignored Coll gesturing to her to sit down. She took a step toward the tall stranger and stuck her face up at him.

"You want to have no leg to stand on?" she asked him with a grim smile. "Need to go get your friends to help you?" Advancing another step, she drew her foot back to kick his other knee. "Are you sure you want to go there?"

"You're all talk," he snarled. "You won't be so cocky when you're outnumbered!"

A grim smile stretched her lips, and she aimed a kick at his good knee. She only managed a glancing blow, as he lurched backward.

"You're bleeding kitey! You're barking mad to hang around with this one!" he addressed the last to Coll who was looking at Laurel with his mouth hanging open.

"We'll finish this later," the tall boy growled and hobbled down the aisle after his friends.

"Anytime, darlin'," Laurel called, sliding back into her seat.

Once the incident was over, she wanted to be sick to her stomach; her hands were shaking badly. She buried her face in her hands.

"Holy crap, he was big and mean."

When was she going to learn to think before she did something? Her dad's voice whispered at her, *Violence is no way to solve your problems, Laurel. You can't just hit people.* Dad didn't seem to understand bullies weren't much on negotiation. Until she stood up to the bullies at school, her life had been horrible. After a while, the group of them left her alone, but started to pick on other kids smaller than themselves. Laurel went to the school counselor, but as one of the biggest bullies was the counselor's daughter, it hadn't helped much. It seemed no matter where she went there was no escape from idiots. The seat cushion sagged as Coll sat down beside her and patted her awkwardly on the shoulder.

"That was great! Barking mad, but great!" he congratulated her. "That group makes life miserable at school for me and my mates."

"I'm not sure I helped." Laurel looked up at Coll through her bangs. "It might just make things worse."

"Nobody stands up to them," Coll said. "Some of us have tried, but they always manage to get us alone, and then there's hell to pay. But you really hurt Stuart; that'll impress the rest of them."

"So we need to be careful when we get off the train in Penzance?"

This is just great, I'm in trouble, and I haven't even gotten off the train yet!

"Sarie will be waiting on the platform," Coll assured her. "She's giving my Gram a lift to the station to pick me up. I didn't know she was meeting you. Nobody messes with Sarie," he finished enigmatically.

She gave him an odd look. It sounded like Sarie was somehow threatening to people. She shrugged. At least she didn't have to worry about getting off the train in one piece and finding Sarie. Coll knew Sarie and could introduce her.

"I just can't stand bullies. I'm in their face before I can stop myself," she confessed ruefully, "and sometimes, it's not such a good thing. What was that kid talking about, shoving my granny or something?"

"It just means you should know when to butt in and when to keep your gob shut," Coll said through his laughter. "Don't push your opinion when someone else bigger or stronger is pushing theirs. Stuart must have picked that up from his Granda."

The train lurched to a stop. There was the general confusion of people gathering their belongings and scrunching their way down the narrow aisle to the exit. They waited until the biggest crush was over before they ventured out into the still busy car to collect Laurel's bag from the rack by the exit. Coll wrestled it down the steps onto the lighted platform for her.

Laurel took a big breath of fresh air and was delighted at the strange new smells. She identified the smell of the sea and damp earth faintly carried on the sharp breeze. She put her backpack down at her feet and tried to tame her flyaway hair.

Coll stood beside her, searching the crowd. She noticed he kept glancing at Stuart until a woman appeared from the station and gave the bully a hug. With a baleful backward look at them, Stuart and his friends followed the woman off the platform into the darkness.

Coll caught her arm and pointed down the platform to the waving figures of Sarie and Coll's Gramma.

"There they are, Laurel. Sarie's the taller one on the left."

Here goes nothing. They moved down the platform toward the terminal. She caught a glimpse of herself in the reflection from the windows. Her hair looked worse than ever for all her attempts to tame it. Mom's words echoed in her ears, "*Try to look tidy when you get there. I don't want Sarie to think I've raised a ragamuffin.*" Her mom teased her when they said good-bye. Her dad was a little more forthright. "*Seriously, Laurel, remember you're representing our family and mind your manners. Behave like a civilized human instead of a dust devil.*"

Ragamuffin, dust devil, either way this is as good as it's getting, she thought, and followed Coll across the pavement toward Sarie and Coll's Gramma.

"Look who I met on the train!" Coll greeted his Gramma with a hug and gave Sarie a huge grin. "This is Laurel."

Laurel stuck her hand out to Sarie, but Sarie engulfed her in big hug.

"It's wonderful to have you here, child," she said.

Sarie was taller than Mom by about three inches, which put her around five-foot-nine. Her greying hair still retained some streaks of its original blond and blew about her face in the wind. Sarie was what people called a handsome woman. She was not pretty in the classical sense of the word, but she was a striking figure all the same. Her wide generous mouth was spread in a grin, and her laughing eyes were bluer than anyone's eyes had a right to be.

Sarie's upturned nose wrinkled as she hugged Coll. "Have you been eating those disgusting dill pickle crisps again?" she asked him in mock exasperation.

"You know it!" Coll grinned back at her, unrepentant.

"Let's get your bags, then." Sarie walked toward where Coll had left Laurel's bag.

"Laurel, this is my Gramma, Emily." Coll introduced his gramma.

"It's pleased I am to meet you, girl," Emily said kindly.

"Nice to meet you, too." Remembering her manners, she extended her hand to Emily.

The three trailed after Sarie down the station platform. The wind was picking up, and it whistled shrilly through the spaces between the train carriages. Sarie was waiting for them by the pile of bags.

"Which bags are yours?" Sarie gestured to the pile.

"I only have one; it's got horses on it." Laurel scanned the confusing pile of assorted bags from a tour group. They must have unloaded their stuff after Coll left hers here.

Coll emerged from the other side, dragging a bag behind him. "This it?" he asked as he hauled it into the light.

"That's the one."

Thank God it was safe! Packed inside were pictures of home: her mom and dad, Sam, her horse, Chance and Carlene. There was one of the butte across the river from her bedroom window. The picture was taken at sunset at the end of a glorious blue and gold September day; the river looked like it was on fire, and the butte was glowing with golden light. There was another of the prairie spread from horizon to horizon in unbroken splendor. It was taken from Sam's back just before she left home. She knew she wouldn't feel so far from home with the photos to remind her how the prairie looked and smelled. *I have to remember to write to Carlene tomorrow and tell her how weird everything is here.*

Sarie hefted the suitcase, popped up the handle, and set off toward the car park with the suitcase trundling along behind her. Laurel followed with her backpack while Coll and his Gramma brought up the rear. She could hear Coll and Emily conversing behind her but couldn't make out the words. Suddenly, she was very, very tired. She looked out toward the sea and the weird hump backed island crouching just off shore. She squinted. It looked like some sort of castle all lit up perched on the summit. She tugged Coll's sleeve and pointed.

"What's that?"

“That’s St. Michael’s Mount. Local landmark, big tourist attraction.” He shrugged and kept walking.

In just a few minutes, everything was stored in Sarie’s little car, and they were speeding along the narrow streets. Sarie pulled up in front of a row of attached stone houses. She shifted into neutral and engaged the parking brake.

“Back in two shakes.”

Sarie got out of the car and helped Emily unearth some packages out of the trunk of the car. With a wave to Coll and Emily, Sarie jumped back in, releasing the brake. The car started to roll down the sharp incline of the street before Sarie even got it into first gear.

“See you tomorrow!” Coll yelled as the car gathered speed.

Laurel waved in return before she looked out the front windshield at the stone houses and buildings crouching on either side of the narrow street. She was too tired to think about tomorrow; all Laurel wanted to do was go to sleep. Covering her mouth as a huge yawn overtook her, she leaned her head against the cool glass of the passenger side window.

“It won’t be long ‘til we’re home,” Sarie said as they left the lights of Penzance behind and headed out into the countryside.

Home, this isn’t home. I want to go home!

She planned to call Dad in the morning and beg him to let her come home. *Coming here was a really bad idea. I know I can convince Dad to let me come home. Why did I let myself get talked into this in the first place?*

It had all seemed kind of exciting. Chance and Carlene said how lucky she was to get a chance to go to England. The reality of leaving kicked in big time when the time came to say goodbye to her parents and friends. Now she was a million miles from home, bone tired, and homesick.

Laurel turned her face into the window, so Sarie couldn’t see the tears tracking down her cheeks. She wiped her nose surreptitiously with her sleeve and tried not to sniff too loudly. The dark landscape whipped past as the car careened down narrow lanes with tall hedges on either side, the branches hitting Sarie’s door. It added to the weirdness of driving on what seemed like the wrong side of the road.

A short time later, Sarie jammed on her brakes and skidded into an even narrower laneway. Ahead the lighted windows of a small house and the faint outline of the roof in the moonlight greeted them. The bulk of another building behind the house was also visible in the faint light. It must be the barn, although it didn't look like any barn she had seen before. It was short and squat, made out of stone of some kind, instead of wood or metal.

Sarie parked the car in front of the house, and Laurel stumbled out. The older woman hefted the suitcase out of the trunk and headed for the door, leaving her to trail behind. Laurel paused on the step to read the small sign on the door post. *Between Cottage.* She followed Sarie through the bright blue door and stood in the doorway for a moment, blinking in the light. A fireplace with some comfy-looking chairs pulled up close to it warmed the small room. The night pressed its black nose against the many windows in the room. Sarie disappeared through a doorway on the far side of the room.

Laurel stepped into the house and pulled the door shut behind her. She wandered toward the door at the back of the living room. The door opened onto a dark hallway; there was light coming from another door at the end of the hall to the left. On her right, the narrow hall led to an equally narrow set of stairs disappearing into the darkness of the upstairs. Dropping her backpack at the foot of the stairs, she headed down the hall towards the light.

Laurel pushed open the bright yellow door to the kitchen. A rush of warm air greeted her. The kitchen was a room added on to the original house at some point a long time ago. The roof slanted downward toward a row of windows running the length of the back wall. There was a big old cook stove producing the vast amount of warmth filling the small room. Sarie put some bread and jam on the table, along with two big mugs of tea.

"Are you hungry, my flower?"

"A little bit, I guess." She hovered at the doorway, not sure what to do next.

"Sit, child, sit. Are you after wanting some tea?" Sarie gestured to the chair across from her own.

"Tea would be nice."

There was silence as she sat opposite Sarie and sipped her tea. The brew was very strong and very sweet.

"Your room is at the top of the stairs on the left. The necessary is down the hall from you." Sarie broke the silence.

"The necessary?"

"The loo, the toilet." Sarie elaborated with a laugh.

"Oh."

The small warmth and comfort the hot tea generated evaporated in a blink. How in the Sam hill was she ever going to figure out what these people were talking about? Her shoulders slumped with defeat, she clenched her teeth in frustration.

"It does get easier, child. Don't be discouraged. We'll have you talking like a native in no time."

She managed a tired smile before pushing away from the table to take her mug over to the wash basin.

"I'll show you up to your room if you like," Sarie said as she led the way back into the cold, dark hall. The older woman dragged Laurel's suitcase up steps to the upper floor.

She stopped to retrieve her backpack from the end of the hall and climbed the stairs behind Sarie, careful where she stepped, as the stairs were narrow and steep. Sarie flicked on the electric light after she opened a door at the top of the landing.

A single bed stood against one wall. There was a worn chest of drawers on the opposite wall and a small table beside the bed. The one window, framed by white curtains, looked out over the starlit moorland. It reminded Laurel of the prairies at home, softly rolling land and big starry skies with the huge moon overhead. The sea gleamed in the distance. She dumped her backpack on the floor beside the dresser and turned to take her suitcase from Sarie.

"If you need anything you can just yell." Sarie hugged her before she left the room. "It's pleased I am that you decided to come."

Laurel didn't know what to say in light of the fact she was going to phone her dad as soon as she could and beg to come home. She mumbled into Sarie's sweater and followed Sarie to the door, closing it behind her.

She was so tired it hurt to think. Laurel forced herself to rummage in her backpack for her PJs. She undressed and dressed quickly in the chilly room and thought briefly about finding the bathroom to brush her teeth. Deciding against an exploration excursion, she slid into bed and immediately muffled a scream; the bed was freezing! Not just cold, but freezing. Her teeth chattered, this was as bad as camping out! Tucking the blankets tightly around her, she hoped body heat would warm things up soon. The long trip and the worry about her mom had taken its toll; before she knew it, she was asleep.

Chapter Two

The White Lady

Warm sunlight and fingers of breeze woke her the next morning. She rolled over and buried her face in the pillow, not wanting to open her eyes. As long as her eyes were closed, Laurel could pretend she was sleeping over at Carlene's, and Carlene's mom was making bacon and eggs down in the big kitchen overlooking the coulee. If she tried hard enough, she could even hear the horses galloping up to the corral from the river.

The high whinny of a horse brought her upright in bed and opened her eyes. She threw back the bed clothes and kneeled on the bed to look out the window. There was a big field behind the house; lined up along the fence by the gate were four large black ponies and two draft horses.

They were solid beasts with long flowing manes and thick tails. The one nearest the gate whinnied again and stamped its hoof on the soft earth. All the ponies pricked their ears up a second before Sarie appeared, wearing a pair of big muck boots and a tattered green jacket. A yellow kerchief kept her grey hair from blowing in the strong breeze billowing the clothes strung on the line across the back garden. Sarie's voice carried easily through the open window.

"Hush you now! You'll wake the girl," Sarie admonished the ponies. "Back off from the git you." Sarie spoke to the largest pony by the gate.

The ponies backed away from the gate and followed Sarie off toward a low stone building. She dropped onto her back on the bed with a sigh. It was no use pretending she was home. Better to think about what to say to her dad when she phoned later. While she washed and dressed, she formulated her argument. Catching her hair up in a ponytail and satisfied she looked pretty decent, Laurel headed down the narrow stairs and into the kitchen. The phone hung invitingly on the wall but better to ask Sarie first. The sides of the big brown tea pot on the table were warm when she checked it with her hand. She poured herself a mug and sat down at the table. Through the windows, she saw Sarie making her way through the back garden to the kitchen door. Finding another mug, she poured Sarie a cup of tea and set it on the table as Sarie hung up her jacket on the hooks by the door.

"Ta," Sarie said. "What would you like for breakfast?"

"Some toast would be good,"

She wasn't sure what Sarie had in the house, toast was safe. Chance teased about how his grandpa used to make him eat kippers and duck eggs when he visited him. She thought kippers were some kind of fish, which sounded totally gross for breakfast. Better not to go there at all. Toast was definitely a safer bet.

Sarie bustled about and in a few moments, set a plate of toast on the blue oilcloth covering the sturdy kitchen table. Laurel helped herself and added some honey from the pot Sarie placed beside her. She tried not to stare in amazement as Sarie ate six slices of toast with honey.

"I'se is as full az an egg!" Sarie declared as she leaned back in her chair and sipped her tea. "I didn't get a chance to eat last night, and the ponies were wanting their breakfast this morning before I could get mine."

Watching the ponies nosing about in the grass in the field, she finished her tea and tried to remember what breed Coll said they were. *Fell ponies, that was it.* They resembled miniature draft horses with their sturdy feathered legs, thick necks, large heads, and rounded barrels. The two larger horses by the barn looked like Belgians, but smaller.

"What are the ponies' names?"

"The biggest one is Lamorna, the other mare is Ebony, the two geldings are Arthur and Gareth," Sarie told her.

"What about the big horses?"

"That's Morgen and Vivienne. Morgen is the one with the most white on her face," Sarie reached to fill her mug with tea.

"Are they Belgians?"

"No, love. They're a breed called Suffolk Punch. They're the same color as Belgians but smaller in stature. It's an old blood line.

I don't imagine you've seen them in Canada." Sarie smiled at Laurel.

"Can I ride one of the ponies?"

"We'll see how you get on with them later today," Sarie promised.

"Can I phone my dad?" Laurel remembered her plan to get back home.

"Of course, just don't be too long, the phone bill will be as dear as saffron if we're not careful," Sarie said as she tidied the breakfast things away.

"Whatever," she muttered. *It doesn't matter because I won't be here that long anyways.*

Ten minutes later, she stalked out the kitchen door and across the back garden. Her dad wasn't very receptive to her plan. He told her in no uncertain terms she was staying in Cornwall and not to make any trouble. She kicked at an unoffending clump of grass and muttered words her dad would skin her for if he heard them. *Well, he can't hear me, can he? Not with me stuck in Cornwall.*

Reaching the fence bordering the ponies' field, she leaned her chin on the top rail. The ponies were grazing in a group about half way down the field. There was a gully and some trees behind them. The breeze rippled the grass and fluttered the leaves of the bushes in the garden. Everything was so green, not just green like the prairies could get after a wet spring, but an almost iridescent green. The grass and the trees radiated a green light which shimmered where it met the sunlight. The strangeness was overwhelming. *This is all just too different. I hate it here.* Homesickness swamped her and tears blurred her vision as she watched the horses graze.

Sarie called from the kitchen. Wiping her eyes on her sleeve, she ducked into the shelter of the hedgerow growing along the ponies' pasture. An ancient, low stone wall lay hidden in the tangled branches of the bushes growing up around it. Clambering up onto the wide top, she tucked her feet under her. She just couldn't face Sarie or anyone right now.

She was furious at her dad. How could he refuse to understand how homesick she was? Mom would understand; she would. But Mom was so sick from the chemo treatments right now it was all she could do to talk for a few minutes on the phone. Laurel didn't want to make her feel even worse by complaining about wanting to come home.

Sliding down off the wall, she peered through the leafy branches of the hedgerow. Sarie was in the back garden weeding the herb beds. Laurel didn't feel like helping right now; she needed time to think.

Feeling more than a little guilty, she set off to explore the pony field. She slipped out of the hedge and began to follow it toward the gully, away from the house. The grass was still damp from the heavy dew. Impatiently she pushed the hair escaping from her pony tail out of her face.

Although the breeze was cool, Laurel's face was damp. It was so much more humid here than at home her normally straight hair curled in little tendrils on her forehead.

Some of the bushes in the hedge were flowering; pale white bunches of blossoms perfuming the soft air. The tension leave her shoulders when she reached the cover of the bunch of trees crowning the lip of the little valley she planned to explore. Sarie couldn't see her in the trees, and if someone came looking, she could stay hidden if she wanted to.

A little path led through the woods, down into the narrow ravine. Under the trees, the air was rich with the fragrance of the damp earth and the small colorful wildflowers growing in abundance under the canopy of interlacing branches. Some of the trees themselves were flowering as well. The trees also had teeth Laurel discovered when she slipped as the path dipped toward the bottom of the ravine and she grabbed at a small bushy tree to keep from landing on her butt. The long sharp thorns hidden in the leaves raked her arm and bloodied her hand. The pain was like a personal assault.

"Even the stinking trees are against me." She slipped and slid the last few yards to the boggy bottom of the gully, stopping to wipe away the tears tracking down her scratched face.

Aimlessly, she continued to walk along the narrow path as it wound through the grassy gully. The ground was wet underfoot and she soon wished for her boots instead of the sneakers on her feet.

"Oh, well might as well be wet *and* miserable, instead of just miserable." She squelched along through the boggy grass.

The marshy area in the very bottom of the gully was full of bright gold flowers dancing above broad emerald green clumps of leaves. The flowers stood above the still water in little hillocks. Marsh marigolds, cowslips her Grampa D'Arcy called them.

The path turned up hill, bordered with dogwood bushes, their bright red bark shiny even in the shadowy light. She could hear water running. *There must be a creek or little stream somewhere.* The path continued to climb slightly as it angled along the side of the gully. White and purple violets grew thickly in the damp earth on the edges of the path.

The peace of the gully began to ease her tumultuous thoughts. The little stream cut across the path, gurgling and splashing as it headed for the marshy bottom below. Laurel sat down on a huge boulder just off the path on the uphill side and watched the water tumbling down the hillside. Laurel gazed at the stream for about half an hour, letting her thoughts drift where they wanted. The boulder was hard to sit on after a while. She felt better now; she still didn't agree with her dad, but at least she wasn't spitting mad. *I still want to go home, like yesterday.*

The path slanted down the hillside from the point where Laurel stood. She was tired of sliding in the mud but not ready to accept her fate and return to Sarie's just yet. In sudden inspiration, she followed the stream uphill to find out where it emerged in the pony field.

The going was tough, the rocky hillside was covered with bushes growing right up the edge of the stream. Branches caught in her hair and pulled at her jacket. It was just as easy to walk on the rocks in the stream as it was to try and bushwhack her way through the brambles. The water was cold, and it soaked through her sneakers, but it was a lot easier going. The stream came to a series of small waterfalls and a short ledge of earth clinging to the side of the gully.

The ledge was twenty feet long and ten feet wide. Ferns and wildflowers covered it, along with some larger trees and saplings. More ferns and flowering bushes hung from the side of the gully as it rose above the spring. The stream ended in a small rock-lined pool in a basin of emerald grass. *Actually, the stream really starts here.*

The air in the little clearing was sun splashed where the light filtered down through the green leaves and lit the bottom of the shaded pool. Water dripped from the stones above the pool, which were moss covered and sprouted more ferns. Sitting cross-legged on a flat rock at the edge of the pool, she pulled her jacket closer around her for comfort. There was no wind in the sheltered gully; the water fell into the pool with a sound like the tinkle of crystal or little wind chimes. She closed her eyes and propped her chin on her hands.

I wish Mom were here; she loves places like this. Mom knows all kinds of stories about the fairies that live by springs and how they have tea parties with the yellow marsh marigolds as tea cups and the delicate leaves of the brambles for plates.

Her mom told her about some water spirits one day while they were exploring down by the river near her house. Undines, her mom called them. They were supposed to live in the still water of pools and springs, but you could only see them if they liked you. She was never sure if her mom was just making up fairy tales for her, or if she really believed in them. Mom never mentioned anything about fairies when her dad was around.

"I miss you, Mom." Laurel spoke softly without opening her eyes.

I wonder what time it is. Her stomach rumbled with hunger; she guessed she really should help Sarie with the chores. Maybe they could ride the ponies this afternoon. *I wonder if Sarie rides.* Coll hadn't mentioned anything about Sarie riding, only that she kept Fell Ponies. Despite her good intentions, she didn't make any effort to figure out how she was going to get back to the pony field.

It's so unfair Mom is going to die. Why my mom? Nobody actually came out and told her Mom was dying. But, that was exactly what was going to happen if somebody couldn't fix things soon. She saw the truth in Mom's eyes when she said goodbye. Her mom was never very good at telling lies.

"I love you too much to lie to you. Even when your dad thinks it's better if you don't always know the whole truth," her mom told her often.

Laurel was glad her mom trusted her to be able to handle most things. Like what happened to Cole, their border collie. Her dad said Cole had gone to retire in B.C. with some nice people. Mom told her the truth; Cole went to sleep and didn't wake up. He was old, and it was time for him to go. She felt better about knowing the truth and didn't fret about Cole missing her. Wondering why she didn't come to give him his dog treats and bring him home.

"I know he's just trying to protect me," Laurel muttered, forcing herself to be fair to her dad, even though she was still currently, pretty mad at him.

How am I going to manage without my mom to talk to? She scrunched her hands into fists and pounded on her thighs in frustration. The floodgates burst open. Sobs tore her throat, and tears clogged her nose, her ribs hurt, and she still couldn't make herself stop. It just wasn't *fair*!

"Mom, Mom!"

Without realizing she had moved, Laurel found herself lying face down on the flat stone with her legs entangled in the bushes. Her tears fell into the pool, making little circular ripples like raindrops. It was a little easier to breathe now, but the tears kept coming. Laurel cried for her Mom, for Cole, for Sam, and mostly for herself.

She was abandoned half way across the world. *Mom needs me; I need Mom; I want to go home!* The tears dripped off her nose into the pool, faster and faster. She needed to stop crying, but she couldn't. The loss of control scared her, and she was very cold now. Her feet felt like ice, her wet jeans clung to her cold legs. In between the sobs, Laurel's teeth started to chatter.

Through the blur of tears, there was a shimmer over the surface of the pool. She hiccupped and blinked. A gentle hand touched her hair, smoothing it back from her face. *Mom*! Mom always smoothed her hair when she was sick or upset. Warmth spread through her...

"Mom?"

The woman about her mom's age, but it wasn't her. The lady had blue eyes, and her skin glowed. Bright and silvery blond hair hung long and gossamer around her face, falling over the weird hooded robe she wore. The fingers on her hands were short and sturdy. She was the most beautiful person Laurel had ever seen, except of course for Mom.

"No, sweet child, I'm not the mother you are missing so badly." Her voice blended with the sparkling voice of the spring.

The woman sat down and rested a hand on her cold shoulder. The touch was comforting. Laurel wriggled around and sat cross-legged with her knees drawn up to her chest. She wrapped her arms around them in an attempt to stop the shivers. The woman wrapped her cape around Laurel. She gathered the soft fabric up under her chin, breathing in the sweet scent of verbena and lavender. Immediately, she was warmer and calmer. With her eyes on the fall of the water into the little rock pool, she searched for something to say, embarrassed at being discovered wailing away like a baby. Even worse, by someone she didn't even know.

"Do you live around here?"

"In a manner of speaking, I do. I can usually be found somewhere near this spring," the woman answered.

"Do you know Sarie?" They must be friends, if this woman hung out in Sarie's pony field.

"Sarie and I are old friends. She is the current custodian of this spring."

"Does the spring have a name?"

"Some call it the Well of the White Lady," the woman said softly.

"Who's the White Lady?"

"She is the spirit of this place, this spring. But she is connected to all the sacred wells and springs, indeed to all the landscape that is Britain," the woman explained.

"So she's like an undine?" She remembered her mom's story about the water spirits.

The woman's laughter spilled into the serenity of the small glade. "Goodness, child where did you hear of undines?"

"My mom tells me stories about them."

"Undines are water elementals. They dwell in any body of water and are small and childlike, although they can be quite helpful at times. The White Lady is the actual spirit of the spring, associated with a particular spring. She is however connected to the greater feminine spirit which inhabits all the sacred springs and dwells in the landscape about us. The greater Spirit is known by many names Mary, Brigit, the Lady of the Lake, and in other lands as Isis, to name just a few." The woman's voice held a strange vibrancy.

"Are you the White Lady?" Laurel's voice was very small. She was pretty sure she already knew the answer.

The woman didn't answer immediately. Stray beams of sunlight flickered in her bright blond hair; a halo of golden light surrounded her. Fear blossomed in the pit of Laurel's stomach. *Maybe Mom's stories are real. Maybe magic does exist in today's world like Mom insists.*

"I have comforted many people at this spring over the years, not one of them has ever had the courage to ask that simple question out loud." The woman smiled. "So, as a reward for your forthrightness I will answer. Yes, I am the White Lady. Do you have a favor to ask of me?"

"A favor?" She hadn't come to the spring to ask for anything. She only wanted to be alone.

"Most of those who come here come to ask for something, a lover, a husband, a child, or to bend others to their will." The White Lady smiled as she spoke.

"Can you do that? It doesn't seem right to ask for that kind of thing."

"You speak with wisdom beyond your young years, little one." The White Lady's laughter ignited sparkles in the sunlit shadows. "What is it you would ask, if you could?"

Do I dare ask? What will it cost me to have my wish granted? In all the fairy tales, there was always a price to be paid for favors given, usually a pretty high one. *Still, I don't care what the cost is as long as my wish comes true.*

"I want my mom to get better. She has cancer, and she's really sick. She can't die. I need her. That's what I want, my mom to be healthy again," Laurel said quickly, before she lost her courage.

"It is not a small thing you ask," the White Lady said thoughtfully. "The decision is not entirely in my hands. Freedom of choice and free will hang in the balance as do the scales of Light and Darkness. Let me consider this for a moment."

Holding her breath, Laurel clenched her hands together so hard her nails bit into her palms. *Please say you'll help me.* The White Lady's face was serene, but her eyes were unfocused as she looked at something far away. Presently the White Lady smiled.

"I have made something of a bargain for you. The outcome rests with you. There is a riddle you must solve. Follow the clues as you receive them and put them together until you can see the whole riddle. Once you see the riddle as a whole, you will also see the answer and the path you need to take."

"Mom will be okay if I solve this riddle?" She wanted to be very certain she understood what the White Lady offered.

"If you solve the riddle and complete the tasks given to you, yes, I think your mother will be healthy again. But beware, you must not waste time. Your mother is very ill, and the decision hangs in the balance. You will need friends to help on your journey; it is not a journey you can take alone and succeed."

Friends, I don't have any friends here. Who can I ask to help me? The only person she knew was Coll, and Sarie, of course. *I can't ask Sarie; maybe Coll will help me. He seemed pretty nice on the train last night.*

"Do you agree to accept the terms of the bargain?" the White Lady prompted Laurel.

"So, I solve the riddle, perform the tasks, and then my mom will be okay?"

"It will be so. Remember your time to complete the tasks is limited by your mother's condition," the White Lady affirmed.

"Then yes, I accept the bargain."

The White Lady placed her hand on Laurel's head and smiled.

"Then let it be so recorded," the Lady said simply.

"When do I get the first part of the riddle?" In her mind's eye, she saw sands draining through an hourglass, like on the soap opera her mom liked to watch.

"Your first clue will come to you on the Fire Festival of Beltane, what you call May Day in these days. Journey to Padstow for the May Day celebrations and keep your heart open to receive the clue. I will add this advice of my own...you must ride on the filly that never was foaled. When you do so, you will know that you are close to your goal. You will literally hold death in your hands. More, I cannot tell you without jeopardizing the bargain. Go gently, child. Blessed Be."

The White Lady shimmered in a shaft of sunlight which found its way through the leaves. Laurel blinked in the sudden brilliance. When she looked again, the Lady was gone. A soft breeze touched her hair, and then all was still in the little glade, the water continuing to fall into the pool.

"I'm going to have to find a way to get in touch with Coll."

She climbed up the steep side of the ravine above the spring and emerged in the pony field not far from the house. The four ponies came trotting over to see if there were any goodies to be had. The heavy horses thundered up behind them. Laughing, she patted each one in turn, letting them sniff her hands. Laurel started toward the gate, her sneakers making wet sucking noises as she walked. The herd followed her single file all the way to the gate.

"Well, I see you've met the ponies." Sarie's voice came from the vegetable patch she was weeding now.

"I'm sorry I ran off earlier." The toe of her sneaker seemed very interesting.

"You look like you've been down in the gully. Did you have any trouble on the path? It can be a bit illy in places."

"What does *illy* mean?"

"It means a bit steep in places." Sarie smiled.

"I guess."

Sarie got to her feet and dusted off her faded pants. Laurel picked up the big basket of weeds and took them to the burning barrel at the far end of the garden. Sarie was just finishing storing her tools in the potting shed when she came back down the path. Sarie took the empty basket, stowing it away before closing the door.

"Shall we go wash up? I think it's time for a croust." Sarie headed for the kitchen door.

I hope a croust *means something to eat. I'm starving.* Sarie dried her hands on the tea towel, which she tossed to Laurel as she came through the door. She put her wet sneakers by the big kitchen stove to dry and busied herself washing the grime from her own hands. Her clothes were a mess; she needed to get into some dry ones before eating. She hesitated, not sure if she should traipse mud all over the house to get to her room. Sarie noticed her dilemma.

"There's a bit of mudroom through that door. You can strip off in there and throw your stuff in the washer." Sarie indicated a low door. "There should be an old flannel shirt of mine you can use to go upstairs in." Her voice followed Laurel into the small mudroom.

Quickly, stripping off her wet muddy clothes, she promptly dumped them into the old wringer washer. Shivering, she slipped into the warm flannel shirt and headed back through the kitchen. The tails of the shirt flapped around her knees, and the sleeves were rolled up so she could use her hands to open the latch on the door to the hall.

"I'll be right back down." She jogged down the narrow hall and up the steep stairs.

Minutes later, she was back in the warm kitchen toasting by the hearth, never having really appreciated the comforts of central heat until now. Her bedroom was damp and chilly in spite of the sunlight coming through the window.

"Will I see Coll at school tomorrow?"

"I was hoping you two could be friends, so I enrolled you at the school in Penzance instead of the little school in Marazion. Luckily, I live part way in between, so we had a choice."

"What books and stuff do I need for tomorrow?" She hadn't really brought a lot of school things with her.

"I have a kit ready for you. Coll made sure there was everything you should need," Sarie reassured her. "You don't need to go tomorrow, if you'd like a day or two off."

"No, I want to get going as soon as I can."

In truth, Laurel wanted a chance to talk to Coll about the Lady from the spring and the bargain she had made. She needed Coll's help. Maybe he would know other kids who could help too.

She spent the rest of the day helping Sarie with chores around the farm and grooming the horses. Shortly after dinner, she went upstairs to read and soon was fast asleep. Sometime later, Laurel was dimly aware of Sarie tucking in the blankets. She wondered briefly, why Sarie stood so long in the doorway, watching her with a strange look on her face. Rolling over, she went back to sleep.

Chapter Three

The Company

Coll was waiting by the entrance to the schoolyard the next morning. A fine misty rain was falling. Mizzle, Sarie called it. Laurel gave up trying to keep her hair from curling into her face and smiled at Coll in greeting.

"Thanks for helping Sarie get the right stuff." Laurel swung her school kit in front of her.

"Sarie wasn't 'zactly sure what was needed." Coll grinned.

He waved his arm in welcome to someone coming up the road behind her. She looked over her shoulder to see who it was. A small thin girl with long dark hair caught back in a braid joined them on the wet cobblestones by the school entrance. She looked inquisitively at Laurel before she returned Coll's grin.

"All right are 'ee?" She said in greeting.

"I'm pretty fair considering," Coll answered.

Coll pulled her forward toward the new girl. "This is Laurel. You know the one that come to stay with Sarie?"

"I'm Aisling." The younger girl nodded her head.

She was puzzled when Aisling glanced down the street, apparently looking for something. It was hard to see very far with the mist gathering in the narrow lanes.

"Have you seen Gort this morning?" Aisling asked Coll. "I stopped by his place, but his uncle was teasy as an adder and just growled at me."

"Not this morning." Coll looked worried.

"You don't reckon Stuart and his gang have got hold of him again, do you?"

"Bloody hell, I hope not. Last time it was all I could do to stop him from running away." Coll swore.

"You mean the same Stuart from the train?"

"The same."

A high thin wail followed by laughter sounded behind a tall stone wall a few yards from where they stood. Coll and Aisling exchanged resigned glances before bolting off toward the noise. Laurel ran after them wondering what small animal was being tormented.

She hoped Stuart was the tormentor; another crack at the big bully would suit her just fine. Aisling and Coll stopped at an opening in the wall leading into a small courtyard and she skidded to halt to keep from pelting into them. A group of six or seven older kids filled the cramped area. The girls stood off to one side, making rude comments she didn't understand. Four big boys gathered around something on the ground making the pitiful sounds. It was like the desperate cries of kittens abandoned by their mother.

The bully she recognized from the train turned at the sound of their feet on the cobblestones, a nasty smile on his face as he stood looking at Coll. Stuart smacked his fist into the palm of his other hand. Coll shifted uneasily but didn't give ground. Beside him, Aisling tightened her grip on her school bag.

"Let him alone," Aisling said fiercely.

"You gonna make me?" Stuart asked menacingly.

Coll stepped in front of Aisling. "Try picking on someone who's at least half your size."

Oh, my God! That's a kid on the ground. Bile rose in her throat. Blood ran from his nose in vivid contrast to his white face, and there was a bruise on his chin. The boy's eyes were wide and terrified. The high thin sounds coming from his throat sent chills up her back. *Stuart hasn't seen me yet!* Laurel looked around for something to use to defend her friends; she grabbed a heavy blackthorn walking stick leaning against the wall by the gate. Clutching it in her fingers she started forward not sure if her hands were shaking more from fear or anger.

Stuart started for Coll, his cohorts following close behind him. Laurel swallowed hard as Coll brace himself for the fight.

Aisling surprised her by smiling fiercely, feral lights glittering in her dark eyes.

She appeared focused on getting Gort out of there, no matter what it took. Laurel barreled around the end of the wall into the tiny courtyard. "Coll, duck," she hollered as she swung the heavy stick with all her might. Coll's eyes widened with surprise and fear, and he dropped under the swishing arc of the stick. Stuart was caught by surprise, and the heavy wood connected with the side of his jaw. He dropped like a sack of hammers.

Seeing her opening, Aisling darted in to stand over Gort, and the fight was on. The two girls with the gang pulled Stuart out onto the narrow lane while the remaining three boys tried to land punches and kicks on the rescuers.

Aisling stood her ground, swinging her heavy school bag as hard as she could. Coll had a bleeding nose and some scraped knuckles but was managing to hold his own, standing back to back with Aisling. Laurel's temper ran away with her; she swung the heavy club wildly. Somehow, she managed to actually land some blows. One of the older boys was limping and another cradled his right arm. The club hit his right shoulder, the force vibrating up the wood numbing her fingers. *I hope it hurts like hell!*

Dimly, she heard voices shouting, and then all the older kids were gone, leaving only Coll and Aisling standing over the huddled figure on the wet flagstones of the courtyard. Breathing heavily, Laurel dropped the walking stick to the ground and moved over to the little group.

"Is he all right? Should we get a doctor?"

She stood uncertainly over Aisling, who knelt on the wet cobblestones and helped Gort to sit up. Using the end of her blouse, Aisling wiped the blood away from Gort's nose. A thin trickle of blood immediately coursed over his upper lip and down his chin. Coll fished around in his pocket and produced a grimy handkerchief. He handed it to Aisling to help stem the flow of blood. Slowly Gort's eyes refocused on the world around him. He managed a small smile at Coll and Aisling.

"Thanks for coming to look for me," Gort said in a wavering voice.

Aisling and Coll each took one of Gort's arms, helping him to stand up on his shaking legs.

Something was wrong here. Why did Coll and Aisling act like this was an everyday occurrence? *Shouldn't they go and find someone in authority to report what happened? Where do Gort's parent's live?*

"Should I go look for a doctor?" She remembered seeing a sign for a doctor not too far away.

Gort shook his head. "M-M-M' unga wond p-p-pay fer un." Gort's voice was distorted by the blood from his nose and his rapidly swelling chin, not to mention his stutter.

"Shouldn't we report what happened to the police?"

Coll grunted in his throat. "No point in that. Stuart's dad is the head of the constabulary. Won't believe a word we say."

"It'll all turn out to be our fault. Stuart will say Gort tripped and fell because he's so clumsy, and we're all just trying to make trouble for Stuart to embarrass his dad," Aisling said in disgust.

Laurel started to launch into a protest but was interrupted by a rough voice behind her.

"Here now, what's going on here? Shouldn't you young'uns be in class?" A large man in a uniform blocked the door of the little courtyard. A short club swung menacingly in his right hand. "You bin fighting again?"

"No sir, Gort just had one of his fits on the way to school, we're just helping him," Aisling lied, looking the constable straight in the eyes.

Laurel caught sight of Coll vigorously shaking his head. "Shut your trap," he mouthed at her. Against her better judgment she closed her lips and waited to see what would happen next.

Coll slipped out of the courtyard as the constable took a step closer to Gort and Aisling. Once he was clear of the wall, he raced off down the rain-slick, narrow street.

"Old Joseph called to say kids was fighting in his yard again." The constable eyed the girls suspiciously. "Who are you anyways? You new in town?" He addressed Laurel directly.

"I'm staying with Sarie Waters," she answered, barely polite.

"Joseph must have heard Gort having his fit and just thought we were fighting," Aisling said quickly.

Gort nodded his head; avoiding looking directly at the constable. Aisling steered him towards the exit to the lane. Laurel hoped fervently Coll would get back from wherever it was he ran off to.

"What's Daniel gonna say about this, young lad?" the constable said in a threatening voice.

The thin boy flinched at the mention of his uncle. Face twisted in a rictus of terror, his gaze flew to the policeman's face. His legs shook so hard he would have fallen if Aisling hadn't held him up.

"D-d-d-don't t-t-tell him, p-p-p-lease."

A smug smile spread across the large man's face. "Well now, I'm thinking mayhap if you come clean out my chicken shed next weekend, I might forget to mention this unfortunate situation to Daniel." The constable fixed Gort with a gimlet eye.

"Now, Ted I don't think that's really necessary; do you?" Emily spoke from the gateway to the courtyard. She stared hard at the constable. "Threatening youngsters isn't very becoming to a man in your position is it?"

"Just see it doesn't happen again," the constable growled as he left the courtyard with a last fierce look at Gort.

Aisling smiled in relief. Emily picked Gort up like he was a toddler and threw the tail of her long cloak around him to keep off the rain. Slowly, she led the quiet group back to her house. Soon they were all sitting in Emily's small, cozy kitchen drinking hot chocolate and warming their cold hands by the fire in the hearth. Emily cleaned Gort's face and applied antiseptic to the cuts. Laurel regarded Gort thoughtfully over the rim of her cup. With his thin pinched-looking face and wild hair, he resembled pictures of homeless children in an old Charles Dickens' book. Without the unfocused look of terror twisting his features, Gort was kind of cute in a waifish, lost puppy sort of way. Aisling sat close beside him, fussing over him like a mother hen.

"I told you to wait for me this morning," Aisling scolded Gort.

"Had to get out early. Uncle Daniel was right ugly this morning."

"So instead of getting your ears skinned by Daniel's caterwauling, you decided to let Stuart and his mates have a go at you instead." Aisling's voice was acerbic with disgust.

"Wasn't 'zactly my original plan." Gort grinned at Aisling from under the tangle of his hair.

"Come here next time," Emily said gently and laid her hand on Gort's thin shoulder.

Gort looked at Laurel directly for the first time since his unlikely rescue. His smile lit up his thin face and she smiled in return.

"A right proper job you did swinging that blackthorn club," Gort enthused. "I could hardly believe my eyes when you clocked Stuart in the jaw!"

"Uhmm, yeah, I don't suppose we could like, not mention that part to Sarie?" *Lord only knows what Dad will say if he hears about this.*

"Not tell Sarie what?" Sarie said from the doorway of Emily's kitchen.

Laurel twisted around so fast she spilled hot chocolate down the front of her blouse. Setting her cup on the floor by her chair, she crossed the small room to grab Sarie's hand.

"Please Sarie, don't tell Dad. He'll tell Mom, and she'll be disappointed in me, and Dad will yell at me for sure. He probably won't even need to use the phone. I'll hear him all the way from home."

"Well, from what Emily tells me, things taint going 'zactly as they should this morning. I think we could just tell your dad you helped a friend out of jam if the subject comes up." Sarie squeezed her hand.

Laurel returned to her chair beside Coll and picked up the cup of hot chocolate Coll refilled for her. Sarie settled into the big rocking chair across from them and surveyed the little group with her piercing blue eyes missing nothing. Sarie exchanged a long look with Emily and then sighed.

"Gort, my son, what are we to do with you?" Sarie said in gentle exasperation.

"Same as always, patch me up and send me back out into the world." Gort grinned.

"I spoke to Ted on the way over. I don't think Stuart will be bothering you for a bit. Seems he's going to need surgery to fix his face and replace a few back teeth."

Laurel's face blanched, and her heart thumped loudly in her ears. *The town constable's kid needs surgery because of me. Dad is going to kill me, let alone what Stuart's dad has the power to do to me.*

"How much trouble am I in?"

"Ted and I had a rather heated discussion about the outcome of Stuart's latest stunt. I reminded him about the dental bills I had to foot the last time Coll stepped in to stop Stuart beating on Gort.

And about the visit from Aisling's mom regarding the torn dress and the lost school bag the time before that. Once Ted cools Angela down and makes her see Stuart isn't the angelic altar boy she thinks he is, everything will blow over." Emily smiled at Laurel.

Coll and Aisling whooped with delight, and Gort joined in somewhat gingerly due to his sore face. Laurel collapsed back into her chair and started to breathe normally again. Coll thumped her on the shoulder, and Aisling hugged her in delight.

"We're the Three Musketeers," Coll cheered.

"Except now there are four of us," Gort pointed out.

"Well, we can be The Company of Four, just like in the book I read last week," Aisling decided.

"Or we could be The Stuart Bashers," Coll offered.

Emily coughed, and Sarie hooted with laughter. Laurel was a little uncomfortable at the mention of Stuart and bashing in the same sentence.

"Let's not rub Ted's nose in it, or Angela's for that matter," Emily said.

"Or Stuart's," Gort said softly.

"I totally agree; let's stick with Company of Four," Laurel added her voice to the discussion.

"The Company of Four it is then," Coll agreed

"We'll have lots of adventures this summer." Aisling smiled at Laurel. "It'll be a welcome change to have some more female input when we disagree."

"Ash, you know you always win anyways," Gort teased her gently.

"That's only because I'm usually the one talking sense," Aisling said tartly.

Judging by the interchange, it sounded like her new friends would be willing to help out on her quest. It would certainly be an adventure. The biggest problem was how to bring up the subject of the Lady in Sarie's gully. *Maybe nobody will believe me. They'll think I'm crazy and make fun of me.*

Once the hot chocolate pot was empty, Emily tucked Gort into the spare bed in Coll's room upstairs to rest for the afternoon. Afterwards, Sarie escorted the other three children back to school.

Laurel and Coll were in the same class. She was very self-conscious as she settled into her desk trying to ignore the stares from the other kids in the room. The girl in the desk across the aisle glared at her and pointedly turned away, the curtain of her long blond hair falling across her face.

The boy behind Laurel whispered in her ear, "That's Stuart's sister, watch your step around her."

Laurel nodded her head slightly so the boy would know she heard. *Great, just great,* another *person who doesn't like me.* At the rate she was going more than half of Penzance would be hating her by suppertime. *I just want to go home!*

Laurel and Coll walked together to the last class of the day. At the door to the classroom, a girl tugged on her arm. She turned sharply to face her, not knowing what to expect. The girl had long chestnut hair, and looked oddly familiar.

"I wish you'd hit him harder. Stuart, I mean," the girl whispered fiercely, while looking quickly over her shoulder. "He's just plain mean. I hate him!"

Then she whisked past them into the classroom. Laurel exchanged a startled look with Coll, who shrugged and led the way into the class.

Coll whispered out of the corner of his mouth. "That was Lily, Stuart's cousin. Her mom is the teacher." Coll indicated the woman at the head of the class with a quirk of his eyebrow. Her heart sank. *Is Stuart related to the whole stinking town?*

Fortunately, the rest of the day passed quickly, and Aisling joined them as they clattered down the stone steps of the school. A small woman in a fit of agitation waited at the foot of the stairs. She pounced on Aisling and holding her firmly by the hand started to lead her away, talking fiercely all the while. She stopped momentarily to catch her breath and glare at Coll. Aisling took the opportunity to wave and cast her eyes heavenward. Coll grabbed Laurel's hand and dragged her away as fast his legs would take him. Once they were a safe distance from the school, he slowed down.

"Aisling's mom was right teasy. Ted or Angela must have been over to her place this afternoon." Coll stopped to lean on the stone wall of a building in the narrow lane.

"Is she always that crazy? Aisling seems so calm and normal."

“Aisling’s mom doesn’t ’zactly agree with her choice of friends. Gort’s uncle is the town drunk; I’m the local hedge witch’s grandson and now you,” Coll laughed.

“What’s wrong with me? She doesn’t even know me.”

“But you’re living with Sarie, the local witch, who is known to keep company with fairies and piskies and such like,” Coll grinned at her. “And now you’ve beaten up on the town constable’s bully of a son and gotten away with it. You might even rank lower than me in Alice’s book. I may actually have risen up a notch in life.”

“Sarie’s a witch?” *Dad so does not know that.* But, she was sure her Mom knew and approved of Sarie.

“That’s so,” Coll confirmed. “I thought you knew.” He looked puzzled.

Laurel shook her head as she started to walk down the street toward Emily’s. Coll pushed away from the wall and hurried to catch up with her.

“You mean like, a witch witch? Casting spells and stirring crappy stuff in big pots?”

“Never seen her do anything with pots. She does observe the old holy days though,” he replied.

“So, is she a good witch or a bad one? Can she put a hex on those kids that ganged up on Gort?”

“Good witch, I think. People ’round here respect her but they ain’t afraid of her. You’re not going to tell Sarie I told you, are you?” Coll looked worried.

They continued walking in silence for a few minutes. “It makes sense now, I couldn’t figure how the Lady could hang around Sarie’s spring and her not know about it.” Now seemed as good a time as any to bring up the subject of her encounter in the gully.

“You’ve met the White Lady of the Spring?”

“Have you?” Laurel answered his question with one of her own.

“No, but I’ve heard stories about her,” Coll said hesitantly. “Have you really seen her?”

She hesitated. *The White Lady didn’t say that meeting Her was a secret, and She did tell me to get help from my friends to solve the riddle. Isn’t this just the opening I need to tell Coll about the riddle and get him to agree to help? If he agrees, I’m sure Gort and Aisling will help too*. That was if Aisling could ever escape the clutches of her over protective mother again. She caught Coll's arm just as they reached Emily's front door. He stopped and waited.

"I'll explain everything once we see Gort. I need to tell both of you, so it'll be easier to tell you together. I can tell Aisling later, when we see her."

Coll nodded before he pulled open the door and stepped inside. They went down the hall into the kitchen where Emily was boiling some fish on the cooker. Gort was sitting in a large armchair pulled up by the hearth with a crocheted rug wrapped around him.

"Some people will do anything to get out of going to school," Coll said as he flopped down into the matching Morris chair on the other side of the hearth. Laurel perched on the overstuffed ottoman between them.

Gort grinned and shrugged. The dark blue-black circles under Gort's eyes didn't look as bad as before. The haunted fey expression had left his features, and his thin face was quite handsome in a fragile kind of way. The long thin nose under high arched brows seemed to have quit bleeding. His lips were still swollen from Stuart's earlier pounding, although the line of his full sensitive mouth was clearly visible. Dark hair fell over Gort's forehead like the heavy forelock of the Fell ponies. Even though the rest of the boy was warmly wrapped in Emily's afghan, Laurel could still see his slight form curled up on the wet cobbles of Old Joseph's courtyard. He probably wouldn't come much higher than her nose if they stood face to face, but she sensed a deep well of courage buried deep inside. The fire popped and crackled, startling her out of her thoughts.

"I rang Sarie and told her I would feed you and take you home later," Emily came around the counter from the kitchen as she spoke.

Emily motioned for Coll to set up the small folding tea trays in front of the chairs pulled close to the fire. Emily set the plates full of boiled fish and potatoes with tinned tomatoes on the trays. Bustling back into the kitchen for the teapot and large pottery mugs, Emily gathered everything they needed and sank into her chair with a sigh.

"I haven't managed to scare Daniel up yet. Somebody mentioned he might have gone to Paul for the day," Emily told Gort.

"That's not such a bad thing," Gort grinned. "He's going to skin me when he finds out I've annoyed Ted and Angela." The grin faded as Gort thought about the inevitable outcome of Stuart's day's work.

"Why don't you leave and live somewhere else?" Laurel asked. The idea of staying with someone who was mean to you didn't make sense.

"It's not so easy," Gort said quietly.

Emily caught Gort's eyes and held them for an instant. Gort nodded his head in resignation.

"She's one of us now. Laurel might as well know how it stands with Uncle Daniel." Gort spoke to Emily over the hiss and crackle of the fire as some rain found its way down the chimney.

"Daniel is Gort's dad's brother. There were never two brothers so different from each other as those two. Brian, Gort's dad, worked hard and never touched the drink. Daniel was a hell raiser from the time he was fourteen, drank and ran with the rough crowd, never worked if he could help it." Emily paused to drink her tea. "There was no other family. Eileen, Gort's mom, came from Ireland, and her family never forgave her for marrying out of her faith. So when Brian and Eileen were killed in the car crash, and the will was read, there it was. Daniel is to take care of Gort until he's of age, and to help him, there is a monthly stipend paid to Daniel in return for his trouble. Luck be to the angels, Daniel can't touch the bulk of Gort's inheritance, but he certainly can, and does, carouse away the monthly stipend."

"Can't somebody do something? You and Sarie look after Gort way more than his uncle does."

"The lawyer Brian used is a brother of Daniel's best friend and a cousin of Ted's. Brian never thought Daniel would misuse Gort the way he has. Brian always was one to look for the best in a person, and Daniel exploited that," Emily explained.

"Complaining only gets me worse treatment," Gort broke in. "Don't try to fix anything."

It seemed trying to make things better would only make it worse. Laurel resolved to talk to Aisling about it the first chance she got.

They cleared away the dishes and replaced the little folding tables against the wall. Emily looked out the rain-streaked window into the back garden as she wound a pink shawl around her head and shoulders.

"I'm off to see if I can scare up your uncle, Gort." Emily headed down the tiny hall to the front door.

"With any luck you won't find him," Gort muttered under his breath.

"Why does she bother?"

"So Daniel can't say Emily is trying to poison Gort against him. He tried to get Ted to enact some kind of by-law or something forbidding Gort from having anything to do with anyone Daniel thinks is unsuitable," Coll told her.

"That's why Emily will go to my house and leave another note on the table telling Uncle Daniel where I am. Then she'll go the constable's office, have it on record she tried to contact Daniel and inform them of my whereabouts," Gort said wearily. "I don't know why Uncle Daniel bothers. He could keep the money and all, if he would just leave me alone and let me stay with Emily. He just enjoys causing trouble, meaner than a snake he is."

Coll suddenly brightened. "Gramma will be gone for a while. Remember you said you'd tell me and Gort about the White Lady when we were alone."

"You saw Sarie's White Lady?" Gort asked, his eyebrows arching in amazement. "I thought Aisling was making that story up."

"Aisling's seen her? Why didn't you tell me?"

"Didn't know." Coll raised his hands protectively.

"Tell us what happened." Gort leaned forward transparently eager to forget about his aches and pains and Uncle Daniel.

Chapter Four

Blood Pact

Laurel pulled the ottoman closer to the fire and jabbed at the logs with the poker. Thoughts buzzed and flipped inside her head, banging into each other and skidding off in all directions. Uncertainty wound its way through her, and she fought down the urge to hurl up her supper into the hearth. *What if Coll and Gort laugh at me, or worse, don't believe me and refuse to help?*

Heat blossomed over Laurel's heart and spread in waves over her body. She stifled her annoyance when her hand shook as she ran fingers through her bangs and lifted them off her hot forehead. Taking one final poke at the logs in the hearth, she leaned the heavy iron poker against the fireguard, closed her eyes for a second, and took a deep breath.

"It was the day after I got here. I was mad at my Dad because he wouldn't let me come home. I ran away from Sarie's house and ended up in the little valley down in the pony field." Laurel twisted her hands together in her lap and noticed absently there were black smudges from the fire on her fingers and jeans.

"That's where Aisling said she met her, too." Gort's eyes gleamed with excitement.

"Anyway, I was upset because my Mom is really sick, and I want to go home. This Lady just showed up out of nowhere beside the pond I was at. She seemed kind of weird at first. Not bad weird, just, oh, I don't know, different I guess. The more I talked to her, the more normal she seemed."

"Who is she?" Coll leaned forward.

"She said she was the spirit of the spring, and people knew her as The White Lady. She must be some kind of fairy, or ghost, or something, I think."

"She's not a ghost. Sarie told me that much," Coll said. "I think she's some kind of old goddess or something."

"Let her finish the story, Coll," Gort admonished him.

"I don't know what she is for sure. What I do know is she offered to help make my Mom better."

"What do you mean?" Gort asked apprehensively with a quick sideways glance at Coll.

"She offered me a deal. I have to solve some riddle, and if I do, the White Lady will make my Mom better. But I have to do it fast, 'cause Mom is so sick, and there's only a little bit of time to save her."

Coll was the key. If he agreed to help her, Aisling and Gort would help, too.

"Did you agree to anything?" Coll asked, his voice sounded strange and far away.

"Yeah, I did. She said she can help my Mom!"

"You didn't ask Sarie about it before you said yes?" Gort asked quietly.

"There wasn't time. What if I had gone to find Sarie and the Lady disappeared before I got back?"

"What did you promise?" Gort prompted.

"Only that I would solve the riddle before my Mom got too sick for the Lady and her friends to help her."

"What if you don't solve the riddle? What do you have to give up? What did you agree to?" Gort persisted. "As far as I know, there are never any dealings with fairies and the like that don't have consequences."

"My mom dies. We didn't talk about any other payment."

"That's it?" Coll was unconvinced.

"What do you mean *that's it*? There's nothing worse. Nothing they could want is worse than Mom dying! Isn't that enough?"

"So it would seem," Aisling said as she entered the kitchen.

"How long have you been here?"

"Long enough to hear most of the story. I didn't want to interrupt you," Aisling said mildly, pulling Emily's chair closer to the fire.

"What do you think? Is there a trick in it somewhere?" Coll asked.

Laurel waited impatiently while Aisling wrinkled her nose and watched the flames play in the hearth for a long moment. "I think unless there was some other payment agreed on, the bargain is as it was explained."

"How did you get away from your mom?" Gort smiled at Aisling.

Aisling screwed her face up in exasperation. "I just listened to the same old saw about what a bad influence you lot are, and what will the neighbors think, and on, and on. And yet here I am, back keeping company with you blackguards."

"They do say some people never learn," Coll said, grinning.

"Let's keep focused here though. What's the riddle you have to solve? Does it make any sense to you?" Aisling snuggled deeper into her chair.

"I don't have it yet."

"Where're you supposed to get it from?" Coll demanded.

"Are you sure?" Aisling's voice conveyed her feelings of unease.

"Of course, I'm sure. She said I have to go someplace called Padstone, or something, on Bel something or other. Beltane, that's what she said."

"You mean Padstow," Gort corrected. "You need to go to Padstow on May first. That's the date for Beltane."

"That shouldn't be hard. Sarie goes to the 'Obby 'Oss Festival every year." Coll smiled in relief.

"Why does she go there? Is that the festival you mentioned before?"

"Yeah, the one I told you about on the train the day I met you."

"It's an ancient celebration that goes back centuries. It celebrates the coming of summer and the new growing season," Aisling explained.

"Did the Lady say how you would get the first clue?" Gort prodded. "What if the whole riddle thing really is a trick, maybe just the fairies' idea of a joke?"

"Tell us exactly what the Lady said," Aisling prompted.

Laurel screwed her face up as she tried to recall the Lady's words. "She said…" Laurel began slowly, "she said…I would get the first clue at the Fire Festival of Beltane. I have to go to Padstone, I mean Padstow, and keep my heart open to receive the message."

"Whatever that means," Coll muttered under his breath.

Aisling gave Coll a quick kick to his shins. He yelped in protest.

"Was there anything else?" Aisling asked.

"Yeah, something about me riding the filly that never was foaled. When I ride her, I'll be close to the answer. She said I would hold death in my hands." Laurel was a little embarrassed repeating the words. It sounded so weird saying them here in Emily's kitchen. When the White Lady spoke the words, they seemed prophetic and beautiful.

"I really don't like the part about holding death in your hands," Coll said skeptically. "You're gonna have to hold a dead horse?"

"Can it be dead, if it never was born?" Gort tried to be logical.

"I don't think she was talking about the horse when she said I would hold death in my hands." It all seemed so clear when the Lady explained it to her, now it was all muddled up.

"I think Laurel's right. The Lady might have meant the Night Mare, when she mentioned the filly that never was foaled," Aisling said.

"For the love of Pete." Laurel used one of her Grampa D'arcy's favorite expressions. "What's the Night Mare?"

Frustration welled up. *How am I ever going to solve a riddle that I don't even have yet, when there are more people, or whatever they are, involved than I can shake a stick at? Aisling and Coll are just making things more complicated.*

"The Night Mare is an aspect of the old goddess of the land. She has something to do with death and transition, I think. Sarie can explain it better than me." Aisling smiled.

"That's why bad dreams are called nightmares," Gort said quietly.

"You would know that better than most." Aisling stood up and hugged Gort gently about the shoulders.

Laurel looked at Coll puzzled. Coll shook his head slightly and mouthed, "I'll tell you later."

"The reason I'm telling you guys this is because The Lady said I can't do it by myself. She said I needed to have friends to help. You three are the only friends I have here."

"Of course we'll help you. Just try to stop us." Aisling hugged her.

"We're the Company of Four," Coll said. "We can all go to Padstow with Sarie and see if we can figure out what the first clue is."

"We should make a pact. Something solemn and binding, to make it official," Gort said.

Coll pulled his jackknife out of his pocket and opened the blade. Reaching up, he took one of Emily's long matches from its holder on the mantle. Coll lit the match in the hearth and ran the flame along the edge of the knife blade.

"We can make a blood pact, all four of us. I'll make a little cut on each of our thumbs. We bind them together and swear to find the answer to the riddle."

"Don't you think Gort's lost enough blood for one day?" Laurel eyed the knife blade uneasily.

"That's exactly what we need to do," Gort said, the light from the fire throwing huge dark circles under his eyes.

Aisling stepped closer to Gort and took his hand in hers. "It is the kind of promise the old ones and the fairies would understand and respect."

Coll knelt in front of Gort and made a quick slice in the pad of his right thumb. As the blood welled up, Coll handed the knife to Gort. Gort turned a little paler as he pressed the blade into his own thumb and handed the knife to Aisling who did the same before passing the knife to Laurel.

Her hand shook as she gripped the handle. The blood on the blade gleamed black in the firelight, then brilliant red as the flames flickered. The knife was slippery in her hand; Laurel wasn't sure if it was blood or sweat. She didn't really want to know. The room shifted and spun, as her gaze fixed on the stained blade of the jackknife. The air thickened, and it was hard to breath. The fire flared brightly, and a woman's face appeared in the flames. The air shimmered between her and the hearth.

"Blood is a binding pact. We will accept the allegiance of your friends and validate your quest once you seal the pact." The voice was at once horrible and comforting. Laurel's bones vibrated with the resonance of the woman's speech. It felt like the time she held a tuning fork to the bone on her wrist.

"Hurry up!" Coll shook her with his hand that wasn't dripping blood.

With one last glance at the hearth, Laurel quickly drew the knife across her thumb. She turned toward Coll, who grasped her hand and held their thumbs together so the blood mingled and ran down their forearms. Aisling joined her thumb with theirs; Gort leaned forward in his chair and added his thumb as well. Coll used his free hand to make sure all four of the small wounds were in contact with each other, and blood from each of them was mixed together.

"Do you know what to say? To make it official, I mean," Coll asked Aisling.

"Yeah, let's not make a mistake and do this wrong," Gort joked.

Aisling nodded before she began to speak in a singsong voice, which made Laurel's stomach feel heavy and cold. *What am I asking my friends to do?*

"By the blood we willingly spill,
By the quest we willingly share,
We pledge to journey for good, not ill,
We bind ourselves to the purpose we share.
Together we are four.
Four for Balance,
Of the Cardinal Directions, there are four.
Four Elements, our luck to enhance,
Bound willingly together as One.
One in our Purpose, we seek healing in our Quest.
We Quest as One;
Until the Quest is fulfilled, we will not rest."

"To this I swear." Aisling finished and looked to her right at Coll.

"To this I swear," Coll avowed.

"To this I swear," Gort answered in his turn.

"To this I swear," Laurel said firmly.

"The pact is affirmed and sealed," Aisling said formally.

The four friends stood silently before the fire for a moment. Coll released his grip on Laurel's hand first; Aisling and Gort removed their hands as well. Coll went to the sink and ran a washcloth under the cold water. He wiped the blood from his hand and arm and then scrounged some bandages out of the medicine chest. Aisling cleaned her hand and applied the bandage to her thumb. Gently, she cleaned Gort and bandaged his hand, too. Laurel took the cloth from Aisling and tidied herself as well.

"We better clear all this mess before Emily gets back." Laurel cautioned. There were little spots of blood on the rug in front of the hearth. The blood-stained washcloth dangled from her fingers.

Aisling took the cloth and folded it carefully into four. Then she bowed to the four directions, starting in the east and continuing in a clockwise rotation. She finished her bow to the north and then flung the washcloth into the flames.

"That should make it pretty official." Aisling grinned.

"I guess," Laurel said doubtfully.

The front door slammed and a second later Emily stamped into the kitchen, bristling with fury.

Does Emily know what we've been up to?

Coll shrugged his shoulders slightly when she glanced at him.

"What's happened, Emily?" Aisling inquired. Taking the woman's coat, she hung it by the fire to dry.

"Daniel's gone too far this time!" Emily raged at no one in particular.

"What's he done now?" Gort asked with resignation and not a little uncertainty.

Laurel stared in amazement; even her dad didn't get this mad. Not enraged like this. Anger flew like sparks in her wake as Emily paced up and down the kitchen.

"Going to have me arrested for kidnapping, is he?" Emily snorted.

"What?" Coll yelped.

Gort hid his face in his hands. Aisling clenched her fists, looking ready to do battle with anything or anyone who wanted to harm Emily or Gort.

"Accused me of getting you lot to lie about Stuart beating on Gort so I could spirit him away to my lair. Says he's going to send Gort away to boarding school in London," Emily snorted again. "Not likely he'd be willing to forego his drink in order to pay for that." She paced faster up and down the rug.

"You won't have to go the gaol, will you Gramma?" Coll asked anxiously.

Emily quit pacing and hugged Coll fiercely about the shoulders. "Of course I'm not going to have to go the gaol. Soon as Daniel sobers up, he'll think twice about trying to get me arrested."

"Bout time you came to your senses." Sarie snorted from the front hall. "I was waiting for you to catch fire from that temper of yours."

Sarie entered the kitchen and pulled a stool up to the fire. "We might have to convince Daniel about Gort though," Sarie continued thoughtfully. "He just might be able to make a good case for sending Gort to boarding school."

"I'm not going anywhere!" Gort struggled to get to his feet, flailing weakly at the blanket wrapped around him. Breathlessly, he finally got himself free and stood swaying slightly on the hearthrug. "I'm not leaving Penzance and the only friends I have." Gort managed to sound quite fierce, and for once, there was no stutter to his speech.

"Calm down now, Gort. Don't you worry your head about Daniel. Let Sarie and I take care of him." Emily took Gort by the shoulders and set him gently back in his chair by the fire.

Laurel looked at Aisling, who had been strangely quiet through the whole conversation. The girl was staring intently at the bottom right square of the rainy kitchen window. She narrowed her eyes trying to see what Aisling was looking at. All she could see was the black rain running down the panes of glass like tears. Suddenly, Aisling sat up, and her face brightened. She jumped out of her chair and headed for the door into the back garden. Laurel looked around the room and met Sarie's inscrutable gaze.

"Where are you going in such a hurry, Aisling child?" Sarie asked quietly.

"There's someone in the garden I need to talk to," Aisling said over her shoulder, as she opened the door on the wet windy night.

"Won't you need a coat?" Laurel got to her feet and grabbed Emily's heavy shawl from the back of a chair. She hesitated, uncertain whether she should follow. Aisling was already out of the door, leaving a waft of cool wet air in her wake as the door shut behind her.

Should I go out with Aisling, or is this something I have no right to interfere with? Sarie shrugged and raised her eyebrows. "Go if you like," she said.

Laurel wrapped the shawl around her shoulders before she opened the door into the dark night. Just out of the patch of light from the big kitchen window, Aisling knelt on the wet grass. Her hair lay still and dry on her back, while Laurel's was already wet and flying about in the wild wind.

Trepidation slowed her steps. This was too weird and way out of her league. Were all her new friends engaged in some kind of supernatural game? The light from the kitchen faded, and the air around Aisling shimmered with rainbow lights. She was only a couple of feet away from the girl, but the shimmer separated them, and somehow it kept the wild night away from Aisling and her secret friend. Laurel peered through the coruscating rainbow light to see who it was Aisling spoke with. There was a twiggy-looking brown man about the size of a small child holding Aisling's hand.

There was an impression of a tiny wrinkled face with a long sharp nose and bright black eyes. Her stomach jumped into her throat as those eyes fastened on hers, and the thin lips stretched into a smile. The small man made a funny gesture, and there was a sudden streak of lightening across the sky. Laurel blinked, and then there was only Aisling kneeling in the wet grass.

Aisling got to her feet and pushed her hair out of her face. The strange shimmer in the air was gone, and the wind was busy making knots in Aisling's hair.

"You gonna share that shawl?" Aisling asked, as if nothing out of the ordinary just happened.

"Who was that?" With one hand, she unwound part of the shawl and threw it over Aisling.

"That was a friend of mine who is going to pay a little visit to Daniel tonight," Aisling smiled, but there was no warmth in her face. "I think by morning Daniel will have changed his mind about sending Gort away. Hopefully, he'll be too scared to bother Gort again for a while."

"But who was it? Why wasn't the storm touching you when you were with him?" *In for a penny, in for a pound*, she figured. Her Gramma Bella used to say that, she remembered suddenly. She also used to say curiosity killed the cat, but Laurel pushed that thought to the back of her mind.

"He's one of the Old Folk, those that some call the Good Neighbors. He's a piskie."

Aisling glared, daring her to disagree.

Laurel laughed at her, the rain running down her face. "Hey, you're talking to the person who cried all over some White Lady and is haring across Cornwall trying to find some riddle I need to solve! If a piskie can help Gort, more power to him."

Aisling hugged her tight. "It's so nice to have a friend who just takes things at face value and doesn't constantly ask for proof or something the way Coll does."

The girls stepped back into the warm kitchen from the windy night. It seemed very quiet out of the wind and rain. They draped the wet shawl over a hook by the fire to dry. Aisling knelt in front of Gort and gently took his hand in hers. He smiled at her from his bruised face.

"I don't think Daniel will bother you for a while," Aisling's voice was soft.

"Ta, Ash. The last time your friend spoke with Daniel, it kept him quiet for a long time."

"So you found who you were looking for, did you?" Sarie said in a dry tone.

"You knew I would," Aisling said with an edge to her words.

"I did that. What I can't figure is how you can be Alice's child," Sarie said enigmatically.

"But you knew my great gram on Da's side." Aisling stared hard at Sarie as she spoke.

Sarie sighed and shrugged. "I guess blood will tell, eventually," she agreed.

Sarie stood up and stretched. Then she gathered up her walking cloak and Laurel's school bag. "It's time we were getting home. Can we give you a ride, Aisling?"

"Sure, as long as you drop me at the corner, so Mom doesn't know how I got home." Aisling grinned.

"Gort, you're to stay here with Emily and Coll for the time being," Sarie told him. Laurel watched her exchange a knowing look with Emily over Gort's head.

“Suits me fine,” Gort agreed, his eyes already closing sleepily in the heat from the hearth.

* * *

Now the threat was gone of Uncle Daniel coming to drag Gort out into the cold wet night and throw him into his equally cold and damp bed, Coll was relieved to see him let himself relax and slip into a safe and dreamless sleep.

Emily picked Gort up as easily a doll and carried him up the stairs to the spare room at the back of the house. Coll followed along behind her, locking the doors after the others left. Turning out the lights on the lower floor as they went, Coll trailed up the stairs in Emily’s wake. He peeked in the door to the spare room just as Emily finished tucking him in and closing the curtains on the damp. The electric fire glowed warmly in the little fireplace. Emily hugged Coll tightly as she met him at the door.

“It’ll all come out in the wash, Coll,” Emily reassured him. “I think Daniel may have had a change of heart by the morning.”

“Do ya think he’ll be okay?” Coll looked at Gort’s small figure in the bed. “He’s tougher than he seems, but Stuart knocked the stuffing out of him today.”

“I think as long as Gort has his friends, he’ll be right as rain.” Emily gave Coll a last squeeze before she let him go. “Now off to bed with you.”

“Night, Gramma,” Coll said as he headed for his room.

The wind was billowing in the curtains of Coll’s window as he entered his room. Swearing under his breath, Coll hurried to pull the sash down against the storm. The floor under his feet was cold and wet from the rain. Coll yanked a towel off the pile of laundry on his dresser and threw it onto the puddled water. Pushing the towel around with his feet to dry the linoleum, Coll reached up to pull his curtains shut. His hand stopped midway, and he gaped at the sight of Gort’s Uncle Daniel staggering down the middle of the lane. Daniel was covered in mud, and wet seaweed hung from his shoulders. His feet slipped on the wet cobbles; he only wore one boot, and his other foot was bare. With his right hand, Daniel brandished a half-empty whiskey bottle wildly in front of him, while his other hand tried vainly to hitch his trousers up over his skinny hips. Coll opened the window again so he could make out what Daniel was shouting. The words were slurred, and the rush of the wind made it doubly hard for him to be sure what he was hearing.

"Ya auld biddy! Setting your demons on me, trying to drown me, knocked me off the pier they did, an me jush a poor man enjoying a drap or two before going back to me hard labor in the marning." Daniel reeled past Emily's front door aiming a kick at it as he passed.

"He's drunk as a hand cart." Coll laughed out loud, as Daniel stopped and shook his fist at the house.

Coll stuck his head out the window to make sure Daniel wasn't trying to break down the door. In a flash of lightening, a small dark creature darted out from the bushes by the front door and raced between Daniel's legs. Daniel went down in a heap. The pale white skin of his buttocks exposed to the rain as he tried to scramble back to his feet.

"Ya demon!" Daniel threw his head back and roared at the sky.

Clutching his trousers with his free hand, Daniel reeled away down the dark lane. Coll saw a dozen small creatures swarming at the man's heels. He narrowed his eyes to see better in the dark and hastily dashed the rain out of his face. *They must be cats.* Although why cats would behave like that, Coll couldn't understand for the life of him. They looked like little brown men, dancing around Daniel, running in to pinch him in the most inappropriate places. Two more of the creatures hung off the waistband of his trousers howling with glee. Coll shook his head and blinked; they *must* be cats, *not* little men. When Coll looked again, all he could see was Daniel running, as fast as a very drunk man was able to run, around the corner into the next street and the dubious safety of his own house.

The sound of wild, unbridled laughter sounded up and down the street above the howl of the wind. Coll closed his window and pulled the curtains firmly across the dark windowpanes. Shivering with more than the cold and damp, Coll climbed into his own bed where he pulled the covers up over his head.

* * *

Down the hall, Emily pulled the curtains shut on her own window. With a slight smile, she climbed into bed. "As you sow, so shall you reap," Emily said with satisfaction into the darkness.

From Daniel's house in the next street over, Emily heard a faint voice yelling incoherently. She pulled the covers up to her chin and smiled again. It seemed Aisling's friends were going to give Daniel a night to remember. Emily's smile faded as she hoped it would be enough to protect Gort from his uncle's nasty rages.

* * *

They waited until Aisling opened her front door and waved before Sarie put the car in gear and pulled away from the corner. The wipers splashed the water around on the windscreen but did little to clear it. Laurel decided it was better to look out the side window and not try to figure out how Sarie could see to drive. She hoped this wasn't the street that ended with a drop into the harbor below. She released a breath of relief when she saw the hedges on both sides of the narrow road; they must be close to home.

"Is Aisling really friends with a piskie?" Laurel spoke over the slap of the wipers.

"She is that," Sarie took her eyes off the road for a moment, "and some other things besides, I dare say."

"What do you mean? What other things, like fairies or something?"

"That's for Aisling to tell you in her own time, if she will. Besides, I don't pretend to know who all Aisling's friends are."

"I suppose. Do you think her friend will be able to help Gort with his uncle?" What could such a little man do to stop Gort's uncle from being such a bully?

"I think Daniel is in for a very long night he won't soon forget." Sarie laughed grimly. "Aisling was plenty furious at Daniel. She's a good one have as your friend, but you don't want Aisling as your enemy."

Laurel thought about the wild feral light in Aisling's eyes as she swung her school bag at Stuart and nodded in total agreement.

“We’ll still have to deal with Stuart. He can’t just get away with treating other people like he does.”

“Be patient, child. Stuart may get sorted out for you. Let it lie for a bit,” Sarie cautioned.

Chapter Five

Stuart is Sorted

"How we view magic is a matter of perception," Emily said in answer to Coll's question.

Coll, Laurel, Gort, Sarie and Emily were sitting in Sarie's kitchen the next evening. The slanting rays of the sun gilded the grass in the pony field and lay warmly across the blue oilcloth of the table.

"What do you mean?" Laurel was confused.

"When we think of magic, as a rule, we think of things like fairies in the garden and mermaids in the bay, or shadows in the moonlight and all sorts of mystical ideals," Emily continued.

"But it's a fine line between the beauty that can be associated with magic and the slide into darkness which can happen if you tip over the edge. You know how the old sayings go, if you follow the fairies home, you return either mad or a poet," Sarie added.

"Aisling says it like magic holds up a mirror to your heart, and what you are inside is reflected back at you," Gort piped in.

"Aisling is not so far from the truth," Sarie agreed. "How we behave and how we view the world comes back to us for good or ill."

"But what did you mean about perception? Don't things just exist as they are?"

"It's how we view things on a personal level that can make two people see the same thing, but interpret it exactly opposite. For example, walking the beach at low tide, a person can see all sorts of glittery bits of sea polished glass and rocks. Some will see them as treasures from the sea; others will walk right over them without really noticing them. Whether we acknowledge them or not, they're still there. Even your own perceptions can change from one moment to the next. Take walking alone in the moonlight for example. You know how one minute it can be all lovely and beautiful, and then somehow, something changes; and suddenly it's not all silvery star shine. Now, the shadows aren't friendly anymore, and they hide secrets in their midst. Where one moment there is harmony, and you feel completely safe, the next it seems danger is everywhere. Some of us will only ever see the beauty and bright side of magic. While we are aware the balancing dark side does exist, it doesn't really touch us." Emily paused.

"But for some," Sarie took up Emily's train of thought and continued, "the dark side is all they know, so only the darkness exists for them. Like Daniel. So in answer to your question Coll, you did see the darker side of the magic last night. Daniel was correct in a way to call them demons, but they were demons of his own making. His anger and rage and just plain meanness of spirit were reflected back at him."

"But I thought the piskie was a friend of Aisling's, and she asked them to torment Daniel."

"Aisling is far too smart to ask a piskie to do anything specific for her. What she did was point out the wrong done to Gort, who is her good friend and therefore, in the piskie's way of reckoning, under Aisling's protection. She let the piskie decide how he should deal with the situation," Sarie explained.

"At least Uncle Daniel agreed I could stay here with Sarie for a fortnight," Gort said happily.

"He would only talk to me through the locked door!" Emily laughed. "He was sure I had a whole flock of "little demons" with me just waiting for him to open the door."

"Did ya get him to agree to let Gort go to Padstow with us?" Coll asked.

"He did say Gort could come with us." Emily nodded and smiled at Gort.

Laurel and Coll exchanged relieved looks across the table. Now they only had to make sure Aisling could come along, too.

"I'll just go along tomorrow and have a word with Alice. I'm sure she'll let Aisling come with us. We're going to visit with my friend, Jane," Sarie said.

Coll grinned, and Gort beamed from ear to ear.

"Jane is Aisling's aunt. Tom's sister," Coll whispered.

"If Alice won't agree, I'll get Jane to give Tom a ring and invite Aisling for a visit. Tom can never figure out why Alice gets so hysterical about Aisling going to the festival." Emily shook her head. "Whatever disagreement a man and wife might have behind closed doors, it won't much matter; Aisling will be allowed to go. Tom will make sure of it."

* * *

Laurel and Coll leaned on the rough fence of the pasture and watched the ponies grazing in the lush grass. Emily and Sarie were deep in some discussion about perception and reality, so they took the opportunity to go visit the horses. They left Gort fast asleep in the big armchair.

"Does any of that make sense to you?" Coll furrowed his brow as he spoke.

"Kind of, but not really."

She narrowed her eyes against the setting sun, making huge rays of light shoot out of the blazing ball as it continued to sink behind the trees. She slipped through the fence and started across the thick grass towards the ponies. Coll followed, catching up with her just as the ponies came mooching over to see if there were any treats to be had. Laurel laid her hand on Lamorna's shoulder and brushed the heavy forelock out of mare's eyes. The pony regarded her with huge dark liquid eyes. Coll scratched Gareth under the chin and searched his pockets for something suitable to offer the inquisitive pony. Laurel laid her hands on either side of the pony's face and rested her forehead against Lamorna's.

"What do we do about Stuart?" she asked Lamorna. "He can't just get away with treating people the way he does."

"Do ya think Stuart's mean because someone else is nasty to him all the time?" Coll cleared his throat.

"I don't much care. He just can't go around acting like poison."

"I guess you're right. But it can't be fun having Angela for your mother, constantly crowing about how great you are and going on about your exalted family history. And Ted, well from where I stand, Ted's a right bully." Coll moved to stand beside her and she lifted her head. Lamorna regarded him thoughtfully from under her forelock.

"Still, we have to figure out what we can do to stop Stuart from setting his gang of bullies on Gort and whoever else they torment. Without getting my dad all hot and bothered," she added as an afterthought.

She pulled away from Lamorna and walked across the pasture with her head down. Coll sauntered along at her side; the ponies and large draft horses tagged behind them like a row of ducklings. Laurel stopped at the old barn and leaned against the sun-warmed granite of the foundation. Some bats fluttered about in the gathering dusk. In the wooded valley of the White Lady's spring an owl hooted. There didn't seem to be much anyone could or would do through official channels. Stuart's dad being the local police was an annoying obstacle as far as she was concerned. Not so much different from Cora-Anne back home being the daughter of the guidance counselor.

Laurel smiled at Coll as he leaned on the wall beside her. Coll bent his knees and slid down the rough stone until he was sitting on the ground beside her feet with his legs stretched out in front of him, his back against the barn. The last vestiges of the sun buried itself in the fringe of the trees, and the first stars pricked out in the twilight sky.

As she watched the darkening sky, Laurel was surprised to realize she hadn't talked to Chance or Carlene in almost two weeks. Alberta seemed more than a world away right now, except for her mom. The doctors were trying some new treatments. Mom sounded so tired but said the pain wasn't as bad. Laurel bent her knees and slid down the side of the barn to sit beside Coll on the still warm earth. The granite wall of the barn felt solid and good against her back. A tear wound its way past her nose. Coll pulled a dirty handkerchief out of his pocket and handed it to her without saying a word. He shifted into a more comfortable position and spoke without looking at her.

"You can't go getting your knickers in a knot about stuff you can't do anything about, ya know."

Laurel's laughter snorted out her nose. "My knickers in a knot..." She giggled. "Wait 'til I tell Carlene that one!"

"I was trying to make you feel better." Coll sounded offended.

"I know you were. Actually, you did make me feel better, I think." Laurel laid her hand on Coll's arm. "I am sorry. I didn't mean to laugh at you. It just sounded so, oh I don't know, like something Emily would say. Not you."

"Do you laugh at me with your friends from back home?" Coll said angrily.

* * *

For some reason he couldn't fathom, Coll wasn't ready to forgive her for laughing at his attempt to make her feel better.

"Of course I don't!" She scrambled to her feet and shouted down at him. "If that's the kind of person you think I am, why do you want to be friends with me at all?"

The ponies snorted and backed away hastily as she stormed back across the field toward the house. Coll sat for a minute longer and then jumped to his feet. He kicked at an unoffending clump of trefoil by his boot. He couldn't decide if he was mad at Laurel or just the world in general. Nothing was working out the way he imagined it should.

"Bloody hell! All I was trying to do was make her feel better," Coll said to the circle of inquiring pony faces.

Arthur nudged Coll with his big black nose and snuffled in sympathy. His wise dark eyes advised Coll not to even try and figure out what the female members of his species thought or even how they arrived at their conclusions. Coll stroked Arthur's sleek black neck. Lamorna gave Coll a shove in the back, knocking him forward toward the lights of Sarie's house gleaming in the darkness.

"I don't know what I have to apologize for," Coll told the mare grumpily.

Lamorna regarded Coll with her dark starlit eyes and snorted all over his shirt.

"All right, all right, I'm going."

Coll backed away from the mare and started across the dew-laden pasture. Before he reached the fence, his feet and pant legs were wet with moisture. *Could the night get any better?* He looked down in disgust. The hooting of the owl in the valley carried across the dark pony field and followed Coll as he made his way up the path to Sarie's back door.

Coll pulled the door shut behind him and turned to see Laurel's white face across the table from a thunderous-looking Sarie. It took a second for Coll to see she wasn't looking at him but at the kitchen door leading into the front hall. Daniel and Ted stood in the doorway. Daniel looked like he was on the verge of being sober; at least, there was no whiskey bottle in his hand. Ted was doing his very best to look officious as he hooked his thumbs in his belt and hitched his pants up on his ample hips.

"Figures you'd be here, a nest of trouble makers that's what you are," Daniel spat at Coll.

He took a step back and closed his mouth, which had dropped open in astonishment at the scene before him. Laurel's chin quivered as she fought to hold back tears. Coll skittered around the edge of the table to stand beside Laurel and glare at Ted and Daniel.

"I asked you to leave my house, Ted. You have no business here this night," Sarie said, her voice low and dangerous.

"I want my nephew you kidnapped from me, you divil spawn!" Daniel made sure he got his two cents worth in, Coll noticed. Coll's breath caught in his throat at the dangerous light which flared in Sarie's eyes when Daniel took a step toward the table.

"Emily has Gort, as well you know. She came around and told you she was taking him to London to see a specialist." Sarie sounded remarkably reasonable, considering she was visibly vibrating with anger.

* * *

This was the first she had heard about Emily taking Gort to London. Laurel returned her attention to Daniel as he shifted his eyes from one place to another.

"Who do ya thinks' gonna pay for the whelp to see some specialist?" Daniel sneered. "It inin't comin' out of what I get. Ain't hardly enough to put bread on the table."

"But it puts whisky in your belly, don't it!"

"That's enough out of you," Ted bellowed at Coll. "I arrest your Gramma, and where'll that leave you!"

His shaking hand gripped Laurel's shoulder. She knew he was making sure she didn't throw something at Ted. Muttering under her breath, she shuffled her feet but didn't challenge Ted or Daniel.

Emily was nowhere to be seen, and Gort was missing from the chair he occupied when they slipped out earlier. She hoped fervently Emily was with him upstairs or somewhere safe where Daniel couldn't lay hands on him.

"I looked through all the sheds on this godforsaken place and can't find him," Stuart said from the back door of the kitchen.

Why is Stuart here at all? Just when you think things have gone about as far south as they can, doesn't this throw a whole new dimension into the drama? Laurel reached up and closed her hand over Coll's in warning. Now it was her turn to worry about Coll losing his temper and jumping Stuart right here in Sarie's kitchen. Coll's knuckles turned white as he gripped the edge of the table before they relaxed slightly. Coll regarded Stuart like he was a snake just come out of hiding.

Sarie pushed her chair back from the table and drew herself up to her full height. She looked down her nose at Ted, pointedly ignoring Daniel and Stuart.

"Ted, I have asked you to leave my premises. You have no right to be here, and if it pleased me, I could charge your son with trespass. You don't have a search warrant, or you would have waved it around before now. If you don't leave at once, I'll call Sam Pritchard over in Mousehole and ask him to come and remove you." Sarie was barely holding on to her anger.

"There's no need to bother old man Pritchard," Ted said uneasily.

"Oh, but I will if you don't leave this instant." Sarie smiled, but it didn't reach her eyes.

Laurel let out her breath when Ted grabbed Daniel by the arm and dragged him down the narrow hall to the front door. As he left the kitchen, he jerked his head at Stuart to leave by the back.

"You haven't heard the last of this." Daniel's nasal voice carried down the hall as Ted thrust him out the front door.

Laurel got up, closed, and locked the back door. She turned and leaned against it with her hands clenched behind her back. Coll picked up the tea mugs knocked over on the table and mopped up the spilled tea from the floor. He finished rinsing the dishrag in the sink just as Sarie re-entered the kitchen.

"Who's Sam Pritchard?" *It's nice to know Ted is scared of someone.*

"He's Angela's granddad and the Chief Constable over in Mousehole." Sarie smiled. Laurel knew she meant the small village of Mousehole even though Sarie pronounced the name as Mouzel.

"Him and Ted don't 'zactly see eye to eye, if you know what I mean." Coll grinned. "That was brill of you Sarie, to think of mentioning old man Pritch."

"I do have my moments," Sarie agreed.

"Where is Gort?"

"He's upstairs in your room. It seemed the best place to hide him." Sarie glanced at the ceiling as she spoke.

"Is Gramma with him?" Coll asked.

"She is. You're both staying here tonight. I've fixed a cot in the spare room for you, Coll."

"What about me?" If Gort was in *her* bed, and Coll was in the spare room, where was she supposed to sleep?

"Why you can have the bed in the spare room," Sarie said, "if you've finished arguing with Coll and promise not to kill each other in your sleep."

"Okay," Laurel said, drawing the word out.

She guessed it wasn't much different than camping out with Carlene and Chance down by the Old Man River. It just felt kind of weird to think about sleeping in the same room with Coll. The more she thought about it, the more she couldn't figure out why she felt that way.

"Is Gramma really taking Gort to London?"

"Emily is leaving with Gort on the first train out of Plymouth tomorrow morning. He needs some help in sorting out his nightmares and how Daniel treats him," Sarie said.

"Why Plymouth? Isn't that pretty far away?"

"It will be harder for Daniel to follow them. He'll just assume they'll leave from Penzance. By the time he figures it out, Emily and Gort will be safely on their way to London. Once they get there, Daniel will have no way of knowing which way they went." Sarie sounded quite pleased with the plan.

"Why's he got to go to London? What's wrong with Doc Eli?" Coll demanded.

"We're hoping the specialist will advise Gort be removed from Daniel's custody and placed with Emily until he's of age." Sarie sighed as she spoke.

"Can they make Daniel give him up? He won't want to lose his monthly dole."

"We'll just have to wait and see. Now it's time you two were off to bed. We have to leave before dawn to get to Plymouth in time for the London train." Sarie waved them toward the stairs. "Mind you don't wake up Gort on your way." Her voice floated up the dark hall behind them.

The bedroom seemed small in the dark. Laurel was very aware of Coll rustling around on the cot just a few inches from her bed. In the faint light from the window, she could make out his face as he lay on his back staring at the ceiling. The starlight glinted in his eyes, so she knew he was still awake.

"How long do you think Gort will have to stay in London?"

"Don't know. I never thought to ask. I don't reckon it should be long. If they weren't going to be back in time to go to Padstow, Sarie would have said." Coll's voice hung in the still air.

"Would you mind very much if Gort came to live at your house?" She wasn't sure how she would feel about having to share her parents with another kid, even one of her best friends.

"No, I think it would be bloody brilliant! Gort's me best mate, and I hate he has to put up with the shite Daniel hands out. You don't know what it's like for him," Coll said fiercely.

"That's good then; night, Coll." Laurel turned over and pulled the quilt up over her shoulder.

"Night."

It seemed she just shut her eyes when a horrible screeching brought her bolt upright in bed. Coll was sitting up as well, but he seemed more worried than scared by the loud wails. Laurel screwed her eyes up against the glare as she groped for the wall switch and turned on the overhead light. The hands on the old alarm clock by the bed said it was two a.m. The volume of the screeching increased. It sounded worse than the barn cats back home when they decided to fight over some female cat.

"What's that noise?"

Maybe it's Daniel come back to take Gort away.

"Let Gramma and Emily deal with it," Coll said, his voice quiet with worry. He twisted the quilt between his hands. "It's Gort having nightmares again." Coll frowned at the nails on his right hand. "Daniel coming here tonight will have set him off. This was one of the places Gort always felt safe." Coll threw the quilt onto the floor in disgust and scrambled from the cot to stand at the window.

"Does it happen often?" *How can anyone keep letting Gort go through this?*

"Often enough," Coll said roughly.

Slowly the screams faded; there were footsteps in the hall and then water running in the bathroom. The floorboards outside the door creaked just before Sarie opened the door and smiled wearily at them.

"I thought you two would be up. Gort's fine now. Emily has got him back to sleep. You best try and get some sleep; we have to be up and away in another hour and a half."

Laurel turned the light out and tried to settle back in her bed. Coll continued to stand by the window. She tried to think of something to say to him, but nothing seemed to be the right thing. Finally she settled for lying on her back and looking at the ceiling waiting for the time to go by.

She was already up and dressed when Sarie came to wake her. Coll was snoring under his pile of blankets on the cot, having finally abandoned his post by the window. Sarie shook him awake and went downstairs to wet the tea. Laurel padded after her and was setting mugs on the table as Coll stumbled into the kitchen. Emily and Gort followed on Coll's heels. The yellow light spilled through the windows into the pre-dawn darkness. *Are Daniel and Ted out there, hiding in the darkness, waiting to grab Gort before we can get to the car?*

It was a subdued group who piled into Sarie's car. The engine sounded loud in the stillness. The headlights of the car pushed back the night. Soon they were speeding north and then eastward towards Plymouth.

"Sorry if I kept you up last night," Gort whispered.

Laurel snorted. "It's Daniel and Stuart who should be sorry."

Coll put his arm around Gort and grinned at him. "Thought you were gonna pop a lung that time."

"Felt like it," Gort grinned back.

She stared from Coll to Gort and back again. *How can they joke about something as horrible as last night? I will never understand boys. Ever.*

The sun swung clear of the eastern horizon as the train for London roared its way into the station. Gort looked very pale and small as he stood with Emily on the platform. Coll kept looking over his shoulder, as if expecting Daniel or Ted to show up at any minute. The dusty oily smell stirred up by the train's arrival made Laurel wrinkle her nose and sneeze. As soon as the train came to a stop, Emily and Gort clambered on board and found seats by the window. Gort waved at them and smiled. Sarie shifted her weight from foot to foot, impatient for the train to get on its way to London. When the train pulled away from the station, the three left behind heaved a collective sigh of relief.

"Well, that's that then," Sarie said.

"Let's get home before anyone knows we were gone." Coll headed for the car park.

On the way back to Penzance, they quietly discussed how they should deal with Stuart. Nothing they could come up with seemed to be the right thing.

Presently, the long night and early morning caught up with Laurel and Coll. Silence descended as both fell asleep, the breeze from the open window ruffling their hair.

Laurel rubbed her eyes and sat up when Sarie stopped at a crossroads. She was surprised to see they were almost home.

"Can we stop and pick up Aisling?"

"I'll stop and see can she come, if you like," Sarie agreed.

Before long, Aisling joined them in the back of the car, and they were headed for Sarie's. After a quick bite to eat, they headed out to the barn to saddle the ponies for a ride.

The late morning sun was warm on their heads as they jogged along the track, not headed anywhere in particular. The chimney of an abandoned tin mine stood out on the horizon, and without really deciding to go there, that's where they ended up. The gorse and grasses grew long and wild around the foot of the tower. They let the ponies graze as they rested, and Laurel admired the view.

"What kind of mine was it?" She was familiar with the coal mines in the Crowsnest Pass back home.

"Tin. This was called the Ding Dong Mine," Coll said.

"That's a weird name."

"No one really knows why it's called that. Some guy wrote a history book and said it might mean 'head of the lode' or refer to the outcrop of tin on the hill. There used to be three mines there, the Good Fortune, Wheal Malkin and Hard Shafts Bounds. The name Ding Dong didn't come into use until the 18th century. There's a bell in Madron church called the Ding Dong Bell that they used to mark the end of the last shift of miners at the mine." Aisling supplied some more information.

"Are all the old mines around here tin mines?"

"Most of them. There are some old granite quarries though," Aisling said.

"How old are they? How long have they mined tin here?" The sun felt good on her back.

"They mined tin way back before the Romans came to Cornwall. They called this the Tin Isles and Cornwall was referred to as Belerion at one time. Some of the old folks say the Phoenicians used to come to St. Michael's Mount and trade for tin. Others say it was the Scillies they went to when they were still part of the mainland before the flood," Aisling said.

"How come you know all that?" Coll demanded.

Aisling regarded Coll regally. "Some people like to know about the place where they live. I love reading the old stories and imagining what it was like when the stories were happening. Some of the older folks, like Old Joseph, know the best stories, the ones that are passed down and haven't ever been written about in the books. Someday, I'm going to write down all the old stories I know."

"I think that's a cool idea."

"Do you know any stories about tin mines?" Coll asked.

Aisling thought for a minute, and then a big smile spread across her face. "Have you heard of the knockers?"

Coll shook his head and slid down off Arthur's back. Laurel jumped off Lamorna's broad back, and Aisling slid off her pony, too. The three ponies shone in the afternoon sun. Laurel was glad they decided to ride bareback. She always felt so much closer to her horse without a saddle. They took the ponies' bridles off so they could graze without being encumbered by the bits. Laurel smiled fondly as the three big black butts of the ponies disappeared over the crest of the hill. She knew they wouldn't go far, and the ponies would come when they were called. Failing that, she knew Aisling could ask the piskies to bring them if they wandered too far.

* * *

"All right then, the knockers." Aisling settled herself comfortably in the grass. "This is a story Joseph told me last week. His Da used to be a miner and so was Joseph before the mines closed up, and he took to fishing for pilchard."

"Joseph's Da was called William, Will for short. Will took Joseph to the mine when he was about thirteen years old. Times were bad, and they needed the extra money, so Joseph quit school and started working in the mine. At first the thought of being all that way underground with no way to get out but up the long narrow shaft with the creaky hoist lift gave Joseph nightmares. It was way better than when they had to scale the long shaky ladders to get in and out, though. But he said that after the first month, he just stopped thinking about it. It helped he always worked on his Da's gang, so his Da looked out for him as best he could."

"It was terrible dangerous, so Joseph said. He saw men in his gang lose their fingers and break bones all the time. There were no safety regulations or anything back then. It was dead hot down at the mine face, over one hundred degrees. You couldn't complain. Your family needed the money. You just went down the hole, did your job, collected your pay, and shut your trap. Some of the mines would fill part way up with water when they got deep enough, and they would have pumps going to keep the water out of where they had to work. Joseph said the worst sound he ever heard was the silence when the pumps broke down, or the petrol ran out."

"It happened one time when Joseph was working a night shift. Someone grabbed him and ran for the lift, Joseph figured it was his Da, but once they got up on top, he saw it was his Da's mate, Tom. Joseph couldn't see his Da anywhere. The sky was covered in low clouds, and it was dark as pitch. Joseph asked Tom where his

Da was, and Tom wouldn't answer him. He couldn't look Joseph in the face at all. Well, Joseph, he gets all upset and angry at Tom. Yelling at Tom, why didn't Tom save his Da instead of him? Joseph knew he couldn't never earn enough to keep his mom and sisters; they needed his Da for that. Tom, he grabs Joseph and lifts him off his feet and holds him out at arm's length so Joseph will stop beating on him."

"'Joe,' he says, 'Your Da weren't dead the last time I saw him! He was after saving some of the others and told me to get yu clear. Joe! Do ya hear me?'

"So Joseph stops trying to do damage to Tom, and Tom sets him back on his own pins.

"'Where's my Da then?' Joseph demands.

"Tom looks all kind of funny and says real quiet like, 'He ain't come up yet, Joe. He shoulda been up by now.'

"Well Joseph, he doesn't know whether to cry, or beat on Tom again when suddenly there's a whole lot of commotion over by the mine head, and Joseph sees them pulling some men from the lift. Joseph runs over there as fast as his legs will take him and looks at the men they've laid on the grass. They're all mates from his gang, but his Da isn't there. Tom comes up behind him and puts his hand on Joseph's shoulder."

"'There's more on the lift Joe, you know your Da wouldn't come up and leave any of his mates behind.'"

"Tom tries to sound like he believes what he's saying. The men on the lift are pulling another man out onto the grass, and it's Joseph's Da! Joseph falls on his knees by his Da's head, but his Da has his eyes closed and is breathing all funny. Joseph sits there holding his Da's hand and praying to anyone he thinks will listen that his Da has to be all right.

"He doesn't know how long he sat there, but then old Doc Ellerly, 'cept he was young Doc then, comes up and moves Joseph away. Doc works on Joseph's Da for a bit and then gets up to go the next man. Joseph grabs Doc's arm and tries to keep him from leaving his Da. Doc kneels down and holds Joseph's arms so he can't move. Doc tells Joseph his Da is going to be fine. He has got a lot of water in his lungs, and he's had a nasty whack on the head, but he should be fine in a fortnight, maybe a month at the most. Doc gets up and moves on the next man."

"Joseph feels like all the air's been let out him. He's happy his Da is all right, but he feels the responsibility of having to be the breadwinner for his house for a fortnight, maybe a month. Joseph's only been down the mine maybe six months now. He still has to rely on his Da and some of his mates to help him find the best spots to gather the tin. Joseph he wonders how he's ever gonna make enough to put bread on the table and pay Doc's fees. He starts to figuring. Maybe they can do without eggs and pay Doc with eggs. It wouldn't cover all of it, but it was someplace to start."

"Then Joseph's mom and sisters show up with half the town behind them. The news of the accident spread like wildfire after Doc Ellerly headed for the mine. His ma gets his Da on his feet and between them they get him home and settled in bed."

"Well, the next night, Joseph has to go to work without his Da. It feels really strange to take that long familiar walk alone. Joseph liked having the time alone with his Da when they walked to and from work. It was like just 'man time.' Joseph always felt closer to his Da when they shared the quiet time walking over the hills to the mine in the predawn darkness or the late evening. But this night Joseph goes alone."

"He meets up with Tom not far from the mine, and they head down into the mine together and meet up with the rest of their gang. Tom tells Joseph he can work with him that night, and so they set off looking for best lode of tin they can find. The hours are long, and the work is hard. Joseph is sure he hasn't got enough tin to justify his night's labors. He's in a part of the mine where the pumps don't sound so loud. Joseph, he sits down and decides to eat his supper. When he's finished, he makes sure to leave a croust of his pastie for the Knockers."

"What's a Knocker?" Laurel interrupted.

"Knockers are small ugly spirits who live in the tin mines. Joseph's Da told him all kinds of stories about them. But most importantly, you must always leave a croust or part of your meal for the Knockers. Some of the miners would spin yarns about Knockers leading miners into dangerous parts of the mine, or playing cruel tricks on them for not sharing with them. The Knockers figuring the miners were coming into their territory, and

they should leave something in exchange for the tin that they took; it being only neighborly and all to do that."

"So now Joseph gets up and adjusts his hat so the little candle on it is shining as best it can. He looks around and tries to decide which way he should go. Somewhere he's got separated from Tom, but Joseph thinks that's all right. He can find his way back to the lift and he'll catch up with Tom there."

"Then, Joseph thinks he can hear someone calling his name real quiet like. He twists his head this way and that but can't make up his mind where they're calling from. The voice seems louder in his left ear, so Joseph he turns to his left and starts along the narrow tunnel. There aren't any side tunnels off the one that he is following, so Joseph is sure he can find his way back. Pretty soon the voice becomes louder, and there is more than one voice calling him. All of a sudden he hears this knocking just ahead of him. Well, Joseph he almost messes his pants."

"He really did say that!" Aisling said as they laughed at her choice of words.

"Anyways, he's scared. It's got to be the Knockers! But Joseph left them some of his pastie, and he always leaves them something, just like his Da and all the men in Da's gang. The voices keep calling him, and he figures he's come this far, he might as well see it through. Besides he wants a word with these guys. Where were they when his Da was in danger? He thought his Da had told him the Knockers would look out for those who treated them with respect."

"Joseph feels a little bolder because he's angry now, not just scared. Next thing he knows, he's in a little room burrowed out of the stone, and there's a whole bunch of these little stringy ugly men with beards. The lamplight is flickering, so it's hard to make out too many details. There's hardly any oxygen for the lamp flame to feed on. Joseph just remembers that they were some ugly."

"Joseph he just stands there not knowing what to do; then one of the men steps forward points to the wall beside Joseph. Joseph carefully looks at what the man is pointing at. He doesn't want to take his attention away from the group of weird guys in case they try something. What Joseph sees makes his stomach drop and his heart jump."

"There's a tin lode in this cavern, loads and loads of top quality tin. More tin than Joseph has seen in one place before. How could his Da's gang have missed this spot? Joseph looks back at the man who pointed. The little man's face splits in a grin from ear to ear, and Joseph realizes the creature's mouth really does go from ear to ear, and it's full of pointy teeth."

"'Are you Knockers?' Joseph asks because he doesn't know what else to say. He never was too quick thinking on the spot. Too late he thinks maybe he has insulted the men by asking that."

"'We are the spirits of the mine. We guard the tin. You can call us that if it suits you.' The creature's voice was deep and gravelly. The other Knockers look at Joseph and laugh. Their laughter is like rocks shifting and grating and rolling under water."

"'We've led you here to gift you with this tin. Your father is a 'ansome one who always leaves us a croust, and he's taught you to respect us proper. The word is you and yours could use a stroke of luck and more pennies in your trousers. For a fortnight, not one day more and not one day less, we will lead you here and help you gather the tin. No one else will be able to see you or follow you. This is our gift to your Da for all the generous croust he has left us over the years.' The Chief Knocker bows as he finishes talking."

"Well, Joseph is dumbfounded, but somehow he manages to stammer out his thanks and then takes his fill of tin. Every night for a fortnight the Knockers are true to their promise, and one of them leads him to the cavern. Joseph's Da is relieved his family isn't suffering for his accident. Joseph tells him about the Knockers and the reason for their generosity. His Da isn't quite sure if he believes Joseph, but he can't argue with the amount or quality of the tin that Joseph is finding."

"Joseph spends a lot of time with his Da when he isn't working, and his Da is getting better. His Da tells Joseph old stories about the Knockers and how they can be beneficial to those they approve of and deadly to those who don't treat them with respect."

"'Myths or no, it costs me nothing to leave a croust for those who might need it,' Will tells Joseph."

"Every day since then, until his last day in the mine, Joseph would leave a whole pastie for the Knockers. He says even now

sometimes he will make an extra big bunch and walk up to the mine and leave them on a flat rock just inside. Joseph says without the Knockers help his family would have starved when his Da couldn't work. Joseph says the Knockers are cousins of the piskies."

Aisling stretched her arms overhead as she finished the story. Laurel wasn't sure she believed everything in the story. But it surely was a fine story to hear sitting in the grass outside the Ding Dong Mine on a sunny afternoon.

"That's an awesome story. Do you think it's true?"

Aisling shrugged. "Old Joseph tells it like it's true."

"Bloody hell!" Coll's hoarse whisper made the girls spin around.

Standing on the crest of the hill behind them was Stuart and three of his mates. A nasty smile hovered on Stuart's lips.

"Well, look who we have here," Stuart crowed. "Where's your snivelly friend?"

Coll leaped to his feet and stood with his hands on his hips to confront Stuart.

"None of your business," Laurel growled through her teeth. All the fun had gone from the golden afternoon.

"C'mon Stu, let them alone," the shorter heavy-set boy beside Stuart said uneasily.

"Just when I have them all the way out here, all by their lonesomes?" Stuart grinned.

"George is right. Let's just go do what we were going to do," one of the other boys said. "My ma gave me bloody hell over that incident at Old Joseph's. I can't see Evelyn for a fortnight."

"I don't think I want to let it go," Stuart said smugly.

"Well, I'm quits then. I bin in nothin' but hot water since you started picking on people." The third boy in the group made a sideways slashing movement with his hand.

Almost simultaneously, the three boys turned and disappeared over the brow of the hill.

Laurel felt the power shift in her direction and let out a small breath of relief. She wanted nothing more than to beat Stuart senseless and leave him lying on the stone strewn ground around the head of the mine. Fortunately, common sense, in the form of Aisling, took the forefront.

"Look, Stuart. Let's just forget about this," Aisling reasoned. "You can still catch up with your friends and go drinking over by the quoit like you planned."

Stuart's eyes widened and a flush swept up his face. "Whaddo you know about any drinking?"

Aisling smiled easily. "Of course, I know. Some friends of mine told me they chased you away last week."

"Friends of yours." Stuart was clearly puzzled. "There weren't nobody around. We just thought we heard voices behind the stones, but it was the wind blowing through those old holes."

"Then how do I know?" Aisling refused to ease Stuart's mind by agreeing with him.

"Blamed if I know." Stuart seemed unsure now. "What kind of company you be keeping?"

"The kind of company who visited Daniel the other night." Aisling smiled widely at Stuart. "I'm sure you know all about it, seeing as how you were at Sarie's with your Da and Daniel, and Daniel raving about demons and such." Aisling took a step closer to Stuart who backed away from her.

* * *

"Not so brave without your mates are ya?" Coll finally found his tongue. He had never heard Aisling openly admit to having any truck with piskies or spirits and such.

"Sod you," Stuart shouted and launched himself at Coll.

The dirt and grass flew in clumps as the two boys wrestled on the ground. Stuart had a size advantage over Coll and used it to end up on top. Blood ran down Coll's face from a cut over his eyebrow, and he grunted as he landed at hit on Stuart's nose. Coll was pleased with the amount of blood that gushed out. *That one's for Gort.*

The air rushed out of Coll's lungs as Stuart's knee made contact with Coll's private parts. The pain, instead of deflating his anger, sent it to new levels. With a massive heave, Coll managed to get out from under Stuart and scrambled to his feet. He saw Laurel jump forward to help him, but Aisling caught her arms. Coll spared a moment to be glad she wouldn't be in range of Stuart's fists.

“Let them figure this out fair and square. Wc’re no better than them if we gang up on him,” Aisling said breathlessly. She looked like she wanted to bash Stuart a few times herself.

Stuart ducked quickly and came up with a large rock in his hand. Without stopping, he threw it will all his might. He missed Coll but struck Aisling sharply on the shoulder. Laurel caught her as she sagged to the ground holding her arm to her side.

Coll was really angry now and systematically worked Stuart around so he was backing up toward the lip of a deep pit. Coll faked a lunge and then came around, caught Stuart by surprise and knocked him to the turf. Quick as a flash, Coll leaped on top of Stuart and held his right arm back with a heavy jagged rock clutched in his hand poised to strike Stuart in the face. Stuart’s face was white under the dirt and blood.

“Give me one good reason why I shouldn’t bash your brains in,” Coll was panting heavily. “All you’ve done is give me and my mates grief and then hide behind your father.” He spat in disgust.

Aisling gently put her good hand on Coll’s shoulder. Coll flinched but didn’t take his eyes off Stuart.

“Let him up Coll,” Aisling said urgently. “What would your Gramma think if she saw you right now?”

“Sarie’d say to smack him.” Laurel growled.

He stared hard into Stuart’s eyes.

“Let him up, Coll,” Aisling repeated gently. “Murdering him won’t do us any good and will make a bigger mess than we want to deal with.”

Slowly, Coll lowered the jagged rock to the ground, and Laurel hastily kicked it out of Stuart’s reach. Coll sat on Stuart’s chest, and his sweat dropped onto Stuart’s chin.

“Touch Gort again, or bully anyone else, and it won’t matter what anyone says, I will hurt you,” Coll said grimly.

She tugged on Coll’s arm, and he got shakily to his feet. The three friends backed away from Stuart as he struggled to his feet. Without looking any of them in the eye, Stuart started back across the moor in the direction he had come.

* * *

Afterward, Laurel could never remember how long the two boys battled in the afternoon sun. It seemed like forever when they were fighting, and when it was finally over, it seemed hardly any time passed. Both boys were sweating and filthy, Stuart's shirttail hung from his pants, and Coll had a rip in the knee of his jeans, which flapped every time he took a step. It struck her as very funny, although she didn't know quite why.

The sound of the ponies' hooves on the turf vibrated in the air as the three black heads appeared over the top of the mound behind them. The ponies must have heard the shouts and came to see what all the excitement was about. Wordlessly, the three friends bridled the ponies and clambered up onto their broad backs. Laurel helped Aisling find a tall rock to stand on, in order to compensate for her sore shoulder. Thankfully, it looked like it was only a bad bruise.

"I'll tell Mum I fell off trying to jump something," Aisling said gaily as they rode along through the orange gold of the sunset.

* * *

Coll was quiet as they walked along; he felt very empty and small now the terrible anger had left him. A film of cold sweat broke out on his forehead as he realized he had really *wanted* to hurt Stuart. What would he have done if Aisling hadn't grabbed his arm. He vowed he wouldn't ever let himself get that angry again, no matter what.

Coll thought about the stories of King Arthur's knights he liked so much. They were always talking about battle rage and how time seemed to slow to a crawl, when in reality the hero was moving very fast. He wondered if what happened to him this afternoon was what they were talking about. Coll always thought it would be cool to be in that magic state where you were virtually invincible. Coll shook his head. He didn't ever want to go there again, if that was what it felt like. It scared him senseless. Arthur tossed his head as Coll's hands trembled on the reins, his unease communicating itself to the pony.

"What do you think Stuart will tell his parents?"

Coll shrugged. He wasn't sure what he was going to tell his Gramma.

“Hopefully he’ll make up a story. Stuart won’t like to have to admit Coll did that much damage,” Aisling said

* * *

They rode the rest of the way home in silence and just as quietly fed and groomed the ponies when they reached Sarie’s. They told Sarie the truth and ate a small supper, all the while waiting for the phone to ring, or Ted to show up at the door. Darkness fell, and still there was no word from Stuart’s father. Just when Laurel was beginning to think it was safe to relax, the shrill of the phone made them all jump. Sarie answered it and talked quietly for a time. They exchanged anxious looks and waited for Sarie to end the call.

“That was Emily. Gort is doing fine. The doctor wants him to stay another week. They’ll be home in time to go to Padstow with us.” Sarie smiled at their white faces.

“That’s great news,” Aisling said and smiled into the fire in the hearth.

“What about Stuart?”

“I’m hoping Stuart is smart enough to leave you lot alone from here on in. Time will tell,” Sarie finished dryly.

Laurel nodded and hoped she was right. Beside her Coll’s face was turning spectacular shades of red and blue. His nose was swollen, and his knuckles were scraped and raw. Sarie gave Coll an ice pack earlier, and he was alternating it between his face and his knuckles.

“Time for bed, you three,” Sarie announced; her voice followed them up the narrow hall as they filed up the stairs to wash and get into bed. “Things will be better in the morning, and hopefully this thing with Stuart has sorted itself out for the time being.”

Chapter Six

The 'Obby 'Oss Clue

When Gort and Emily returned at the end of the week, Sarie and Laurel met them at the train in Penzance. Daniel was nowhere to be seen.

Once back at Emily's house, Coll opened the door before anyone had a chance to touch the handle. He wore one of Emily's house aprons tied over his jeans with a dishcloth slung over his shoulder. Gort grinned at him as he went through the hall and into the kitchen. Laurel suppressed a laugh and followed Gort into the kitchen. Coll had a high tea consisting of cold meats, eggs, cakes, and sandwiches spread out on the kitchen table. Sarie had once explained the term to her. Generally an early evening meal, high tea was given the name because at one time, it was eaten while sitting on high stools with raised tables. People believed the meal would be digested easier when sitting at a high angle.

"What a smashing tea, Coll," Sarie said.

"Not even a great mess to clean up after," Emily teased.

Coll turned a brilliant shade of red when Laurel impulsively hugged him. Gort punched Coll lightly on the arm.

"Missed me, did you?" Gort grinned.

"Bloody right, I did." Coll returned the grin.

They sat down and made short work of the lovely tea. As they savored the sweet, the conversation turned to Gort's visit with the specialist in London.

"So what did the doctor say?"

"He said he was going to recommend I don't live with Uncle Daniel in the future." Gort's relief was evident in his voice.

"But mind you, you have to stay with him until after the court date," Emily cautioned him.

"I know." Gort looked down at his plate.

"That doesn't seem fair!" Laurel pounded her fist on the table.

"We have to follow the laws, child. Until the courts declare Daniel is no longer Gort's guardian, we have to abide by the standing court order. Either that, or Gort goes into the custody of the crown and has to go to a foster home," Sarie told her.

"When is the court date?" Coll asked.

"The first week of August," Emily said. "If Daniel gives Gort a bad time before then, Gort has a number he can ring and report it. If that happens, things may move a bit quicker."

Aisling let herself in the front door and joined them in the kitchen.

"Did you save any sweet for me?" Aisling asked, eyeing the cake crumbs on Coll's plate.

"Of course we did, my love," Emily assured her.

Emily and Sarie began the washing up at the kitchen sink while the rest of them settled by the hearth in the parlor.

"How am I going to know where to look for the clue once we get to Padstow?" Laurel frowned.

"Did the Lady give any indication where you would find the clue?" Aisling asked.

"I don't think so."

"Think harder," Coll growled.

"I am."

"What did she say again? I don't remember exactly," Gort broke in quietly.

"She just said I would get the first clue on May Day in Padstow. She talked about the filly that wasn't born yet and holding death in my hand."

"So do we have to find a pregnant mare somewhere in Padstow? That'll be easy," Coll snorted.

"Quit being so negative," Aisling admonished Coll. "I don't think we'll have to look too far. I think the clue will find us."

"So we just go to Padstow, join in the festival, and wait and see what happens?" Gort asked.

"I think that's best." Aisling nodded.

"What about what I think?" Laurel broke in.

Coll sighed. "What do you think we should do, then?"

"I don't know. I just feel like I should have a plan of some kind." Her frustration was plain in her tone.

"Let's just wait and see. Maybe we'll come up with something before we get there," Aisling said.

The bright, clear May Day morning found their small group looking for a parking spot in Padstow. The town was crowded with tourists and locals, all vying for the best place to see the festivities. Those who weren't actively involved in the festivities jostled for space on the edges of the narrow streets. Soon the 'Oss would start his journey. Laurel was no closer to figuring out how to find the clue than she had been the night they talked about it in Emily's parlor. She just hoped with all her heart she would recognize the clue when it was in front of her.

Sarie's friend emerged through her back gate just as they parked in the tiny spot behind her cottage. Aisling greeted her Aunt Jane and introduced Laurel. The woman led them down a narrow back alley to emerge onto the main thoroughfare. The voice of the crowd swelled to a new level as the 'Obby 'Oss began to make his way through the narrow street. The girls craned their necks trying to catch their first glimpse of the 'Obby 'Oss in his bizarre costume.

The crowd hemmed them in. Sarie held tight to Laurel's hand as the crowd vibrated with excitement as the 'Obby 'Oss drew near. She lifted herself up on her tiptoes as high as she could in order to catch a glimpse of the alien-looking creature with its large hoop depicting the head of a horse, and a scraggy tail hanging from the rear of it.

The traditional song rang high and loud as thousands of voices joined in celebration:

"Unite and Unite. Let us all unite. For summer is a cummin today, and wither we are going, we will all unite, in the merry morning of May."

Periodically the 'Obby 'Oss lunged into the crowd and captured a young woman, prompting good-natured jesting and howls of laughter. At intervals the 'Obby 'Oss would falter, stagger and fall to the street where he lay motionless for a moment, when this happened the joyous song changed to a sad dirge. As soon as the 'Obby 'Oss rose and danced again, the song spun back to its joyous celebration. Laurel didn't know where to look first; this was all so different than anything she ever experienced. Even Stampede in Calgary wasn't this crazy. The song filled the air and rose from the stones of the street under her feet. It vibrated in her bones and eardrums.

There was a sudden break in the crowd; the 'Obby 'Oss was right in front of them. She watched entranced, as the 'Oss made an exaggerated grab for Sarie, who waved him off, laughing. The strange hooped face of the creature paused, his painted eyes looked straight at her and the sound of the celebrations faded. It seemed only Laurel and the strange beast existed in a world somehow one step sideways from the world she knew. She couldn't even feel Sarie's hand on hers, and the words of the song, though faint still echoed in her ears.

The 'Obby 'Oss regarded her for a long minute before a voice echoed in her head. It was both soft and deep, young and old, gentle and intimidating, all at once and yet none of them at all. A part of her was afraid, but another part was braver than she would ever have imagined and allowed her to listen to the message.

"Greetings, child who searches for answers. On this May Day, the 'Obby 'Oss grants you a boon. Neither husband nor child will I give you, but the answer to part of the mystery you seek to achieve your heart's desire."

Laurel started as the voice took on a deeper tone; she could hear the ringing of great brass bells underlying it as if they rung from the depths of the ocean.

"Find the great lizard as it emerges from the foam and follow its path to the secret caverns of the crystal guardians. You must remember…to gain entrance, you and your companions must be found worthy, and so I tell you that it takes not the courage of a man, but the selfless sorrow of a woman for the Selkie guardian to admit you."

"Thank you," Laurel whispered.

Suddenly, the world came back into focus. Although Laurel felt like a lot of time had passed, it seemed only a tiny second elapsed to all those around her. Sarie was still waving the 'Obby 'Oss away and giggling like a girl.

"Go on with you, I'm too old, and she's too young."

The 'Obby 'Oss shook his hooped head at Sarie and bowed before he continued on his way. The May Song rose high and strong over the throng and slowed to the awful dirge as the 'Oss stumbled and fell once more.

"Why does he do that?"

Sarie smiled. "Don't let it bother you, girl. It symbolizes the death of winter and the birth of the spring. If winter doesn't come, the summer never ends, and there can be no spring. It also mirrors mankind's cycle of life: we are born, we die, but we live on in our children and our children's children."

Laurel doubted if her mom was comforted by the thought of her daughter going on without her.

"Come on you lot, let's go find some market stalls and some goodies to stuff your gobs with," Sarie invited.

They shouted their agreement. The 'Obby 'Oss leaped to his feet again and cavorted down the street out of sight, though his song continued to echo in the air.

As the group made their way to the market stalls, Coll dropped back. "What happened back there? You looked all mazed for a minute, like you could see something the rest of us couldn't."

"The 'Obby 'Oss spoke to me," she said.

"It never," Coll exclaimed. "It's not supposed to speak to anyone."

"I don't think it was the man inside the costume who talked to me. It sounded deep, like it was inside my head, but faraway at the same time. It was spooky."

"Bloody Hell," Coll exclaimed loudly.

"You mind your tongue, young man!" Sarie said over her shoulder. "You'll have your Gramma down my throat for allowing you to behave like a ruffian." Jane and Emily laughed at her words.

"Sorry, Sarie," Coll said, and then spoke in a quieter voice. "What did it say? Why couldn't the rest of us hear it?"

"I don't know why you couldn't. I wish you were all there with me. It was creepy,"

"What do you mean there with you; you didn't go anywhere. I was still hanging on to you and so was Sarie." Coll looked confused.

"It was weird," she paused, trying to find a way to describe it, "as if I took a step sideways or something. Like I was apart from everything somehow. All the noise faded, I couldn't feel you or Sarie. All I could see was the painted face of the 'Obby 'Oss and hear that voice. But I could still hear the May Song faintly, all I could make out was *unite, unite*. It was freaking weird."

"What did it say?" Coll asked impatiently. "Who would have guessed the 'Obby 'Oss would talk to you!"

"Weird stuff, all in riddles. You know those stories your Gramma and Sarie tell at night in front of the fire where the faeries or piskies or whatever give the person the information they need, but they never tell it right out. The people in the story have to figure it out for themselves if they want to finish their quest or get out of the faery hill, or whatever."

Coll danced a jig of delight on the cobbled street. "This is great, isn't it just? We get to go questing like King Arthur's knights. Gort's going to be beside himself."

"You don't think I'm crazy, or making it up?"

"Naw, I believe you. We knew you were going to get a message here. You even had that faery struck look on your face for a moment when the 'Oss stopped in front of you. You know, the one Sarie always makes as she describes how the person in the story would look." Coll stopped talking long enough to make sure Sarie and the others weren't too far ahead. "What did the bloody thing say," he asked plaintively.

Laurel giggled at his tone. "Something about lizard tails and paths." She trailed off and her eyes unfocused for a second. "In order to find the answer to my heart's desire, I have to *find the great lizard as it emerges from the foam and follow its path to the secret caverns of the crystal guardians.*" She shook her head. "I don't have any idea what it means."

"Anything else?" Coll vibrated with excitement.

"There was something about gaining entrance to the secret caverns. Me and my companions have to be acceptable, I think he said 'worthy,' so the Selkie guardian will admit us. What the heck is a Selkie?" she asked crossly. "How am I supposed to figure this out when I don't even know what the stupid things are?"

"That's why you have companions. A Selkie is some magic kind of seal man." Coll grinned. "Do you remember anything else?"

Laurel pushed aside her resentment and frustration at the riddles to try to remember the last piece of the riddle.

"He said *it takes not the courage of a man, but the selfless sorrow of a woman* to gain entrance." She kicked at piece of litter. "I haven't the slightest idea what that means either."

Coll grabbed her hand and pulled her through the crowd. They could just see the top of Sarie's head in front of them.

"Hurry up, we don't want to get lost," Coll said over his shoulder and then in a louder voice, "Sarie, Gramma, wait for us!"

Panting slightly, they caught up with their group just at the edge of the market stalls. Aisling and Gort looked at them questioningly; Coll winked at them.

"Just wait 'til you hear the story we have to tell you later when we're by ownselves." Coll grinned at Gort. "You're going to either love this, or think we're bleedin' kitey."

"As long as it doesn't involve anything illegal." Gort muttered.

* * *

After saying good bye to Jane, the children piled into the back of Sarie's little car as the sun was setting over the roofs of Padstow. Sarie and Emily sat in the front.

"All set?" Sarie asked.

"As we'll ever be," Gort answered for all of them.

They were full of fair food and a scrumptious tea. Not as good as the ones in Mousehole, Coll allowed afterward, but very good all the same.

The little vehicle hummed its way south along the coast to Newquay and then inland along the A3075 toward Redruth. Laurel laughed as they passed a sign pointing to the little village of Goonhavern. Sarie followed the A30 from Redruth through Camborne, Hayle, Lelant and St. Erth, finally coming out into the open countryside and welcome respite from the lights of the towns.

They were soon asleep, all piled in a heap like kittens. They were too tired to talk about the great secret, and besides there were too many adult ears to hear. They woke up when Sarie reached the outskirts of Penzance, stopping to drop off Coll and his Gramma.

"Don't forget we're going to Land's End tomorrow," Sarie reminded them.

“No worries, we’ll see you in the morning.” Emily stepped out of the car.

The windows at Gort’s were all in darkness when they stopped by the door.

“S’okay, Sarie,” Gort told them. “I’m used to making due. Daniel will be home from the local before too long.”

“You call if you need anything, Gort child.” Sarie held his eyes with hers for a moment. “I don’t mind coming back up here to fetch you if need be,” she assured him.

“’Preciate it, Sarie.” Gort smiled at her. “Night, girls.”

“Night,” both girls chorused back at him.

Sarie put the small car in gear and headed out east toward Longrock and the turnoff for Between Cottage.

Aisling snuggled up with Laurel under the rug in the back of the car.

“I’m glad you’re staying the night,” Laurel said. “I can’t wait ‘til tomorrow to tell you what happened today.”

“Was it exciting? Does it have to do with the ‘Obby ‘Oss?” Aisling whispered back.

Laurel’s gasped in surprise. “How do you know about the ‘Obby ‘Oss?”

“The piskies told me,” Aisling said. “I think we both have secrets to share with each other.”

“No way.”

After having the ‘Obby ‘Oss talk to her, Laurel wasn’t about to question Aisling’s assertion the piskies spoke to her.

“Later,” Aisling said, “when we’re alone.”

Laurel nodded her agreement and let her head rest against the window of the car. The dark night roll past, hedgerows looming against the sky and slowly her eyes closed again.

Chapter Seven

If It Barks Like a Seal…

The faint pink light of dawn threw a strange half-light across the bed where the girls sat leaning against the headboard. Aisling wrapped her arms around her knees and regarded Laurel seriously for a moment. She just finished telling Aisling about the clue the 'Obby 'Oss gave her.

"You believe me, don't you? The horse really did talk to me; do you think he's the horse that hasn't been born I'm supposed to ride?"

"Of course, I believe you. The piskies told me something special would happen while we were in Padstow, something involving 'the big horse' and a message. But the 'Oss can't be the right horse, didn't she say it was the filly that never was foaled? The 'Oss is male, so it can't be him."

"Rats, big, fat, ugly rats! How am I supposed to make sense out of any of this?"

Aisling patted her arm. Her eyes smiled before her mouth. "I expect it will work its way out, it always seems to. But I have a secret to tell you, too."

"What?" Laurel twisted around and sat on her knees facing Aisling.

"You remember the man we talked to in Emily's garden the other night, the piskie," Aisling began.

She nodded, wondering where Aisling was going with this.

"Well, I see him all the time. His name is Gwin Scawen, and he says he will help us with the riddle. As long as the *big uns*, as he calls them, don't get wind of it and get their backs up." Aisling grinned. "It's brill, isn't it just, that he'll help us."

"Wow, that's amazing! Maybe he can help us make sense of some of the stuff we don't know."

"That's what I was thinking, too. He gets all kinds of interesting gossip, he knows all sorts of stuff before it happens." Aisling paused. "He's the one who told me about the horse and the message, but I couldn't tell you. Anyway I didn't know what horse he meant at the time."

"Has he told you anything else?"

"No. But he was right happy to have some mischief with Daniel the other night." Aisling grinned.

"Maybe he can keep Stuart away, too."

"I think Stuart will keep his distance for a bit after his set-to with Coll the other day. I really don't think he understands how much damage he does with the way he acts. It's what he sees at home all the time. Ted bullies Angela terrible. Angela talks to my mum a lot, and I think Ted beats on her sometimes. But I don't know that for certain." Aisling paused to push her hair out of her eyes.

"I still think it would be good if your little brown man kept an eye on him for a bit. If we knew Stuart was planning something, we could head him off at the pass before he can get to Gort." Laurel wasn't ready to cut Stuart any slack. She didn't trust him within a mile of Gort.

Aisling stretched her arms over her head and then slid out of bed. The sun was fully up now, and the small room was filled with soft light. Laurel could hear the ponies in the field whickering as Sarie doled out their morning grain.

"The boys are here. Sarie went to get them, so we can ride early today. Who gets the bathroom first?"

"It sounds so funny to hear you call the loo a bathroom." Aisling chortled as they hurried down the hall.

"Better than water closet. Sounds like you fill a closet with water and then expect to go to the toilet there."

They both reached the door at the same time and tried to get in ahead of each other with wild laughing and pushing.

"Okay, okay," Laurel said breathlessly. "Let's just share."

"I'm still first!" Aisling ducked under her arm. "Pays to be short and scrawny sometimes."

A few short minutes later, they joined Sarie and the boys in the kitchen. They finished the toast and tea before heading out to exercise the ponies and brush Vivienne and Morgen. They left

Sarie to tidy the kitchen and gather up the things they were taking with them for their picnic out at Land's End.

By nine-thirty, the ponies were ridden and put away safely. Everyone cleaned up in the mudroom; Coll had to change his shirt because Arthur smeared green horse slobber all down the front of his jumper. They tumbled out the back door of the kitchen like a pack of puppies as Sarie's voice split the morning air.

"C'mon, you lot. Shake a leg," she called as she turned the ignition. They raced around the front of Sarie's cottage and piled into the back of the small vehicle, leaving the front seat empty for Emily.

"We're all here," Laurel said.

"Gramma said she'd be ready by eleven." Coll squirmed trying to get comfortable.

Sarie put the car in gear, and they were off. Laurel decided not to watch as Sarie took the turns on the narrow road more than a little too fast for safety.

"How far is Land's End?" Laurel wondered.

"We should be there in about twenty minutes once we pick up Coll's Gramma."

"Land's End is about nine miles from Penzance," Gort chimed in.

Sarie glanced in her rear view mirror and caught Laurel's eye for a second. "Land's End is the most southwesterly point in the British Isles. It's as close as you can get to Canada without getting wet."

"Years ago, I think in the 1700s, there used to be more land, out as far as the Scillies," Sarie continued, "but it flooded, now there's only Land's End and the Scillies. Fishermen used to pull up window frames and such like in their nets when they fished for pilchard." Sarie paused for a moment. "Lyonnesse it was called, the land that now lies under the sea, mostly called *Lost Lyonnesse* in all the tourist literature. The old tales say that when the wind is right, you can hear the bells from the drowned churches tolling under the waves."

"It sounds like Atlantis, you know, the story about the land that sank under the sea and all the ancient knowledge was lost. One of my teachers said there was evidence the Mayans in Central and South America were related in some way to the people from

Atlantis." Laurel paused, thinking. "Something to do with the way so many Mayan and Aztec temples aligned to the sun and the equinoxes."

Sarie smiled. "There are stranger things in the world than we can imagine, so your teacher may very well be right."

Sarie pulled up in front of Coll's house with a flourish. "Here we are, then. Hello, my gold." Sarie addressed Coll's Gramma as she clambered into the front seat. Emily passed a large picnic hamper back to the kids.

"Keep that safe, you lot," she told them.

Coll rolled his eyes as the four in the back tried to balance the large basket and not tip anything out.

"Are there raisin cookies, Gram?" Coll asked, while sneaking his hand under the cover.

"There are Coll, and you be taking your fingers out of the basket now, you," Emily admonished him. "Those are for your sweet, after our picnic tea."

Coll had the grace to blush as he withdrew his hand from the cover. He flashed a brilliant smile to his cohorts and showed them the two cookies he managed to filch. Coll broke both cookies in two and shared them.

The wind chased the sun and clouds across the sky in blustery gusts as Sarie drove past a building that boasted it was the "First and Last Pub in England", and pulled into the car park. Every one buttoned up before exiting the car and following the path leading to the look out at Land's End. Because they were local they didn't have to pay the entrance fee at the gate. The paved courtyard was bounded by attractions and food booths. Sarie led them right on through and out to the right past a small stone circle that Laurel found oddly intriguing. The granite stones gleamed in the sunlight and she imagined there were small figures cavorting in and around them. Aisling grinned at her.

Leaving the grownups behind they charged off down the path toward the Land's End sign post to take Laurel's Picture. They stood just off the path and looked out at the Longships Rocks and the lighthouse perched on the highest one. Beyond them Aisling pointed out the Armed Knight formation and Enys Dodnan. The latter looked a lot like Los Arcos which Laurel had seen at Los Cabos, Mexico.

Laurel leaned against an outcrop of rock to catch her breath. The wind snatched each breath from her before she had a chance to actually breathe. Hunching her shoulders, she turned her back to the wind and grinned at Coll.

"It's just like the wind when the Chinook is blowing back home," she shouted.

"What's a *Shin-uck*?"

"It's when the warm air from the west coast comes through the mountain passes and blows across the prairie. It makes a big cloud archway in the sky, and the temperature changes really fast. Sometimes, we can wear T-shirts in the middle of winter in southern Alberta." Laurel answered him. "Mind you," she continued, "Lake Louise still has ice on it on the twenty-fourth of May long weekend, and it can snow in July!"

"Sounds barmy to me," Coll told her.

Sarie and Emily caught up with them, having sent the young ones on ahead to show Laurel the view.

"We'll have to find a more sheltered spot to picnic," Emily told them. "Why don't you childer go explore? Sarie and I will look for a place to eat. Don't stray from the path and stay near to these rocks here, so we can find you."

Laurel turned her face into the wind to look out across the blue expanse of the Atlantic. The sun bounced diamonds of light off the waves, and the water itself was a deep intense cerulean blue. Viewed from the high vantage point of the rocky green cliff where she stood, the effect was spectacular.

A ways out into the water were more groups of rocks, and far, far out in the distance were the faint smoky outlines of the Scillies.

"Do you think," she asked as she turned to Aisling, "that there really is a lost part of Cornwall lying under the water?"

Aisling looked out over the restless water. "Sometimes I think I can hear the bells ringing if I listen hard enough," she said earnestly. "I love to come here and imagine what it must have looked like to have land, farms, and villages all the way out to the Scillies. Who lived there and if they managed to get to high ground with their animals before the waves came. Sometimes, I get happy stories where everyone made it, and other times it's sad; people, animals and homes are lost. That's when I hear the bells." She shook her head, "You must think I'm daft, talking like that, but it's what I feel."

"Didn't anyone survive the flood?"

"Stories say a man named Treyvelan raced ahead of the first huge waves on a white horse and made it to high ground. Legend has it the horse lost a shoe and that's why you'll see three horse shoes on some old Cornish family crests," Aisling explained.

Laurel smiled at her. "There's a place in Alberta called Writing on Stone. There are all these really old Indian paintings on the rocks. Petroglyphs and pictographs, I think Mom said they're called. I love to go there and put my hands on the warm rock and imagine what the person who painted the figures was thinking about, or seeing. Mom says they painted them while they were on *spirit quests.* It was young men doing some kind of coming of age ritual involving not eating, meditating, and ritual drumming. Then the boy's guardian spirit or...totem, I think, would appear or speak to him, and the boy would record his message on the rocks. But it's like I can almost see them and hear them chanting as they paint. This place feels just like Writing on Stone."

A gull caught in the updraft off the cliffs flew directly over their heads screaming in its high-pitched voice.

"He was close!" She laughed. "At least he didn't crap on us."

They watched the gull wheel in the sky and then join some others as they headed to the car park to mooch at the trash bins.

"They say that gulls are the spirits of drowned sailors. I wonder if that one knew me?" Aisling spoke softly.

Laurel shrugged. "We can go ask him if you want."

Aisling looked at her quizzically. "You just accept all this legend and spirit stuff as normal," she said. "Most everyone thinks it's all bunk, but you think we should just go ask the thing."

She shrugged again. It was just Aisling was so easy to talk to about this kind of stuff. Carlene would think she'd lost her mind.

"Maybe it comes from talking to my horse too much or spending too much time alone on the prairie."

Aisling looked toward the flock of gulls raiding the trash bins by the car park. "I guess if he wanted me to know, he would have told me."

"It's amazing; there's really nothing but ocean between here and Canada," Laurel mused, not taking her eyes off the horizon.

Aisling grabbed her hand. "C'mon let's go see what trouble Coll and Gort have gotten into."

Holding hands, the two girls started off down the path that wound along the headland and was part of the coastal path encircling the Cornish peninsula. They headed north away from Land's End toward the beautiful curving sand beach in Sennen Cove. The wind continued to gust from the west, making conversation difficult. It was hard to hear anything except the waves booming on the base of the cliffs and the wind screaming in their ears. The girls contented themselves with sharing smiles as they walked along.

To the east, the moor stretched away from them in waves of heather and gorse. Gulls rode the waves of the wind high above their heads. Aisling tugged on her arm and pointed to Coll and Gort just a little ahead of them on the path climbing up on a pile of rocks to peer down over the edge of the cliffs. They broke into a run to catch up with them.

"You best not be letting your Gram see you doing that," Aisling shouted to Coll.

Gort, not quite so adventurous, was only sitting on top of the pile, not leaning over as Coll was doing.

Coll looked down at the two girls on the path. "It's bloody amazing," he yelled with his face alight with adventure. "You can watch the waves hit the cliff and feel it in the rock." Coll turned his face back into the updraft off the cliff face. "Blimey, I think I can fly!"

Gort looked over at Coll, grinned down, and grabbed hold of Coll's coat.

"I...I...I'll k-k-keep him fr-fr-from p-p-itching over th-th-the edge." When he was excited Gort's stammer always got worse.

Aisling grinned back at Gort and began to clamber up the rock pile.

"You coming? I'm not going to miss this!" she called to Laurel.

The rock pile did not look safe at all, perched as it was on the edge of the cliff. Heights were not Laurel's favorite thing. Looking out from Land's End while standing on the solid earth was one thing, perching on top of a pile of boulders on the edge of a cliff was something else again. Looking up she saw her friends' three faces peering down at her.

"C'mon, it's marvelously amazing!" Aisling called.

Laurel shuffled her feet and then squared her shoulders. *What was it Grandma used to say? "In for a penny, in for a pound"; that was it.* She might never get to come here again, and the view sounded wonderful. She wormed her way up the pile before she could change her mind.

"Make room for me," she called as she reached the top and squeezed onto the flat surface of the large boulder topping the mound.

There was enough room for all four of them to sit and look out at the waves making their first land fall since New Foundland. To the right of where they perched was a small cove; the waves there were gentler than the ones hitting the rocky wall to the left where it jutted out and took the full brunt of the ocean. The sand in the sheltered cove was snowy white, the waves an intense blue as they washed up on the shore. The beach was littered with flotsam, and small shells glittered in the sunlight on the sand.

"Do you think there's a way down there?" Coll asked, eyeing the cliffs for a possible path. "I bet there's chough's nests somewhere." His eyes scanned the cliffs.

"M-m-maybe," Gort replied, as he too swept the cliff for possible ways down to the beach.

Aisling shook her head. "Even I am not so barmy as to go looking to break my neck, just to explore some little beach or annoy some birds."

Laurel looked closer at the funny looking rocks in a corner of the cove. "Oh, look," she cried excitedly. "There's a whole mess of seals down there, or whatever it is you call a bunch of seals."

Coll, Gort and Aisling all looked as well, and sure enough there was a colony of seals.

"Listen," Coll said, "you can hear them barking."

It was hard with the wind roaring and the ocean crashing, but she could hear a harsh croaking sound.

"Is that them?" she asked incredulously. "It sounds like…I don't know what. Not what I thought seals sounded like."

Coll, Gort and Aisling burst into laughter.

"What's so funny?"

"You've never heard a seal bark?" Aisling managed to get out, while Coll and Gort continued to laugh.

"I live on the prairie," Laurel reminded them haughtily. "There's not a lot of ocean for seals to live in. Have you ever heard a prairie dog whistle?"

Coll wiped the tears from his eyes on his sleeve. "Sorry," he apologized. "I just thought everyone knew what seals sounded like. Anyone I've ever known has seen seals. Just like everyone knows pilchard are sardines."

She stared him down, not ready to forgive any of them for laughing at her just yet.

"Your circle of friends must be very limited then," she said and turned her nose up at all three of them, refusing to even look at them. She turned her gaze back to the colony of seals far below them.

Aisling put her hand tentatively on her arm. "I'm sorry. I didn't mean to laugh at you. You just looked so dumbfounded and amazed; if you could only have seen your face."

Laurel relented and smiled at her, "It's okay Ash. I know you were just influenced by the rabble over there." She indicated Coll and Gort, both of who tried to look innocent and contrite at the same time.

Gort swallowed. "S-s-s-sorry," he stammered. "Really," he added.

Coll reached over and put his arm around her shoulders. "Sorry. Be a good sort; forgive me for being a git." He grinned at her.

Laurel snorted. "I'll think about it."

Aisling looked at her watch. "We should go back and find Sarie and Emily. They must have found a place to picnic by now."

"They'll have eaten all the cookies," Coll howled. "Let's get off this bloody heap of stone."

The four friends slid down the rocks much faster than they climbed up and took off back down the path at a run. As they rounded the turn and came in sight of the point at Land's End, Sarie and Emily appeared, waiting for them by the sign post.

"We were starting to think that you'd kept on going all the way to Sennen Cove." Emily smiled at them as they gathered around her and Sarie.

“Lunch is right over here.” Sarie indicated a blanket spread on the ground in the lee of a large granite boulder.

They wasted no time in finding themselves a spot on the blanket and tucking into the sandwiches and fruit set out for them.

“Are there still some cookies left?” Coll asked around a mouthful of deviled ham sandwich.

“You mean other than the ones you filched in the car?” Emily fixed Coll with a gimlet eye.

Coll had the grace to squirm in his place and then looked at Emily widening his eyes pitifully. “They are so-o-o-o good Gram, and I just couldn’t wait for Laurel to taste your amazing baking.” Coll nudged her with his elbow as he spoke.

“They were the best I’ve ever had.” She smiled brightly at Emily, trying to help Coll out, not sure if Emily was really angry at him or just teasing.

“Oh, go on with ya, you silver-tongued devil.” Emily flapped her hand at Coll. “Charm the silver off a dead man’s eyes, he could.”

Emily rummaged in the haversack sitting beside the picnic basket and brought out some saffron buns, along with another package of cookies. They all pitched in and made short work of their sweet and then lay back on the blanket to watch the wind chase the fluffy white clouds across the sky overhead.

Aisling raised her head to glance at Sarie. “We must go over to Mousehole for a cream tea,” she said.

“Aye, we should,” Sarie agreed. “They do have the best ones around.”

“Better than the one at Padstow?” Laurel asked, not taking her eyes from the clouds hurrying towards the horizon overhead.

“The best,” Coll interjected excitedly. “A big pot of tea, with lots of sugar, of course and scones with clotted cream and preserves.”

“I l-l-love them,” Gort said.

“We’ll make plans to go next week, I think,” Sarie said.

“Yes,” agreed Emily, “cream tea for the six of us.”

Sarie and Emily got to their feet. “Em and I are going to take a short walk to wear off lunch,” Sarie told them. “Don’t go too far, it’s getting late.” Sarie and Emily set off along the Coastal

Pathway to the east in the direction of Greeb Farm and the craft shops on the other side of the iron age hill fort.

Laurel and her friends headed north toward Sennen Cove. They raced along the path, grinning at their own daring as they didn't slow down, even when the path curved sharply and ran along the edge of the cliffs.

As they neared the cairn of rock that they climbed earlier, Laurel stopped to catch her breath. Holding her hand against the stitch in her side, she waved to the others and indicated she would catch up with them when she could. She walked until she reached the rock cairn and leaned on a large boulder at the foot of the pile. The wind came up the face of the cliff and ruffled her hair across her face.

The sound of the seals also carried on the wind. She held her hair out of her face and looked down at the seals, squinting against the bright sun. There seemed to be a lot of them, and they appeared to be upset about something judging by the odd barking noises. Mixed in with the wind and the sea on the rocks, it sounded like voices.

Never knew what a seal sounded like before and now I'm thinking I can understand them.

She laughed at herself and straightened up from her comfortable spot on the boulder. She jumped as something tugged at her jeans.

"Drat…" Her voice faltered as she turned and looked down at the small figure tugging on her jeans. "Oh my goodness, I didn't hear you come up…"

Her stomach clenched and her mouth fell open. Standing beside her, tugging urgently on her jeans, was a small brown man. At first she thought it was a lost child, but as soon as she looked into his eyes, she knew it was no child. The little man was wiry and brown and wearing dusty russett colored clothes and a pointy hat with a brim. The hat had a wide band held in place by a coppery-colored buckle. His wise old eyes crinkled at the corners as he met her gaze.

"Mistress, mistress, sorry it is to bother you, but yon Selkie needs your help," he implored her.

"Are you Aisling's friend?" Laurel found her voice with difficulty.

She tore her gaze away from the little man's face and looked frantically up the path. Where were the others? Why didn't they come back to find her? The path remained distressingly bare. She couldn't tell if this was the same piskie she had seen with Aisling or not.

Tugging at her jeans again to get her attention, the little man cleared his throat.

"Gwin Scawen, I am, young miss. I used to work in the wheal over in the nance by the loe."

Work the what, in the where, over by the who? Laurel's thoughts bumped against each other as she searched for words. "What do you mean, I don't understand. What language is that?"

Gwin Scawen twitched his shoulders straight and spoke proudly, "Why, 'tis just old Cornish, Mistress."

He wrinkled his brow for a moment and then smiled brightly. "What I said was I used to work in the mine that is the valley next to the creek."

"Oh." She couldn't think of anything more intelligent to say. "What was the thing you said about a silkie? Do you mean silkie chickens?"

"It's a Selkie, miss. A seal man and sore hurt he is. He is by the carrick down in the porth." Laurel frowned at the strange words. Gwin Scawen shook his head and rephrased, "I mean he is by the rock down in the cove. He needs your help."

"What can I do? Wouldn't a veterinarian be better? I don't know anything about seals, only a little bit of horse first aid."

Gwin Scawen shook his head. "No, 'tis you he needs. He saw you earlier and tried to call you. When you didn't understand, he called me to find you."

Looking down at the beach far below her, the rocky cliffs didn't look very climbable to her. There was a large seal lying in the lee of a rock, with a ring of seals surrounding him.

"Is that him, the Selkie?" she asked pointing down.

"Aye, 'tis," replied Gwin. "And we must be helping him soon, before the tide comes in and the light goes."

He took Laurel's hand in his dry papery one and pulled her with him toward the cliff edge.

"Are you crazy?" She gulped. "There's no path there, and besides I'm scared of heights. I can't climb down there!"

Gwin stopped and looked over his shoulder at her. "But you must, miss; it is you he needs. He says he has a message for you as well." He looked at her imploringly. "He won't last the night without your help."

She looked down into the cove again. As if he could feel her gaze, the large seal raised his head and met her eyes as if they were only a few inches apart. Laurel felt a great pull in her stomach before a soft deep voice vibrated between her ears.

"Please, Daughter of Eve, I need your assistance. If there was any other way, I would not trouble you. Please."

She couldn't ignore the pain, or the pride in the deep voice. She could feel the deep tiredness seeping into his bones.

"I suppose you know a safe way down from here?"

"Oh yes, Miss Laurel, this way, this way." Gwin pulled her closer to the edge of the cliff.

"Wait! How do you now my name? I know I didn't tell you." Laurel looked at the little man suspiciously.

"The Selkie told me, just now. You gave him your name when you allowed him into your heart to speak with you," he explained. "And you were with Miss Aisling the other night in the rain as well."

"Oh," was all Laurel could think of to say as she allowed Gwin to pull her to a small, narrow and very crumbly path snaking down the face of the cliff.

"Are you sure this is okay for someone as big as me?"

Gwin Scawen took a tighter hold and led her further down the path.

"Close your eyes if you are affrighted and trust me. I will lead you safe to the Selkie."

The earth tilted, and her head swam, as it always did when she was near heights. It was either trust Gwin Scawen, or pitch over the edge.

"Okay, lead on, Gwin, and don't let me fall."

She closed her eyes and gave her trust to the little piskie; she felt the touch of the Selkie in her mind.

"You will be safe, little one. Allow Gwin Scawen to bring you to me; it will benefit us both."

Laurel moved forward on the path with her eyes tightly shut, Gwin kept talking to her, telling her when the path turned or dipped sharply. She could feel the warmth of the Selkie inside her, holding her fear at bay. After what seemed like hours, Gwin Scawen stopped and gave her hand a shake.

"Open your eyes. We have arrived."

The sea crashed against the shore sounding like thunder; the heavy smell of fish and seaweed hung in the air. The ground under her feet no longer slanted downward but was level and sandy. She opened her eyes a crack. Sure enough they were at the bottom of the huge, tall cliff which now towered above her. "Holy crap," Laurel whispered tilting her head back so she could see all the way to the top. "How am I supposed to climb back *up*?"

Gwin Scawen tugged on her hand to get her attention. "The Selkie is here by the carrick."

She pulled her gaze from the terrifying cliff and took a deep breath to stop the racing of her heart. She looked down in front of her at the immense, black bulk of the Selkie lying by the boulder. Somehow, he hadn't seemed so *large* from up on the cliff. She tried to swallow and found her throat wouldn't co-operate. Instead, she unclenched her jaw and approached the massive creature, at what she hoped, was his head.

"H-h-hello," she managed to squeak out. "What's wrong with you? Where are you hurt?"

The hulking mass shifted; the Selkie lifted his sleek head out of the shadow of the boulder. Laurel felt the foreign touch inside her head again, but it wasn't so frightening now; although, on some level of her consciousness, she was gibbering madly and screaming at herself to get the heck out of there.

"*Daughter of Eve, my thanks for your bravery in coming to my call.*" He dipped his head to her in a kind of seal-like bow.

"Are you hurt somewhere?

"*I am,*" he acknowledged. "*I have a wound that needs tending; it is more than Gwin Scawen can manage on his own.*"

Laurel moved closer to the Selkie and knelt by his massive shoulder. The strong odor of brine and fish guts stung her nose and her eyes watered. Underlying it, she detected a trace of pipe tobacco. From this close, fine lines of pain creased the corners of the Selkie's eyes, and there was tenseness in his face. She watched the little hairs on his muzzle move slightly as he breathed.

"Where are you hurt? Are you lying on it?" She grimaced thinking how hard it would be to get the sand out of an open wound.

"*It's a little more complicated than that, I'm afraid.*" The Selkie shifted his huge mass slightly. "*Do you ken what a Selkie is?*"

Laurel tried to remember if Coll or Aisling ever mentioned Selkies. "I don't think so. What are you; I mean you're some sort of seal, right?"

The Selkie made a sound almost like a human chuckle, "*In a manner of speaking yes, some sort of seal.*"

Gwin Scawen held his sides and shook with laughter.

"*It's not quite that funny, you,*" the Selkie admonished him.

Gwin Scawen continued to whoop with laughter, "The King of Selkies described as *some sort of seal!* Oh my, oh my, wait 'til I repeat that, when next we meet at the Dancing Maidens!"

Laurel cleared her throat and fixed her gaze firmly on the Selkie.

"Well, what *is* a Selkie, then?"

She didn't think anything she said was quite *that* funny. *What else could he be?*

"*My apologies, little one, a Selkie is a man who can turn into a seal and back again. We are magical creatures who the modern world no longer wishes to see, much like our friend Gwin Scawen here, who is a piskie.*"

Laurel shook her head hard to see if rattling her brains made what the Selkie said make any more sense.

"You're a man who can turn into a seal or a seal who can become a man? What were you first man or seal?" she demanded. "This is too freaky."

The Selkie frowned, if indeed a seal face can frown. "*I don't remember which was first. My mam was a human mortal, so I suppose I was born in a human shape. I never asked her when I had the chance. and Da would never speak of her again once she was gone.*"

"Where did she go?" Laurel was distracted from her original question by the mention of the Selkie's mom and his obvious love for her.

The Selkie looked surprised. "*Why she died of course. Humans do not live anywhere near so long as Selkies. I used to come and visit her every moon or so, but the time came when I couldn't help her prolong her life any longer, and she stepped onto the next wheel. Still, she lived to be a hundred and five years, by your reckoning.*"

"A hundred and five years? That's a long time for a human."

"*But it's only a moment for us,*" the Selkie said softly, "*and then we grieve them for the rest of our lives.*"

Laurel returned to the thread of their original conversation. "Assuming I believe you are a Selkie, and you can turn into a man, and that you're a magical being, what do you need me for?"

The Selkie cast a quelling glance at Gwin Scawen and shifted uncomfortably as if he as was embarrassed.

"*As I said, it is complicated. I was interrupted during my transformation from man to seal; it seems that I am rather stuck where I am.*"

"What happened?"

Gwin Scawen stuffed his knuckles in his mouth to keep from shrieking with mirth.

The Selkie closed his eyes for a moment.

"*I got caught up in fishing net. I was careless and not paying attention to what was around me, and here I am.*"

He rolled over away from the boulder; Laurel could see pale flesh protruding from his far shoulder.

"*I seem to still have a human arm and leg.*"

Am I having a weird dream? Did I fall down the cliff and really whack my head? This can't be real.

The Selkie chuckled again. "*This is as real as the moon and stars, little one.*"

Laurel tripped over a piece of flotsam as she backed hastily away from him and sat down hard in the sand, staring at the Selkie.

"*Don't look so startled. I am speaking mind to mind, and you have no shields in place, so I can hear you rather plainly.*"

"Oh."

Gwin Scawen scurried up them. "The tide is coming in; we need to finish this quickly, Vear Du."

"Is that your name? Does it mean something?"

"It means Great Black," said Gwin Scawen.

Vear Du frowned at Gwin Scawen. "*Our friend here forgets himself. The giving of one's true name is a powerful trust not given or taken lightly. Although I see no darkness in your heart, I must ask for your pledge never to reveal my true name to any creature or entity. Do I have your pledge*?"

"Of course, I can't think who I could tell could hurt you anyway."

Vear Du nodded. "*You would be surprised*," he said enigmatically.

"The tide," Gwin Scawen reminded them.

The waves were much closer than before, and the wind was picking up. It was also getting dark. The cliff towered above her; it was not something she wanted to climb in the dark, even if the moon was waxing almost full.

"What do you need me to do?" Laurel turned her attention back to Vear Du.

"*I need you to cut the net free from my arm and leg. Then I must find a place to put it where it can't get back into the sea*."

She moved around Vear Du, squeezing in between him and the boulder. The tough netting dug into his skin where the metal fittings left raw burns on the pale flesh. The pale human arm and leg looked pathetically ridiculous lying limply against the sleek black hide of the Selkie.

"What do I cut it with?"

Gwin Scawen stepped forward and a silver blade flashed in the fading sun. "You may use this, Daughter of Eve." He handed her a small silver knife with the handle towards her.

"Why couldn't you cut him loose then?" Laurel asked as she set to work on the net.

"The metal fittings on the net contain iron, which is causing the burns you see on Vear Du," Gwin told her. "It makes me weak to even contemplate touching them."

Vear Du grunted and shifted while she worked at the netting; it just seemed to get tighter the more she tried to get it loose.

"Stay still!" she ordered him. "My Dad would be telling you to cowboy up and quit being a princess!"

"*I see*," Vear Du's voice was dry with amusement, "*well then I will try to, what was it you said, cowboy up*?"

"That's better." She freed his shoulder. "You've got some nasty burns though, Mr. Selkie. Can you roll a bit more onto your other side?"

Laurel squeezed further into the space between Vear Du and the boulder and reached her arm under his huge fishy-smelling chest.

"Man, you stink," she exclaimed, trying to breathe through her mouth, so she couldn't smell his odor.

"*I stink*?" Vear Du's voice was full of outrage. "*I stink*?"

Gwin Scawen put his hands over his mouth to smother his giggles.

"Like you've been rolling in mounds of dead fish guts."

"*Oh*." Vear Du sounded mollified. "*Well, I guess I have at that*."

"Great." She sawed at another length of netting.

"*Oh, that's much better*." Vear Du sighed as the net pulled away from his upper body.

Laurel wriggled out of the small space she occupied between Vear Du and the boulder. She was surprised to hear water lapping at the side of the boulder nearest the sea.

"Darn, the tide is coming faster than I can free you. Can you wriggle your rump away from the boulder so I can get at your leg?"

With a mighty heave Vear Du shifted his body further away from the boulder. "*Is that better*?"

"Yeah, I think that'll do it."

She stepped between his tail fluke and his human leg. Kneeling down, she sawed at the net as fast as she could, the sea lapping at her sneakers and wetting her jeans.

"Almost there," she said over her shoulder to Vear Du, "just one more bit to come free."

Laurel glanced at the encroaching tide now starting to creep around the boulder and pool in the sand beside Vear Du. Frantically she tugged at the net where it was caught under the black belly, finally it came away from his body far enough for her to slip the silver blade of Gwin Scawen's knife between the net and his skin. With a swift movement, the severed twine pulled away from the pale human leg protruding grotesquely from his black hide.

"There, you should be able to move now." She scrambled back from Vear Du and the boulder.

The wind whipped her hair across her face as she straightened up. The sea water was up to her ankles and even colder than the wind, if that was possible. Gwin Scawen was perched on top of some small rocks closer to the face of the cliff.

"Now what? Why isn't he moving?"

Gwin shrugged his thin shoulders and continued to watch the huge bulk on the sand anxiously. Finally with a great shudder Vear Du shook himself and floundered away from the boulder.

"If you would be so kind as to look the other way, little one, I will complete my transformation."

Laurel averted her eyes and turned her back to the sea, although she felt a little foolish. *What does a seal have that I shouldn't see?* She started violently as a hand gripped her shoulder from behind, whirling around she stared straight into the brown eyes of a very cold, wet man. Laurel staggered backwards as fast as she could, her mouth working but no sound managing to come out. The man held out his hand again and smiled slowly.

"At least I no longer smell of fish guts," he said gently.

"Where did you get those clothes?" It was the first thing that came into her mind.

The man glanced down at his loose pants and shirt. "I keep them here in a niche in the rocks for emergencies. I would have thought you would ask who I am before questioning my sense of style." He smiled again.

Gwin Scawen giggled. "She is too smart for that, Vear Du. She knows you are the Selkie. It's a good thing I did not bet with you on her intelligence, you would owe me."

Laurel gulped and forced herself to take a better look at the man in front of her. After that first quick look into his eyes, all she could do was look at his sturdy wet feet in the sand. He was a little taller than her dad, with black, black hair, brown eyes with huge lashes, a relatively small nose and a generous mouth. His jaw was strong and his neck short; it merged into his wide powerful shoulders. The shirt was blown against his broad chest, which tapered down into a narrow waist and slim hips. *He can't be more than seventeen or eighteen and he's hot.* She returned her gaze to his face.

"I thought you would finish turning into a seal." She felt heat rise in her face. "Was that very rude?" she asked Gwin Scawen who was howling with laughter again.

"No, no, just unexpected."

Vear Du smiled a little uncertainly. "I thought you might be more comfortable speaking with me as a man."

"Ummm, well, I guess so."

A small wave washed around the boulder and wet her to the knees. She looked at the water and then up the cliff in apprehension. Soon the water would cover the little beach; there didn't look like anyplace to get above the tide line. To make matters worse, the sun was just a glimmer of red on the western horizon, and the night was drawing in. The round dollar of the almost full moon glimmered in the sky as the deep blue of twilight threatened to fade into night.

"How am I going to get back up the cliff?" Laurel looked from Vear Du to Gwin Scawen. "I know I can't climb it in the dark."

Although, at least in the dark I won't have to see just how far I'll fall if I take a wrong step.

Vear Du sighed. "I haven't enough strength at the moment to magic you to the top. Even the moon with all her strength cannot help me tonight." He looked at Gwin Scawen. "Can you help?"

"I have an appointment I must keep." Gwin Scawen danced on the top of the big rock he stood on. "I promised her I would come when the moon was newly risen." He glanced at the silver circle riding higher in the sky. "I am already late."

With an apologetic glance, he turned, stepped sideways off the rock, and vanished.

Laurel's mouth dropped open, and she turned to stare at Vear Du. "But what am I supposed to do?" she exclaimed in anger. "I agreed to help you, but I don't want to drown, and I don't want to spend the night cold and hungry stuck on some rock! What are you going to do, leave too?" Her voice rose sharply at the end of the sentence.

Vear Du reached out and took her hand; his was surprisingly warm. She was freezing, what with standing up to her knees in sea water and the wind blowing sharply against her.

"You have done me a great service, never fear. I will find us a place to spend the night and get you warm," Vear said. "There is a place just up the path a bit, high enough to be out of the way of the tide and offer warmth. I use it sometimes when I tire of being a seal and yearn to be a man, just for a time."

He led the way towards the foot of the cliff. A short climb up the path, he stopped and laid his hand on an outcrop of stone jutting from the cliff. A glimmer of light outlined his hand; the outcrop shimmered and disappeared. In its place was the dark opening of a cave.

"Very cool. Do you have any dry clothes or food in there?"

Laurel was shaking so badly she knew Vear Du could feel it and hoped he would think it was from the cold and not the fact she was scared spitless. It was a lot to take in a day, Selkies and piskies, and rocks turning into caves.

"Don't be scared, Laurel," Vear Du said. "You have shown extraordinary bravery this day. Nothing evil is going to befall you. Come in and be welcome."

He led the way into the mouth of the cave, which was much larger than it appeared from the outside. Near the entrance was a fire pit, which burst into smokeless flame at a glance from the Selkie. She sidled nearer to its warmth and held out her frozen hands.

Soon Vear Du had a small kettle suspended over the flames, and the smell of beef stew tantalized her nose. Vear Du also set a small kettle to boil for tea. Then, he brought some blankets and an old pair of trousers from the depths of the cave.

"These may be a little large for you, but they should do until we can dry yours," he said, as he handed her the trousers. "You can change in the back of the cave if you like."

Laurel took the pants and found her way into the darkness out of the ring of firelight. Quickly she changed and was happily surprised at how much better she felt now she was warm and dry.

Returning to the fire, she draped her wet jeans over a rock near to dry. She accepted the large mug of hot tea Vear Du pressed into her hands and settled in the soft sand by the fire pit.

"Where the heck did Gwin Scawen have to go in such a hurry? Sarie and my friends will be worried sick about me, and I have no way to let them know where I am. Oh, God, I hope they don't phone Mom and Dad and tell them I'm missing! They have enough to worry about."

Vear Du sat cross-legged. "I think everything will be okay. Gwin Scawen will never tell me his business, but I think he will get a message to your friends somehow. He has certain connections he will never share with me. Piskie Business, he calls it."

"I hope so."

There is nothing I can do about it right now, anyway.

She hadn't brought her cell phone with her, and it probably wouldn't work from inside the cliff anyway. *Maybe Gwin can get a message to Aisling.* Laurel yawned in spite of herself as the warmth seeped into her cold bones. Vear Du threw off as much heat as the fire.

"Why aren't you cold?"

"I don't feel cold like you mortals," he answered her. "I like the fire for its light and company when I watch the moon rise over the sea."

He pulled a pipe and some tobacco out of a pouch around his neck, tamping the tobacco down into the bowl before lighting it with a coal from the fire.

"That's why I could smell pipe smoke on you, even over the fish guts. Now you smell mostly like pipe smoke and only a little bit like fish guts."

Laurel took the wooden bowl of stew Vear handed her and grinned at him over the rim before she ladled the rich broth into her mouth. Vear Du shrugged his shoulders and smiled back at her. He took a huge pull on his pipe and leaned back to blow the smoke at the roof of the cave.

"Ahh!" he exclaimed. "I do miss my pipe when I am my seal self."

Her mind formed a mental picture of the huge black seal with a pipe in his mouth floating in the sea. She giggled as the mental picture began to blow smoke rings at the sea gulls hovering overhead. Vear Du's eyes crinkled in amusement as he caught the image from Laurel's mind.

"I do dream of it," he admitted. "But logistically it wouldn't work." He held up his hand and wagged it at her. "Flippers do not make good tobacco tampers or pipe holders."

She put her empty bowl down in the sand behind her. In spite of herself, she yawned again and pulled the blanket close around her shoulders. Vear Du moved around the fire to sit beside her; Laurel moved closer to him to take advantage his warmth. Soon her head was nodding against his shoulder.

"Would you like to lie down? You can use my leg as a pillow."

She was too tired to refuse and smiled sleepily at Vear Du as she stretched out on the fire-warmed sand and laid her head on Vear Du's strong thigh. The last thing she remembered was Vear Du tucking the blanket more snugly around her knees before she drifted into the soft darkness of sleep.

* * *

Laurel was walking through a bright mist; nothing looked familiar. But it wasn't scary either. The mist billowed and swirled, but there was no breeze. As the mist brushed against her skin, she heard voices and caught bits of words, but again, nothing she could understand. Somehow it didn't matter, and she kept moving through the mist.

Imperceptibly, the mist became brighter and thinner. Soon Laurel could see through it like looking up at the sky while you are under water. Wavering images floated past her gaze; all of them out of focus, until one image sharpened and came to rest in front of her.

Two figures were perched on top of a weird-looking pile of stones. The stones stood on top of a ridge of rock rising out of the moor. The ones at the bottom of the pile were smaller than the ones closer to the top. They were huge flat stones and roughly circular in shape, like some giant child had been piling pebbles haphazardly, and then growing tired of the game, left them there. On top of the strange pile, she saw herself and Vear Du sitting knee to knee facing each other and holding hands. She was considering how to climb up the inverted pile when she realized she didn't need to climb. She could float up!

Up through the thin mist she floated, until she was even with the topmost rock. Laurel sat down beside the gossamer figure of herself and with a small whuft of misplaced air and a pearly swirl of mist, joined her dreaming self.

Vear Du's hands were warm on her own and his deep voice comforting. The stone beneath her buttocks vibrated with his voice, and the mist shimmered.

"What is it that you seek, little one?" Vear Du looked deep into her eyes as he spoke and his hands tightened fractionally on hers.

For a moment, she was lost in the depths of Vear Du's eyes. It was like looking into a deep still pool, where everything terrible might happen, but also everything wonderful. There were eons of pain and laughter, joy and sorrow, Dark and Light. Laurel forced herself to concentrate. There *was* something she needed help with. She needed to unravel the words of the 'Obby 'Oss. There was a Selkie that guarded something; somewhere she needed to go to help her mom get better. What did the 'Oss say?

"I was told there is a Selkie guarding caves with crystal guardians…." Laurel's voice faltered. "Are you the Selkie?"

Vear Du smiled "Ah. That explains why you could see me and hear Gwin Scawen. The 'Oss already opened your eyes to the secret world that lies just beyond the veil of your own. No, I am not the Guardian of the Crystal Hollows, but one of my kin is. You may use my name to prove your worthiness, also a talisman will I give you."

Vear Du let go of one hand and rummaged in the pouch at his neck, which held his pipe and tobacco. He drew out a strangely glowing crystal and a cowrie shell linked together by a shimmering silver chain. Vear Du pressed the talisman into her hand; she tucked it into the front pocket of her jeans.

"Thanks…but how do I find a big lizard and follow him like the 'Oss said?"

Vear Du sighed. "It is never simple, and you must find your own way." He paused and his brow furrowed with his frown. "The great lizard emerges from the sea, not far from where you live. If you look with your heart, you will see him. Follow his spine to the rocks that can't be eaten." Vear Du paused and looked pointedly at Laurel and then down at the stones they sat on; he didn't look away until she nodded in comprehension. "From there you should find direction to the meeting place where you must greet and ride the filly that never was foaled to her home under the hill. You will recognize the meeting place by its stone markers, a century plus one. From there, it is up to the Crystal Guardians to decide if you are worthy. To gain entrance from my kin, you must remember it will not be the courage of a man that will win your way but rather the selfless sorrow of a woman. Don't fret child, I will help you all I can, you may use the talisman to call me."

"Help me to remember everything exactly right." She was terrified she would forget something *really* important.

Vear Du tightened his grip on her hands again, leaned forward, and kissed Laurel in the middle of her forehead. The spot tingled and grew warm, for a moment she felt an instance of perfect love.

"All you need do is hold the talisman in your hand and follow your heart, little one." Vear Du's smile was like warm sunlight on a winter's day. "Let your friends help you, four heads are better than one. Share your quest with them, for they, too, have paths they need to walk."

The mist shimmered and blew between them, Vear Du's face blurred, and the black sleek head of the seal from the beach was superimposed over the human features. They really were one and the same; it was amazing she wasn't terrified. A small part of her was screaming she should be very afraid. The mist thickened and became more opalescent, swirling moistly about them.

"Come, little one, it is time." Vear Du's voice came out of the mist. Laurel could no longer see him, but his fingers warm on her own.

* * *

She stirred and opened her eyes; she was lying on the sand in the Selkie's cave. The fire still burned brightly, and there was a pot of tea sitting on one of the hearth stones. Her head was still on Vear Du's thigh, and pale light was pearling the sky outside the cave entrance.

"Is it morning?"

"'Tis. Soon we can get you back to your friends and Sarie."

"How do you know Sarie? I never mentioned her name."

"Sarie and I have a mutual friend from when Sarie was very young, only a little older than you, in fact," Vear Du answered. "You may give her my greetings, if you like."

"What mutual friend?" It seemed very important she knew who it was.

Vear Du frowned slightly and opened his mouth to reply. In the same instance, the shadows on the other side of the fire shimmered and brightened; out of the glow, Gwin Scawen stepped sideways into their presence.

"About time you came back," Vear Du growled at him. "What business has kept you away for so long?"

"Well, yes." Gwin Scawen looked sheepish. "It didn't seem to be so very long where I was; no time at all."

"Did you manage to remember to deliver your message?" Vear Du asked him.

"I did too, so there!" Gwin Scawen screwed up his leathery little face and stuck his tongue out at Vear Du. "I needed to visit with her anyway. It's been awhile, and the gull who checked on her yesterday thought she seemed lonely."

Laurel's mind raced. *Does Gwin Scawen mean the gull that flew so low over me and Aisling, yesterday? Aisling said she thought it was trying to speak with her.*

"Do you mean Aisling? Is that how my friends will now I am okay and where to find me?"

Gwin Scawen regarded her soberly before smiling mysteriously. "You'll have to ask her yourself. Not my secret to tell."

Laurel refrained from telling him Aisling already confided in her. Vear Du got to his feet and brushed the sand from his trousers. He glanced at the fire, and it immediately shrank in on itself and went out. Gwin Scawen blinked, the pots and dishes vanished from the hearth and stowed themselves in the shadows at the back of the cave.

"You should change into your own jeans as they are dry now. Make sure you have everything with you." He looked at her significantly.

Laurel picked her jeans up from the rock and headed to the back of the cave to change. She folded the borrowed trousers and left them on a crate. She checked the pockets, but they were empty. Frowning she pulled on her own jeans, feeling like she was missing something. She tucked her shirt into the waistband of her jeans and smoothed her hands down her thighs. Her palm encountered something sharp and hard in her left front pocket. *I don't remember having anything in my pocket.* Curious, Laurel pulled the object out into the dim light.

The small crystal shone and glimmered in the palm of her hand, and a spot in the middle of her forehead felt warm. With sudden clarity, she remembered her dream. Here was physical proof it was real; this was the talisman the Vear Du in her dream gave her. As she watched, the crystal dulled and transformed itself into a silver grey granite stone. The shimmering silver chain became a leather thong. Only the cowrie shell remained unchanged. Laurel tucked the talisman back into her pocket before stepping back into the front of the cave.

"We have been discussing the best way to get you back to the top of the cliff." Gwin Scawen informed her. "I would be honored to lead you back up the path." He bowed so low his long nose brushed the sand. "Our large friend here," Gwin indicated Vear Du with a dismissive wave of his twiggy brown hand, "thinks he should magic you back to the top where your friends should be arriving at any time."

She would really rather not climb back up the cliff, coming down was hard enough. Laurel looked at Vear Du and then at Gwin Scawen who was smiling hopefully up at her.

She swallowed dryly, "If it's all the same to you, I would rather not climb back up. I'm afraid of heights."

Vear Du smiled triumphantly at Gwin Scawen. "It shall be as you ask."

The three odd companions scrunched across the sand to the mouth of the cave. Laurel knelt down and hugged Gwin Scawen.

"We will see each other again," Gwin Scawen promised her.

"I hope so. I will miss you if you don't show up."

Laurel straightened and looked up into Vear Du's dark eyes. "What about you, will I see you again?"

Vear Du's eyes crinkled at the corners as he grinned at her. "As often as you wish, little one. I am usually somewhere about this cove. On rare occasions, I will visit the Mount of Michael, or seek human company in the pubs of Penzance. Call me, and I will find you."

"Thanks for keeping me warm and fed last night." She hugged Vear Du around the waist.

Vear Du smoothed his large hand over her bright hair. "It was the very least I could do, little one, after you came to my rescue. And now I think it is time."

"What do I have to do?"

"Just close your eyes and think of the cairn of stones by the top of the path, that is all," Vear Du instructed her.

Laurel took one last look at Gwin Scawen who was smiling encouragingly at her.

"Miss you," she whispered to him. "Wait, will I be able to find your cave again if I come here?"

Vear Du rested his large warm hand on her shoulder. "If I am here in the cove, or at the cave, yes, you will be able to enter; otherwise, no. You only have to call me if you need me."

"Okay, I'm ready," she whispered.

Vear Du turned Laurel to face the sun-sparkled sea below them and placed his arm about her shoulders, his hip pressed against her. He turned and took a step sideways, pulling her with him. Vertigo gripped her. It was black. Black as if no light was left in the world. As suddenly as it came, the darkness was replaced by the pale radiance of the newly born sun flooding the moor with gold. Mist hung over the gorse, grey and smoky in the dawn light. It swirled around her knees, and she shivered in the light breeze beginning to blow in from the sea. The mist made it hard to see if anyone was coming up the path from Land's End.

"Should I wait here, do you think?"

"They will be along in a few minutes, I believe." Vear Du gripped Laurel's shoulder tightly for a second. "I must leave you now, little one. Remember, you only have to call if you need me. Gwin Scawen will always be somewhere nearby as well."

"Be careful," she admonished him. "Stay clear of nets, enchanted or otherwise." She let go of his hand, stepped back, and raised her hand in farewell. "Go gently," she whispered. It was what her Gramma had always said to her when she left.

Vear Du placed a hand over his heart. For a second, she imagined tears glistened in his dark eyes. The mist swirled, and Vear Du was gone, but his voice hung in the air. "And you, little one."

Laurel raised her hand to reach out to the mist, seeking to hold Vear Du to her, but she was interrupted by the sound of voices coming out of the mist further down the path.

"She has to be here somewhere," Coll's voice echoed strangely through the mist. "They didn't find her when they searched the cove last night."

"Just a little further, I think." Aisling's light tones slipped through the thinning mists.

"Over here! Here I am."

"D-d-did you hear that?" Gort shouted excitedly. "Sh-sh-she's o-o-ver there!"

Sarie's worried voice reached her.

"Stay where you are, Laurel," she cautioned. "Keep calling to us."

"I'm right here! By the big rock pile we climbed yesterday."

The wind off the sea sharpened as the sun broke free, and the mist disappeared, scarpering off across the moors in rags and streamers of sun-lit pearl.

On the path stood Coll, Aisling, Gort, Sarie, and Emily, all looking at Laurel like she was a ghost.

"Where did you come from?" Emily asked a little breathlessly. "You weren't there just a minute ago."

"But I was. I heard you talking, and I called to you."

"We could hear you Laurel, but we couldn't see you at all," Sarie told her gently.

"Where did you spend the night? We looked everywhere for you. They even had men from Sennen go down the cliff and search the cove in case you fell."

"I told you we'd find her here this morning," Aisling interrupted.

Aisling linked her arm and started back down the path toward the car park.

"I followed a path down the cliff and got lost. I found a cave and spent the night there."

"I didn't know there was a cave down that path," Coll chimed in. "I never saw one the one time I crawled down there."

"I don't know if I could even find it again myself," she lied. *As if I could ever forget the way to Vear Du's cave.*

Aisling whispered, “I knew you were okay. Gwin Scawen came and told me you were safe last night.”

Laurel tripped over her own feet as she gave Aisling a startled look. “You were who he went to meet last night? I knew it,” she whispered back.

Aisling nodded, “He really likes you, thinks you’re very funny. You have to tell me the whole story once we can get alone.”

“Why don’t you sleep over tonight?” She raised her voice, “Sarie, can Aisling stay over tonight?”

“I suppose as long as you’re not too tired. Why don’t we wait and see how you feel this afternoon.”

Chapter Eight

The Clue to the Great Lizard

Laurel and Aisling decided to spend the rainy afternoon going through the books in Sarie's spare room, which doubled as her library. They had all the books that even remotely looked like they might contain a clue to the Great Lizard in a haphazard pile by the bed. The rest of the books they returned to the shelves, although maybe not quite as neatly as they were before.

"My goodness," exclaimed Aisling brushing her hair back out of her eyes, "let's hope there's something here to at least point us in the right direction."

"Do you think it might be something on the Lizard Peninsula, maybe at Lizard Point?" Laurel narrowed her eyes to squint at the faded map pinned to the wall. "My friend had a thoroughbred called Cornish Prince and his aire was Lizard Point. Kind of a coincidence, don't you think."

Aisling laid the book she was holding down on the quilt beside her and studied the map, too. "I thought you said the seal guy told you it was close to where you live. The Lizard is a fair distance from here," Aisling pondered.

"I guess."

The Cornish idea of a far distance was very different from her experience in Alberta, where Calgary is considered fairly close to Edmonton as it's only about three hours north on the Number 2 highway.

"What's closer to here that even has lizard in its name though?" Laurel said with exasperation.

She walked over to the map and glared at it. *We should have figured this out by now.*

“Look with my heart he said. How am I supposed to do that? I’ve tried and tried.” She threw herself down on the small bed under the window.

Aisling turned, leaned on the wall by the map, and watched the rain hit the window.

“We’ve got to be missing something really obvious,” Aisling mused. “Lord, I feel like I’ve gone Bodmin.” She rubbed her forehead.

“What’s that mean?”

“Means going mental,” Aisling replied. “There’s a mental hospital on Bodmin Moor.”

“Then I should check in, too.”

Aisling turned back to frown at the map. “Maybe the boys will find something today. Coll said they were going over to Church Cove to visit old Mr. Albion. They promised to see if they could get Mr. Albion to tell some old stories about the area.”

“Let’s hope they’re having better luck than we are.”

Laurel leaned over to take another book from the pile. She over balanced and knocked the whole lot of them flying. Aisling jumped out of the way as the books crashed around her feet.

“Damn it all to hell!” Dad’s favorite phrases came in handy when things did not go as planned.

Aisling knelt and began to gather the books up.

“Maybe we should try to sort them into…” Aisling began.

Sarie’s voice echoed up the narrow stairwell. “What are you girls up to?”

“It’s all okay, Sarie. I just knocked over some books. Sorry.” The last thing she wanted was for Sarie to think they weren’t being careful with the old books.

“Lunch will be ready in about fifteen minutes,” Sarie called back. Her footsteps retreated to the kitchen at the back of the house.

Aisling already had most of the books back into some semblance of order. Laurel picked up an old tattered book with a smeared title on the frontispiece and a bunch of papers fluttered out of it.

Aisling looked horrified. “Bloody hell,” she whispered. “Did we do that? Sarie will be flaming mad.”

Laurel picked up the topmost paper. “It looks like a letter, it’s all handwritten. I don’t think it was actually part of the book,” she told a relieved Aisling.

The date on the letter was May, 1965. Carefully putting the letter on the bed, she gathered the rest of the papers. The corner of an old photo was stuck under the edge of another book. Laurel pulled it free and gasped; there staring up at her were two girls about fifteen or sixteen. The girl on the left was Sarie.

“Ash, look at this! It’s an old picture of Sarie and someone. Do you know who the other girl is?”

Aisling studied the photo. “I don’t think it’s anyone I know,” she said slowly. “But look where they are. They’re by the big rock cairn out at Land’s End. You know the one where we lost you and then found you again.”

Laurel’s heart started to pound against her ribs. “Do you think this is a clue? But that can’t be. There isn’t any place that has anything to do with a lizard near there. Is there?”

“I don’t think so,” Aisling said and turned the photo over in her hands. “There’s something written on the back.” Aisling moved closer to the rain-drenched window to take advantage of the extra bit of light filtering through. “It says *Sara and Arabella, Sept 1961*.”

“Did you say Arabella? My grandma’s name was Arabella.”

“Really,” Aisling squealed softly. “Maybe it is a clue of some kind. It seems too much of a coincidence otherwise.”

Aisling passed her the photo. Laurel looked at the laughing young woman closely, trying to see some resemblance to her dad. Their eyes were the same and the smile. She turned the photo over to look more closely at the writing.

“Look, Ash, someone else wrote on here, too. I think it says,” she peered at the faded pencil inscription, “‘me and Bella at Seal Rock.’ Seal Rock. It says Seal Rock, and it’s definitely the same rock pile where I met Gwin Scawen and Vear Du. This has to mean something!”

“Where’s the book that they fell out of?” Aisling scanned the floor for the tattered old book.

“It’s right here.” Laurel fished the book out of the folds of the quilt. “It looks like it’s all about St. Michael’s Mount.” She handed the book to Aisling.

"It is." Aisling looked at the faded smeared cover. There was a sepia-tinted engraving of the island in the bay topped by the castle. "That's a landmark very close to where you live." Aisling handed the book back.

She started to thumb through the pages, looking for something written in the margins, or on the inside of the covers. Her nose started to twitch suddenly; she held the book close to her face and inhaled.

"Ash, what does this smell like to you?"

Laurel excitedly handed the book to Aisling and bounced from foot to foot waiting for the answer. Aisling took the book, crinkling her nose as she sniffed carefully. She put the book safely on an empty shelf.

"It smells like musty old book and tobacco."

Her fist punched the air. "I knew it!"

"Knew what?"

"It smells like Vear Du's tobacco. This must be a clue, but what does St. Michael's Mount have to do with a great lizard?" She clapped her hand over her mouth. "But St. Michael's Mount *is* an island. Vear did say the great lizard emerges from the sea!"

"If we can just put all the pieces together. I wonder why Sarie never said she was friends with your grandmother?"

"Do you think I should ask her? You know how crusty she gets when you ask something she doesn't want to talk about."

"Maybe wait and see what kind of mood she's in at lunch."

Laurel put the photo on the shelf beside the old book and picked up the letter from the quilt.

"Maybe there will be some answers in here." She started to read. Aisling sat beside her so she could read it at the same time.

"Girls." Sarie's voice called from the foot of the stairs making both girls jump. "Lunch is on the table."

"Coming, Sarie," they chorused.

Reluctantly, Laurel folded the old letters and placed them safely back inside the front cover of the faded book. Together, the girls clattered down the stairs.

"Just wait 'til we tell the boys," Aisling whispered as they hurried down the narrow hall to the warm kitchen.

Sarie had a lunch of cheese sandwiches and tea set on the table along with some scones and clotted cream. The rain beat against the windows lining the back of the little kitchen. Under the windows was a long counter Sarie used for preparing meals and countless other things the girls could only guess at. A cheerful fire in the hearth sent lovely warmth through the kitchen. Laurel loved to sit and watch the patterns the flames made and the soot pictures that emerged on the back of the hearth as the flames made the residue collected there flare and glow.

The wind howled and whined as it found the cracks around the windowpanes and whooshed past the chimney with a hollow roar. The wet grass whipped in the wind; the ponies huddled in their shelter trying to keep out of the wet. The pony field was just outside the back door of the kitchen, and the little stone barn was a shapeless blur through the driving rain. Laurel wondered if they should go and rescue the poor ponies and tuck them into the warm, dry barn. Sarie turned from the cooker to put the teapot on the trivet sitting on the oilcloth-covered table. She caught the direction of her gaze.

"We can go out after lunch and put the poor souls in 'til the wind drops a bit," Sarie said over the noise of the storm. "They look like seals."

Laurel and Aisling exchanged startled looks at Sarie's reference to seals. She opened her mouth to ask Sarie about Arabella and the old picture but caught Aisling's eye and stopped. It was better to ask Sarie when her mind was on something else. She might just answer them without thinking about it.

"Let's ask her while we're with the ponies," Aisling whispered quickly.

She nodded and bit into her cheese sandwich. Sarie turned back to the cooker, scooping broiled tomatoes onto a plate, which she deposited on the table.

"So, what mischief have you two hooligans been up to this morning?" Sarie inquired.

"Oh, we were just looking at some of the old books you have in the spare room." Laurel replied.

Sarie frowned slightly, "Are you being very careful with them?"

"Oh, yes, Sarie," Aisling answered quickly. "I know how you value those books."

"Well then, did you find anything interesting?" Sarie asked a little too casually, a slight frown between her brows.

The girls tried hard not to look too guilty.

"Uhmm, not really, yet," Laurel said. Then with a sudden inspiration, she asked, "Do you know anything about a big lizard that has something to do with St. Michael's Mount?"

Sarie looked up startled and dropped her spoon into her tea. "Goodness, child, why would you ask such a thing?"

"It's something I overheard in the bookstore in Marazion the other day. Some tourist asked about it."

Inside, she was delighted with Sarie's reaction. *Sarie knows something!* She risked a quick glance at Aisling while Sarie cleaned up the spilled tea. Aisling eyes gleamed with triumph.

The girls let the subject drop, finished their lunch, and helped Sarie with the cleanup.

Looking out the window at the still lowering weather, Sarie reached for her old canvas hat and coat hanging on the hook by the back door. "It's certainly blowing a gale," she remarked. "Let's go put those ponies in out of it for a while."

Laurel shrugged into her oilskin, glad the old coat would keep out the Cornish rain as well as it did the Alberta winds, and stuffed her feet into boots. Aisling was suited up as well when Sarie opened the kitchen door. They hurried out into the blustery rain. Sarie secured the door quickly so not too much of the warmth from the kitchen could escape.

Heads down and with their faces full of rain, the trio headed for the pony field. Aisling ran ahead to the stone barn to open the doors to the boxes and make sure there was hay in each manger. Laurel and Sarie slogged through the rain to the gate of the field. The ponies saw them coming and left their shelter to splash through the poached ground toward them. Laurel put her hand out to stroke the wet forelock away from Lamorna's eyes. The black pony stuck her cold, wet muzzle into her chest and whickered.

Sarie led the way toward the barn. The ponies followed in a line, heads bent against the driving rain, and their tails wet and straggling, stuck to their rumps by the wind. Laurel followed them into the barn, her hand still on Lamorna's shoulder.

It was strangely quiet in the barn out of the howling storm. The ponies trooped into their own stalls and snuffled about in the oat boxes for grain. Laurel shook the rain from her hat and set it on the dusty windowsill. She picked Lamorna's rug from the hook on the wall and took it into the black mare's stall.

Her heart contracted with homesickness as the smell of wet horse and straw assailed her nostrils. She leaned her head against the wet, black mane for a moment. Lamorna turned her head and lipped her hand. Laurel threw the rug over Lamorna's back, ducked under her neck to buckle the straps at the chest, before she fitted the roller around the mare's girth and buckled it snuggly.

It had taken a bit to get used to English rugs, all her blankets back home had belly straps that were attached. Laurel went to fetch another rug to put over the first, as steam started to rise from the black pony. Aisling and Sarie were doing the same for the other three ponies. Soon the barn was brimming with the sound of horses eating, the rustle of straw in the boxes, and the lovely smell of horses in a warm barn mingled with the damp smell of wet grass and mud.

Sarie pulled out a bale of straw to sit on; the girls joined her. Sarie stuck a piece of hay in her mouth.

"Tastes all warm and summery," she said. Her eyes on the ponies' rumps, which were all they could see of them, as the ponies buried their heads in their mangers.

Aisling met Laurel's gaze and nodded. Laurel cleared her throat nervously and settled a bit on her bale of straw.

"Uhmm, Sarie?" she began tentatively. "Did you know my Gramma Bella?"

Sarie pulled her gaze from the ponies and looked at Laurel. "Why would you ask that?"

Aisling nodded encouragingly, so she plunged on.

"Well, Ash and me, we kind of found something this morning that made me think you might know her..."

"What exactly did you find?" Sarie's voice was quiet and hard to hear over the wind and rain that lashed the stone barn.

"We, well I guess it was actually me. There was a picture of you and someone named Arabella. She looked like my Gramma."

It didn't seem wise to tell Sarie they had found letters, too.

"Bella and I were friends growing up. She left here when she was twenty." Sarie's words were hard and clipped. "It's how I know your mom and dad."

"Why didn't anyone tell me?"

"Your dad didn't want you to know," Sarie said.

"But how did they know how to reach you? Gramma Bella has been dead, since I was really young..."

Sarie looked uncomfortable and couldn't meet Laurel's eyes. She got up from her bale of straw and went into Arthur's stall to straighten his rug.

The pieces came together in a rush.

"She's still alive," she whispered. "Isn't she?" Laurel demanded in a stronger voice. "Isn't she?" She leapt to her feet and shouted at Sarie's back.

Sarie turned to face her. "Yes, she is. But your parents, well, your dad, don't want you to know."

How many times have I asked about Dad's mom? Both of them lied to me!

"Why?" The words came out strangled. "Tell me. You know!"

Sarie looked sad. "It's not my story to tell. You must ask your dad, if you want to know that badly."

"Where does she live, at least tell me that?" Tears were forming in her throat.

"You have to ask your parents," Sarie refused. "It's not for me to say."

Eyes swimming with tears, Laurel pivoted on her toes and banged out of the barn door, running across the yard with the storm demons at her heels. She crashed through the kitchen door, stopped briefly to latch it against the wind, and raced up the narrow stairway into her room. Shedding her oilskin in a heap on the floor, she threw herself on the bed, muddy boots and all. She would be trouble for the mess later; right now it just didn't matter.

Laurel hardly remembered her Gramma Bella. She used to live in a little house behind her parents' house. Her house smelled of lavender and baking and so did she. *How old was I when they told me Gramma Bella was gone? It was just after I started school, if I remember right. So, I must have been five or six.* She couldn't remember if her parents actually told her Gramma Bella died, or just that she had gone away. Laurel ground her teeth savagely. She *believed* Gramma Bella died, and her parents encouraged the belief.

Laurel pounded her fist in her pillow. "Why would they *want* me to believe that?"

A noise at the door distracted her. She whipped around on her bed ready to blast Sarie with questions. Instead it was Aisling who stuck her head in the door.

"Are you okay?" Aisling asked hesitantly. "I can leave you alone if you like."

"Where's Sarie?"

"Still in the barn. She said she needed to think on some things."

Laurel snorted and swung her legs off the bed. Kicking her sodden oilskin out of the way and stopping to drag off her muddy boots, she headed for the door.

"Where are you going?" Aisling asked as she moved out of the way.

"I'm getting those letters and the picture before Sarie hides them on me," she said over her shoulder as she pushed open the door to the spare room.

"But those letters belong to Sarie."

"They're from my Gramma Bella," Laurel said fiercely as she gathered up the letters and the photo but returned the book to the shelf.

Turning on her heel and marching back into the bedroom, she pried up the loose wall board she had discovered behind her bed and tucked everything safely away. Her fingers itched to open the letters and read them, but it would be safer if she waited 'til Sarie was either asleep or gone to the village.

Aisling didn't come back to the room, so Laurel padded back to the spare room to see what she was up to. Aisling was carefully putting all the books back on the shelves. "I'm glad it's only you. I don't know what Sarie would say if she saw this mess after what happened in the barn." Aisling continued to set the books on the shelves.

Laurel dropped to her knees after a moment and helped. Downstairs, they heard the kitchen door open and close, but Sarie did not come up the narrow hall to the foot of the stairway. The girls continued tidying the small room as the light faded into darkness outside. The rain still hit the windowpanes, shiny in the lamp light, but the wind seemed to have dropped from its former ferocity.

Leaning down to retrieve a small book from under the edge of the bed, Laurel read the title so she could put it back in order. Suddenly, she blinked her eyes and took a second look at the book. The title in faded gold letters read, *The Dragon Line in Cornwall.* Laurel tucked the little book under her shirt and into the waistband of her jeans.

"I think that's all of them." She straightened up. "I guess I should go apologize to Sarie for being a brat."

Aisling grinned at her. "Want me to go to first and see if it's safe?"

"Let's just go together," Laurel suggested. "You know, the united front, even though you didn't do anything."

Aisling led the way out the door. Together they traipsed down the dark stairs and into the warm bright kitchen. Sarie was sitting at the table with her hands clasped around a mug of tea. She looked up when they came through the door. Laurel hugged Sarie around the shoulders before Sarie could say anything.

"I know it's not your fault, Sarie. I'm sorry I took it out on you."

"I would tell you if I could. I made a vow to Bella many years ago to always keep her secrets, no matter what," Sarie spoke softly.

"It's okay, Sarie."

Laurel grinned at Aisling across the warm lamp-lit room. They would find the answers themselves and end the mystery once and for all, secrets or no.

The sound of the phone ringing ended the conversation. Sarie got up from the table to pick up the receiver. With a smile, Sarie turned and handed the phone to Laurel.

"It's Coll."

"Hey, did you have a good time in Church Cove? Did you hear any good stories?" Laurel was careful not to ask about lizards.

"Not lizards, but a dragon. It's got nothing to do with Church Cove or the Lizard though." Coll named the two towns where his Gramma had taken Gort and him to visit friends of hers.

The small book pinched her ribs. "That may be more useful than you think."

"Did you find something in the old books?" Coll's excitement showed in his voice.

"Yeah we did."

"Is Sarie in the kitchen?" Coll guessed.

"Uhmm-hmmm."

"Gort and I will come over first thing after breakfast tomorrow. The ponies will need exercise anyway; we can ride and talk. The weather is supposed to break tonight sometime."

"That sounds great. I'll make sure it's okay with Sarie to take the ponies out tomorrow. I'll see ya then."

"Ta."

They spent the rest of the day helping Sarie around the cottage. After supper, they all gathered around the hearth in the kitchen and wound some wool Sarie had just finished dyeing. The repetition of movement left her mind free to wander. Absently, her gaze followed the play of the flames as they devoured the log on the hearth. The wind blew over the chimney from above and made sparks fly up the flue, and the flames flared and flickered.

Laurel thought about the little book that was upstairs under her pillow. *Could Vear Du's lizard really be a dragon? Dragons do kind of look like really huge lizards.* She had seen some pictures of Komodo Dragons; they did seem to behave like big aggressive lizards.

She wound the wool faster as some of the pieces of the riddle started to make sense. *If the lizard really meant this dragon line that is supposed to rise out of the sea at St. Michael's Mount, then it makes sense our next step should be to visit St. Michael's Mount.*

Still watching the dance of the flames in the fireplace, Laurel suddenly let out a little gasp. There in the flames, she could see a red and orange lizard creature twinning through the fire. Its bright blue eyes looked directly into her soul before it winked at her and disappeared into the flames as the fire flared sharply. She turned her astonished face to look at Aisling and Sarie. Sarie was concentrating on her winding, but there was a secret kind of smile on her lips.

Aisling was grinning like a loon, her wool sitting idle in her hands. "Did you see him?" she whispered.

"What did you see? Was it like a lizard of some kind?"

Aisling giggled. "It was a salamander." She hugged herself in excitement. "I don't see them very often, only once in a while."

"So it…he was real?"

"As real as you or I are," Sarie said, joining their conversation.

Both girls stared at her, startled at the matter of fact tone of her voice.

"You can see them, too?" Aisling asked.

"It is my fireplace," Sarie pointed out dryly. "Do you think they go where they are not welcomed?"

"Oh," the girls said at the same time.

"The question," Sarie raised her eyebrows at the girls, "is what have you been doing to garner their attention?" Her eyes rested longest on Laurel.

"I've always been able to see them." Aisling spoke quickly to distract Sarie.

"Why am I not surprised?" Sarie said, without moving her gaze.

Should I tell Sarie about the quest? Quest sounded very adventurous and mysterious, much better than search. *But how am I going to explain about the 'Obby 'Oss and Vear Du and Gwin Scawen?* Laurel thoughts about the old photo of Sarie and Gramma Bella; if Sarie could keep her secrets, she could keep some secrets of her own.

"Darned if I know," Laurel answered, "it is your fireplace after all. It was way cool though. I'm glad you both saw him, too, or I'd have thought I was seeing things."

Aisling sighed. "They always make me feel happy and warm inside."

"How do you know it was a he?"

As far as Laurel could tell it was hard to see any difference, what with the flickering of the fire and the sheer improbability of it all.

"He told me," Aisling said. "It's the same one who visits me at home sometimes."

"How can you tell?" Sarie asked, watching Aisling carefully.

"He gifted me with his name." Aisling looked straight into Sarie's eyes.

"What is it?" Laurel asked.

Sarie opened her mouth and then closed it, gazing at Aisling instead.

Aisling smiled slowly. "I can't tell you. It's his name, and only he can gift you with it."

Laurel looked mutinous for a second and then shrugged.

"You mean," said Sarie softly, "it's not your secret to tell."

Aisling nodded; Laurel snorted as she wound her wool.

"It's not the same thing as not telling me about Gramma Bella," she muttered mutinously.

Later snuggled in bed, Laurel filled Aisling in on the information Coll relayed earlier. Just as they were quietly settling down to sleep, she sat bolt upright.

"What's wrong?" Aisling cried softly.

"The salamander showed himself to me just when I finally came to the conclusion the lizard Vear Du talked about was actually a dragon, and we need to go to St. Michael's Mount! He winked at me just before he disappeared."

Aisling sat against the headboard and drew her knees up to her chest. The faint light of the stars touched her features as the last of the rain clouds cleared from the night sky.

"I think the salamander was telling you you're on the right track. They always have reasons to show themselves to those they don't know," Aisling spoke thoughtfully.

"Can you ask him? You said he visits you."

"I know him as well as anyone can know an elemental creature, but they don't see the world the same as us. Their answers, when they actually give you one, are usually just another riddle to try and unravel."

"Just wait 'til we tell the boys what we've figured out! Let's hope their dragon stories keep pointing us in the same direction."

Aisling slid back down and turned her face to the window where the stars were peeking through the veil of the night. "Let's hope," she agreed.

The morning dawned bright and clear. A stout wind blew from the west, but it was reasonably warm. Coll and Gort arrived in time to share the last of the griddlecakes Sarie prepared for breakfast. Soon the four friends were headed out the door to tack up the ponies for their ride.

"Have fun," Sarie called. "Keep an eye on the weather."

In a few minutes, the riders trotted out the lane to the track leading west toward Madron. Laurel on Lamorna, Coll on Arthur, Aisling astride Ebony, and Gort with Gareth. The girls quickly related what they found the previous afternoon.

"So, I think our next step is to go to St. Michael's Mount and see what we can find. I wish this wasn't taking so long. Mom sounded really sick when I talked to her a couple of days ago. The chemo is really hard on her. She's losing all her hair," Laurel's voice broke on the last words.

Coll moved Arthur up beside her as the track widened out a bit.

"Turns out there is an old legend about a dragon track starting at St. Michael's Mount and running across Cornwall northeast toward Glastonbury and Avebury. Maybe, you're right and the lizard is really a dragon," Coll informed the girls. "Some guy discovered the alignment again in the late '60's and wrote a book about it."

"We can l-l-look at S-Sarie's map and see if we can make a line from Mount's Bay to Glastonbury and see what it crosses on its way," Gort offered. As always Gort's stutter got worse the more excited he got.

"Do you think it has anything to do with the King Arthur stories?" Laurel asked. "What's the name of the book that guy wrote?" Maybe we should try and find it."

"Maybe," Aisling sounded doubtful. "Tintagal is quite a bit north and on the coast, not really in any kind of line that would join Mount's Bay and Glastonbury. The book was called View Over Avalon."

"That doesn't sound like it would help much." Laurel chewed on her bottom lip.

"What about Lanyon Quoit?" Coll interjected. "Gramma tells an old story sometimes about how Arthur was supposed to have used Lanyon Quoit as a table for him and his knights to have dinner on the night before he fought at Lyonnesse, where he killed Mordred and was wounded himself." Coll thought for a few minutes and then grinned. "I'm just brill I am. Do you know where they took Arthur after he was wounded and dying, from Lyonnesse, I mean?"

They looked expectantly at Coll. Laurel's heart quickened, at last, finally, this whole riddle thing seemed to be starting to make sense. Maybe, somehow she could find the answer to getting her mom well again. The doctors in Calgary didn't seem to be having much luck.

"They took him to Avalon," Coll said triumphantly.

Aisling dropped her reins on Ebony's neck to clap her hands. "That is brill, Coll, really!"

Gort nodded enthusiastically. "First rate!"

"Where is Avalon? What does it have to do with the dragon line or Arthur?"

"Avalon is at Glastonbury," Aisling said. "So the dragon line that starts at Mount's Bay on St. Michaels Mount runs straight to Avalon-Glastonbury. Glastonbury comes from the old name Ynis Witrin or Isle of Glass, hence Glas-ton-bury."

"I think we should try and find that book you mentioned in the book store on Market Jew Street in Penzance. It mentions Avalon too," Laurel insisted.

"The lady at The Edege of the World Bookshop might carry it," Aisling agreed.

"Maybe there is a clue at Lanyon Quoit," Gort said. "Sarie asked me what I want to do for my birthday next week. I'm gonna suggest we go for cream tea at the Lanyon Tea Room."

"My Gramma always says this is Arthur's country," Coll said. "With any luck, we should find something at Lanyon."

The ponies jigged a little, tossing their heads impatiently. Their actions plainly saying they had been walking way too long. In a few moments, all four were cantering into the wind across the moor. Laurel flung her head back and laughed; it was so great to be riding. The feel of the pony under her was so familiar; she urged Lamorna into a gallop and drew ahead of her companions.

Before too long, the group was trotting past Chyndour, headed roughly toward Heamoor. They stopped at a flat grassy spot at the top of a rise. Aisling and Gort dismounted and pulled the lunch they packed out of the saddlebags. Coll took Ebony, Arthur, and Gareth to find some water at the little rill that ran sparkling at the foot of the rise.

Laurel sat on Lamorna and gazed across the moor as it ran toward the sea. It was so much like her beloved Alberta prairie, except the prairie ran to the mountains. Like the sea, the mountains had a power and life of their own; they were, after all, the bones of the earth. The pony lowered her nose to the grass and took advantage of her rider's preoccupation with the country before her. *This is Arthur's land,* she remembered Sarie telling her, echoing what Coll said earlier in the day, *but it belonged to itself long before Arthur was born.*

Laurel liked the idea of that. The country stretching before her seemed to shimmer with a life force which had nothing to do with what humans did, or did not, do to it. She tugged gently on the reins and pulled the pony's head out of grass. The wind coming across the moor from the sea carried music with it. It wasn't a familiar music, but she seemed to follow the notes all the same. It was a mixture of old cowboy songs sung around the campfire to keep the night at bay. It carried the shiver of mystery from the ancient stone works dotting the Cornish peninsula. There was fiddle and harp and drum and guitar and harmonica. The music called up bird song, the voice of the sea, and the bass voice of the rock itself that held up the land. She could hear the reverberating sound of the bells in the lost land of Lyonnesse out past Land's End. She could hear words that were somehow inside her head and also part of the wind. The sound vibrated through the pony's hooves and into Laurel.

"The land lies dreaming under the sun,
So much different it is,
So much the same it is.
All things are one when the day is won."

"Come and get some grub!" Coll's voice broke through her reverie.

Laurel slid down from Lamorna's broad back and led her over to the other ponies. She removed Lamorna's bridle, slipped on her head collar and left her with the other ponies to graze. She dropped down onto the grassy turf and took a ham sandwich from the pile Aisling set out. Everyone was silent while they devoured the sandwiches and cookies, which they washed down with sweet tea.

Once they were full, Laurel pulled the little book about the dragon line out of the waistband of her jeans. She handed it to Coll, who looked at it in surprise.

"Where did you find this?"

"Ash and I found it yesterday on Sarie's book shelf. I read it last night, and I think it confirms what you said about the dragon line cutting across Cornwall. See what you think."

Coll skimmed through the pages and whistled softly between his teeth. He handed the book to Gort who took it eagerly.

"It does seem to agree with what we found out yesterday," Gort said.

"I think so, too," Coll said.

The group was silent for a time; each following their own line of thinking with regard to the book and the dragon line.

Finally, Coll got to his feet and stretched. "We should get a move on if we want to be back before dark." He moved over to the ponies to bridle Arthur.

The girls collected the bits of litter and the remains of their lunch, stuffing them back into the saddlebags. In just a few minutes, they were all headed down the track back toward home. The sun was warm on Laurel's back making her sleepy.

"Let's trot!" She set off at a brisk pace with the wind at her back. The others followed suit, and soon Laurel forgot about riddles and her mom being sick. She soaked in the feel of Lamorna underneath her and the sound of all the ponies' hooves drumming the soft earth. The wind lifted her hair and tossed it forward over her face. The ponies' tails and manes were black streamers ribboning in the shifting currents.

Laurel laughed in exhilaration. All the ponies quickened their pace until they were cantering down the track two abreast. In no time at all, they were at Sarie's gate and turning down her lane. Sarie came out of the cottage to meet them as they trooped past the kitchen.

"I was starting to worry you wouldn't get home before full dark," Sarie said as she opened the gate to the pony field for them.

Laurel glanced at the dusky sky. "We went a little further than we planned."

"No harm done," Sarie assured her. "The ponies look like they enjoyed themselves as well."

Once the ponies were un-tacked, rubbed down, fed, and turned out for the night, the four friends headed for the bright warmth of Sarie's kitchen. Sarie had a large tea waiting for them as they came through the door.

"Once you've eaten, I can run Gort and Coll home. I told Emily I would drop by this evening so we can plan our trip to Glastonbury at Alban Heruin," Sarie said.

Laurel frowned at the strange name. "What's Alban whatever you said?"

"It just means Summer Solstice, it's the Celtic name for it," Sarie replied.

Coll grinned at Laurel across the table. Now all they had to do was convince Sarie and Emily they needed to go along as well.

"Sarie, I'm staying at Coll's for tonight. My uncle's gone to the Arms for the afternoon, and I'd just as soon steer clear of him for the night." Gort looked imploringly at Sarie.

Sarie rested her hand on Gort's shoulder. "I'm sure it will be all right with Emily, Gort. You know one of us will always take you in if you need it."

"Ta, Sarie," Gort sighed. "I just hate to ask. You know how Uncle Daniel gets when he thinks I'm telling the whole town he can't take care of me."

"It would be nice if he acted like he wanted to take responsibility for you once in a while," Sarie said acerbically.

The girls pleaded tiredness, staying home while Sarie and the boys headed off to Penzance. They had plans to meet at school the next day to strategize about Lanyon Quoit and Sarie and Emily's trip to Glastonbury.

Laurel was so tired she totally forgot about the letters hidden behind her headboard.

* * *

School proved beastly all week, leaving little time for anything other than studying, and it wasn't until the following Friday night she remembered the letters.

Sarie was over at Emily's for the evening, and Laurel was snuggled by the hearth, studying her math, three cats curled around her. The fire flickered, and she shook her head to clear her eyes.

She looked up at the fire to determine if she needed to add some turf. She blinked and looked closer at the flames. There, curled around the log, was the fiery salamander, his blue eyes urging her to look at him. Laurel put her books down on the floor and knelt at the edge of the hearth as close as she could get to the fire.

"Hey there," she said softly. "I'm glad you came back."

The little salamander writhed with delight and wound himself around the flames. Then he sat up on his haunches and folded his little forelegs across his chest. He reminded her of the gophers back home with his solemn face above his crossed paws. The salamander's blue eyes locked on Laurel's with an intensity that startled her.

"*I have answers for your riddle.*" The salamander's voice was high and breathy in her mind.

"Can you tell me whom I need to ask to make my mom better?" She spoke softly in case she scared the creature.

"*I can tell you this: The answer lies in the stoned hole, close by the literate stone.*"

Laurel shook her head and sat back on her heels while she held his gaze.

"Can't you be clearer?" she asked. "I'm running out of time, and my mom is getting sicker."

The salamander cocked his head to one side and regarded her thoughtfully, and she hoped sympathetically. *What is it with this stuff? Everything is a riddle, and nobody can, or will tell me outright what I need to know.* The salamander spied Laurel's math books on the rug, and he grinned in satisfaction. It was hard to tell, what with his thin lizardly little lips.

"*You must solve the problem which follows.*" His voice was earnest in her head.

"*One plus none plus one, write it down, one plus none plus one. When you find the answer, you must follow it through nine times.*"

Grabbing her notebook and pen, she scribbled down the ridiculous, annoying riddle.

"That's all you can tell me?" Laurel said rather brusquely.

The salamander reacted instantly to the tone in her voice and vanished into the ashes with a flick of his tail.

"Rats, rats, rats! I'm sorry, little guy," Laurel spoke uncertainly into the flames in the hearth. *Where did he go when he disappeared, up the chimney, or into another plane of existence?* "Really, I'm sorry. Please come back so I can thank you properly," she wheedled.

The peat flared in the fire, and two blue eyes regarded her out of the flames. The salamander balanced on top of the log and bobbed his head.

"Thank you for the information," Laurel said very formally. "Thank you for coming back. I'm sorry I was rude."

"*You are forgiven, Daughter of Eve.*" The salamander's voice was more formal as well. "*You are young yet. Learn patience and to see what is right in front of your nose.*"

The fire popped again. When the flames settled down once more, the salamander was gone... *What the heck was a stoned hole? Is it a real stone, or is it something to do with some drug-induced hallucination you need to be stoned to see? And a literate stone, can the stone talk?*

Laurel decided she would leave the talking stone part until Coll, Aisling, and Gort were there to help her. On Sunday, they were going to Lanyon Tea Room for Gort's birthday tea. There should be plenty of time to figure out what the salamander was trying to tell her.

"One plus none plus one," she muttered trying to reason it out. Finally, she rang Aisling.

"Two heads are better than one," Aisling agreed, once Laurel explained why she called.

"If you add them up, they come to two. Does that mean anything to you?" Aisling asked.

"What about eleven?" Laurel fiddled with different combinations of the numbers on her page.

"For something that's supposed to be plain and simple..." Aisling's voice trailed off.

"I read in the little book about the dragon line there are actually two lines. They call them the Michael and Mary lines, and they both kind of twine around each other. The Mary line seems to touch water and wells. The Michael line is the one with all the St. Michael's churches built along it. Maybe that's what the two means?"

"Maybe so," Aisling mulled the thought over. "But how does that tell us what to do. We already know the dragon line goes from Mount's Bay to Glastonbury and beyond."

"What about one hundred and one? That could be a date, like October first," Aisling continued.

"October will be way too late for Mom! It can't mean it will take us 'til October to figure this out."

"Let's try and get to St. Michael's Mount tomorrow. When is the best time to go?"

"If we go at low tide, we can walk out on the causeway. Otherwise, we'll have to wait to take the little boats that go out at high tide," Aisling answered.

"When is low tide?" Laurel still had no idea how to figure out when low and high tide occurred.

"Wait 'til I check Dad's tide chart to be sure." After a few minutes, Aisling came back on the line. "We should be able to walk out around eleven in the morning, when the slack tide is."

"Do you want to come here, or should I meet you guys in Marazion in front of the Godolphin Arms?"

"I'll have to ring you in the morning. I think Emily will give us a lift to the Godolphin Arms. We can wait for you out front," Aisling said.

"Okay, I'll talk to you in the morning."

After she rang off, Laurel gathered her school books, smoored the fire like Sarie taught her, and headed up the stairs to her bed. As she dumped her books on the chair by the door, she remembered the letters hidden behind the headboard.

Suddenly not quite so tired, Laurel pried the loose board out and retrieved the old letters along with the photo of Sarie and Gramma Bella. She spread the letters on the quilt. There seemed to be quite a few of them. Judging by the dates, they encompassed a long period of time. The last one was dated in 2008. Laurel's heart quickened as she picked up the paper; her hand shook, making the letter quiver in her grip. Quickly, Laurel looked for a return address. There it was.

"Bragg Creek, Gramma Bella lives in Bragg Creek! Or at least she did last year."

Laurel couldn't believe it. Bragg Creek was not far from where she lived. It was a pretty little village with a mixture of high-income residents who worked in Calgary and a vibrant artistic community. Just before she left for Cornwall, Chance and Carlene and their parents took her to Elbow Falls in Kananaskis Country. On the way home, they stopped in Bragg Creek for ice cream.

"As soon as I get home, I'm going to go look for Gramma Bella."

Carefully, Laurel tucked the letter with the vital address into her backpack. She could read that letter later. She selected the letter with the earliest date and settled down on the bed near the lamp to read. She hadn't read more than *Dear Sarie*, when the kitchen door banged and Sarie herself called up the stairs to say she was wetting the tea.

Laurel gathered the letters and stored them in her knapsack to take with her tomorrow. Aisling would enjoy reading them.

"I'll be right down. There's still some treacle pudding left from supper."

Chapter Nine

The Mount In The Bay

It was just shy of ten-forty-five the next morning when Sarie dropped Laurel off in front of the Godolphin Arms in Marazion. The beautiful old inn sat right on the sea front, directly above the start of the causeway to St. Michael's Mount. Sarie waved as she put the car in gear and headed toward Fore Street.

"I'll be here to pick you up at ha'past two," she called through the open window.

Sarie was meeting Emily for lunch and gossip at the Mount Haven Hotel and Restaurant on Turnpike Road. Emily needed to leave her car at the garage for repair, so she would ride home with Sarie afterward.

Laurel waved back and turned to survey the causeway laid across the sandy tidal flat. The old rocks gleamed wetly in the sun, and the fishy smell of the sea filled the air. Laurel found a rock and perched on top of it, her back to the sun.

Soon she saw Emily's car coming along King's Road from the west. Getting to her feet, she dusted off the seat of jeans. Coll, Gort, and Aisling were out of the car almost before Emily fully stopped.

"Don't lose track of the time," Emily admonished them. "Sarie and I will be here at ha'past two; don't be late."

"We won't," they all chorused together.

With a wave, Emily headed off the same way Sarie had just gone. The four friends linked arms and headed down to the sandy beach where the causeway began; a sign said St. Michael's Way. It was only a short walk out to the island, which sat in front of them like a huge sand castle perched on top of the rocky island. The pathway curved gracefully across the tide flats. Made of native stone, it shone faintly with damp, but was not too slippery. Laurel was able to take her attention from where her feet were stepping and watch the details of the castle-like building perched on top of the hill become clearer the closer they walked.

"Gramma says it used to be attached to the shore and surrounded by trees," Coll said.

"But then the sea rose, and it became an island," Aisling joined in.

"I r-r-read there used to a giant and his wife who lived on St. Michael's Mount; his name was Cormoran. Before him, there was supposed to an elderly giant who used to steal people's cows," Gort said.

"What happened to them?"

"The giant-killers got the last one. Old Cormoran, it was," Coll said.

"Why did they kill them, the giants?"

"I don't rightly know. Gramma just says their time was past, and they went away. She thinks it's quite sad they were forced out of existence."

It took about ten minutes to reach the island. They explored the buildings on the relatively flat part of the island where the Pilgrim's Way ended. After paying the higher admission price which included access to the gardens they clambered up and around the narrow and high paths that took them right up against the granite cliffs of the island. The castle itself hovered high above them. After pausing by the old well for a moment to look out over the bay, they left the gardens and made their way around to the beginning of the way up the mount. They followed the pathway past the old dairy and dodging a bus load of German tourists made their way up the step cobbled paths to the summit. The way was overhung with trees and the cobbles were uneven underfoot. They paused at the Giant's Well but there were too many people crowded there taking pictures so they climbed higher to where a sign proclaimed The Giant's Heart. There were some big boulders sitting on end almost lost in the lush foliage. Aisling giggled as tourist posed with the boulders, smiling and pointing at the giant slabs. Coll and Gort stood back grinning.

"What's so amusing," Laurel demanded.

"Those stones aren't the Giant's Heart at all. Unless the tourists read the brochure they think they are. The heart is actually a fairly small stone set into the pavement. Look, right there." Aisling pointed to a small heart shaped stone set innocuously into the cobbles.

"Do you think we'll be able to see where it is we're supposed to go next from the top of the castle?" Laurel asked turning her thoughts to more important things..

"I don't think we can actually go through the whole castle. It's owned by the St. Aubyn's, they live here," Aisling said.

"Really?"

Getting to the top and trying to find a clue from there was the plan. The climb to the entrance to the castle was steep and Laurel was winded by the time they emerged on the grassy summit. Large rocks poked through the soil and people had picnics spread out on them. Once they caught their breath, Aisling led the way up the stone steps to the public entrance. Laurel followed the rest of the tourists through the public areas of the building. She paused in the doorway to the dining room to examine the frieze which encircled the walls. A tiny sense of vertigo swept over her, but passed when she descended the two steps down into the room proper. While the artifacts displayed were interesting, there didn't seem to be any clue to the riddle that she could see.

The small chapel was beautiful with the sunlight shining through the stained glass and purple African violets set in the wide masonry window sills. The shadowy expanse exuded a sense of peace and love, it made her Mom feel very close. Laurel wanted to pause there but the press of people behind moved her forward. Out on the open court of the crenelated tower she studied the island and the sea, searching desperately for some sign of a lizard or dragon. Anything that might qualify as a clue to the riddle. She glanced at Coll leaning beside her. "See anything that looks like a clue?"

He shook his head. Aisling shrugged in an apology. Gort stared off over the gardens and seemed oblivious to the rest of them at the moment. Coll tugged at his sleeve as they moved off back into the castle through the Blue Room, which Laurel found quite pretty. Once back out of the building, they gathered on the brow of cliff, sitting on a sunny ledge of rock overlooking Mount's Bay and Newlyn in the distance. Mousehole hidden by an outcropping of the shore.

"I didn't find anything, did you guys?" Laurel looked around the group.

"Sorry, Laurel," Coll said.

"Me, too," Aisling replied.

Gort shook his head.

"Rats, on to Plan B." Laurel sighed.

"What is Plan B?" Gort wanted to know.

"Darned if I know." She grinned at him. "We need to come up with one, I guess."

The sun shone warm on her face, and the breeze coming in from the sea was refreshingly cool. She stood up and wandered over to a faint path. The others followed her. There was an offshoot to the path they were on, leading to a small lookout over Mount's Bay looking back toward Marazion.

"Let's stop here for a bit," Laurel suggested.

The little group followed the short path to the lookout. Coll jumped up on the low stone wall and drummed his heels against the side. She leaned beside him while Gort and Aisling took advantage of the little stone seat built into the wall.

Gazing out over the blue water of Mount's Bay, she admired the panoramic view. To the north, Marazion and the Cornish moors were laid out at her feet. To the west was Penzance, and to the southeast, she could just make out Cudden Point. Brilliant points of light danced on the swells of the bay, St. Michael's Way was still laid bare by the low tide as it wended its way back toward the Godolphin Arms.

"It's so beautiful, but what does it have to do with our riddle?"

Coll narrowed his eyes against the sun's glare. "Maybe this is just the starting point, and we have to use it to navigate to the next point."

"Wasn't there something about rocks that you couldn't eat?" Aisling asked.

"Vear Du said we have to go to the rocks that can't be eaten to find the clue to where I have to meet some filly that hasn't been foaled yet. None of it makes sense!"

"Remember," Aisling said, "the salamander said it was simple and right in front of us. Maybe we're looking too hard?"

"Maybe," Coll jumped down from the wall. "Let's keep walking, it's almost ha'past noon."

"L-l-let's get a bite to eat at the Island Cafe," Gort suggested.

Quickly, they rejoined the main path and retraced their path down the steep Pilgrims Steps. Soon were sitting at a little table on a large flagged patio with a marvelous view of Mount's Bay. Laurel took a sip of her lemon ice and tipped her head back to watch some gulls as they wheeled overhead. Aisling waved to the gulls as they headed off to look for better scavenging elsewhere. Coll reached for another pastie. A large elderly gentleman, standing in the middle of the flagged entranceway as if lost, caught Laurel's eye. Glancing about, she saw most of the tables were full; there was very little room to find a place to eat.

"Do you think we should ask that old man if he wants to join us?" she asked, indicating the empty chair at their table.

"Sure," Coll said, as he wolfed down the pastry in his fist.

"He looks nice, I guess," Aisling agreed.

She pushed back from the table and approached the gentleman across the sunny patio, smiling at him as she stopped in front of him.

"Excuse me. Would you like to join my friends and me?"

The tall man looked down at her upturned face. "That's very kind of you, young lady."

"You look like you need a place to have your tea, and it's really crowded in here. There's an empty spot at our table if you like." She indicated her friends at the table by the edge of the patio.

The man looked from Laurel to her friends and back again before he spoke.

"That would be lovely," he told her.

They crossed the crowded patio to the table.

"I'm Laurel," she extended her hand to the old gentleman who took it in his own. "This is Coll, Aisling, and Gort."

"I'm Corm." The old man settled himself in the chair next to Aisling. Corm's hand shook as he took a sip from his cup of tea. His blue eyes looked watery in the bright sunlight.

"H-h-have a pastie." Gort offered Corm the plate.

Corm smiled at Gort and took a steak pastie from the proffered plate.

"It's been a long time since I had such a kind offer," Corm said.

“Please, have a scone, too. Before Coll eats them all,” Laurel said with a sideways look at Coll.

Corm smiled his thanks and accepted a scone which he slathered with preserves. After they finished and were enjoying some ices and the view, Corm leaned back in his chair and regarded his new friends.

“What brings you out to St. Michael’s Mount?” Corm asked.

“Laurel’s never been,” Coll said. “She’s from Canada.”

“And we haven’t been out here for ages,” Aisling chimed in.

“I thought maybe you were too young to have come here seeking answers,” Corm said with his eyes on the waters of the bay.

What does Corm mean about answers? “What kind of answers do people look for here?” Laurel asked.

“Why, all kinds, girl.” Corm looked surprised. “The island has been a place of holiness for centuries. Legend has it in the fifth century St. Michael appeared over this very island and its twin, Mont St. Michael in Brittany.”

“So they come here for religious reasons, like looking for God?” Aisling asked.

“Some do.” Corm agreed. “Others come looking for older answers. The island was a Druid sanctuary long before it was Christian.”

“D-d-do you know anything about rocks that can’t be eaten?” Gort broke in. “Any old stories like?”

Corm regarded Gort for a moment and then smiled at Laurel. “Perhaps I do know a story you would be interested in. It seems only fair to share after you young ones have been so generous to an old man.”

Corm’s voice was quiet in the sunlit afternoon and took on a sing song tone as he began his story:

“A very long time ago, out on Bodmin Moor it was, a Saint and some of the old Cornish Giants engaged in an argument. The Giants felt the Saints were raising too many Christian crosses and claiming too many of the wells of the Goddess as Holy Wells sacred only to Mary. The Giants also believed the Saints were taking too many tithes from the scant harvest of the region. The Giants met on Bodmin Moor. They were angry with the Saints for

taking what the Giants had recognized as their own for far longer than the Saints had been around.

A Giant known as Uther was their leader. He was known to be very smart and very strong. A Saint who was named St. Tue was out on Bodmin Moor at the same time, having just claimed yet another well. St. Tue was a small man, but all the same, when he heard the Giants arguing over how to oust the Saints from the land without vexing the local people, he approached the Giants with a proposition."

Corm stopped and took a sip of his tea and then continued.

"St. Tue proposed a challenge, a test of strength; he challenged Uther to a rock throwing contest. St. Tue said if the Giants won, the Saints would leave Cornwall forever. But, if the Saints won, the Giants must henceforth follow the way of the cross.

"Now, Uther was a champion at rock throwing. He could hurl large stones with great accuracy. Uther was very good and loved to prove it by balancing bigger rocks atop smaller ones with perfect balance. The Giants thought they had this contest in the bag. St. Tue was such a small man, and Uther was a rock-hurling champion. The Giants gathered up twelve flat round rocks, somewhat the shape of wheels of cheese. Uther went first as was only fair as it was St. Tue who challenged Uther. Uther picked up the smallest rock and hurled it a hundred feet, in the direction of Stowe's Hill. The first stone came to earth on the southern summit. St. Tue threw next. Legend says the hand of God took the rock from St. Tue and set it atop the first rock. On and on the challenge went, Uther hurling his ever larger rocks onto the pile by might and main and St. Tue's stones easily capping the top each time as the hand of God placed the rocks gently on top of the growing pile. As the pile of rocks grew, the task became harder and harder. The Giants were in awe of St. Tue as the small man continued to place his stones with ease. St. Tue had the last throw; his rock sailed to the top of the stack and landed perfectly.

"The Giants were enraged and felt they had been tricked in some way. They argued it was customary to throw one more stone for luck. Uther picked up the thirteenth stone and with all his strength and determination threw the stone toward the top of the pile on the southern summit of Stowe's Hill. In disbelief, the Giants watched as the stone failed to reach its destination and rolled back

down the slope to St. Tue. St. Tue prayed to his God for strength. If St. Tue was successful, the Giants would follow the Christian faith whether they wanted to or not, for that was the rules of the challenge. An angel appeared who was not visible to the Giants and placed the final stone as the crown on the pile of stones, which is still there today.

"The pile of stones is named the Cheesewring and is there for the visiting. If you follow a straight line from where we sit here on St. Michael's Mount to the northeast, you will find it still perched on the south summit of Stowe's Hill."

Corm drank the last of his tea and wiped his beard with a napkin. He smiled at them as he rose. He placed his hand on Laurel's shoulder and squeezed it gently.

"I trust my story will help you find what you seek."

"Are you leaving?" Coll asked. "Can you tell us another story?"

"I think one is enough for the now." Corm smiled. "Perhaps we'll meet here again one day. In the meantime, thanks for your kindness to an old man."

Corm turned and walked away across the patio; as he passed through the shadowed arch, he disappeared. Although Laurel kept close watch on the spot where Corm should have reappeared, she couldn't see him. *It's just one more mystery to think about.*

Gort was talking quickly to Aisling when she turned her attention back to the table.

"Did you hear what he called the pile of rocks in the story?" Gort said.

"Yeah, something weird. I know; he called it the Cheesewring."

Gort looked at her expectantly.

"What?"

"It's a pile of rocks out on Bodmin. Why would you call it the Cheesewring?" Coll was as frustrated and puzzled as Laurel.

"It's a pile of *rocks* named after something we eat." Aisling watched their faces, waiting for the penny to drop.

Laurel and Coll looked at each other.

"What am I missing?" Coll asked.

"Beats me."

"Oh, for goodness sake," Aisling exploded. "The rocks are named after cheese. Cheese is something we eat, but you can't eat rocks."

Slowly a smile spread across Laurel's face, like sunlight after the storm. "Vear Du said I have to follow the spine of the lizard to the rocks that can't be eaten."

"It is as simple as the nose on my face, now we know the answer. He meant the Cheesewring," Coll said in disgust. "Why couldn't he just have said *Go to the Cheesewring*?"

"Right at the end of the story, Corm said the Cheesewring is on a straight line from here at St. Michael's Mount if we travel northeast." Aisling reminded them.

"A s-s-straight line could be the spine of the lizard Vear Du was talking about," Gort contributed.

"I think you're right."

"Bloody hell," Coll exclaimed. "We'd better get a move on it we want to meet Gramma and Sarie in time."

They put their rubbish in the trash bin, headed down to the shore of St. Michael's Mount, and back across St. Michael's Way. The tide was coming in, lapping over the edges of the causeway as they hurried along, but they were hurrying, so they reached the beach behind the Godolphin Arms before the water was more than ankle deep. Laurel collapsed on the sand to catch her breath. Aisling sank down beside her. Coll and Gort went up to King's Road to watch for Emily and Sarie.

Looking at her watch, she saw it was just two-thirty. "With any luck, they'll be so busy gossiping with their friends they'll be late." Laurel laughed.

"Stranger things have happened," Aisling replied.

Laurel reached into her backpack and extracted one of the letters from her Gramma Bella and handed it to Aisling.

"What do you make of this? I haven't had time to read it all yet, but it proves my Gramma Bella is alive, or at least she was last year." Laurel wrinkled her forehead as she looked out across the shimmering water of Mount's Bay.

"It sounds like your Gramma was from Cornwall originally, actually from Penzance," Aisling's voice rose in surprise at the end of her sentence.

"What? I never knew Gramma Bella was born in Cornwall."

"It says right here." Aisling pointed to a spot partway down the page and handed her the letter.

"I never looked past the return address and the date when I first saw it," Laurel admitted.

She glanced up toward the road to see if Coll and Gort had seen Emily and Sarie coming along. The boys were engaged in pitching stones into a tin can they found, so the girls surmised Sarie's little car was not about to pull up at any minute.

"Let's read it all the way through right here. It looks like Sarie and Emily are late," Aisling suggested.

Laurel wriggled her butt in the sand to get more comfortable and spread the letter out on her knee so Aisling could read along with her.

"June 20, 2001
General Delivery,
Bragg Creek, Alberta
Dearest Sarie,

Well, I am all settled into my little cabin in the trees. The creek runs through my property at the back, and I can hear it rushing along as I lay in bed at night. Early in the morning when it is quiet, I wake up and imagine the sound of the water is the tide coming against the shingle by Vear Du's cave. I never told you before, but he comes to me in my dreams, and we talk the night away. When I am gardening, or standing by Elbow Falls with the water resonating through the stone under my feet, I often feel his arm about me and his strength by my side. Like a waking dream, I know he is actually with me at these times. You were always more practical than me, and I know you are probably shaking your head at this minute as you read this. Maybe you are right, maybe it is just a trick of my mind, taking my longings and forgotten memories and forging them together. But my heart tells me I am right in believing Vear Du can come to me here by these majestic mountains. There is magic here, strong and clear. Not the same as the magic I knew in Cornwall but here all the same. All enchantments and magic and Light comes from the same source to comfort and guide us if we just reach out our hand. I miss Laurel more than I imagined I would, which is saying a great deal. My heart hopes Colton will have a change of mind about banishing me from his family's life, but my intellect tells me it is not very likely to happen. I have been thinking about accepting your kind offer to come and stay with you for a while. I would love to see the house in Penzance again. Do the new people look after the front garden like Da did? Something is holding me back, I'm not sure what, but I will trust my instincts and see where this new path I am on leads me.

Love always,
Bella"

Laurel raised her head and met Aisling's bewildered gaze.

"Gramma Bella knew Vear Du." Her voice was almost non-existent as she struggled to speak through the tension gripping her chest and throat in an iron band.

"Did he look that old?" Aisling asked. "You made him sound like he wasn't much older than eighteen or so."

"He didn't look old enough to have known Gramma Bella when she was a teenager."

Aisling leaned back on her hands and watched the gulls circling over her head. Laurel stared blankly out over the water.

"Maybe Vear Du is a god," Aisling mused, her eyes still on the flight of the gulls. "That would make him immortal so he wouldn't age."

"It doesn't seem right. Who ever heard of a god who was a seal or Selkie, or whatever he is?"

"Mmm, maybe he's just immortal because he *is* a Selkie?" Aisling revised her thoughts.

"Do you think we could ask Sarie?"

Aisling shrugged her shoulders.

"We could try, I guess. I don't know how far we'll get though," Laurel said.

"Hey!" Aisling suddenly sat up straighter and turned to face Laurel excitedly. "Do you have the rest of those letters?"

"Yeah, I have some of them right here." She patted her backpack.

"I bet we might find the answer to some of our questions in those letters." Aisling reached for the backpack.

Laurel folded the letter they just read, stuffed it into a different pocket on the backpack and reached to pull out the next unread letter.

Coll's abrupt arrival made both of them jump and swivel around to face him.

"Sarie's here." Coll stood a few feet behind them grinning. "What's so interesting you didn't hear me yell from up above."

They scrambled to their feet and knocked the sand off their clothes.

"We'll show you when we get back to Sarie's." Laurel promised as she hefted her backpack out of the sand and swung it onto her back.

The three friends hurried up to where Sarie and Emily waited. Gort was already in the back seat where he scrunched over to make room for them.

Aisling grinned at him and whispered, "We have some really interesting stuff to show you."

Laurel pulled the corner of an envelope out of her backpack.

"What did you find?" Coll whispered none too quietly.

"Later," she shushed him as Sarie and Emily both turned to look at them.

"Find something interesting out at The Mount?" Sarie inquired.

"Not really," Coll tried to do some damage control.

"Nothing at all?" Emily prodded with a smile.

"Well, we met a really nice old man named Corm," Laurel said to distract them, and it *wasn't* a lie.

Emily frowned at Sarie. "Do you know anyone by that name from here?"

"No, not off the top of my head, I don't," Sarie agreed.

"Did he say he was from around here?" Sarie fixed a gimlet stare on Coll.

"He didn't say, but I think he is," Aisling supplied. "He told us the greatest story about how the Cheesewring out on Bodmin Moor was supposed to have been created, all about giants and saints and a contest."

"So he must be local, or he wouldn't have known so much about it," Laurel chimed in.

"What did he look like?" Emily asked. "You said he was old; was he tall?"

"Actually, he was really tall," Coll said.

"N-n-not j-j-just tall but b-b-big all over," Gort said.

"You said his name was Corm?" Sarie asked.

The four friends in the back looked at each other in consternation. *Why are Sarie and Emily so interested in some old man we shared our table with?*

"Did we do something wrong?" she whispered stealthily to Aisling.

Aisling shook her head and looked at Coll.

"Is he a lunatic or something?" Laurel whispered, figuring Coll would be the authority in their group on things like that.

"Maybe an axe murder on the loose?" he whispered back.

Emily swiveled so she could see their faces better as Sarie put the car in gear and pulled out onto the road.

"That's right," Coll said, "should we have known him?"

"No, I don't think so," Emily said.

"Some people have told stories about how they met a very large man on St. Michael's Mount, and he has given them very useful advice or help. The unofficial story is that it is a manifestation of the giant who used to live on St. Michael's Mount," Sarie told them.

"Do you remember what the giant's name was, Coll?" Emily asked her grandson.

"Sure, his name was Cormoran. I was telling Laurel all about him when we were walking out there," Coll said somewhat boastfully.

Aisling leaned forward as far as she could. "Are you saying our Corm who we asked to share our table was really the ghost of the giant Cormoran?" she asked in disbelief.

Laurel let her breath out in a gasp. "Holy cow, a real giant," she whispered incredulously.

Sarie caught her eye for a moment in the rear view mirror.

"I gather you went out there looking for some kind of answer for this quest you're on," Sarie stated.

In answer to Laurel's startled look, she grinned. "I'm not as dense as you think, missy. You must be onto something to have the salamander in the hearth so interested in your wellbeing. If you don't want to tell me about it, at least let Emily and I help if we can. It appears you have the blessing of not only the salamander in your quest."

"Did you do a kindness for your friend Corm? How did you meet him?" Emily brought the conversation back to the original topic.

"Laurel offered to share our table at lunch with him. There was nowhere for him to sit and have his tea," Coll said.

"Did you offer to share your food with him?" Sarie asked.

"Well, yeah, I guess we did share our sandwiches with him." Coll mused.

Sarie and Emily smiled at each other as if everything was settled then.

"Did you see him leave, or did he stay at the table after you left?" Emily wanted to know.

"He left before us and kind of disappeared under the arch…" Laurel'svoice tailed off.

"I thought he just got swallowed up by the shadows under the archway," Aisling stated.

"But I watched for him to come back out into the sunlight on the other side, and I couldn't see him there or on the path outside."

"I think," Emily said, "in return for your kindness, Cormoran has given you some knowledge or answer you were seeking. Random acts of kindness are usually rewarded in kind."

"It's not often anymore the spirits of the land bother to become involved in the trivial pursuits of the human race," Sarie agreed. "You have been very lucky."

Chapter Ten

One Plus None Plus One

Clouds scudded across the sky as Sarie drove west out of Penzance. The car was full of talk and laughter from the four friends crammed into the small back seat. It was Gort's birthday, and they were headed for a luscious cream tea at the Lanyon Quoit Teahouse.

The moors stretched away on either side of the narrow road in a glorious vista of late May color. Wild flowers bloomed against the green backdrop of the moors, caught in glimpses in the gaps in the hedgerow bordering the road. Birds sang in the hedges and filled the sun-warmed air coming in the open windows of the car with music.

A little time later, Sarie pulled into the car park by the tea room. The windows of the Lanyon Farm House reflected the sun, and flowers danced in the window boxes. The tea room was an old milling house made of single brick construction. There were no frills, just a pleasant sunny white-walled room with small tables and chairs scattered about it. The windows offered spectacular views of the surrounding countryside, and the sun poured warmly through them as Sarie and Emily led the way into the welcoming room.

The majestic bulk of the Lanyon Quoit was visible to the southeast. The huge ancient stone monument consisted of a huge slab of rock resting on three upright stones. The sun threw it into stark relief against the moor behind it.

Laurel settled into her chair and was struck by how alone the stones looked sticking up from the surrounding countryside.

"What's that pile of rocks called?" Laurel asked Sarie.

Sarie glanced out the window and smiled. "That's Lanyon Quoit."

Laurel wrinkled her forehead. "What's a *quoit*?"

"A quoit is a stone structure consisting of large stones, three or four of which are upright and support a large flat stone. Lanyon looks like a table, some of them are more rounded or beehive shaped almost," Sarie answered.

"I thought I read somewhere those structures were called *dolmens*," Laurel said.

Emily laughed. "In the rest of Britain they are called dolmens, but in Cornwall, we call them quoits. It means the same thing."

"Where did it come from?" Laurel asked as she continued to stare out the window at the monument.

"It was here when Cornwall was still called Belerion, longer than memory," Emily said her eyes fixed on the stones.

"King Arthur used the top of it to have supper on with his men the night before he fought with Mordred and was wounded," Coll, ever the King Arthur expert, contributed.

"Some believe it used to be covered with earth and grass and used as a burial chamber. The structure today is not as it used to be," Sarie said.

"How do you mean?" Laurel asked. She couldn't imagine anyone actually *moving* the thing around.

"I did a project on the Lanyon Quoit in school last term," Aisling said. "The quoit was tall enough for a mounted man to ride his horse under. It used to have four stones supporting it. During a storm in 1815, the quoit fell. It took nine years until people raised enough money to try and restore it. One of the supporting legs was broken when the upper stone toppled, and that's why there are only three supporting stones now. Also, they made the three remaining stones shorter, which is why it's no longer possible to ride under it. The top stone used to stand seven feet off the ground. It weighs thirteen and a half tons and measures nine feet by seventeen and a half feet. It is twenty inches thick."

Emily smiled at Aisling. "That's a very good description, Aisling. Did you know that originally the monument was on a northeast-southwest axis, but when they rebuilt it in 1824 it was positioned at a right angle to the original orientation? Some people believe it used to be instrumental in seasonal rituals. "

"I forgot about that," Aisling admitted.

"Maybe we can stop on the way home, and you can have a closer look," Coll said to Laurel across the table.

Just then the pleasant owner of the tea room approached their table to take their order.

"It's a fine morning, isn't it just?" she greeted them.

"It is," Emily agreed. "I think we will have six cream teas, please."

"You must save some room for our lovely chocolate cake creation," the woman said as she made a note of their order on her pad.

"I-I-I will." Gort grinned widely. "They make the best home-made cake here!"

In no time, the table was laden with their cream tea. Laurel had never seen a cream tea this elaborate, although she heard its praises sung by Gort all the way to the tea room. Everyone got their own pot of good strong English tea served with milk. Then there were two fresh, warm scones spread with clotted cream and topped with strawberry preserves. Not whipped cream, but clotted cream. Sarie insisted whipped cream was just not suitable for a Cornish Cream Tea.

"What's the difference between whipped cream and clotted cream?" Laurel wanted to know as she prepared to bite into her scone, which smelled absolutely divine. She eyed the heavy yellow cream in the ceramic pot by her plate.

"Cornish Clotted Cream," Sarie began, and Laurel noticed Sarie pronounced the words Cornish Clotted Cream as if they were capitalized, "is thick and yellow, whipped cream is white. Heating unpasteurized cow's milk and then letting it stand in a shallow pan for several hours produces clotted cream. If you use pasteurized milk, it won't clot properly. While the milk stands in the pan, the cream rises to the top and the clots form. The best clotted cream is made from the milk of Cornish cows."

"It tastes amazing," Laurel said around the mouthful of scone in her mouth.

Quickly the cream tea disappeared. Coll and Gort each indulged in a large piece of three layer chocolate cake. Laurel chose some Roskilly's ice cream, which she shared with Aisling, while Emily and Sarie drank another pot of tea. The wind was picking up as they stepped out of the tea room door.

"Smells like it might rain," Sarie observed, holding her hair out of her face with one hand.

Aisling looked across the moor to the northwest, squinting into the whipping wind. "Look! I can see the Men an Tol from here," she said loudly over the wind.

"Where? I don't know what I'm looking for," Laurel complained.

"It's pretty hard to see from here," Coll said.

Gort pulled on Laurel's sleeve to get her attention. "Ask Sarie if we can go there," Gort said urgently.

"Why? Does it have something to do with the riddle?" Laurel responded to the urgency in Gort's voice.

"I-I-I'm not sure if I remember right, but I think it has something to do with the salamander's riddle. I-i-if I'm right, you'll see when we get there."

Laurel hurried to catch up with Sarie who was almost at the car. "Sarie," she called.

"Ask me in the car," Sarie shouted over the wind, as she got into the driver's seat.

Laurel willingly hopped into the back seat and took a moment to catch her breath. The wind blew bits of dirt against the side of the car.

"Sarie, can we go to the Men an Tol?" Laurel asked hopefully.

Sarie looked doubtfully out the windscreen at the clouds blowing in over the hills.

"I'm not sure it's such a good day for a walk across the moor to the stones," Sarie said. She caught sight of Laurel's disappointed face in the rear view mirror. "Is it that important, then?"

"Gort thinks it is," Laurel said. "He thinks it might be the answer to the salamander's riddle."

"What was the riddle exactly? Tell me again, my gold."

"One plus none plus one, seemed to be the most important part of it, and something about a literate stone. Did he mean the stones will talk to us?" Laurel was still puzzled by that reference.

Their conversation was interrupted by the rest of the group crowding into the car. Laurel waited impatiently while Sarie repeated Laurel's request to Emily and filled her in on the salamander's riddle.

"Well now, that is interesting," Emily pondered. "Do you think the salamander may have meant there is writing on the stone, like literature?"

"Maybe," Laurel was unsure of the new concept. "What do you think, Ash?"

"It's possible," Aisling conceded. "I should ask Gwin Scawen the next time he visits."

"There is a menhir, a standing stone, between the Men an Tol and the coast with writing on it. It's called the Men Scryfa; the name means *inscribed stone*. It's supposed to be the burial marker of a king who died in the battle of Gendahl Moor," Emily said.

"What's written on it?" Coll asked.

"Some say it is a local form of Latin, and others translate it into Cornish. It says *Rialobranus Cunovali Fili,* which might mean Son of Chief Royal Raven, or Cornish Royal Raven, son of the glorious Prince. The writing is on the north side of the stone," Sarie said.

"H-h-how t-t-tall is it?" Gort asked.

"Two meters," Emily supplied.

"Maybe that is what the salamander meant, and it is near the Men an Tol. Can we *please* go there today, Sarie?" Laurel pleaded.

Emily looked across the front seat at Sarie. "We did ask them to let us help them with this mystery."

"True, too true," Sarie agreed. "So, it's off to the Men an Tol with us then."

She backed the little car out the parking spot and headed off down the Morvah Road on the way to the un-surfaced track leading to the Men an Tol and the Men Scryfa.

Not too much farther up the road, the track came in view on the right hand side of the road. The car skidded a little in the muddy tracks as Sari turned into the layby. The dirt road led north between banked hedges. Laurel buttoned her jacket and followed the others out of the car. By now, the wind was blowing gusts of rain ahead of it, and the ground was muddy.

"Emily and I will stay here, if you have no objections," Sarie said, turning the up the heat in the car a bit further.

Laurel nodded and let Coll lead the way up the rutted lane. An old stone barn appeared on the left where some cattle were huddled taking shelter from the rain. Just opposite it was the stile and a wooden sign that indicated the Men an Tol was that way. She paused at the top of the stile and looked across the gorse and heather toward the odd arrangement of stone that stood in a cleared irregular circle of grass. Laurel had a hard time actually looking at the stones. The rain kept filling her eyes, and the wind blew great gusts of rain about the stones almost obliterating them from view. She hopped down the rest of the steps and continued down the rough path toward the stone circle. Standing by the round holed stone she waited for the rest to catch up with her.

"What are we looking for?" Laurel shouted at Gort over the storm.

Gort peered into the rain and then danced on the spot in glee. "Look, look at the stones. What do you see?" Gort was so excited he lost his stammer, a reversal of what usually happened.

Aisling paused on a little farther up the path and tried to peer through the rain.

"Oh, I see it," she exclaimed.

Panting a little from the wind and the rough footing, she stepped away from the stones and retreated to stand by Aisling. Laurel's mouth fell open, while Aisling gripped Laurel's arm tightly. Coll stopped dead and stared.

"It's just like the salamander said," Laurel's voice was awestruck. "Look, one plus none plus one"

"Really simple and right in front of our faces," Coll said disgustedly. "You'd think we could have figured this out without coming out in a gale and catching our deaths."

Aisling hugged Gort. "Gort, you're just brill! You're the only one of us who figured this out."

There in front of them stood the ancient Men an Tol. Two upright stones on either side of a round holed stone, looking for all the world like the number 101.

"What were we supposed to do once we got here?" Aisling asked Laurel.

"I'm not sure," Laurel spoke over the roar of the wind. "Oh, look Aisling! By the hole in the stone, it's Gwin Scawen."

Gwin was seated on the top of the lower edge of the hole, kicking his heels against the stone and as dry as if it was a sunny summer day. Laurel would have sworn he wasn't there a minute ago. When he saw he had their attention, Gwin beckoned them to come closer. Squelching through the wet grass and shivering in the wind, the four friends made their way across the bit of grass separating them from the piskie. As they reached the first upright stone, the air shimmered, and Laurel felt a gentle hand smooth her hair.

Suddenly the wind and rain were gone; the sun shone warmly on their skin. A gentle breeze brought the scent of gorse and wild flowers to them. Coll looked around him in astonishment and then took a good long look at Gwin Scawen. The little brown piskie was rubbing his hands together in glee and excitement.

"I thought you might show up here today. I told that uppity salamander you would figure it out!" Gwin spoke to Aisling.

"Actually, Gort figured it out, not me," Aisling admitted.

Gwin Scawen turned slightly and regarded Gort closely for a minute. Laurel thought she saw a golden light glow about Gort for a second, but as quickly as it was there, it was gone.

"Ahh," Gwin Scawen smiled and bowed slightly to Gort. "You begin to find the threads of your destiny."

Gort gaped at Gwin Scawen like an idiot. "Huhh?? W-w-what d-d-o y-y-you mean? Why w-w-would you bow to *me*?"

Gort turned his astonished gaze to Laurel and Aisling. Gwin's neat brown coat flapped gently in the breeze as he danced from one foot to the other.

"In time, little warrior, all in good time, everything will be clear to you," Gwin said enigmatically.

Coll finally found his tongue. "How did you do that?"

"Do what, oh brave protector?"

Laurel grinned as Gwin answered a question with a question in the way of piskies, who like to confuse mortals if they can. Just for fun, of course. She recalled Aisling warning about just such a thing.

"How come it isn't raining here, but it is out there?"

Coll indicated the storm raging just a few feet away from them. They could see another Men an Tol outside the gossamer barrier being battered by the windy rain.

"Are there two sets of stones?"

Gwin Scawen skittered about the hole in the stone in rhapsodies of glee. He jumped down and danced across the sunny grass to hug Aisling around the knees.

"I was wondering when you would notice. We are here at the Men an Tol. There is only one set of stones," Gwin said, looking adoringly up at Aisling.

Laurel hid her smile when Gort moved a little bit closer to Aisling and laid his hand on her arm. It was obvious Gort wasn't sure he liked the little brown man, who had such a proprietary air about him regarding Aisling. Aisling smiled at Gort and covered his hand with her own.

"Gwin means no harm Gort. It's just his way."

"Aisling is one of my best friends," Gwin Scawen said solemnly.

Coll cleared his throat nosily and coughed. "Back to the rain and the stones?"

"Oh, of course, what was it that was troubling you about the rain and stones?" Gwin said wickedly.

Laurel stayed on the fringe of the group, watching the tableau play out before her. Coll's face darkened with frustration and the beginnings of anger. Aisling knelt down and looked Gwin Scawen squarely in the eyes. Gwin shuffled his feet in chagrin at the look on Aisling's face.

"Ah, now my flower, I was only teasing him, wasn't I just?' Gwin Scawen turned his large expressive brown eyes on Aisling's face. She grinned and hugged the little piskie.

"Would you please explain why it doesn't rain here?"

"You had only to ask." The little piskie bowed to Aisling and settled down on a piskie sized rock near her feet.

"We are in a *between* place. The storm is still there; we are not. There is only one Men an Tol, but it can exist on more than one plane at a time. Because the Men an Tol is immortal, it is part of the earth and the sky, and the powers move through both. You can come to this place only because I brought you here. We are *between* here," Gwin indicated the grass at his feet, "and there." He pointed to the raging storm. "I have led you through the veil between the world you know and the world as it truly exists. Very few humans can come through at all. You must be pure of heart and purpose to come here and return unscathed."

Gwin Scawen looked up into Aisling's face and smiled a beatific smile. "Is that sufficient, oh Light of my Life?" Gwin asked her.

Aisling giggled at him and tweaked his nose. "I know I've been here and came back all right, but can all of us?"

"Yes, you four seekers shall return unscathed to your own world with the answer you seek. Even without me, you could all return, as one of you carries the talisman of the Selkie to guide and protect you." Gwin surveyed them all with a grin.

Laurel was visibly startled. *How could Gwin Scawen know about the talisman?* She was sure he wasn't there when Vear Du gifted her with it. Laurel looked at Coll, who was frowning. She guessed Coll was disturbed she hadn't confided in him that Vear Du gave her a special talisman.

"Did Vear Du tell you about the talisman?" Laurel asked Gwin Scawen.

Gwin Scawen grinned back at her. "Now, now, Crystal Seeker, a piskie must always have his secrets you know."

"Why did you call me Crystal Seeker?" Laurel was distracted from her previous question, just as Gwin Scawen had planned.

"In the fullness of time, you will have your answer. For now, you must be content to seek it."

"What is so special about these stones? I-I-I m-m-mean to our search?" Gort's stammer returned as all the attention was focused on him.

"You must still seek part of the answer at the rocks you can't eat, but I can tell you this. You must travel through the hole, nine times, holding your intention clear in your mind and ask for assistance with pureness in your heart." Gwin was about to say more when his head jerked up suddenly.

"Oh dear, someone is looking for you. You must go now." Gwin Scawen jumped back into the lower ledge of the hole in the stone and suddenly the calm, sunlit patch around them started to shimmer and shrink. Gwin Scawen looked for Aisling and held her eyes as the patch became smaller and Gwin became increasingly transparent.

"Wait!" Laurel cried. "What else were you going to tell us?"

Gwin Scawen waved at Laurel, his voice floated through the air even as he became a wisp of smoke in the air. "Go to the rocks which can't be eaten. The answers wait for you there. Use the talisman!"

Suddenly, the wind knocked the breath out of Laurel's lungs, and the rain poured down her neck. Through the storm, Laurel could see Sarie struggling up the path towards them, her head down in the rain. Coll, Gort, and Aisling were all gathered close around her. Laurel laid her hand on the cold, rain soaked top of the circle stone and felt an answering tremor from the stone run through her body. *I'll be back,* she promised the stone silently.

The four friends wound their way back across the rain-swept moor and down the lane to meet Sarie. Laurel answered Sarie's smile of relief when she saw them, bringing up the rear while Sarie shepherded them back along the muddy path to the car. Once they were all inside and wrapped in the blankets Emily produced from the boot of the car, Sarie turned the car around in the muddy layby and headed toward Penzance.

"Enough exploring for one day. We'll have to leave Lanyan Quoit for another day," Sarie exclaimed as the car fought the gale and bucketed from one side of the road to the other.

"Did you find any answers out there?" Emily asked.

"Gort was right. We did find the answer to the salamander's riddle there," Laurel said.

"Can we tell you about it later?" Aisling asked through her chattering teeth. "I'm all wrung out from the weather."

"Of course, my loves," Sarie exclaimed and turned the car heater up another notch.

The slap-slap of the wipers on the windscreen and the warmth of the car soon lulled the occupants of the back seat to sleep. Aisling's head slipped over onto Gort's shoulder just as he was on the edge of slumber himself, and he smiled as he let Orpheus take him away.

Laurel scrunched close to Coll for warmth, and she saw him grin, as he too fell asleep. *Consorting with piskies in the middle of a storm is very tiring,* Laurel thought as she drifted off.

Chapter Eleven

Alban Heruin

Laurel and Coll carried the last of the bags out to the car and stowed them in the boot. She giggled as she shut the lid.

"I still think *boot* is a weird name for the trunk of a car," she said to Coll.

"I think *trunk* is a barmy thing to call a car boot," he retorted.

"Whatever." She climbed into the back seat and scooted over so Coll could get in as well.

Sarie came bustling around the corner of the cottage and dropped some car rugs onto the passenger seat as she slid behind the wheel. Emily arrived just after her, coming from the barn. She carried a canvas bag with what looked like bits of hay and straw poking out of the top. Emily carefully set the bag on the floor of the front seat and then settled herself into the seat. They exchanged puzzled looks in the back seat.

"What's in the bag, Gramma?" Coll asked.

"Just some clean hay and straw Sarie and I need," Emily answered.

"What's it for?" Laurel persisted.

"You'll just have to wait and see," Sarie said. She put the car into gear and proceeded down the lane and out onto the road leading to the A30 which would take them north toward Glastonbury.

"It's too bad Gort and Aisling couldn't come with us," Emily remarked as they bowled along the highway.

"Gort's uncle wouldn't let him come," Coll said with disgust in his voice. "Says he needs him to clean out the back shed."

"Aisling's mom didn't want her going to Glastonbury because of the rock festival thing going on," Laurel said. "Are we going to that?"

"No, we're going to watch the summer solstice sunrise from the top of Glastonbury Tor. There will be lots of people there, but it's not the festival with rock and roll music," Sarie told her.

"Gort's uncle said something about not holding any truck with all the New Age nonsense that goes on there," Coll added.

Emily smiled. "It certainly has enjoyed a revival in the past twenty years or so, although the term New Age is misleading. There is nothing *new* about the ceremony on the Tor celebrating Alban Heruin. It is one that has been enacted longer than recorded history. There used to be bonfires lit on all the high sacred places from Cornwall to Avebury and beyond at dawn the morning of the summer solstice."

"Avebury was the focal point of the ceremony, but all along the countryside ceremonies were performed that strengthened the energy in Avebury. Most of the sites now have churches or shrines dedicated to St. Michael, but those were built on older sites sacred and holy to those who followed the old religion that was supplanted by Christianity," Sarie added.

"The fires followed a straight line from Cornwall all the way to Avebury?" Coll asked.

"They did," Emily affirmed.

"How did they know where to go? They couldn't have mapped it from the air or anything." Laurel was puzzled.

"There are old straight tracks across most of Britain marked out by Dod Men, or Ley Men using sighting staves to go from one high point to another. These men made notches in the hillsides on the horizon. Small and sometimes quite large artificial hills topped with trees and surrounded by moats marked the direction. Ponds in the bottom of valleys were specially placed so the water reflects the light, and you can use them to site the next high point you want to head for. Some believe the routes were used for trade, to move say, tin or serpentine stone from Cornwall or salt from the coast. Many of the places which have whit or white in their names are on the old salt route. There are other old tracks like the Ickneild Way and the Ridgeway which are ceremonial paths leading to significant stoneworks like Avebury and Stonehenge," Emily supplied.

"Others believe the major routes follow lines of natural or magnetic energy which flows through the earth itself. There are two lines flowing from Carn les Boels in Cornwall, through Glastonbury to Avebury and all the way to East Anglia. They are called the Mary and Michael lines. The Michael line is more famous and tends to stay to the high places. The Mary line is more sinuous and likes to visit ponds and springs, many of which are dedicated to her or female saints," Emily continued.

"Most of the researchers believe the lines represent male and female energies within the earth. They enrich the sacred balance of light and dark, winter and summer, spring and fall, and all the male and female energies. Fire is one of the four sacred elements, and it was used to enhance the energies along the line which culminates in the sacred marriage of the two lines as they come together in The Sanctuary at Avebury," Sarie chimed in.

"The two lines meet in a church?" Coll was confused.

"No. The Sanctuary is a stone circle which is part of the large Avebury complex of stones. The long avenues of stone surrounding Avebury mark the lines as they approach The Sanctuary. In ancient times, thousands used to make a pilgrimage to Avebury to be part of the great procession that started before the sunrise and reached The Sanctuary as the sun rose," Sarie continued.

"How did they know when to start to reach the spot all together at the right time?" Laurel couldn't figure it out. *They wouldn't have had any kind of electronic device to help them that long ago.*

"Silbury Hill is a large, man-made hill with a flat top sitting in the middle of the plain to the south of the Avebury circles. The select people who knew exactly when the sun would rise lit a fire on the flat top of the hill and performed their pre-dawn ceremonies there where everyone could see them. Then, when the time was right, one signal from that high flat point gave the leaders of each procession the go ahead to start," Emily added.

"So all across the country, as the sun started to rise over the plain, or the hills depending on where you were in the country, the hill top fires would be lit, and the light passed on to the next point along the line," Sarie said.

She broke off the conversation to pick up the road map from the seat beside her. "Emily, can you look and see just where I'm supposed to pick up the M5?"

“It looks like just past Exeter,” Emily told her after carefully surveying the map. “It shouldn’t be too much farther.”

Laurel sat back to look out the window and watch the expanse of the Exmoor Forest as it rolled past. The A39 skirted the top edge of the vast moorland. “Why is it called Exmoor Forest when there are no trees?” she asked Coll.

Outside her window was just a vast expanse of open land, which Laurel privately thought of as prairie. It looked just like the rolling prairie near the foothills of the Canadian Rocky Mountains.

“Something to do with it being an area reserved for the kings to hunt on a long time ago,” Coll answered.

“It’s from the medieval meaning of forest which simply means anyplace where deer and other beasts worth hunting were found that was reserved for only the king to hunt. There were never any trees here except for along the little river valleys.” Emily fleshed out Coll’s explanation.

Laurel nodded her head and resumed looking out over the moor. *I miss Alberta, and the prairie, and Sam. It must have really sucked to an average Joe in medieval times when the kings and their friends got all the good stuff.*

“How long will it take to get to Glastonbury?”

“Gramma said it takes about three and a half hours from our house.

“That’s not too bad then. It takes about the same amount of time as going from south of Calgary up to Edmonton at home.”

Coll shook his head, but didn’t say anything. Her idea of what was a long way and Coll’s just didn’t add up to the same thing.

They were past Exeter now and on the M5 headed toward Bridgewater, where they would turn a bit more eastward on the A39, which was also known as the Bath Road. Time passed quickly; they made good progress, as there weren’t many motorists on the road.

Sarie left the A39 and took the A361, which Laurel was amused to see was also called Street Road. They followed it along as it eventually passed through the outskirts of Street. Laurel was intrigued by the names of the towns and villages they passed. They had a strange and exciting flavor to them. She repeated them in her head so she could remember them to tell her mom and dad: Knowle, Bawdrys, Shapwick, Street, and the best of all Butliegh

Wooton. *Chance and Carlene will hoot when I tell them about these weird names.*

Although, in all fairness, there were some odd place names at home, too. They were just so familiar they didn't seem strange to her at all. She smiled as she thought of a few of them: Medicine Hat, Moose Jaw, Pincher Creek, Many Berries, Seven Persons, Grassy Lake. Laurel made a mental note to share her thoughts with Coll sometime when they were alone and could be as silly as they wanted about the ramifications if one expanded on some of the names. She giggled as she thought about it.

The huge mound of Glastonbury Tor hovered on the horizon before they reached the town proper. Laurel found the hill with the tower looming over the landscape compelling and kept her gaze on it. Before she knew it, they were driving into the outskirts of Glastonbury. The streets were crowded with people—all sorts of people. There were some ordinary holiday goers long with others who were dressed in what looked like some kind of ceremonial robes, some who had wreaths of flowers on their heads, and a vast majority who looked like they had come to take part in the rock festival.

Sarie navigated the narrow streets carefully before turning onto a little lane called Chilkwell Street. Emily pointed out the bed and breakfast where Sarie booked a room for them. It was right on the shoulder of the lower slope of the Tor.

"What luck, Sarie, to get a room so close to the Chalice Gardens. I'm so glad Elaine has room for all of us," Emily congratulated Sarie.

"I booked it last summer. It's wonderful to be so close to the White Spring and the Chalice Gardens."

"Where's the water coming from?" Laurel peered out the window at a spout protruding from the stone wall that spilled water down into a grated gutter.

"That's the public access to the Red Spring water," Sarie said. "There's another by the White Spring on the other side of the lane."

"So anybody can come and get water from here?"

"That's so," Emily explained. "Both springs have their source under the Tor."

"What's so special about the springs and the hill?" Laurel wanted to know.

"Since before recorded time, this hill has been considered holy ground. It is the location of the first Christian church in England and has been referred to in old manuscripts as *the holiest erthe in Englande*. Joseph of Arimathea is supposed to have traveled from the Holy Land and landed on Weary All Hill, which is on the other side of town." Emily gestured with her arm. "When he set foot on land, he planted his staff made from a thorn tree into the soil, and it blossomed and grew. The ancestor of that original thorn still grows on Weary All Hill, where it blooms every year at Christmas and Easter time. It and its offspring are the only thorn trees in England to bloom at Christmas. Joseph and his followers built a wattle and mud church on the site where Glastonbury Abbey was later built. This place is called the birthplace of the Mother Church in England. It's a real shame that the poor tree has been vandalized recently, all that's left is the trunk."

"Although long before Joseph established his church, there were followers of the old Mother Goddess religion who dwelt on the slopes of the Tor. Nine priestesses, sometimes called The Morgens, healed the sick and taught those who were called to them about The Mysteries. Druids are also supposed to have been involved." Sarie took up the story.

"On the ceremonial days of the year, the priestesses and the Druids led the sacred processions up to the top of the Tor and performed the appropriate ceremony for the Holy Day they were observing. It usually had to do with position of the sun and the changing of the seasons."

"Is that why you and Emily come here, to participate in a ceremony?"

"We do," Sarie confirmed, "not just for the ceremony, but for the wonderful energy that exists here. You'll see. We're going to visit the Chalice Gardens after we unpack and have some lunch."

Sarie parked in the small drive of the B&B. Laurel gathered her belongings from the back seat and went around to the boot of the car to collect some of the bags.

The cheerful woman who ran the bed and breakfast greeted them at the door. She hugged Sarie and Emily and ruffled Coll's hair.

"Elaine, this is Laurel, the daughter of an old friend of mine." Sarie introduced her as Elaine led the way into the kitchen at the back of the house.

"The room is upstairs." Elaine indicated a narrow stairway in a little hall off the kitchen. "It overlooks the back garden. I left the window open. The vine is blooming and smells heavenly. I'll wet the tea while you get settled." Elaine busied herself setting the kettle on the stove.

"We can take the stuff up, if you and Gramma want to visit," Coll offered.

Laurel followed Coll into the dark hall and up the narrow stairs to a small landing. The door to the room at the top of the stair stood ajar. Coll kicked it open wider and stood back. There were two double beds in the quaint room with flowered wallpaper and sloping ceilings set into the eaves of the house.

White lacy curtains billowed in the light breeze coming through the window. Laurel could hear the contented humming of bees as they collected the pollen from the blossoms nodding against the windowpanes. Coll dumped his load of baggage on the nearest bed and leaned out the window to survey the back garden. Large trees provided plenty of shade, and the emerald grass was short cropped and velvety. Flowerbeds in a riot of colors lined the paths through the garden, and roses draped themselves over the numerous arbors set picturesquely into the pattern of the paths.

Coll craned his neck and leaned further out the window, looking for something Laurel couldn't make out.

"Be careful, Coll! What are you looking for?"

"I wanted to see if I could get a look at the Abbey from here," Coll answered, his upper body still extended out the window.

"What's so interesting about the Abbey?"

She had looked at some pictures of it in a brochure she found in the back seat on the drive up to Glastonbury. It was just a bunch of old ruins with some partial walls still standing and most of the footings marked out in the grass. In Laurel's opinion, it wasn't much to get excited about. She wished they could have gone to the Cheesewring instead.

"There's a spot where they say King Arthur and Queen Guinevere were buried. When they dug up the coffin his name was inscribed on it, and the skeleton of a large man with blond hair was in it," Coll said as he finally pulled his body back into the room.

"Where's the skeleton now, can we look at it?"

"I don't know where it is. I don't think anyone knows what happened to it. Wouldn't that have been brill, to be able to actually see his skeleton?" Coll enthused.

"I guess."

"C'mon, let's go back to the kitchen and see if lunch is ready yet."

Sarie, Emily, and Elaine were sitting at the table in the sunny kitchen sipping tea when Laurel and Coll came in from the narrow hallway at the back of the room. They settled themselves in the two vacant chairs at the table. Coll immediately helped himself to a warm scone and smothered it in butter and strawberry jam. She poured tea for herself and Coll before reaching for a cookie from the plate in front of her. The oatmeal raisin cookie was still warm from the oven and melted on her tongue.

The talk swirled around Laurel, but she wasn't really listening to the conversation. She was worrying about her mom, turning the pieces of the riddle over and over in her head. *I have to find the answers soon and do whatever it is I'm supposed to do to make her better.* She strained to remember exactly what the Lady said. The gist of it being if she were truly sincere, her wish could be granted, but only if Laurel could unravel the riddle. It couldn't be won by tricks or deceit, only by the gold of friendship and silver of inspiration. *I don't have a clue what she was talking about.* The only thing concrete so far was the 'Obby 'Oss in Padstow speaking to her and giving the first bit of information as the Lady promised. She tried to picture the Lady in her mind; the vision kept drifting and changing like mist in the wind.

Sometimes it seemed as if she imagined it, and it was just some fantasy she invented to keep from admitting her mom was dying.

Quietly, Laurel picked up her tea and another cookie and slipped out the back door into the sun-streaked shade of the garden. She followed the path until it ended at a bench made from an old tree stump in an arbor covered with cascades of red roses. Bees hummed lazily among the blooms in the afternoon sun, the sound oddly soothing.

She sat down and leaned her head against the high back of the bench. Through her closed eyelids, the sunlight spilled down through the leaves above her, flickering like flames in the hearth. A smile touched Laurel's lips as she thought about the little fire salamander that sometimes visited in Sarie's hearth fire. The little creature's vivid blue eyes so in contrast to his rich red and golden orange body. In her mind's eye, the little creature stood on his haunches and clasped his little hands in front of him. There was his typical sweet smile on his thin lips, and he bowed slightly.

"The Lady comes," Belerion said and vanished.

Laurel heard the soft swishing of fabric a second before she felt someone sit beside her on the bench. She supposed it was Coll, come to see what she was up to and cracked one eye open enough to confirm her suspicions. Both eyes popped wide open, and Laurel sat up with a start almost spilling her teacup from her lap. Beside her was the White Lady from Sarie's spring. The Lady smiled gently and laid her hand on her arm.

"How did you know where I was? Are you a friend of Elaine's? Are you who the salamander was talking about just now?"

"Go gentle, I'm sorry to startle you." The Lady's voice was lilting water sliding over river rocks. "In a manner of speaking, yes, I am a friend of Elaine's."

"How did you know where I was?"

"You called me to you, so I came."

"I didn't mean to; I was just thinking about when I met you at Sarie's spring."

"Your emotions are strong, and your thoughts were loud," the Lady said with a small laugh. "Your need for comfort is great."

Laurel looked away from the radiance of the Lady's face and fiddled with her teacup.

"I'm really scared for my mom," she muttered. "I can't find the answers to the riddles fast enough. I'm scared she'll die, and I won't get to say goodbye."

The Lady slid her hand under Laurel's chin and cupped her cheek. A soothing calm filled her at the touch of the Lady's hand. She leaned her head on the Lady's shoulder.

"Lay your burden down for a bit, child. It is hard work to push Destiny from the path it has chosen, but it can be done." The Lady's breath stirred her hair as she spoke.

"Your mother's condition hasn't worsened since you spoke to her, and the closer you get to the riddle's conclusion, the stronger she becomes. I don't think you fully appreciate the enormity of the task you have undertaken, or how few people could have gotten as far into the mystery as you and your friends have. You have the respect of many powerful, if unseen friends; your little Salamander being one of them."

A smile stole across Laurel's lips at the mention of the Salamander. "He's so cute, and he really does try to help me. I just wish he would say what he really means."

"He helps because you do not demand things of him as your right. He also feels your true affection for him. It does not hurt you are also trusted and loved by two of his favorite mortals."

"You mean Sarie and Aisling?"

"I do. Sarie is a familiar soul to those of us who walk the old paths, and Aisling is the embodiment of a spirit who is older than time. You have chosen your companions well for your quest." The Lady's voice drifted away, although she could still feel her arm around her shoulders and the cloth of the Lady's robe under her cheek.

"I didn't really choose," Laurel admitted, not wanting to take praise where it wasn't warranted. "They chose me."

"No matter how it happened, it was well done." The Lady's voice was lost in the whisper of the rose leaves in the sudden breeze, and dozens of red rose petals rained down.

"Laurel?" Coll shouted for her from somewhere in the garden.

Startled she straightened up and looked around for the Lady; there was no sign of her. No footprints besides hers marred the soft earth by the bench. She shook rose petals from her clothes and watched them flutter to the earth.

"Thanks," she whispered. "I'm over here, Coll!" Laurel answered the summons and headed back to the house.

"C'mon; Sarie and Emily are ready to head out for the Chalice Gardens." Coll took her hand and pulled her toward the front of the house.

"Isn't Elaine coming?" They rounded the corner of the house and joined Emily and Sarie.

"Not this afternoon," Sarie said. "She'll be coming with us tonight to keep vigil on the Tor until dawn."

"Blimey!" Coll said. "We get to stay up all night."

"If you can manage it," Emily said dryly, being well acquainted with the slothful side of Coll's nature.

"Hey!" Coll took mock offense to his grandmother's comment.

Laurel grinned at him. "If the shoe fits…"

"The moon is full tonight. The Vale of Avalon will be beautiful illuminated with her Light," Sarie said.

"And it might help keep Coll awake."

Emily snorted through her nose in amusement and slung her arm across Laurel's shoulder. They trooped across Well House Lane and turned onto Chilkwell Street. Chalice Gardens was only a few steps from the junction of the two streets.

Emily turned into a cobbled laneway with a wooden arch over the entrance. The words *Chalice Well* were written on the huge cross beam. The lane was over hung with archways of living plants and seemed to open its arms in welcome they entered from Chilkwell Street. Laurel noticed odd symbols in the cobbles and made a mental note to ask Sarie what they meant. They paused at the quaint red gatehouse to purchase entrance tickets and a guidebook.

There were a lot of people inside the Gardens. Some wandered about, exclaiming at the natural beauty of the gardens. Others sat in quiet meditation on the grass or benches, oblivious to the chatter flowing around them. Sarie led their little group toward a spot where water flowed down into some largish pools. The water was reddish in color and glowed like rubies in the afternoon sunlight. There were two pools in the shape of the symbol she noticed in the cobbles.

"What's that weird symbol that makes up the pools?"

"It's called a *vesica piscis*. It is made up of two identical circles where the circumference of one circle goes through the center of the other. It is a symbol sacred to many religions. The *vesica* is the bit in the middle. The top of the circles forms a gothic arch, and if you extend the lines on one end of the symbol, you get the Christian symbol of a fish."

"I knew it looked kind of familiar, but I couldn't figure out why." Laurel was familiar with the fish symbol from the church at home.

A series of rock steps led down to the cobbled area around the red pools. The whole thing was set into the side of a low bank, and the water fed down into them by a waterfall created by a series of molded concrete containers which directed the water. Sarie explained were called flow forms.

"Flow forms are vessels or organs with a narrow entrance and exit, between which are placed lateral cavities. These make the water swirl around before it exits. The carefully placed exits make the water move clockwise in one cavity and counter-clockwise in the one below it, forming a figure-eight."

"Why does it matter how the water runs?" Coll asked. Laurel knew he was impatient to do whatever it was Emily and Sarie wanted to do by the pools and get to the King Arthur's Courtyard part of the Gardens.

Emily smiled at Coll and gave him a look cautioning him to patient. "It's quite complicated, and I won't bore you with it, but it has to do with creating positive energies in the waters of the stream."

"Oh," Coll said, obviously grateful his Gramma opted not to explain the whole procedure.

Laurel was astounded to see Emily and Sarie slip off their sandals and step into the lower pool. She was about to open her mouth to say something, when Sarie and Emily joined their hands turning their faces to the sky as they raised their joined hands. Looking at the expressions of joy and worship on both their faces, she closed her mouth and knelt down to trail her fingers through the red water. Coll squatted beside her and indicated his Gramma and Sarie with a jerk of his head.

"They do this every time we come here," he whispered in exasperation. "I don't get it at all, and Gramma won't explain it to me. You're not supposed to go into the pool here, but they always do."

The red water was cold on Laurel's fingers, thicker and with more substance than she expected. The sun's reflection off the pool dazzled her eyes, for a moment. She could have sworn she saw a beautiful silver-gold light surrounding Emily and Sarie. Laurel blinked her eyes, but the image was gone.

"Did you see that?"

Coll looked at her blankly. "See what?"

"Around Emily and Sarie, like a light or something." She couldn't find the words to explain it properly.

"It's just the sun on the water," Coll said disgustedly. "Don't you go getting all weird on me, too."

"Who else gets weird?"

"We brought Aisling once, and she kept saying she saw all these weird things. Her mom won't let her come again. Her dad was really mad a Sarie for a while."

"But why?"

"I don't know…some religious thing. I just kept my head down and waited for the whole mess to blow over, and Aisling could hang out with me and Gort again."

"Are you ready to go?" Emily asked.

While they were talking, Emily and Sarie left the pool and slid on their sandals.

"Let's go." Coll got to his feet and headed up the hill towards some big old trees. King Arthur's Courtyard was just ahead.

"What kind of tree is that?" Laurel pointed at huge old gnarled tree whose trunk split just above the ground and then grew back together further up, leaving a large hole in the trunk like it had grown around something no longer there.

"It's a yew tree," Emily said.

"Really, it doesn't look like any yew tree I've ever seen." The only yew trees she knew were small and usually in some sort of hedge or under a window.

"These yews are ancient trees. They grow bigger and live longer in this climate than they do in Canada," Sarie told her.

"I guess."

She stared at the yew as they walked closer; there was a visible presence about the tree, like a personality. The slight breeze in the yew's branches sounded like whispering voices. They walked between the two huge yew trees and came to a wooden gate with a wrought iron grill in an arch over it.

"Finally," Coll said loudly. "This is King Arthur's courtyard; that's his sword over the gate."

Laurel looked up; there was a sword in the iron work and another of the circle symbols. *What was it called again? Vesica—something to do with fish*; *I'll have to ask Sarie what it is again, so*

I get it right when I talk to Mom. I hope her new treatment is working.

Inside the courtyard was another shallow pool of water fed from a stone channel with a flat bed and raised edges. The water from the spring farther up the hill sang happily as it dropped down into the pool in an almost vertical descent. The bright red water framed by lush greenery. A sign proclaimed it as the Pilgrim's Pool. Coll was busy exploring around the bushes and ferns growing in profusion around the low stone walls of the pool.

"What's he doing?" Laurel asked Emily.

"He's looking for King Arthur's sword." Emily smiled affectionately as she spoke.

"What? You mean the Excalibur sword; the one he's always talking about? What makes him think it's here?"

"He thinks because this is called King Arthur's courtyard, and the sword is displayed so prominently over the gate, it has to be hidden here waiting for the right person to find it and bring it back into the world."

"Really." It would be so cool if he actually found the sword.

"Most people think the name has some connection to the fact the Michael and Mary lines meet here before they carry on up and around the Tor," Sarie said.

"C'mon Coll, time to go," Emily said.

Coll emerged from a huge bank of ferns and brushed the earth from his knees.

They left the courtyard and continued on toward a large thorn tree surrounded by flowers around its base. Just below it, was another cobble-stoned area surrounded by a low stone wall topped with flowers. In the center of the wall was a fountain shaped like a lion's head with the red spring water pouring from his jaws. The stones were stained red from the water. Under the stream of water was a round stone pedestal the water fell down onto.

"Why is the water red?" she finally asked the question bothering her since they entered the Gardens.

"There is a lot of iron in the water, which makes the water and everything it touches red. It's why the spring is called the Red Spring, or the Blood Spring," Sarie said as she rummaged in her bag for something.

"I thought it was called Chalice Springs?"

"This is Chalice Gardens, but the spring is the Red or Blood Spring." Sarie emerged from her search with a clear glass lidded jar in her hand.

"There's a White Spring, too," Coll said to further confuse her. "We'll have to go there too before tonight."

"The water there is, let me guess, white?"

"Got it in one." Coll grinned at her.

Emily and Sarie knelt down by the lion head fountain and filled their jars with the water. Emily produced a folding camp cup out of her bag; she and Sarie each drank a cupful of the water. Sarie handed her the cup, inviting her to drink, too. Laurel stuck the cup under the flow of cold water and looked dubiously at the red water glowing in the sun. Sucking in her breath, she took a cautious sip of the water; it was cold enough to make her teeth ache with a bit of the same taste she got from holding nails in her mouth when she helped her dad. *It doesn't taste too bad.* She handed the cup to Coll when she was finished, and he drank from the spring as well. The thorn tree above the fountain was big and looked ancient.

"The tree is one of the Holy Glastonbury Thorns. It is descended from the original one sprouted from Joseph of Arimathea's staff. This is the smallest. There is a larger one by the well head and another down by the *vesica piscis* pools," Sarie said.

Emily led the way along a flag-stoned path bordered by a wide garden blooming in a riotous profusion of color. The path led into the shade of a large hedge with a wrought iron gate set in it. Laurel took a big breath of the flower-perfumed air as she followed along behind the others. The well-head was in a tiny area cobbled with stones. It was a round hole in the flat stoned area, the edges decorated with flowers and vines. The lid stood open and was made of oak and more wrought iron. The design was the circle symbol again, and it was pierced by a sword. *Bet Coll says that's Arthur's sword, too.*

"This is the Chalice Well, where the Blood Spring rises," Emily said. "The spring is capped, and the water rises through the stone well shaft."

They stood for a minute or so in silence. The late afternoon sun slanted across the stones and down into the depression where the well-head sat open; the stones and the well cover glowed orange red in the light. *Mom would love this!* For a second, Laurel could feel her mom beside her, holding her hand.

"Let's head back now so we have time to visit the White Spring before we pick up Elaine and get ready for this evening." Sarie's voice broke the stillness.

Soon they were passing the Lion Head Fountain before coming out of the trees above the pools. The water was flame red in the slanting light, liquid red gold poured down the flow forms and into the molten waters of the pools. *Mom would love to do a painting of that.* They passed the red gate house and walked briskly down the cobbled lane under the arches back out to Chilkwell Street. Sarie turned down another street, called Wellhouse Lane.

"The other spring is down this lane, just past where we're staying" Coll said as he dawdled along behind. "Staying up all night on the Tor better be worth all this walking."

"Didn't you stay up on the Tor all night last time you came?" She dropped back to walk beside Coll.

"Nah, Gramma thought I was too young, and it rained like crazy."

Emily and Sarie stopped in front of a brick building with bright blue doors. Emily tried the door, but it was locked.

"We'll have to try again tomorrow if we want to go inside and see the shrine," Emily said over her shoulder.

"We can still collect the water we want from the alcove at the side." Sarie led the way around the corner to a niche in the brick wall. From the left side of the niche, a thin stream of water flowed down onto a stone platform and then ran into the lane. Sarie filled another of her lidded jars she produced from the depths of her bag. Emily filled hers as well.

There were a few branches with green leaves on them woven into a wreath placed in the niche and some ribbons hung from another branch someone else stuck into a gap in the bricks. *Wow, this is kind of lonely; I hope the inside is nicer.* She waited for Emily and Sarie to fill their jars.

Soon they were back in the kitchen at Elaine's preparing sandwiches and packing some fruit to take with them later in the evening. Laurel and Coll clattered up the narrow stairs to fetch the ground sheets and the sleeping bags. Coll picked up Emily's satchel as well and brought it down to the kitchen.

Emily and Sarie were busy weaving the long pieces of hay and straw Emily brought from Sarie's barn. The two women wove five wreaths; intermingling the green hay and the golden straw. Both were heavy with seed heads which Emily and Sarie left hanging artistically down from the wreath. Elaine came in the kitchen door with her arms full of flowers from the back garden.

The blossoms and loose petals covered the table as the children helped to decorate the wreaths with the brilliant flowers. Laurel filled her wreath with red, white, and yellow roses along with green ferns and some white frothy flower that mingled sweetly with perfume of the roses.

Coll used mostly greenery on his wreath and some twiggy branches sticking up in a representation of a stag's antlers. He added some small blue flowers with yellow centers and some of the white frothy flowers.

"What are the wreaths for?" she asked.

"For our heads, silly; we'll wear them as we walk up the Tor this evening," Sarie said.

Laurel figured that would be all right; the wreath really was very pretty, and it smelled wonderful. Coll grimaced at her behind Emily's back. She grinned back, knowing he wouldn't complain for fear he would find himself spending the night alone in the room upstairs.

Elaine sprayed the finished wreaths with a fine mist from a bottle of the combined waters of the Blood and the White Springs. Emily and Sarie carried them outside to place the wreaths in the cool shade of the garden house.

"They'll be safe there until it's time to go," Sarie said.

After a lunch of tomato and cucumber sandwiches and tea, everyone retired for a nap. Laurel lay on the bed beside Sarie, listening to her even breathing. The sunlight shimmered through the white lace curtain. It fell on Coll's face as he slept, highlighting the soft gold in his hair and the fine hair beginning to grow on his cheeks. She felt a surge of affection for him, which took her by surprise.

Absently, she mused Coll would be pleased to know he looked like pictures of the young King Arthur with the light illuminating his features. Presently the warm sun and the bird music from the garden lulled her to sleep.

* * *

The sun was still high in the sky, riding over the tops of the trees, as they joined a larger group of people outside the White Spring on Wellhouse Lane. Laurel was amazed at how strangely some people were dressed. There were people wearing long cloaks and what looked like white nightgowns underneath. Other people dressed in clothes, which reminded her of the pictures in her history book from the middle ages. Most people wore flowered wreaths on their heads or carried bunches of flowers and greenery.

There was an odd excitement in the air, and the crowd shifted expectantly as the front of the procession started to move along the road to the path at the foot of the Tor. Emily, Sarie, and Elaine produced sky blue cloaks from the depths of Emily's satchel. The cloaks gave their familiar figures an otherworldly appearance, and it was vaguely disturbing for a minute. Coll shrugged uneasily and reached for Laurel's hand as the movement of the procession reached them, and they started to move forward.

The way was cool and shadow-filled as the path led under the trees at the foot of the Tor, before emerging out into the brilliant sunshine of the Fair Field. Laurel blinked, and for a moment, she saw the slopes of the Tor covered in a forest of trees before her vision cleared. She decided it was just a trick of the light. The climb up the side of the large hill was steep and hard, even though the path was well maintained. The higher up they climbed, the more beautiful the view was. Laid out on either side, the green English countryside glowed emerald in the afternoon sun. The Somerset Levels flowed away from the Tor, and it was easy to imagine the Tor surrounded by water.

The procession snaked its way slowly up the southwest spine of the Tor, past a bench by a fallen stone, moving ever upward toward the tower perched on the top of the Tor. The women's cloaks billowed in the light wind, which sprang up as they neared the top of the hill. The silken material whispered against itself as the wind blew it close to their bodies.

They reached the highest point of the Tor as the sun was starting to sink toward the horizon in the west. Emily, Sarie, and Elaine spread the ground sheets out while Coll and Laurel placed the sleeping bags and the satchel with the food in it beside them.

Coll threw himself on the ground with his head on a sleeping bag, his wreath slipping down over his face to rest on the tip of his nose.

Laurel gazed all around her; no matter which way she looked, the view was amazing. It was like standing at the center of the world with all creation was laid out around her. *It's almost like being on top of Sulphur Mountain back home.* There was the same feeling of wonder; like the wind could just lift her off the ground, and she could fly wherever she desired.

She wasn't sure what some of the people gathered on the Tor were doing: a cluster of people appeared to be meditating; a group near to her was performing some sort of ceremony, with crystals and other things she couldn't identify. Everyone seemed to be following their own agenda. She thought it would be one unified ceremony, kind of like communion in church.

"Is there any sort of plan for the ceremony?"

"There are groups from all kinds of religions and beliefs who come up here on the special days," Sarie explained. "Everyone is free to practice what they wish. So, each group will have a plan for their ceremony or ritual, but there isn't an overall plan or any ceremony involving the group as a whole. There's just the landscape and the sun uniting us all."

"Sarie, Elaine, and I are going to take part in our ceremony now. You and Coll wait here please; we'll be about forty-five minutes."

"We'll be back shortly after the sun sets." Sarie smiled as she picked up Emily's satchel and followed Elaine and Emily.

Coll was still sprawled on his back with his eyes closed.

"How are you going to stay up all night if you can't even make it until the sun goes down?" Laurel prodded him with her toe.

Coll rolled onto his side and sat up. "We might as well unroll the bags and sort out supper."

They organized their little campsite and then sat side by side to watch the sun slide down the western sky sinking behind Weary All Hill. Laurel rested her chin on her bent knees. The sunset was making her extremely homesick. She thought about riding up the butte across the river with Chance and Carlene to watch the sun set over the prairies. It was fun to ride home in the twilight, which lingered a long time on the Canadian prairie.

Coll stood up as the sun sank below the horizon to drown itself in the sea and got the sandwiches out of the insulated bag. "They'll be along soon now. We'll eat, and then they'll want to watch the moon rise."

She sat staring at the spot where the sun vanished for another long moment. The sky above still glowed golden.

Is that what it will be like when Mom dies? Here one minute and gone the next? Just...gone? A tear slid down her cheek, and she brushed it angrily away. "She's not going to die," Laurel whispered fiercely. "I'm going to solve that stupid riddle, and they'll have to keep their promise and save her."

Sarie, Emily, and Elaine appeared out of the gathering dusk. Their cloaks billowed around them like the wings of huge blue-hued ravens. Over by the tower someone chanted, the sound floating over the Tor as the darkness closed over the land. Bright stars pricked the velvet of the night sky and softly illuminated the Tor. The grass was already wet with dew and glistening in the starlight. The world held its breath waiting for the moon to rise.

In no time at all, the sandwiches disappeared. Everyone was hungry from the climb up the Tor and the excitement of the day. Laurel zipped up her sweatshirt with the kangaroo pouch on the front. She grinned. Chance's mom called her jacket a bunny hug. She was from Saskatchewan and always laughed and said that was what people called the jacket where she came from. Chance and Carlene could never convince her to call it a kangaroo sweatshirt. The breeze from the west picked up a little after the sun went down, and the temperature on the top of the Tor dropped a few degrees.

The horizon started to glow with a tiny bit of silver light as the moon prepared to show her face. A ragged cheer rose from some of the people gathered on the Tor as the moon pulled free of the horizon and swung into the sky. The majority of the gathering was silent and absorbed in the spectacle of the swollen moon rising into the starry sky. Laurel took her eyes away from the sky to look around her. People stood with their arms spread wide over their heads embracing the moon and the sky, some kneeled in supplication with their heads bowed, and others swayed to an unheard music, chanting softly.

By the St. Michael's Tower, voices rose high and clear, the sound hanging on the crystal air of the night. Laurel couldn't understand the words though the music was beautiful; soon other voices joined in. The sound swelled as the moon rose higher in the sky, and the moon was lifted ever higher by the sound. She looked over at Sarie and saw tears traced in the silver moonlight running down Sarie's cheeks. A wonderful stillness and calm filled her; she felt so light, it seemed possible to float on the currents of the breeze like the ravens. The silver light illuminated the tower behind their campsite, the edges of the stones rimed in argent.

"Doesn't the tower look like a guardian knight?" Coll said quietly.

"I guess," she replied. The tower seemed friendly enough, but there was some sort of weird feeling of power coming from it Laurel couldn't name. It sent skitters of unease down her spine.

Emily, Sarie, and Elaine settled themselves on the ground with their sleeping bags draped over their shoulders for warmth. Their eyes never leaving the shining face of the moon as it poured silver fire over the land. Coll crawled into his bag and immediately fell asleep. Laurel giggled a little as she wriggled to get comfortable in her makeshift bed.

She blinked and looked directly into the light of the moon. There were little creatures, half human, half something else playing in the moonbeams. They slid down the silver light squealing with glee until they hit the grass, disappearing to blink back into sight again at the top the moonbeam slide to do it all over again. Laurel watched them in delight as the moonlight washed over her. Her mind drifted from thought to thought; she felt warm and loved lying in the embrace of the Tor and the moonlight. Somehow she knew everything would be all right; she would solve the riddle and her mom would be okay. The moonlight led her into the dark comfort of sleep.

Chapter Twelve

The Monk in the Marsh

Loud crashes and cold water running down her neck woke Laurel. Her ears rang with the sound of people shouting. She struggled out of her soaking sleeping bag and tried to make sense out of her surroundings.

The top of the Tor was pitch-black; the moon buried in the boiling storm clouds overhead. To make matters worse, rain sluiced down from the sky in torrents. Lightening split the night in two, and a huge growl of thunder followed closely on its heels. She looked around wildly in confusion, trying to get her bearings in the suddenly stormy night.

"Coll, Sarie, Emily!" The wind whipped the words from her lips.

Laurel wiped the rain from her face. As quickly as she cleared it away, the wind blew more into her face. She ducked instinctively when thunder rolled over her head. In the flashes of lightening, she looked for the tower; at least she could get out of the rain there. She got a good look at the structure in the flare of the next lightning bolt and moved toward it. The wet grass was slippery, and the uneven ground caught at her feet as she stumbled toward the tower.

"Sarie!" *She must be here somewhere.*

Laurel continued to battle her way in the direction of the tall structure. Other people in the storm pushed past her, some of them traveling in the same direction, some of them fleeing in the opposite direction. No one noticed her calling for help. Her jacket was soaked through, and the cold wind made her shiver even more than the thunder and lightning.

Suddenly, she tripped and rolled head over heels down the steep side of the Tor. A scream tore from her lips as she fought desperately to grab something to stop her headlong flight down the slope. The grass and mud were greasy in her hands; her fingers slid off any hold she managed to find. Finally, she hit a level spot and stopped with a thud.

"Holy crap," Laurel swore as she tried to get breath back into her body.

Gingerly, she tested out her arms and legs and was relieved to find they all seemed to be in working order. Other than feeling like she'd been run over by a herd of longhorns, she appeared to be in one piece. Shakily, she scrambled to her feet and started in surprise when her flailing hand touched the rough bark of a small tree. Laurel grabbed the sapling for support and pushed her straggling hair out of her eyes. The night was full of wind and rain, and visibility was limited to a couple of inches in front of her nose.

"Where am I?" Laurel spoke just to hear her voice. She didn't remember seeing any trees on the climb up the Tor. "The only trees I saw were the ones at the end of Wellhouse Lane, and they were way bigger than these trees."

Thunder rolled in the distance, and the flashes of lightning were further away now. Laurel shivered harder; the shock from her swift descent down the hill and her soaked clothes combined to make her teeth chatter. She had no idea where she was, or how to get back to anywhere familiar.

Sarie must be looking for me.

"Sarie, Coll, Emily!"

She walked into the trees where there was a faint path running downhill. The trees blocked a lot of the wind, and it wasn't raining quite as hard under the canopy of the little wood. Laurel's feet squelched in her wet sneakers, once or twice she stopped to yank her shoe out of the muck where it stuck fast.

"Am I having a good time yet?" She slipped and slid her way along the narrow path.

The slim trees lining the narrow path provided some support; Laurel clung to them to keep from landing on her butt in the slimy muck. The force of the rain lessened; the sky was becoming lighter in what she supposed must be the east.

"Do I want to go east or west?" She was completely disoriented, with no idea where she was in relation to the town, or anywhere else for that matter.

"What would Dad do?" Laurel talked out loud to give herself courage. She was cold, wet, and hungry and just wanted to sit down in a heap to wail her lungs out.

Figure out where you are; then figure out where you need to go. Her dad's voice echoed in her ears telling her what to do if she got lost on the ranch.

"I need to get out of the trees to see where I am," she muttered under her breath.

She surveyed the path in front of her, where one set of interconnected paths led upward and another downward. Laurel decided on the downward set. She was tired, and the thought of trying to clamber up the path while she slid backward in the mud was less appealing than sliding downward, on her backside if need be. The rain was almost gone now, and birdsong was breaking out all over the copse of trees. *Where on earth are Sarie and Coll and Emily?*

"Isn't anybody looking for me?" Laurel growled as she squished her way down the slope. "It's freaking morning! You'd think they would have noticed I'm gone by now."

Getting angry also made her warmer. She moved quicker as the path leveled out. The sky lightened, and Laurel looked in astonishment at a large flooded marsh. There were some high parts serving as makeshift paths through the area.

Mist hung in sheets over the watery levels, getting thinner and tattered as the sun grew stronger, and the slight morning breeze began to blow. The hum of insects registered a split second before the first of a thousand insects bit her. Laurel swatted them away and looked for a way back to higher ground. The wood she just left was swallowed up in some of the thicker mist gathering behind her.

"This just keeps getting better and better. Lost and mosquitoes, too." Laurel filled her lungs with a sense of futility. "Sarie, Coll!"

Is that someone shouting back? The sound came from out in the marsh.

"Am I that lost?"

"Hello!" A shout answered her. It came from the mist-shrouded marsh in front of her. She hesitated before she took a step and sunk into the muck past her ankles. She couldn't tell where it was safe to walk and what would sink under her feet.

"Help! Over here."

"I'm coming; stay where you are." The voice was male, with a funny accent much different from the English accents, which were actually starting to sound normal.

Laurel kept yelling at intervals to guide her rescuer to her. *I hope he's not some axe murderer lurking in the swamp, waiting for unsuspecting victims. Where is Sarie?*

Laurel could hear the soft squelch of feet making their way through the boggy marsh. The mist swirled a bit as the morning breeze moved through it. A patch cleared, her rescuer stepped through it and stopped by her side.

Laurel looked up at the man. He wasn't much taller than she was, but he was very wide. He was the stoutest man she had ever seen. His brown robe reminded her of the robes the priest in the Catholic Church at home wore. His short dark blond hair stuck up all over his head. It was hard to tell the color properly, because dampness from the mist and rain darkened it to almost brown. The man leaned on his tall walking staff and breathed heavily for a moment. His blue eyes crinkled at the corners as he smiled.

"Is it lost ye be?"

"Were you out looking for me?"

"Why no, child," he seemed surprised. "I heard you calling through the mist when I was on my way to my favorite fishing place."

Laurel was silent, trying to figure it all out. The man's speech was funny, English but the phrases sounded wrong. He sounded like the old Italian man in the general store in Fort McLeod who only spoke English when he couldn't avoid it.

"Well, I'm lost." She kicked herself mentally. *Brilliant, just brilliant. At least he doesn't seem to be an axe murderer.*

The man heaved his bulk onto the trunk of a fallen tree and pulled some rounds of bread from his pocket. He offered her some, so she took them and sat down beside him. He chewed in silence for a time, tilting his head back to watch a flight of ducks as they winged overhead through the thinning mist. The marsh was alive with life as the sun brightened, and the mist flowed away into the bushes.

"I'm Laurel." She finally remembered her manners and extended her hand.

"I am Brother Ioho." The man gravely shook her hand.

"I'm visiting Glastonbury, but I got lost in the rain."

"I'll take you to the Abbey. I'm sure your people will come there for help if they can't find you. Elsewise, we can send a messenger to them so they can come and collect you." The man threw some of his bread crust to some ducks that swam nearby.

"The Abbey?"

"Glastonbury Abbey, the lovely big church with the wonderful bells. I live there and serve God as is my wont," Brother Ioho explained.

"You're a monk who lives at the Abbey."

"I am."

"But the Abbey isn't there anymore, just part of the old walls."

"It was there, and fine and beautiful when I left this morning," Brother Ioho told her. "I have met some in the marsh before who have told me the same thing, but the Abbey is always there when I return from my wanderings."

Laurel's heart beat a little faster in apprehension. Somehow she had taken a step sideways, like they did at the Men an Tol. Only this time, there was no Gwin to show her the way back. *Don't panic; don't panic.* She forced herself to breathe around the tightness in her chest. *Get him to lead you out of this swamp and then find a policeman as fast as you can.*

The monk seemed in no hurry to get back to whatever it was monks did. The sun shone brighter, and the day got hotter as they sat on the log and talked about all manner of things. Brother Ioho loved animals so Laurel told him about her dogs and cats at home, about her horse Sam, and about Sarie's ponies in Cornwall. Brother Ioho talked about the creatures in the marsh; the ducks and swans came to feed from his hands. The sparrows and wrens liked to sit on his shoulders as he wandered through the fenland. The longer she talked to him, the calmer Laurel felt; she trusted her instincts and allowed herself to relax in the sunshine.

"Animals don't judge you," Brother Ioho said. "They pay no never mind I am three stone overweight, or my hair never lies flat. The creatures of the marsh care only that I am kind to them and don't hunt them or kill their young. When I am with them, my world is in harmony, and I am happy."

The sound of bells pealing sounded faintly over the noises of the marsh: the high pitched peeping of the frogs, the annoying hum of the stinging insects, and the splashes and voices of the water fowl as they hunted for food. A huge blue heron swept from the sky and landed ten feet from where they Ioho sat. The big bird twisted his long snake-like neck to regard them with a knowing beady eye. Satisfied they meant no harm, the bird turned his attention to fishing and soon caught his fill of small silver fish. The heron launched himself into the air as gracefully as a bird that size can. He circled three times before flying away. His harsh rusty krawking sounded loud in the relative quiet of the marsh.

A small brown duck waddled out of the reeds at the edge of the water. It shook its feathers like a dog shedding water from its coat, muttering to itself in little quacks which sounded like words. The duck headed straight for Brother Ioho and settled itself onto his ample lap. Brother Ioho smoothed the duck's head and offered it some bread from his pocket.

"How is it you've been doing, my little friend?" Brother Ioho asked the little duck.

The duck lifted her head up and fixed her beady eyes on Brother Ioho's face as he leaned down. Very carefully, she stretched up and tapped the monk's chin with her bill. The duck took the bit of bread from Brother Ioho's hand and settled in his lap again with a great ruffling and arranging of feathers. Brother Ioho laughed.

"You always were vain, little one."

"How did you make friends with the duck?"

"I rescued her from a fox," Brother Ioho explained. "The fox already had this one's mother and siblings for breakfast. I heard the little one piping under a log after I disturbed the fox. I took her back to the Abbey and raised her, after which, I returned her here to the marsh. There were some as looked at her as dinner in the stew pot." He shook his head. "It's a pity some see only what will contribute to their own comfort and not credit this life with the sanctity it deserves." Brother Ioho stroked the duck's feathers, which shimmered in the morning sunlight. The duck pushed her head against his hand in utter trust and confidence.

"Can I pat her?"

"To be sure."

"Hi, pretty one." Laurel stroked the duck's head with her forefinger and spoke to her as if she was one of the foals back home. "Is she safe here?"

"As safe as she will be anywhere. At any rate, this is her home and where she is meant to be. I'm only glad I can still visit her and be remembered." Brother Ioho spoke quietly, an expression of love softening his round face.

After the duck exhausted the supply of bread crusts from the monk's robes, she rose and flipped her feathers into place before she jumped to the mossy ground. The duck rubbed her bill against Brother Ioho's hand one last time and then marched off into the shallow water. Five little ducklings appeared from under an overhanging bush and joined her in single file as the duck led the way out into the reeds.

"Go safely," Brother Ioho said under his breath.

Laurel tipped her head back to look at the clouds gathering in the blue sky above her. She should be making an effort to find her way out of the marsh and look for Sarie, but somehow it was too much effort. The sun was warm, and the marsh was oddly peaceful. Time was standing still; there was no hurry or rush to do anything or go anywhere.

"Do you think it's going to rain again?" Laurel asked Brother Ioho.

"Chance that it might." Brother Ioho watched the reflection of the clouds in the still water of the shallow pool in front of their log seat.

"What's it like, being a monk and living in the Abbey?"

"I love the Abbey; it is so beautiful. Oft times we sit in the gallery under the west window with the sunlight streaming in as the sun sets. The organ sounds, and some of us sing in answer, hidden behind the great rood screen. The sounds echo even outside the Abbey, and all the little organs in the other churches in town join in the triumphant sound. Then the bells ring out over town and marsh. It is a wondrous thing to hear." Brother Ioho paused and watched the fingers of the breeze stroke the surface of the pool with a soft caress. His voice was quiet and dreamy as he continued.

"I am happier in the orchard or here in the marsh communing silently with my God and nature than I am performing the rituals of the choir. I was never meant to be a monk. They placed me here in the choir, when I would have rather drawn a sword."

"Can't you just go and do what you want with your life?"

Brother Ioho shook his head. "I love the Abbey herself too much to ever leave her now. I sleep up high beneath the eaves. The Prior decrees those of us who are fleshy and weighty must sleep there so we must exercise as we climb the stairs. There are some who make comments on my weight, saying I will never get through the portals of Heaven with my bulk."

"Can't you get someone to make them stop? It's mean to tease someone because they're different." Laurel was indignant anyone would try to make this sweet man unhappy.

Brother Ioho smiled. "I told them the gates of Heaven are wide enough for all, so none of God's creations should stick in the opening. I ignore them and spend all my spare time walking the lanes and the woods."

"Is it cold where you sleep up under the eaves?"

"'Tis damp sometimes, but I love to listen to the rain on the roof. At night from the tower and the high roofs, it sounds like a waterfall. There are gargoyles on the roof, and they shout to each other as the water streams from their carven lips." Brother Ioho patted her hand. "Don't be distressed for me, child. I love the Abbey for herself and her beauty which will far outlast those who tease me."

"It's still not right."

"What are you seeking?" Brother Ioho looked down into her upturned face.

"Seeking?" Laurel was puzzled. "I guess how to get back to Sarie?"

"No, child, what are you seeking in your heart?" The monk prodded her gently.

"I want my mom to get well." The words fell from her mouth before she could stop them. "My mom has cancer, and I had to come to stay with Sarie. I made a wish at an old spring at the back of Sarie's pasture, and a lady told me my wish would be granted if I could figure out the answer to a riddle."

"We are all seekers of something, child. Yon hill is at the end of your quest, but the time is not yet come; you must find all the pieces of the puzzle before you return here, or nothing will you find. Go to the place where the giants were routed by the saint. There you will find the last clue and use it to return to this place." Brother Ioho indicated the Tor rising behind them. "It has been a place of miracles before and will be again. Have courage. You have a good and pure heart; your quest will be a successful one."

"Do you really think so?" *Is he actually telling me Mom will be okay?*

"By all I hold holy, I do believe it. Now you must believe also and continue your journey. It will bring you full circle back to this hill of vision. More I cannot tell you." Brother Ioho placed his hand on her shoulder as he spoke. "Now, I hear the bells calling. Come, I will take you up to the Abbey."

A light rain started to fall as they made their way through the marsh. Brother Ioho unerringly leading the way as mist began to gather on the water. After a time, the monk stopped and pointed through the trees.

"Look, you can see the towers and gables of the Abbey there." Pride and love shone in the monk's expression.

Laurel looked up beyond the trees through the falling rain and mist. Her breath caught in her throat; there indeed was a magnificent building shining in an errant ray of sunshine that escaped the clouds. It was a huge structure with many arches and bell towers, the voice of the bells sounding sweetly down over the wet countryside.

She would have remembered seeing the church when they walked through town yesterday. *How can I have missed such a big building, and why didn't Sarie and Emily want to visit it?* She missed her footing and ended up in the marsh up to her knee.

"Son of sea cook," Laurel swore, using one of Grampa D'Arcy's favorite phrases.

Brother Ioho stopped and looked behind him. He was laughing as he offered a hand and pulled her back onto a relatively dry hummock of long grass.

"I have done that myself many times walking while I lose myself in the glory of the sight of the Abbey," the monk told her kindly.

“Is it much farther?” She was beginning to get cold again, and the need to find Sarie filled her with a new urgency.

“We’re almost to the edge of the fens now; then it is but a short climb up to the Abbey grounds,” Brother Ioho assured her.

The mist continued to thicken as the rain increased. Laurel took the hand Brother Ioho extended to her; she could hardly see where she was putting her feet. The path they were following started to rise, and she was careful not to slip in the muddy footing.

“Almost there,” panted Brother Ioho.

There was a gate in the stone wall just ahead of them. Brother Ioho stopped at the wooden gate.

“It has been most delightful to talk with you. I will remember you for a very long time.” Brother Ioho smiled and kissed her on the forehead.

Laurel hugged the short stout monk hard. “Thanks for rescuing me and never mind what other people say about you. You’re an awesome monk.”

Brother Ioho rested his hand on top of her head for an instant before he pushed the wooden gate open on its hinges. For a second, a huge stone building soared into the heavens over her head, the gargoyles Brother Ioho mentioned spewing rain from the eaves out of their mouths that fell in silvery torrents to the ground. There was a brilliant flash of light. Caught by surprise, Laurel stumbled and fell to the ground.

A hand gripped her arm and shook her. She slipped and slid as she tried to stand up.

Sarie’s voice sounded very far away.

“Laurel, Laurel. All right are ye?”

“‘M okay.” Her voice sounded strange, even to her.

“Sit up slowly. There that’s it.” Emily knelt and helped her to sit up.

“Wow, you look as rough as a rat.”

Muck and bits of bushes and weeds clung to her clothes and her hair. Sarie wrapped a blanket around Laurel’s shoulders and helped her to stand up.

“Where’ve you been to? We’ve been all around the bal looking for you,” Sarie asked gently.

The sun was shining, and it wasn’t raining anymore. It didn’t seem possible.

"What happened to the rain?" she asked stupidly.

She saw Sarie and Emily exchange worried looks. "The rain stopped early this morning, right after the storm."

"No, it was just raining. When I walked through the gate in the wall of the Abbey, it was raining."

"You must be mazed. We found you here, lying under this bush," Sarie said gently.

"I fell asleep; then when I woke up it was storming." Laurel paused. "I remember, I tried to find the tower to get out of the rain, and I fell down the side of the hill. I ended up by a swamp, and there was a monk who knew the way out. He brought me through a gate into the Abbey grounds."

"You are in the ruins of the Abbey, though Lord only knows how you managed to get here," Emily said.

"No, I just *saw* the Abbey and the gargoyles. And it was raining cats and dogs."

She looked around and saw all that remained of the beautiful building she had seen were the remnants of some walls and arches.

"I don't know. But I know what I saw, and Brother Ioho, the monk, said he was from the Abbey, and he would take me there. I heard the bells ringing." Laurel shook her head and then wished she hadn't. It hurt.

"It's too confusing," she murmured.

"Finally." Sarie sounded relieved.

Coming across the short grass was a medic van with its light flashing.

"Cool, can we ride in the ambulance, too?" Coll wanted to know.

Emily cuffed Coll lightly on the head. "It's for Laurel, idiot child."

She was more than happy to let them bundle her into the medic van. She was tired and the heated blankets they wrapped her in were wonderful. Laurel smiled faintly as Coll clambered in beside her, his eyes wide as he tried to take in all the equipment crammed into the van. She let her eyes drift close.

Chapter Thirteen

Non-edible Rocks

The doctor at the hospital declared Laurel none the worse for wear, but he insisted on keeping her overnight for observation. Laurel spoke to both her mom and dad on the phone and assured them she was fine. Her dad was all for hopping on the next plane and coming to bring her home. She was surprised herself by refusing. *I miss Mom and Dad so much, but I have to stay here and figure out the riddle. We're so close, and there's things I'll miss about Cornwall when I do go home. Coll for one.*

The next morning she settled herself in the back seat of Sarie's car and let Emily tuck a car rug around her. Coll climbed in beside her and handed over a thermos of hot, sweet tea. Soon they were bowling along Glastonbury's High Street ready to turn to the southwest and head home for Cornwall.

Leaning her head against the window, she watched the countryside flow by. Before too long she closed her eyes; the motion was giving her a huge headache. With her eyes closed, Laurel reviewed the clues, the images forming and re-forming themselves on the insides of her eyelids. The Lady at the spring, Vear Du, Gwin Scawen, Corm—who Coll now insisted was Cormoran, the last resident giant of St. Michael's Mount—Brother Ioho, the little salamander in Sarie's fireplace.

They found the lizard as it came out of the sea. That was the ley line of energy known as the Michael Line. It was supposed to point them in the right direction. That led them to visit the Men an Tol, and the knowledge about rocks not being able to be eaten referred to the pile of rocks at the top of Stowes Hill on Bodmin Moor known as the Cheesewring. The Michael line, or the backbone of the lizard, ran right through the pile of stones on Stowe's Hill and continued northeast through the Tor at Glastonbury. Brother Ioho gave encouragement, but no real new information. *He did confirm the Cheesewring is the rocks that can't be eaten, because that's what Corm told us about, the giants and St. Tue.* Laurel wondered if she should have asked him more questions or maybe different questions. *It looks like the Cheesewring is the next place we should go and investigate. I hope Sarie will take us and not be all crazy about what happened in Glastonbury.*

She was still a little achy from her roll down the side of the Tor. She knew Coll was rightly impressed by some of her more spectacular bruises. Laurel glanced at Coll from under her lashes; he was looking out the window as the rolling landscape of the Dartmoor Forest flashed by. She touched his arm to get his attention.

"Do you think Sarie will agree to take us to the Cheesewring?" Laurel asked in a voice she hoped wouldn't carry to the front seat.

"Jeez, I don't know," Coll whispered.

"We need to go soon; time's running out, I just know it."

"Let's wait and talk it over with Aisling and Gort. I heard Gramma tell Sarie, Ash and Gort are coming out to the farm this afternoon once we get home."

She wanted to get Sarie to agree to the trip right here and now but curbed her impatience and leaned back into the cushions of the back seat and closed her eyes. She didn't release her grasp on his hand, keeping her fingers entwined with his, fighting back a smile at the strange thrill of excitement arcing through her. Behind closed eyes, Laurel planned the trip to the Cheesewring. She wasn't sure what would happen once she got there, but she knew she needed to go soon. They could take the ponies and camping gear and ride all the way to the Cheesewring. It was a long way though. Maybe Sarie wouldn't like them to take the ponies so far on their own, especially if Sarie refused to drive them up to Bodmin.

Maybe, they should just ask if they could go pony trek camping and not ask Sarie to drive them first. If Sarie didn't know where they were going, she couldn't very well forbid them to go. But Sarie and Emily both said they would help, and Laurel's conscience pricked her at the thought of deceiving Sarie, especially when Sarie's beloved ponies were involved. Coll was probably right in saying they should talk it over with Ash and Gort tonight.

Aisling was always so smart about seeing the correct way to do something.

Before Laurel realized it, Sarie's little car bounded up the narrow lane and came to a stop by the cottage. She was grateful she was excused from helping unload the bags. Her bumps and bruises were painful after sitting still for so long.

Laurel hobbled into the kitchen and set about remaking the fire in the huge cook stove. It was fun to cook using the wood-burning cooker. It reminded her of the weekends her family spent at their cabin in the mountains; the smell of the freshly started fire reminded her of Gramma Bella. A thrill of excitement wound through her stomach. *Gramma Bella is alive! I'm going to Bragg Creek first thing when I get home.*

"*First things first,*" she reminded herself. *I need to concentrate on the next clue and finish this riddle once and for all.*

Soon the car was unloaded, and everything stowed away where it belonged. Coll, ever the chivalrous knight, carried her gear up to her room. The kettle on the cooker just started to boil when Aisling and Gort arrived. Aisling's dad stuck his head in the door to stay hello and then was gone, off on an errand for Aisling's mom.

"H-h-holy c-c-cow, wh-wh-what h-happened to you," Gort exclaimed as he caught sight of her many colored bruises. "You l-l-look like m-m-e after Uncle D-d-daniel's had one of h-h-his m-m-oods!"

"Wait 'til you hear." Coll snorted with laughter at the look on Gort's face.

"Only you could turn a simple trip to Glastonbury into a right crash up." Aisling smiled affectionately and settled in the chair beside her.

"It wasn't my fault," Laurel protested. "I didn't plan to fall down the side of the hill!"

"You fell off the Tor?" Aisling was incredulous.

"Kind of," she said sheepishly.

"In the middle of a great thunderstorm," Coll broke in.

"It was nice when I went to sleep, but then I woke up, and it was teeming rain and thunder and lightning. I couldn't find Sarie or anyone. I was trying to get to the tower thing on the top, but I slipped and kind of rolled and bounced down the side of the hill into a bunch of trees. I got lost in the fog and ended up in a swamp. Then I met this old guy who was a monk. His name was Brother Ioho. But this is where it gets weird. He said he lived in the Abbey, and when we walked out of the swamp, I saw the Abbey through the trees. Just before I left him, he opened a gate in a stone wall, and I saw the Abbey again, all in one piece. Afterward, when Sarie found me, the Abbey was all in ruins. But I know what I saw, I wasn't dreaming. I know I wasn't."

"You should have seen her Ash, all covered in mud and burrs and soaking wet," Coll enthused.

"The doctor said it was the bump on her head made her hallucinate," Sarie joined in the conversation.

"Did the monk have another clue for you?" Aisling asked quickly.

"In a way."

"Wh-wh-what did h-h- he say?" Gort prodded.

"He said the time to solve the riddle wasn't yet, but the Tor was where I needed to end up. I need to go to the place where the giants were beaten by the saint and many roads lead to the Tor." Laurel paused for a moment and wrinkled her face in thought. "He did say I would be successful in my search though."

"The giants and the saint, Corm told us about them; this confirms it. The Cheesewring is where we need to go next," Aisling spoke up.

* * *

The fire crackled in the hearth, and a small explosion of sparks flew up the chimney. In the resultant glow, the little salamander twined himself around the coals in the grate and waited for the group to notice him. After a short period, he perched on the top of the glowing flames and clapped his small paws together three times. A shower of embers swirled in the fireplace and some landed on the rug.

"What the bloody hell is that?" Coll gaped at the figure in the flames.

"Hush, Coll, you'll scare him off." Aisling knelt on the rug and scooped the glowing embers back into the hearth with a little shovel.

"It's the salamander I told you about. The one who gave me the clue about the none plus one plus none. You know, the Men an Tol," Laurel said to Coll without taking her eyes off the salamander.

The salamander executed a very courtly bow and smiled benevolently at them.

"Wow," Gort breathed without stuttering at all.

"It's welcome you are to my house and fire," Sarie greeted the salamander formally.

The little creature bowed again to Sarie with a flourish of his tail. His bright blue eyes twinkled as he regarded each one of the company in turn. With a small scattering of sparks, he seated himself on the edge of the biggest heap of coals in the fire and folded his front paws around his knees.

"Well met searchers," the salamander greeted them. "You have journeyed well and answered each clue as it presented to you." His voice was the high, sweet sound of wind chimes and bells tinkling. "You must not falter now when your goal is close to you. As you have deduced, the Cheesewring is where you must go. There you will receive the final clue and a message of much importance."

"Who are you?" Gort asked.

The salamander regarded Gort solemnly for a brief moment, his bright eyes thoughtful. Gort raised his hand to his forehead for a moment. The salamander nodded his little head haloed by the golden flames.

"I am known as Belerion, the Shining One."

"I've seen you before. In Uncle Daniel's fire. I thought you were my imagination," Gort said quietly.

"I have watched over you when your friend Aisling was worried for you," Belerion told Gort. "I couldn't speak to you until you acknowledged me."

"Oh," Gort managed to say.

"So, Little One," Sarie broke into the conversation. "This lot needs to go up to the rocks on Stowe's Hill by Minions?"

"'Tis so, Mistress Sarie," Belerion affirmed with a nod of his gold-red head, "as soon as ever it is possible."

"We should wait for this one to heal up a bit before we go haring off on another adventure." Sarie indicated Laurel's bruised face.

Belerion smiled, and his blue eyes glittered. "I can fix you up right smartly."

He rose gracefully to his hind legs, pulling himself up to his full height. The fire glowed brighter, and the flames created a halo of orange-red and gold around his small figure. With his small paws, Belerion gathered bits of the fire and formed them into a glowing ball. The ball retained it shape, but flowed like water in his hands, the colors of the fire pulsing across its surface in waves. Belerion turned his gaze to Laurel, and his eyes sparkled as he suddenly tossed her the ball.

"Catch!" Belerion's silvery voice shimmered in the air as the small ball soared directly at her.

Instinctively she reached out her hand to catch the small missile. As it came in contact with her fingers, the ball broke apart into hundreds of small shimmering spheres of light. The spheres organized themselves into a spiral and danced about with Laurel at their center. Belerion clapped his hands in glee from the hearth.

As the tiny brilliant lights swirled around her, the aches and pains faded away. She looked down at the big bruise and scrape on her forearm and watched as the colored spheres concentrated on the spot and leached the bruise and soreness away. The scrape faded as she watched. Laurel gave up trying to follow the pattern the spheres made and lost herself in the beautiful colors and the wonderful feeling of warmth and happiness they produced inside her. The spheres organized themselves back into a single sphere and returned to Belerion's hands in the hearth. With a graceful movement of his hand, Belerion returned the ball of colored light to the flames.

"Wow, thanks. I feel so much better."

"This is my personal gift to you, Laurel the searcher. Now you must take full benefit of my gift and make your journey soon." Belerion bowed.

* * *

Coll watched the lights encircle Laurel and return to the creature in the fire in disbelief. This was the kind of magic his Gramma talked about but Coll never really believed existed outside of the old stories. Until now. It was one thing for Aisling to have a piskie for a friend because everyone knew there were piskies in Cornwall. But to have little lizard guys in the fire talk and heal up bruises right in front of him was more than Coll would have been willing to believe if he didn't see it with his own eyes.

"*Ah, the protector.*" Belerion held Coll's eyes with his bright blue ones. *"You do well to not trust easily. That is your job, to keep the searcher from danger she may not perceive for herself. Guard her well, Knight Protector,*" Belerion said for Coll alone to hear.

With a cheery flick of his tail and a wink of his eye, Belerion disappeared into the heart of the flames, and the bright glow of the fire decreased a bit.

"Well then, shall we plan on visiting Minions this Saturday?" Sarie said brightly into the silence after Belerion's departure.

* * *

Saturday morning found the company of four, along with Sarie and Emily in the cramped confines of Sarie's car. The headlights pushed back the pre-dawn blackness as they wound their way through the narrow lanes. A rabbit dashed across the road, appearing suddenly from the thick hedge on one side of the road and disappearing just as quickly into the heavy growth on the opposite side. Laurel smiled at Aisling; rabbits were good luck.

Dawn was beginning to lighten the eastern sky as Sarie drove into the outskirts of Minions. On the drive up from Penzance, they finished off the breakfast of scones and hot tea Emily brought along. Gort and Coll were ready for a more substantial meal. With that in mind, Sarie pulled into the car park by the Cheesewring Hotel. The hotel boasted a pub, which was open at this hour of the morning for hikers and locals who needed an early start. The atmosphere inside the square white two-story building with the pub on the ground floor was warm and welcoming. Laurel wrinkled her nose in appreciation of the enticing smells coming from the kitchen area. Before long, they were all tucking into sausage and eggs with fried potato planks and toast. Coll and Gort finished first and amused themselves telling smugglers' stories Old Joseph had shared with them.

"Can we start soon?" Laurel pleaded with Sarie, anxious to get to the Cheesewring and start looking for the final clue. Somehow, she was sure a clue wouldn't be just sitting there waiting for her to find it.

"Of course we can, love."

"Where do you think we should look first?" she asked as the group trooped out of the pub and climbed back into Sarie's car.

"We could start at the museum," Emily offered.

The museum was housed in the engine house of the old South Phoenix Mine, the official name being the Minions Heritage Centre. Laurel and Aisling wandered around the building, taking in the exhibits and displays, which consisted mostly of the mining ventures which were the main reason Minions had been established in this lonely spot on the southeastern portion of Bodmin Moor.

"Look, it says here Minions got its name from a barrow which lies just west of the village. It's called Minions Mound. Do you think we should look there?" Aisling read the information off the notice in front of a picture of the barrow.

"I don't know. Do you think it might be the right place? What's a barrow anyway?"

"A barrow is an old underground burial place, usually covered over with turf and containing the remains of warriors and their weapons." Coll spoke up from behind the girls.

"Blimey, Coll. Don't sneak up like that," Aisling exclaimed.

"I suppose we could go and take a look," Laurel said slowly. She really didn't think the barrow was the place she was looking for. But neither was she willing to pass it up, just in case it was important somehow.

"D-d-o you th-th-think we'll have to t-t-talk to gh-gh-ghosts?"

"You can stay outside and guard the door if you like," Aisling assured Gort.

The group left the museum and scrambled back into the car. A short time later, Emily and Sarie dropped them off close to the track leading to the barrow. Emily and Sarie decided to stop at Minions Post Office, which also boasted a tea shop, to gossip and enjoy some hot tea and scones. The little group set off toward the barrow situated a short distance along the track.

"Coll, you go first." Laurel was reluctant to enter the low doorway of the barrow. The granite stone outlining the opening shone silver grey in the morning sun but didn't look at all inviting.

Coll stuck his head and shoulders in the opening and then ducked back into the sunlight. Gort stood a safe distance back from the dark hole, making a great show of admiring the wide sweep of the moor shining in the late morning sun.

"Ya can't really go in, it's all blocked off," Coll said with more than a little relief in his voice.

Laurel kicked a small tuft of grass with her shoe. Now she was at the barrow, she knew it wasn't the place she was supposed to find. Something just didn't feel right or safe to her. Little tingles of electricity ran up and down her spine; her skin felt jumpy and itchy.

"I don't think this is the place. Let's walk back and find Emily and Sarie." She wanted to be gone from the place.

"You're sure you don't want to look around a little, or try to call Gwin Scawen and see what he thinks?" Aisling asked.

"I'm sure, really, really sure," Laurel said emphatically, starting back down the track toward the village.

They met up with Sarie and Emily outside the Post Office. It was almost one o'clock, and they were no closer to finding her final clue than that morning before they left Penzance.

"Why don't we just stay the night at the Piper's Stone?" Emily spoke to Sarie quietly.

"We could at that," Sarie agreed. "It's such a lovely cottage, and it will give Laurel more time to find whatever it is she's looking for."

Sarie went back into the Post Office to ring the owner of the Piper's Stone and make arrangements. The cottage was available for the night as it was still too early in the season for most tourists. In a few minutes, Sarie parked by the beautiful, granite cottage with its leaded glass windows and profusion of flowers blooming around it.

"Oh, it's lovely," Aisling exclaimed. "Do we really get to stay here tonight?"

"It is lovely, isn't it?" Emily said happily. "You girls can take the small room upstairs; Gort and Coll will have to camp out in the lounge on the sofa bed."

"Thank you so much for doing this." Laurel hugged Sarie around the neck. "I'm sorry it's taking so long to find the clue."

"Just so long as you find it. Where do you want to search this afternoon?" Sarie inquired.

"I guess we may as well walk up to the top of Stowe's Hill and check out the Cheesewring rocks," Laurel said.

"M-m-maybe we sh-sh-should look in D-D-Daniel Gumb's c-c-cave," Gort interjected. "I r-r-read about it for school."

"It says here there's a cave on the south side of Stowe's Hill under the Cheesewring." Aisling waved a brochure she picked up from the table in the kitchen. "A man and his family lived there in the nineteenth century. It says he was kind of an odd man and preoccupied with mathematics and geometry. This must be your man Gort; it says his name was Daniel Gumb."

"It seems as good a place as any to start," Coll said.

"Let's go now then." Laurel was anxious to get started.

Sarie drove along the narrow winding roads of Minions out to the small car park on the eastern outskirts. The bulk of Stowe's Hill dominated the horizon, with the odd pile of rocks known as the Cheesewring perched on the edge of the Cheesewring Quarry.

They stopped to read the information sign posted by the head of the track.

"Wow, the top of Stowe's Hill is twelve-hundred and forty-nine feet above sea level. That makes it the highest point in Cornwall." Coll was impressed.

"Sulphur Mountain, back home is just under seven thousand feet above sea level. Me and my mom took the switchback trail to the top once; at least this shouldn't be as hard."

"This is interesting. It says the rock formation got its name from its resemblance to "cheeses" which are cloth bags full of pulped apples cider is pressed from. I wondered how it got its name. Another interpretation is it looks like an old press used to wring the milk out of cheese." Aisling read from the sign.

“C’mon then, let’s go.” Coll started off up the rugged track. “Let’s find the cave.”

It was a short half-mile walk up the track to the stones, and then they scoured the slopes on the south side for the cave.

“The cave’s over here.” Coll’s voice echoed slightly off the granite boulders before it was carried away by the wind.

“Do ya think we should go inside?” Aisling sounded unsure.

“Is it safe do ya think?” Laurel hesitated uncertainly.

“If we’ve gotta go, let’s go now,” Gort said with a show of forced bravery.

“I’m with you on that, mate,” Coll agreed.

They walked carefully into the interior looking about expectantly. Laurel closed her eyes and concentrated on asking for the final clue. There didn’t seem to be any feeling of life or other presences in the cave. Frustrated, she opened her eyes. Aisling was scrounging around at the entrance examining the stones of the doorway. Coll and Gort drifted away to the back of the cave. The light was strong enough Gort appeared to feel comfortable being so far from the door.

Laurel walked aimlessly over to Aisling, and together they left the cave and climbed up onto the flat roof over the doorway. The roof was made from a huge single slab of granite. Looking away across the moor, homesickness stabbed in her belly. The moor was so much like the Alberta prairie—miles and miles of short grass and stubby bushes sweeping beneath the arch of the endless sky.

“Look what you’re standing on.” Aisling squealed in excitement.

“What?”

There were some odd lines and figures scratched or engraved into the rock surface. The girls stood back to get a better look.

“It looks kind of familiar,” Aisling said slowly, “like I should know what it is.” Her voice trailed off as she continued to study the markings.

“Does it look like geometry to you?” The markings weren’t making any kind of sense. Scratched on the silvery grey granite was what looked like a square within a square with two smaller squares on the bottom right and on the bottom of the right side of the original square.

"Hey!" Laurel tipped her head back and spoke to the bright blue sky and golden sun. "Is this what I'm supposed to find? If it is, I need some help 'cause I have no idea what it means."

"I know where I've seen this before." Aisling looked both satisfied and disappointed at the same time. "It's a copy of the Pythagorean Theorem. They mentioned it in the brochure back at the cottage."

"Do you think this is the clue?"

"What do you think? Does it mean anything to you?"

She closed her eyes and concentrated as hard as she could; this had to be the final clue she needed to get on with putting it all together. The harder Laurel tried to make the scratching on the rock mean something, the more it eluded her. Her stomach was sick, and her hands shook with frustration as she clenched them at her sides. Blinking away the tears of frustration, she dropped to her butt on the granite and rested her head on her knees. Dizziness swept over her. The rock moved underneath her.

"All right are 'ee?" Aisling's voice came from a long way away.

"I don't think so." Laurel shook her head and wished she hadn't. "I need to get away from here." Staggering to her feet, she began walking up the hill towards the misshapen pile of rocks at the crest. The further away from Daniel Gumb's cave she got, the better she felt. Aisling hurried after her.

"What happened?" Concern made Aisling's voice shrill.

The sweat on Laurel's face felt cold; her eyes teared, blurring her vision. Aisling caught her hand and pulled her to a halt.

"Did you see something? Was that the clue?"

"No, I just had to get away from there. I don't know where the stupid clue is."

"I'm going to go over to The Hurlers." Aisling indicated the stone circles in the distance with a wave of her hand. "I'm hoping Gwin Scawen will be about and willing to offer us some advice. Do you want to come with me?" Aisling frowned.

"No, I think I'll keep on up to the Cheesewring thing and see what I can find. Will you let Coll and Gort know where we've gone?" Laurel looked up the hill at the imposing bulk of the stones above her head. "I think I'm headed in the right direction, but you go on ahead to the Hurler circles, at least we'll be covering more ground than if we stick together."

"Are you sure you're all right?" Aisling dithered with indecision.

"I'm fine, Ash, really. Once I got away from the cave." She looked back down the slope and shivered. "You reckon Coll and Gort are still in there?"

"I'll check on them before I head to the Hurlers." Aisling headed down the slope and soon disappeared from view.

Stopping at the crest, Laurel spread her arms wide to the wind blowing sharply over the hill. Her hair flew out behind her head; the wind smelled of dry grass and gorse with a touch of saltiness from the sea. Now she was at the top of the hill, Laurel was unsure what to do next.

The odd shaped pile of granite reared itself over her, the main bulk of it supported by what looked like fat stubby legs of smaller rounds of granite. It resembled a short squat giant crouching on the edge of the quarry. Laurel wondered if it ever thought about launching itself into the air.

She walked around the base of the pile. *How can I get up onto the top*? Without hesitating, Laurel put thought into action and began to scale the granite rocks. It was much easier than it looked to reach the flat stone on the top of the pile. *That seemed too easy;* I *should never have been able to climb up here.* She pushed the thought to the back of her mind and stood with her feet apart and gazed over the surrounding countryside.

Gort and Coll emerged from the cave down the slope of the hill and Aisling was standing in the center of one of the stone circles to the north. Laurel squinted against the sun; there was small figure capering about Aisling's legs. It looked like Gwin Scawen showed up to help them after all.

"Now what?"

She sat cross-legged on the sun-warm granite and stroked the silvery surface with her fingers. A lump in the front pocket of her jeans reminded her of the talisman Vear Du gave her. Leaning back a little, she slid her fingers into her pocket and pulled out the talisman, holding it up to the sun. The stone swung in the wind on the end of the leather thong.

Music sounded from the object in her hand. Tinkling, like ice breaking up in a lake before the wind, or crystals on a wind chime. The talisman was no longer a plain stone and cowrie shell on a leather thong, but the glowing crystal and cowrie shell Vear Du gave her in the dream. The chain they were attached to shone silver in the sunlight. Joy and relief flooded through Laurel. *This must be the right place to look for the final clue. Now if only I could figure out where the darn thing is, or even what it is.*

A shadow crossed the surface of the rock blocking the sun for a moment. She looked skyward to see if clouds were blowing in and promptly forgot to breathe. High above her, a huge creature was circling. It descended quickly in tight spirals, coming ever closer.

The creature's short stubby wings didn't seem sufficient to hold the rest of the beast in the air. He had a long neck and a small head attached to a large body with a long tail and stubby legs. Fascinated, Laurel watched it come lower and lower. For all its bulk, the creature moved with a certain gracefulness in the air. The beast was just overhead, and she wondered if she should move and give it more room to land. Its smooth skin was mottled brown and grey. The creature had large expressive eyes, and he dipped his head and winked at her. Clapping her hand over her mouth, she wasn't sure whether to laugh or scream.

The creature landed gently on the granite stone. She felt the stone rock slightly under her. She got to her feet, still holding the shining talisman in her hand. She took a quick step back and almost toppled off the side as something slid down the creature's shoulder and landed in front of her.

Vear Du leaned forward and pulled her back from the edge. The wind blew his dark hair across his face as he grinned at her.

"I thought you were never going to remember to use the talisman," Vear Du said in greeting.

"You're the final clue?"

"Not exactly. Come sit, and we'll talk." Vear Du indicated the sun-warm rock.

"Who's your friend?"

"That's Morg," Vear Du said affectionately.

"And what is a Morg?" The large creature stretched himself out in the sun in the lee of the Cheesewring and, for all intents and purposes, looked like he was going to take a nap.

"Why he's an old friend of mine is Morg."

"But what is he?"

"Morgawr, that's his proper name, is a sea creature descended from the Ancient Ones. He's an immortal like me, or nearly so."

"But, he was flying. How can he fly, if he's supposed to swim in the sea?"

"I don't know. I've never thought to ask him. He just can."

"Oh," said Laurel, studying Morg intently as he slept. His gusty breathing sent little dust devils whirling with each exhalation of his breath.

"Now, back to business, my gold," Vear Du reminded her. "You have a riddle to solve."

"Do you have the final clue for me?"

"So far, you have successfully figured out each step. Next will come the final test of your courage and the strength of your company. You have been to the holed stone once; you must go there again. Only the four of you may go, although you may take the horse friends as a means of transportation." Vear Du's dark eyes smiled warmly with approval.

"Sarie and Emily can't help us this time?"

Vear Du shook his head. "The ones who can grant your miracle are very clear on this point. You and your company must complete this last task on your own. Are you ready for the clue?"

Laurel nodded her head, while the talisman glowed warmly in her fingers, lending her the courage she needed at the moment.

"As I said, you must return to the holed stone. This time as the full moon is rising. When the moon begins to gleam on the horizon, you have to crawl through the hole nine times. You must finish the ninth pass before the moon swings clear of the hills. From there, you go forward as you see fit; the choice will be yours to accept the challenges or reject them. Only you can determine if your miracle will happen. If things go as they should, you will greet the Filly Who Never Was Foaled and embark on your journey. If your company stays true to form, they will accompany you. If not, you must choose if you will journey on alone, or give up your quest." Vear Du looked gravely into her face. "Will you remember these things I tell you?"

"You bet I will. Where is the holed stone? I don't know what stone you mean."

"Think carefully. You have been there. Remember the voice of Belerion." Vear Du took Laurel's cold hand in his large warm one.

"Belerion?"

What does the little salamander have to do with the holed stone? She started in surprise as Morg roused himself from his nap and raised his long snake like neck so his bright eye was even with the top of the Cheesewring. Morg gazed intently at her and gently blew a great gust of breath. His breath smelled salty and slightly fishy, overlaid with the scent of hot dry stone and wild flowers. Shimmering in the air before her was the Men an Tol where they met Gwin Scawen the day of Gort's birthday cream tea at Lanyon Quoit Teahouse. With a small, satisfied snort, Morg shook himself and rose to his feet.

"The Men an Tol! I should have known that. We need to go the Men an Tol at the next full moon. Thank you, Morg. Thank you."

Morg dipped his head in a small bow.

"What am I, chopped liver?" Vear Du cleared his throat and tried to look annoyed.

"I'm sorry, thank you, too." Laurel flung her arms around Vear Du and hugged him tightly.

Morg made a sound remarkably like someone clearing his throat to get attention. Vear Du turned toward him with his arm still around her.

"I know, my friend. It is time we were leaving," Vear Du said ruefully.

"Wait," Laurel cried as Vear Du made to mount Morg once more.

"What is it, little one?"

"Did you know my Gramma Arabella?"

The big Selkie turned a pale shade of grey at the sound of Arabella's name. He looked like someone punched him in the stomach.

"Why do you ask?" Vear Du tried to sound like it was of no consequence.

"You know why," Laurel said quickly. "I found some letters Gramma Bella wrote to Sarie a long time ago, after she left Penzance."

"What did the letters say?" Wearily, Vear Du sat down on the hard granite. His legs didn't seem to want to hold him up anymore.

With an impatient sound, Morg settled himself back down in the sun with his head turned to catch everything being said. Sea monsters do so enjoy a good gossip.

"He'll listen to every word you know; he quite likes his gossip this one." Vear indicated the attentive creature with a resigned wave of his hand.

"Gramma Bella used to meet you out by the bay where I met you. She called it Seal Rock in her letter. She said she loved you. Did you love her back?"

"Aye I did, very much, I still do. Love between humans and Selkies is a complicated thing. By now Bella is older and I…I still look much the same as I did when I met her," Vear Du said sadly. "Your Gramma Bella chose to leave and find a human to love."

"She did not! Her father sent away to Canada and made an arranged marriage for her."

"I never knew that." Vear Du said in a small voice. "Why would she go? She could have moved in with Sarie."

Laurel snorted in exasperation. Selkie or no, Vear Du was as dense as Coll could be sometimes.

"She was pregnant with my father," Laurel shouted at Vear Du. "Didn't you ever think of that?"

"She was what?" Vear Du leaped to his feet. Below them Morg reared up in alarm.

"Didn't you ever ask Sarie why my Gramma left? Didn't you even try to find out?"

"I only saw Sarie once after Bella left. I was afraid to ask her where Bella was gone or why," Vear Du said quietly. Silver tears traced their way down his bronzed cheeks.

"So you're my real Grandfather. If I hadn't come to Cornwall, I never would have known you existed at all."

"That's true, isn't it? You're my granddaughter. And I have a son." A light glowed in Vear Du's dark eyes, and a brilliant smile split his face. "I knew there was something familiar about the feel of you when I realized you were up on the cliff top the day I was caught in that damnable net."

"How will I ever visit you?"

"I'm not sure. Morg and I do have to get going. We have tarried longer than we were supposed to. I think if you use the talisman you can call me, no matter where you are." Vear Du moved toward the edge of the stone where Morg waited for him.

Laurel ran after him and flung herself into his arms. "I'll miss you. I'll try to let you know how everything turns out."

Vear Du seated himself on Morg's neck, just behind his head. Morg made ready to take off when Vear Du raised his hand.

"How is Bella?" His dark eyes were huge and seemed to swallow Laurel.

"She's fine as far as I know. I'm going to go find her as soon as I get home."

"Give her my love," Vear Du said softly and lowered his arm.

Morg launched himself into the air with a whuft of displaced air. Laurel staggered back a few steps and tipped her head back, waving to Vear Du. In a very short time, they were a small dark speck in the wide blue sky. Soon she couldn't even see that.

Laurel scrambled back down the granite rocks to the crest of Stowe's Hill. The little village of Minions was cradled between the hill where she stood and Caradon Hill in the distance. She looked toward the stone circles of the Hurlers; Aisling and Gwin Scawen were nowhere to be seen.

"Laurel." Coll's voice came from below.

"I'm right here."

"Where the bloody hell were you?" Coll huffed as he jogged the last couple of feet to Laurel.

"I was right here on top of the Cheesewring."

"We looked and looked for you. You were nowhere," Gort said slowly. He was looking at her hand.

"What've you got? Is it the clue?" Coll followed Gort's gaze.

Laurel held up the talisman. The crystal still glowed, and the cowrie shell glittered on the shimmering chain. As Coll and Gort watched astonished, the glow faded, and the crystal reverted to the silver grey of granite, and the shimmering silver chain faded back into the leather thong. The talisman still retained a faint warmth as she tucked it back in her pocket.

"No, that's the talisman Vear Du gave me. I do have the final clue though," she said triumphantly.

"What is it?" Aisling broke into the conversation. She joined them on top of the hill. Gwin Scawen capered at her side. Grinning broadly, Gwin bowed, his long nose touching the ground.

"It is most delightful to see you again, Miss Laurel," Gwin Scawen greeted her. "You have found that for which you were searching." Gwin made it a statement, not a question.

"Well, yeah. How do you know that?"

"I saw the great sea horse and the Selkie," Gwin said. He seemed most pleased at the reaction his statement got from Coll and Gort.

"A sea horse," Coll said derisively. "This is the middle of the bloody moor. We're nowhere near the sea."

"Am I wrong?" Gwin Scawen grinned wickedly.

"He's right. Vear Du was here, and he was riding this huge creature. He looked like the Loch Ness Monster, now that I think about it. Only nicer."

"Vear Du was here?" Aisling broke in. "Did he have the last clue?"

"He did. He thought he was making it pretty simple, but I couldn't figure it out. Then Morg, that's the sea horse's name, showed me the answer."

"What do we have to do?" Coll asked.

"We have to go to the Men an Tol at the next full moon. We have to go on our own, without Sarie or Emily. Just us, but we can bring the horses."

"What d-d-do we h-h-have to do once we g-g-get there?" Gort asked.

"I have to crawl through the hole nine times. I have to start just as the moon begins to rise and finish the ninth time through before the moon comes clear of the horizon. Vear Du said I would meet the Filly Who Never Was Foaled."

"Then what happens?" Coll said. It all sounded way too simple.

"It depends on me, on us. We all have to make some kind of choices we won't know about until it happens. I guess we just have to wait and see."

Somberly, the little group made their way back down the hill and followed the track back to the car park in the slanting light of the setting sun. By the time they reached the car park, the sun had set, and the lovely blue glow of the twilight sky burned over them, still offering enough light for them to see Sarie and Emily waiting for them.

"Well, did you get it?" Emily asked.

"We did, but we can't tell you everything," Laurel replied.

"We'll tell you as much as we're allowed," Aisling promised Sarie.

In very short order, they were all gathered around the table in the kitchen of the Piper's Stone Cottage. Over the good dinner Emily prepared for them, Laurel filled Emily and Sarie in on the details she felt they could share. Sarie asked the most questions about Morg. There were many legends and stories about long necked sea monsters being sighted out in Falmouth Bay as well as other places up and down the Cornish coast. She could tell Sarie very much wanted to meet one of them for herself.

* * *

The twilight faded outside the mullioned cottage windows, and true night descended while they talked long into the night. The fire crackled and sputtered; from deep in the golden glow Belerion's bright blue eyes glittered and then disappeared. The seeker was in possession of her final clue, now it was all in her hands. Belerion sent her his blessing.

Chapter Fourteen

Through the Men an Tol

"When's the next full moon?" Laurel muttered, riffling through the calendar on the kitchen table. "Bother and damn, the last full moon was when we were in Glastonbury. The next one won't be 'til near the end of July."

"What are you whingeing about, my heart?" Sarie asked as she came into the bright kitchen from gathering eggs.

"The next full moon isn't until the twenty-first. That's two whole weeks away." She was on the verge of tears.

"We can't hurry the tides or the moon in her dance." Sarie smiled as she hugged her about the shoulders over the back of the chair.

"Does it have to be the full moon?" Laurel leaned back her head resting against Sarie.

"It does, my love. Vear Du was very specific was he not? I don't think anything will happen if you try before the full moon."

"Do you think I could try? Would it screw it up if I tried too early and nothing happened? Do you think it would mean even if we went back when the full moon was rising and did everything right it wouldn't work 'cause we already tried?"

"I don't know, child," Sarie said thoughtfully. "I don't know if it's a one-time only thing or not. Perhaps you could see if Aisling can get a take on it from her little man."

"You think we should ask Gwin Scawen, or maybe Vear Du?"

The more Laurel thought about it, the more she didn't want to see Vear Du. It was all weird now she knew he was her grandfather. All that stuff about Gramma Bella and him, it was very unsettling.

She needed to talk to her mom about it, but it was hard to bring up the subject on the phone. *I wonder if Dad knows who his real dad is.* Maybe that's why he's so crusty about anything to do with magic or fairy stories. Her mom only talked about those kinds of things when her dad wasn't around. *Gramma Bella must have told him who his real dad was though. You would think!* She would be pretty upset if someone knew things about her and didn't say anything. It was all too confusing.

"Laurel! What are you thinking?"

"Sorry, Sarie." She clambered out of the chair. "Is it okay if I call Ash and see if she's talked to Gwin Scawen lately?"

"Of course, just don't be too long. I need some help with the weeding in the herb bed. Come out when you're done with Aisling." Sarie picked up her gardening gloves from the counter by the back door and jammed an old hat on her head as she left the kitchen.

Five minutes later she burst into Sarie's garden. Whooping, she grabbed Sarie in a wild hug. Words fell out of Laurel's mouth too quickly to make any sense. Sarie gave her a small shake.

"Slow down child! What is it that's got you in such a tizzy?"

Laurel took a deep breath and tried to contain her excitement. *This news is just too good.*

"I just rang off with Ash. Emily heard from the authorities, and since Daniel's gone off again, Gort can stay with Emily until the courts decide if he can stay there for good! Can you believe it? Isn't that just the best news ever?"

"Thanks be to the heavens." Sarie's face wrinkled into a huge smile. "That's the best news in a while, innit?"

"I asked Aisling about going to Men an Tol before the full moon. She thinks we should wait and follow the instructions to the letter, but she's going to ask Gwin Scawen when she sees him. I just want to go and get it done. Mom sounded really awful when I talked to her this morning."

"Why'nt we wait and see what Aisling's little man has to say before you go throwing the baby out with the bath water?"

Sarie knelt down beside the bed of basil and started to weed. Laurel sighed and moved over to the patch of rue and dropped to her knees on the springy grass. The sun beat down on the back of her neck; she wished she had thought to bring a hat from the mudroom.

The monotonous task of weeding allowed her mind to work itself around in circles. She wished Gwin Scawen would say it was a good idea to go to the Men an Tol before the full moon. Then she wished he would say no, they needed to wait until the full moon. The whole idea of crawling through the hole in the rock scared the bejeebers out of her. *What'll be on the other side after the ninth time through?* She couldn't deny the existence of magic and things that really shouldn't exist in this world. After all, there was Gwin Scawen, Vear Du, and Belerion. They were certainly magic. What would a horse that hadn't been born yet look like? A horse that hadn't been foaled must be one which hadn't been born yet, but... There was the whole thing about holding death in her hands, what was that supposed to mean? Sweat ran down Laurel's back and stuck her hair to her forehead. The sweat wasn't entirely from the heat of the sun, although she wouldn't have admitted it to anyone.

Laurel finished with the rue and moved on to the patches of mint, peppermint, spearmint, and a type of mint, which actually smelled like chocolate. Who would have thought so many weeds could grow so quickly in the week since they weeded this part of the herb bed? The sun inched its way toward the zenith as she inched her way through the herb garden on her hands and knees, ferreting out the invading weeds. Just when she thought her knees were going to be permanently bent, Sarie straightened up and wiped her face with the sleeve of her shirt.

"That's good for now." Sarie surveyed the neat patches of herbs glowing greenly in the July sun. "Lordy, it's hot, innit?"

"I'm gonna go and wash up. Everyone's coming around one to take the ponies for a ride." Laurel wobbled to her feet and stretched her arms above her head.

"It does seem like it's time for a croust."

"Ash and I thought we'd make a picnic, if it's okay with you." They stowed the weeding baskets and tools in the shed at the foot of the garden.

"Why of course, it's all right, my love. I'll pack up some of the pasties we made the other night."

"Coll loves your pasties the best, but don't tell Emily."

The kitchen felt wonderfully cool when she stepped inside out of the bright sun.

"We'll find something for a sweet as well. We need to put some meat on Gort; the lad's all skin and bones." Sarie threw her a towel from the pile by the washer in the mudroom.

"Ta." Laurel caught the towel and washed up at the kitchen sink while Sarie used the sink in the mudroom.

Just a little over an hour later, they were jogging along the narrow lane north of Sarie's. The thick bramble hedges on either side were fragrant with blossom, and the happy buzzing of the bees filled the sunlit afternoon. She jammed her battered cowboy hat further down on her forehead.

Lamorna tossed her head to dislodge an annoying fly. Arthur snorted to clear his nostrils of the bit of dust stirred by the feet of Aisling and Gort's ponies ahead of them. She couldn't make out what they were talking about. Gort's thin face looked serious as he turned his head to answer something the dark haired girl said.

Laurel tipped her head back and took a deep breath of the soft warm air. The fragrant blossoms mingled with the earthy smell of the grass crushed by the ponies' feet and the dry dirt of the track. As always, there was a slight salty hint of the sea. For the moment, the thought of the upcoming full moon and the trip to the Men an Tol were the farthest thing from her mind. It was so good just to feel Lamorna beneath her and savor the golden afternoon.

"Laurel?"

"Hmmm." She turned her head to meet Coll's eyes.

"What do you mean to do? At the Men an Tol, I mean?" Coll seemed unsure.

"I'm gonna crawl through the hole nine times like they all say I have to."

"But then what," Coll persisted. "What happens next…the whole holding death in your hand thing?"

"How should I know? Nobody's shared that part of it with me."

"Are you planning on taking a knife or something with you?" Coll kept following his line of questioning.

"No. Do you think I need a weapon?"

Coll shrugged and looked away. "There's just the whole death thing. What if it's dangerous for you? How are the rest of us supposed to protect you?" She watched Coll twist Arthur's coarse black mane in his fingers.

"I'm not sure a knife is a good thing, unless maybe it's made of silver."

“Maybe we should ask Old Joseph if we can borrow his blackthorn walking stick,” Coll suggested. “You know the one you bashed Stuart with.”

“I guess we could. If you really think we need to. My dad always says you have to be careful about carrying a weapon because whoever you’re trying to protect yourself from could use it against you.”

“I s’pose.”

Her answer caught in her throat as Lamorna came to a sudden halt. Lamorna’s nose was only inches away from Gareth’s sturdy hind end. Gort and Aisling were stopped in the middle of the track and sitting half turned in the saddle waiting for them.

“It’s a good thing ‘Morna’s got brakes.” Amusement sparked in Gort’s eyes. “We thought you were gonna bash right into us.”

“Anything you care to share?” Aisling asked.

“Let’s talk about it while we picnic. Are we almost there yet?” Laurel said.

“We can cut across the field here and picnic by the bend in the stream.” Aisling waved her arm in the general direction of a small valley visible through a break in the brambles.

The ponies pushed through the narrow opening single file. Coll uttered some foul words as the brambles caught in his shirt and almost pulled him off Arthur. She managed to get through only snagging her hair once. Gort and Aisling came through unscathed much to Coll’s disgust. Grunting, Coll put Arthur into a canter and headed off down the narrow grassy path towards the stream. Aisling laughed and followed him on Ebony, leaving a trail of golden dust hanging in the still afternoon air. Gort brought Gareth up even with Lamorna, and they meandered quietly after Coll and Aisling.

“What were you and Ash talking about back there?”

“You,” Gort said, “and the M-M-Men an T-T-Tol.”

“What about it?” She hoped Gort and Aisling hadn’t changed their minds about helping her, although she could hardly blame them if they did.

“I d-d-don’t know how I can h-h-help. How am I s-s-supposed to know what to d-d-do?” Gort’s forehead wrinkled in distress. “I w-w-want to h-h-help.”

"I don't know what I'm supposed to do either, Gort. Other than crawl through the darned thing. I'm scared half to death thinking what if it doesn't work and what if it does."

"R-r-really…you always s-s-seem to b-b-be so sure that this is wh-wh-what will m-m-make your mum better."

"I have to believe, or I'll just crawl into a corner and cry." Laurel blinked back her unshed tears.

"Ash says th-th-that we'll know wh-wh-what we n-n-need to d-d-do when the t-t-time comes."

"Did Aisling say if she'd had a chance to talk to Gwin Scawen?"

Gort shook his head. "I didn't a-a-ask her."

Gareth lifted his head and whinnied for Ebony and Arthur, who disappeared into the green folds of the small valley. Laurel grinned at Gort, and they let their ponies break into a canter.

By the time they caught up with Aisling and Coll, the picnic was unpacked and waiting for them in the shade of the trees overhanging a small pool formed by a bend in the stream. The sunlight filtered through the leafy branches falling in golden strands onto the grass.

In very short order, the ponies were taken care of, and they all settled down on the grass. It was quiet in the glade except for the sound of the stream and the ponies' teeth tearing at the grass. The picnic Sarie prepared disappeared in record time. Coll lay back on the grass with a sigh.

"Those are the best pasties ever," Coll said contentedly.

"You best not let Emily hear you," Aisling teased him.

"'Course not." Coll opened one eye and grinned at Aisling.

"Did you talk to Gwin Scawen?" Gort didn't stutter as he spoke with his mouth full of oatmeal raisin cookie.

"I saw him this morning. He had to scamper though; my mum almost caught me talking to him," Aisling said.

"Did you get a chance to ask him about the full moon thing?" Laurel asked anxiously.

"First off, he said he thought you should wait for the full moon. He muttered something about the *big ones* not liking it when *us ones* don't follow direction. I didn't get a chance to ask anything else 'cause my mum showed up."

"Huh," Laurel said disgustedly. "The full moon is two weeks away."

"We'll just have to wait and use the time to figure out what we need to bring with us." Aisling patted her arm.

"I think we should take a weapon or something," Coll said.

"Are you sure that's a good idea?" Aisling cautioned.

"Coll thinks we should borrow Old Joseph's blackthorn stick."

"The Stuart basher," Gort said with satisfaction.

"Oh, that reminds me. I saw Stuart and his sister this morning in the high street, and he was actually civil to me," Aisling said.

Coll snorted loudly and sat up to snag another cookie from the bag on the grass. "The sun must have risen in the west then this morning," he said derisively.

"No, seriously, I think Stuart was actually trying to be nice," Aisling said with puzzlement in her voice.

"Maybe we should give him the benefit of the doubt," Laurel said. "Maybe he's finally figured out there's more to life than beating on someone."

"Can if you want. Me, I'm gonna keep my guard up, just in case, like," Coll said.

Gort said nothing. He just sat with his face all creased up with thought.

"I still reckon we need to talk about how to protect Laurel at the stone." Coll returned to their earlier conversation.

"I don't believe I'm gonna need protection. I have Vear Du's talisman, and I'll make sure I have it in my pocket the whole time."

"That's a pretty strong protection, innit?" Gort spoke quickly.

"I think so, too, you," Aisling agreed.

"I still want something, you know, bigger," Coll persisted.

"You should only carry the protection of your convictions," Gwin Scawen said, stepping into a strand of sunlight by the stream.

"Bloody Hell," Coll swore as he leapt to his feet.

Gort swallowed loudly and fixed his eyes on Gwin Scawen as he strode purposefully across the grass. Laurel smiled at him in welcome. Aisling extended her hand to Gwin as he scrambled into her lap.

"Do sit down, Coll," Aisling said mildly.

“We don’t need to take weapons, do we?” Laurel addressed Gwin Scawen.

“It would be a grave mistake to go bearing instruments of aggression,” Gwin Scawen said, after he polished off a bit pastie he found in the folds of Aisling’s trousers.

“How’re we supposed to protect her then? Little rough with nothing to hand, innit?” Coll blurted out belligerently.

“There is a time for physical protection, I agree,” said Gwin Scawen looking at Gort. “However, she will require the protection of your company and the quality of the conviction in your hearts to accompany her into the Otherworld.”

“We have to go to outer space or something?” Coll clearly wasn’t sure exactly what the little brown man meant.

“No, you only need go through the mist into the world parallel to this every-day one.” Gwin spoke, holding Coll’s eyes with his own.

“Is it where the Filly that Never Was Foaled is, the one I need to meet?” Finally, someone to ask about the questions banging around in her head.

“She is there, yes. She will come partway into this world to help you on your journey, and you others as well.” He nodded at Coll, Gort, and Aisling.

“Wh-wh-what if I’m t-t-too scared to follow her?” Gort said. Sweat shone on his forehead, and his hands trembled.

“It is the desire in your heart that counts. If what you truly wish is to go and help her in whatever way you can, then the fear clouding your mind won’t stop you. The desire must be stronger than the fear, or you must stay behind and guard the stone for their return.” Gwin Scawen slid down from Aisling’s lap.

“How will I know what to do?” Laurel asked.

“Cease worrying about what you will do and what choice you will make. You know you must go through the hole nine times at moonrise on the night of the full moon. When the choice or decision is before you, the best course of action will be clear to you.” Gwin Scawen stood by her knee and rested his gnarled brown hand on her leg. “Remember to carry Vear Du’s talisman with you. If you must relinquish it to the Guardian for his scrutiny, be sure to bargain for its immediate return to you before you let it leave your hand.”

She nodded her agreement. Suddenly, Gwin lifted his head and looked to the west.

"I must away now. Heed my words well, Little Seeker," Gwin spoke. "I will see you this evening, will I not?" Gwin Scawen addressed Aisling.

"By the stones, are the others coming?"

"To be sure, tonight we dance and sing and celebrate!"

Gwin Scawen stepped into a strand of sunlight and winked out of sight.

"Damn me, I hate it when he does that." Coll rubbed the back of his neck.

"C'mon, it's getting late." Aisling gathered up the remains of the picnic and stowed them in the pouch on Ebony's saddle.

Laurel turned Lamorna's nose up the path out of the clearing by the stream. The closer the full moon got, the further away it seemed. A part of her was glad it was still a couple of weeks away, the part of her that woke her up in the middle of the night drenched in sweat and breathing hard.

She wasn't sure it was a good idea for her friends to come with her. What if she was required to die or go with death, or whatever the whole hold death in her hands thing meant? She knew she couldn't allow the others to die because of her. Saving her mom was Laurel's problem, not theirs. At any rate, four lives for the price of one was a poor bargain.

There was no way of stopping Coll, Gort, and Aisling from coming to the Men an Tol with her. She did think she could she could manage to leave them at the stone after the ninth time through. Gort was so scared and Coll was too, in spite of his big talk. Aisling was the only one who seemed comfortable with the concept of the parallel world Gwin Scawen talked about.

Laurel rejected the idea of Aisling coming with her after some consideration. *What would Gort do without Aisling? And what would Aisling's crazy mother do if Aisling disappeared, or was found dead out on the moor?* All hell would break loose, and Emily, Sarie, Coll, and Gort would suffer for it. *The best thing to do is to go with the horse lady alone, if the horse shows up at all.* Now she had a sort of plan, and it was good to know no matter what happened her friends would be safe.

* * *

The next two weeks passed too slowly for Laurel. Her mind was set on a course of action, and she just wanted it to be over and done with. She ignored Aisling's efforts to discuss what she wanted to do after she crawled through the Men an Tol and just kept saying she didn't know. Fear crawled up Laurel's spine whenever she thought about the upcoming full moon. It would be too easy to confide in Ash, let Aisling talk her out of going on her own. She spent a lot time talking to Lamorna; the big black pony was a willing listener, and best of all, the horse couldn't tell anyone what she knew.

* * *

Finally, the evening of the full moon came around. Laurel talked to her mom twice on the phone; she sounded so tired and far away. It seemed her mom was using all her strength just to keep her soul in her body. Dad relented and promised if Mom wasn't feeling a lot better in a couple of days, Laurel could come home and be with her. The fact her dad was agreeing to bring her home scared her more than anything else so far. *Mom must be really weak.* Laurel went with Sarie to pick up Emily, Coll, Gort, and Aisling, late in the afternoon. After a light supper of soup and toast, the four friends left Sarie and Emily drinking tea in the kitchen, while they went out to get the ponies ready for their ride to the Men an Tol.

"I wish Sarie and Emily could come with us," Aisling said. Ebony turned her large head and nudged Aisling in agreement.

"Me too, but we have to go on our own."

"I think Sarie and Gramma are planning to come out in the car after the moon is up. I heard Gramma talking to Sarie when she thought I wasn't listening." Coll slipped Arthur's bridle over the pony's ears.

"Th-th-that's not s-s-such a b-b-ad thing. Wh-wh-what would happen to the p-p-ponies if we don't c-c-come back?" Gort stroked Gareth's wide forehead.

“As long as they don’t show up before the moon does,” Laurel said absently.

She toyed with the idea of asking Sarie and Emily to come in time to stop the others from coming with her. But that would break the stupid rules she agreed to. Laurel figured she would just have to give them the slip while she crawled through the stone. She would just wing it as the situation developed. Her mind wouldn’t stay focused long enough for her to formulate any kind of real plan.

The sun was just sinking below the western horizon as they swung up on the ponies outside Sarie’s cottage. Emily and Sarie stood in the yard to see them off.

“Good Luck and God Speed.” A worried frown marred Emily’s features. “Stay safe,” she added, gazing on Coll and then Gort’s slight figure.

“Take care of my ponies, you,” Sarie said gruffly.

“I will,” Laurel promised. “Thank you for everything, Sarie.” She wanted to be sure Sarie knew how grateful she was for the loan of the ponies and getting to stay with her. Just in case.

“Go on with ya. I’ll see you before moon set.” Sarie flapped her hand.

The last light of the sun illuminated the small cottage and barn, laying long shadows across the garden. Gathering up Lamorna’s reins, Laurel lifted her hand in farewell and started down the lane. The others filed after her in the gathering dusk, the reflective tape on their stirrups and bridles shining in the dark.

Crickets sang, and the first calls of the night birds echoed across the fields. The shadows gathered faster in the narrow lane between the thick brambly hedges. Laurel was glad once they were out on the open moor where the twilight lingered much longer. The faint twilight continued to fade as the little group silently made their way toward the Men an Tol. The first stars of the evening were sparking in the night blue sky before anyone spoke.

“You’re sure ya want to do this?” Coll tried one more time to talk her out of it.

“You know I have to,” Laurel said quietly. “You guys go back if you want. I would really feel better if you did, actually.”

“You’re not getting rid of us that easily,” Aisling said stoutly. “We promised to come with you, and we will.”

“M-m-me too,” Gort chimed in. His face was paler than usual even in the starlight.

Coll grumbled under his breath as he turned to look across the starlit moor in the direction of the holed stone. Unlike the last time they visited, the night lay quiet and tranquil around them. The twilight deepened to night, more stars appearing in the clear sky. Mist began to gather in the hollows and along the low stone wall. It drifted across the track as they rode along; soon it swirled in waves around the ponies’ legs. Aisling checked her watch with the torch she took out of her jacket pocket.

“We have about twenty minutes before the moon should start to come up,” Aisling said quietly as they rode side by side.

“Thanks, Ash. You don’t have to do this, you know. I can do it alone.” She reached over and squeezed Aisling’s hand as she spoke.

“No more of that now,” Aisling admonished her. “We’re coming and that’s that.”

There was a luminous glow on the horizon heralding the coming of the moon when Laurel slid down from Lamorna’s back. Around her, she could hear the rest of them dismounting as well. It was hard to make anything out clearly; the mist was thickening, and the sky was still lit only by the stars. The glow on the horizon strengthened while they removed the tack from the ponies. The ponies wouldn’t stray far from where they were. Sarie and Emily would come and fetch them if Laurel and her friends didn’t come back. She still hadn’t figured out how to leave the rest of them behind. At the moment, she was too scared to think about anything except her mom. Aisling appeared out of the mist on her left, and Coll and Gort came up on the right.

“Right then; it’s time,” Coll said.

Holding hands, the four friends walked through the mist toward the low stones. Coll’s hand shook in hers. Laurel tightened her fingers around his, as much to keep her own from shaking as to comfort Coll. The rise where the Men an Tol stood was clear of mist as they arrived; around them, the vapors formed a circle rising higher than their heads. Above them, the sky was clear and bright. Aisling checked her watch again. It was hard to see the horizon for the thick mist, but mist or no, the moon was beginning to rise.

“I think you should start now,” Aisling said softly. She hugged her tightly. “Good luck, you.”

Laurel’s fingers closed around Vear Du’s talisman, and she sent a prayer out into the night. *This has to work. It has to make Mom get better. I don’t care what it costs me.*

She smiled at Gort and Coll before squatting down in front of the hole and peering through.

“Does it matter which way I go through?” *Why didn’t we think to ask that particular question before now?*

“Go sun-wise, east to west, I think.” Aisling sounded worried.

“Okay, here goes nothing.” Her voice broke.

Before she could chicken out and run screaming into the mist, Laurel stuck her head into the hole. She wriggled through and landed in a heap on the dirt and grass on the other side. Nothing felt any different, nothing looked any different. Well maybe the mist was a little thicker and beginning to glow as the moon started to peep over the horizon. She repeated the process while Coll, Gort, and Aisling watched anxiously. Laurel could tell Coll was seriously creeped out and probably wishing he borrowed Old Joseph’s blackthorn cane. Gort trembled, looking like he wanted to be sick. Aisling watched the hole intently and monitored the growing light of the rising moon.

“One more time, this is the ninth time through,” Aisling said encouragingly.

Chapter Fifteen

Riding The Filly

Laurel finished crawling through the hole in the Men an Tol for the eighth time. Scratched and dusty, she looked up her friends.

"Does anything look different to you?" she asked, it being difficult for her to judge from her position on the ground.

"Bloody hell," Coll whispered in awe.

There was a strange light coming from the sky above the stone; it was gold and silver, sunlight and moonlight together; suddenly it was neither day nor night, even though the full moon was clearly starting to show itself above the horizon.

A bright light bathed her as she made the final turn around the stone and crawled through for the ninth time. The gold and silver light intensified, blinding the little circle of friends surrounding the dolmen.

"Hold on to her," Aisling cried in a voice somehow larger and brighter than her own.

Laurel felt them take a hold of her as she slid through the hole in Men an Tol for the last time. Light flared again…the four friends were above the moor looking down at the stone.

It stood in two worlds—the one she was born into and another marvelous one, somehow familiar even though she had never been really aware of it before. Liquid lines of pure light crisscrossed the land, pinpointed by brighter spots where the lines met or crossed each other. Many of the landmarks they knew as ancient stone works were situated right where the lines crossed.

The line coming out of the sea from Brittany shone clearly at St. Michael's Mount on the edge of Mount's Bay. It was a different color than the rest, more blue and silver. It pulled at her, so she followed its path with her eyes, and her heart reached out for it with her inner strength. *A Dragon Line, the path we've been seeking.*

She looked around the circle of her friends; all of them returned her gaze with shining eyes and expressions of profound joy. Holding hands still, they began to follow the line of light as it led them up country, the whole of Cornwall spread out before them. Indeed the whole of England and the world was laid out before them if they cared to look.

Laurel never experienced such pure joy before; the light buoyed and carried her safely through the heavens. The full moon shone so brightly she could see each blade of grass, each leaf on the trees. She was part of the luminescence; she looked in wonder at her friends; they seemed to glow with their own inner light.

I wonder if people think we're comets?

The whimsical thought crossed her mind before she turned her attention to the line of light they were following. It went straight across the land—twined with it was another softer line of light flowing the same direction but wound around the brighter line. It looked like the serpents wound around the staff thing on all the doctors' medical certificates. She'd spent enough time in waiting rooms staring at them while waiting for her parents to come back. *A serpent, a dragon, they're a lot alike...*

She knew she was seeing the living Michael ley line Sarie talked about and the softer line twining it was the Mary line. Where the two lines met, there was a flaring of brighter light, St. Michael's Mount, St. Michael's Brentnor, Hurler's Stone Circle and Burrowbridge Mump, the Tor at Glastonbury, and on to Avebury and Hopton St. Mary's in East Anglia.

There was a lessening in speed as they approached Burrowbridge Mump and a swelling of the music, which accompanied them on their journey from the Men an Tol. The light around Glastonbury Tor was becoming brighter; it pulled on her breastbone so intensely she ached.

Out of the light came living crystal horses, more beautiful than anything Laurel had ever seen. The crystal was all colors and clear at the same time. The colors pulsed through the horses and emanated from them as well. On their backs were knights, clad in crystal armor shining with all the glory of the moon and stars, backlit by the golden glow of the sun.

She realized she should be afraid, and on some level of her consciousness, she was terrified. Somehow it all seemed too wonderful in this moment to worry about it. She looked at her friends and saw the same awe and glory reflected on their faces. Laurel and her friends floated motionless, waiting as the horses approached them.

Below them, a thorn tree bloomed white and shining in the moonlight. The first knight and horse came toward them using the stars as stepping stones. He bowed his head and reached out a crystal gauntlet.

She must be careful what she did, think before she acted. Sarie explained Faery was very different from human; they did not think in the same patterns and stood much on ceremony. This was the answer she asked for, a way to help her mom; she couldn't turn aside now and besides it was all too glorious not see it through to the end. *Are the horses warm, or cold like ice?* Holding her purpose firm in her heart, Laurel reached out her hand and placed it in the crystal gauntlet of the knight.

"Welcome, little one." The voice was kindly and terrible at the same time.

She inclined her head in acknowledgement but couldn't take her eyes from the rider-less crystal horse following him. The horse came forward and stopped in front of her. The horse's mane flowed like water in the small wind from the stars. The eyes, no *her* eyes, were wells of light revealing glorious vistas: the land of Cornwall, all of the world, including her own little part of Alberta, and her beloved prairie.

Laurel was startled to see the lines of light continued through the oceans. They connected everything through the bones of the earth. *How wonderful; how totally amazing.*

The Crystal Mare shook her head and blinked. Although there was plenty of the wondrous light, there were also dark areas where the lines were disrupted, and horrid putrid colors muddied the crystal. The darkness was fascinating in its own right, red pulsed there, the dark red of power and domination.

"Come to me," it whispered. *"I can give your heart's desire, but first I require your heart."*

The darkness hiding in Laurel's heart, as it does in all humans, reared its head and listened. There was a blackness shot through with a diamond green.

"Listen to me; come to me," it whispered, adding its voice to the sibilant tones of the dark red. *"I can heal, or I can destroy, but you can choose. I only require one of your friends in exchange for your mother."*

The Crystal Mare continued to watch. Laurel was aware of her presence outside the voices in her mind. She shook her head to stop them and shouted as loudly as she could.

"Get out of my head. I want no part of you. Get out; get out; get out!"

The great Mare shook her mane once more. The voices faded though the discordant colors still fouled the brightness of the lines in places as she traced them around the world and back to herself in the heavens high over the stones of the ancients. The crystal nose pushed Laurel.

"What are you waiting for?"

She gazed into the Mare's eyes in bewilderment. "What do you mean?"

The Crystal Mare raised her head, her mane flowing with rainbow light. The full moon was cradled between the large ears. The horse glowed brighter, and strange music filled the air.

"I am the Filly that Never was Foaled," the Mare intoned. The sound vibrated in the air; the stones of the earth shivered with power. *"I believe you were looking for me?"* Humor tinged the Mare's voice mingling with the power.

Never in her wildest imaginings did she ever envision this! Her hand shook as she reached out to touch the strands of hair in the Mare's mane; her fingers tingled with electricity.

"How can I ride you?" Laurel whispered, the fathomless eyes inches from her own.

"I will carry you Little Seeker; you only have to agree willingly to accept my offer," the Mare said with grave dignity. *"It is a bargain between only you and myself."*

"You can make Mom better?"

"I can take you to those who can. I myself don't have the power to grant your desire."

There were beings more powerful and magnificent than this living crystal being in front of her? Laurel wasn't sure she was ready to meet them. It was hard to be near such beauty. It actually hurt with a physical ache. The thought of her mom fighting for her life in Calgary straightened her back. If Mom could stand the chemotherapy and radiation, Laurel guessed the least she could do was see this riddle through to the end. She looked the Crystal Mare straight in her magnificent, terrible eyes.

"Let's go," she said.

The Mare tossed her head at the crystal knight. Some communication passed between them, because the crystal knight lifted Laurel up onto the broad back. The Mare shifted under her seat, and she was amazed at how much like a real horse she felt.

"You won't fall no matter what happens. Remember that," the Mare commanded.

Laurel looked for her friends; they were all seated behind other knights of the company. Fear and awe filled their faces. The Mare was suddenly flying at a high speed along the sparkling, opalescent path of power snaking along the earth below them. There was no wind, only the crackle of star fire. The stars burned brighter as the horse danced along the path they made in the moonlit skies.

Laurel was lost in the brilliant patterns of the flowing, living lines of the earth beneath her. It was all too beautiful to be scared, although on some level her common sense screamed in protest. The world spread before her was layered with choices affecting the past, present, and future. All the possibilities of all choices—if this person chose to end their life and step onto another wheel, then the future and children they would have, slid to another layer, all the endless possibilities waiting for decisions to make them a reality.

There are so many possibilities, so many threads waiting to be woven into the weft of our lives.

Her gaze followed the shining earth lines below her as they drew the Crystal Horses over the Tor of Avalon. She looked at the high egg-shaped hill below her and knew she was back in her own head again. The great Mare reached backward and touched Laurel with her nose.

"You'll do." The melodious words in her inner ear were accompanied by the music she could always hear in the back of her mind.

Laurel glanced at her friends' faces as the other knights gathered about them in the moonlit velvet black brilliance of the night. All eyes were turned to her and the Mare.

Except for Gort. He was looking at the leader of Crystal Knights with naked longing on his face. The knight did the most curious thing; he dipped his head to Gort in recognition and respect. Gort's eyes widened even further as a most beatific smile spread across his features and bent his own head in return.

Before Laurel could wonder about the exchange, the Mare turned her head and descended toward the Tor. The rest of the crystal company followed in a bright comet trail behind them. *Are they meant to protect us, or to keep us from running away?*

All other thoughts fled from her mind as she watched the terraced hill coming closer. The horses moved with a sound of bells chiming when their hooves lifted and fell in the midnight air. The company circled down toward the hill, following the path of spiraling streams of light, which joined at the summit.

Light spiraled out of the earth into the heavens and out of the heavens into the earth. Each spiral balanced the other in the dance, colors and power joining and intermingling while still maintaining their own integrity. No matter what happened after this, she would never be the same, she would always seek to find this perfect point of balance, light and dark, good and evil, birth and death. It was such an old mystery and truth, hidden in plain sight for anyone to see it.

Laurel thought they would end up at the tower on the apex of the Tor where she tried to find shelter during the storm at summer solstice.

"Ah, but it was here and sacred long before the Christians took it for theirs." The bell-like voice sounded in her ears. The great Mare turned her head. *"Trust in the light within you, in what you know to be true,"* she said enigmatically and turned her head forward once more.

What is that supposed to mean? She watched the silver crystal wonder of the movement of the Mare's mane as it flowed.

The knight on the crystal stallion in front drew his sword from the scabbard. Sparkling trails of light flew from it like snow. A great sound of cosmic winds ringing with harp strings and bells accompanied his action; all the knights behind them did the same.

Laurel forced herself to concentrate on where they were She didn't want to be so distracted by the show of arms she didn't pay attention to where they were going.

"Look below." The Mare read her thoughts. *"See the Druid's Stones; the Living Rock marks the entrance to the mystery path encircling our home. You can walk it anytime you wish to visit us."*

Laurel looked down, on the southwest side of the Tor directly on the line of light stretching back to the Men an Tol; she saw the Stones and the faint silvery line of the path of the Tor labyrinth. The path glowed with the magic of the ancients and the land itself, leading both inward and outward at the same time echoing the spiral paths of light.

"*Thank you."* Without thinking, Laurel spoke mind to mind.

"You are very welcome, child."

We're going to go right into the hill! Fear warred with excitement, and Laurel wrapped her fingers more tightly into the glowing mane clenched in her fist.

The knight in the lead stopped on the southern flank of the Tor. In front of him, a large egg shaped stone protruded from the hill. The shape looked like the head of a seal. *This must be the guardian Vear Du spoke about.*

The Crystal Mare whinnied loudly; the knight raised his sword towards the moon where it swam in the velvet sky above the Tor and shouted words in a strange language. The music that accompanied them from the Men an Tol swelled again; the seal shaped stone moved. The Stone opened his eyes; Laurel felt his touch in her mind as he accepted her before turning his gaze on each of her friends.

His mouth appeared along a fault in the Stone, his voice the raspy sound of stones grinding and rocks rolling in a swollen river.

"You have something to show me?"

What could she possible have to interest the guardian? The moon's brilliance faded for a heartbeat, and Laurel heard Vear Du's voice soft in her ear.

'The Guardian will require a token to allow mortals to enter. Show him the talisman I have given you. It will be his choice to either keep it in payment, or return it to you. Remember to ask for its return. Either way, he should allow your company to pass.'

She dug in her pocket and closed her fingers around the slate blue stone.

"I want this back when I leave."

The stony lips moved in what could have been a smile, the head wobbled slightly in agreement.

She pulled the talisman out and offered it to the stone seal. The seal's mouth opened further, Laurel placed Vear Du's talisman into the open maw. She could have sworn she saw a stone tongue lick the talisman, tasting it. The stone jaws closed, and the stone eyes turned inward for what might have been a second or an hour.

The seal focused his eyes on Laurel again, and his lips curved impossibly into a stony smile. He opened his mouth and barked three times. With much grinding and groaning, the stone seal shifted aside to allow them to pass into the Tor. Swallowing hard and closing her eyes, she approached the solid wall of earth behind the Stone. There was a small pressure like wind against her body and a whufting sound of displaced air. Laurel opened her eyes a crack to see where they were. Still holding hands, she saw Coll and Aisling and Gort.

The only one with his eyes wide open was Gort; he stood with his hand resting on the shoulder of the crystal horse nearest him. It wasn't saddled and seemed younger than the rest of the company, and there didn't appear to be a knight attached to it.

"Bloody Hell," Coll whispered in awe, "the stories are true. We're inside the bleeding hill!"

Aisling was talking to herself. "It all makes sense now…the inner is the outer, and the outer is the inner. The only separation is the one we make ourselves."

Laurel stood where she was, the great Crystal Mare beside her. She was waiting for something she wasn't sure what, but she knew there was more than all this wonder. She needed an ending for her quest, an answer to her wish, a lasting healing for her mother.

The great Mare pushed her forward with her nose. Laurel could feel her breath, reassuringly warm on her shoulder blades. For the first time, she took in her surroundings. It was a large cavern with many entrances and exits. Music wove softly through everything, the quiet music, which echoes a heartbeat in the still of the night, always there in the quiet places of your soul waiting to be acknowledged.

The cave was bright with light; for all it was deep inside the earth. Crystal shimmered from the ceiling, and the walls were streaked with pink quartz and black obsidian, all the colors of the bones of the earth. This was a birthplace, a birthplace of magic, wonder and awe, but also chaos, despair, and grief.

"Balance," she whispered, "the sacred balance Sarie talked about." Everything separate but a part of the whole.

A man appeared without her seeing how he got there. *"Welcome, Daughter of Eve. I am Gwynn ap Nudd."* He pronounced his name Gwin ap Neeth.

"Light, Son of Dark," the Crystal Mare translated.

The tall figure dressed all in black turned his gaze on the Mare. *"What is your stake in this, Mare?"* he asked with a dangerous edge in his voice.

"I am the guardian for the Great Mother, as you know, and this Daughter of Eve has business with Her." The words vibrated.

"It seems to me," Gwynn ap Nudd replied, *"she seeks an answer for Death. Which is definitely my field of expertise, wouldn't you agree?"*

The Mare sighed softly. *"Perhaps, but the questions she asks concerns one who has not yet been claimed, and so does not yet wait for The Wild Hunt to bring her home."*

"Do you mean my mom?" Laurel couldn't stand it any longer, the two of them talking about her as if she wasn't standing here listening.

Gwynn ap Nudd looked from Laurel to the Mare. *"Are you interfering again?"* he asked darkly.

The Mare shook her head sending particles of color floating about her. *"She has learned to hear us on her own—surely that should tell you something."*

Gwynn ap Nudd regarded her thoughtfully; she returned his gaze without flinching. If he could help her mother get better, Laurel was all for listening to what he had to say.

"A bargain perhaps," he mused. *"But it must mean something; it must be a sacrifice."*

"What do you want?"

She heard Coll behind her somewhere. "Remember, be careful what you agree to; spell it out. Remember!"

* * *

Coll couldn't see what Laurel was looking at; she was conversing with thin air near as he could tell. The giant crystal horse stood behind her and seemed to be supporting and protecting her. All Coll could hear was the chiming of bells and a sort of buzzing sound in the air.

Bloody Hell, he thought, *I hope there's not some bloody great bee's nest down here.* He hated bees.

Coll saw Aisling deep in conversation with a group of small dark people. She appeared mesmerized by what they were saying. He could hear a little of the conversation, something about secret paths that existed if you knew where to look and mysteries hidden in plain view.

He looked for Gort and found him at the far side of the cavern, standing close to one of the crystal horses. The horse lifted his head and looked right at the slender boy, some communication seemed to pass between the two. The light around them wavered, and the floor of the cave rocked under Coll's feet for a fleeting second.

Gort raised his hand and rested it on the horse's shoulder. Tears ran unchecked down his face. The boy and horse stepped closer to each other, and the stallion rested his head against Gort's.

* * *

"What do you want?" Laurel asked Gwynn ap Nudd impatiently.

"So quick to want a bargain. This should prove most interesting."

"Remember she is under the protection of the Great Mother," the Mare spoke.

"Yet she still has freedom of choice, does she not?" Gwynn ap Nudd addressed the Mare.

"She does," the Mare agreed with reluctance and misgivings.

"Talk to *me*," Laurel shouted, totally losing her patience. She was tired of these two talking about her like she wasn't there with no thoughts of her own.

"I forget she can hear us," Gwynn ap Nudd muttered. *"Most tiresome."*

"Deal with it. What do you want? I'm beginning to think you're bluffing, and you have nothing I want," Laurel told Gwynn ap Nudd boldly. She figured the best defense was a good offense, that's what Dad said about hockey strategy anyway.

Gwynn's eyes narrowed. *"Nothing you want, Daughter of Eve?"* he asked softly. *"You come here to bargain for your mother's life, and you can still suggest I have nothing you want?"*

Oh shoot, now I've made him angry.

"That you have," the Mare agreed. *"But I'm not so sure it's a bad thing."*

How does he know what I want to ask? Is it him I've been talking to when I sensed the presence of something sacred at the Men an Tol the first time I was there? Her heart told her it couldn't be so; the presence felt so decidedly female. *Can Gwynn ap Nudd be male and female as he chooses?* Panic clawed at her throat. *I'm in way too far; I don't know enough about Faery, or wherever this place is. What if I make it worse?*

Her thoughts ran round and round in her head; her heart raced and sweat broke out on her skin. A calming influence touched her mind as the Mare poked her with her nose.

"Find the center and be still," the Mare advised.

Grasping the tendril of thought she followed it down into the seething mass of her fear. Followed it down and passed through it to the stillness inside her. She forced herself to breathe in and out, to calm the wail of her thoughts, to think clearly once more. Laurel sent a rush of gratitude to the Mare who stood so stalwartly behind her.

"That is what you want, is it not Daughter of Eve, to make a bargain to save your mother?" Gwynn ap Nudd asked.

Laurel cleared her throat. "Not exactly a bargain, I don't think. I want magic to make Mom better, but I don't think you'll do that."

"Everything has its price," he answered her. *"The question is—are you willing to pay the price?"*

"You can make my mom better, so she and my dad can live a long, happy life together?"

"Is that your bargain," Gwynn ap Nudd asked with a small smile. *"No other conditions?"*

"Let me think," she told Gwynn to buy some time.

Gwynn ap Nudd fixed the Mare with an odd stare. *"No interference from you, this is her free will, freedom of choice and all that."*

The Mare nodded her head reluctantly.

Laurel's mind whirled. *Mom can get better. There is hope; all I have to do is make this deal.* Somewhere at the back of her mind was a niggling thought she was missing something important. *It doesn't matter, as long as Mom gets better and stays that way. Dad will be so happy.*

"That's what I want out of the bargain."

The Mare stamped, obviously unhappily. Laurel couldn't think what she might have forgotten to stipulate, and at any rate, Gwynn ap Nudd was correct. It was her bargain to make.

Gwynn ap Nudd seemed to grow larger and darker; he smiled, and it swallowed some of the light in the crystal cavern.

"Then I will take your life in exchange for hers, Daughter of Eve," he told her. Before she could disagree, he waved his hands in an intricate pattern and spoke words in the same language the knight used to open the Seal Stone.

"It is done."

"You can't. I never agreed to that." She was never going to see her mom or her dad again. "Damn, damn, damn," she swore softly.

Gwynn ap Nudd regarded her tear-stained face. "*Ahh, but you did. Your bargain, freely given from your own lips, was for your mother to get better and live a long happy, healthy life with your father. There was no mention of you being with them, or even of you ever leaving this place."*

"I didn't know. I didn't think it through. It's not fair. You took advantage of me!" she raged at him.

Suddenly the cavern was filled with a wondrous light and music. A tall, unbearably beautiful woman appeared beside Gwynn ap Nudd. The Mare moved beside Laurel and bowed her nose to the floor in front of the Lady. She was at once the most beautiful and terrifying thing Laurel had ever seen. Coll, Aisling, and Gort moved to stand beside her. The riderless stallion stood on Gort's right side. The Crystal Mare regarded the pair solemnly and then snorted softly as if to say it was out of her hooves.

The luminescent figure addressed the visitors to the crystal caverns.

"I am called by many names: Lady of the Lake, Great Mother Goddess, Bridget, Mary. It matters not what I am called, but what I am. I am all that was, all that is, and all that will be. I rule the light half of the year, from Beltane to Samhain, yet even while I wax, I am ever moving toward waning. I am a part of birth and of death, of fruition and harvest. My consort Cernunnos rules the dark half of the year. At Beltaine we mate, and I wax as I give birth to the light; at Samhain we mate, and I wan as I give birth to the darkness. It is all balanced, neither of us all good or all evil."

As the Lady spoke, the friends watched her change from young and fair, to middle aged, and finally to an old woman. Her image shimmered back to the beautiful, terrifying being she first manifested as.

The Lady bent her gaze on Laurel. A painful burning sensation invaded her senses, and then it was gone. The Lady smiled as she looked at Coll who seemed very relieved the bee buzzing he worried about finally resolved itself into words he could understand. Her presence made it possible for the humans to hear when the Shining Ones spoke. When the Lady came to Gort and GogMagog, she paused and frowned. The big crystal horse trembled and then steadied as Gort laid his hand on his cheek.

"We'll speak of this in a moment," she promised the two darkly.

The Lady turned her face to Gwynn ap Nudd. "The bargain was ill made," she informed him. "The Daughter of Eve came at my call not yours."

"Yet where were you when she arrived?" he answered coolly. "She came first to me."

The Lady looked purposefully at the Mare.

"I couldn't interfere," the Mare spoke quietly. "She invoked her free will, and I could not interfere." She stamped her hoof which set off an angry bell-like sound. "Gwynn ap Nudd pushed her to bargain too quickly."

"And yet she was eager for the bargain," Gwynn ap Nudd returned easily. "I wish to claim my part of the bargain."

It was true she bargained, bargained without asking the price first, without spelling the terms out exactly as she wanted it to turn out. She sighed and a strange calmness and sense of the inevitable settled around her. A bargain was a bargain, no matter how ill made.

Laurel stepped forward toward the Lady on trembling legs.

"He's right; I did make a bargain with him. Stupid as it was. If he will keep his half of the bargain, I will keep mine." Her voice broke on the last word, but she squeezed it out.

Gwynn ap Nudd smiled a terrible smile of invitation. "Come ride with me then, Daughter of Eve."

Her friends finally understood what it was Laurel's bargain involved; they all spoke at once in a babble of voices.

"Laurel you can't," cried Coll. "Your mom wouldn't want you to. I bet she would rather die than have you give up your life for her."

Aisling held her hands to her mouth and just kept whispering, "No, no, no." Her small dark friends tried to comfort her while sending poisonous looks at Gwynn ap Nudd.

Gort and GogMagog stepped up beside her as one and looked Gwynn ap Nudd straight in the eye.

"Take me instead," Gort told him firmly.

"And me," said GogMagog.

Gwynn ap Nudd laughed at GogMagog. "I can't take you, you idiot. You're an immortal, but I could take your friend," he added thoughtfully.

"Then take my immortality as well." GogMagog turned to the Lady. "Gort and I are as one. I am his charger; he is my knight. We are two parts of a whole such as we have not seen in eons. We are mortal and immortal, the light of the sky and dark of the earth, fire and water, both endless life and endless death. In me, he is born again in fire; in him, I die in water, and yet we are both reborn as we die because we are one." GogMagog paused to place his nose on Gort's cheek. "I offer you this, if you will release the Daughter of Eve from your bargain. The Lady will make it so if I ask."

The Lady nodded her head, although she didn't appear happy about it.

"The bargain is mine, and I intend to keep it. I love all of you for offering to help, but the bargain is mine to keep."

Laurel looked straight at Gwynn ap Nudd. "But first, you will show me you have kept your part. Bring my mother here to me. Let me speak to her and see she is well, hear it from her own lips."

"Can you tell me if it is real, or if he is playing tricks?" she asked the Mare and the Lady.

Both nodded.

"Then show me!" she challenged Gwynn ap Nudd.

Gwynn ap Nudd rolled his eyes, made some movements with his hands, and spoke in the strange language. The air shimmered between them, and then her mother stepped through the veil. She looked around her in confusion and astonishment for a moment. Seeing Laurel, she gathered her in her arms in a quick swoop.

"Oh, baby girl. I prayed I'd get to see you one more time. There just wasn't time to get you back from Sarie's." Her mom hugged her tight. "I'm going to miss you so much."

"Mom, you're not going to die. You're going to live a long, happy, healthy life with Dad. He promises." Laurel indicated Gwynn ap Nudd with a nod of her head.

"Who are you?" Her mom addressed Gwynn ap Nudd.

"For all intents and purposes in your world, I am Death."

"Why are you willing not to take me?" she asked, distrust plain on her face.

"Because Anna Dara Rowan," Gwynn ap Nudd used her mom's full name, "your daughter has offered herself in your place."

Laurel's mom looked her full in the face. "Is that true? Did you actually make a deal with this creature?"

"Careful now," Gwynn interjected. "I prefer God, or at least Greater Being, to creature."

The Lady snorted through her nose in derision, and the Mare stamped her hoof again.

"I did," Laurel answered. "I didn't exactly mean to trade him me for you, but that's what I did."

Anna turned on the Lady in anger. "You *let* her do this? She's a child!"

The Lady raised her shoulders in regret. "She invoked Free Will. Our hands were tied." She indicated herself and the Mare.

"Well, I *don't* allow it," Anna shouted turning on Gwynn ap Nudd. "You will take me and not her. I have lived a full life even it is a short one. You *will not* take my baby!"

Her voice rang against the walls of the cavern sending crystal notes flying every which way. The crystal horses whinnied loudly as sparks and streamers of color flamed from every corner and crevice of the chamber. "That's *my* Free Will!" Power flared and darted.

"Enough!" The Lady raised her arms and every one fell silent.

The echoes of the wild music still rang through the hollow hill and were heard in the town below. The crystal horses shifted uneasily; their knights drew their swords and moved to stand with Laurel. All of them bowed to Gort and GogMagog as they passed.

"It appears sides have been drawn Gwynn ap Nudd." The Lady looked at the mass of her crystal army aligned with Laurel and her friends.

"So it would appear," he answered easily.

"Since Anna," the Lady inclined her head briefly to her, "refuses to go along with the bargain and challenges it, you have a problem Gwynn ap Nudd. How will you fulfill your side of the bargain?"

Gwynn ap Nudd was simply vibrating with frustration. Laurel heard his thoughts, though he spoke no words out loud. *The Daughter of Eve tricked me somehow, but I'm not even sure how. I'm so close to winning, taking someone young was so much sweeter than someone older. The young cling so tenaciously to life.*

"I'll take them instead then." Gwynn ap Nudd indicated Gort and GogMagog. "They offered freely. The woman and child can live."

"No. Not Gort! The bargain was mine to keep."

Laurel wound her left hand tightly into the Mare's mane. The crystal colors reflected on her face and in her eyes, coursed through her carrying renewed strength and conviction. The Mare leaned lightly into her for support and stamped her hooves making the chamber chime with the deep thrum of war drum and the belling of a stag.

"Will you fight them all?" The Lady asked Gwynn ap Nudd, indicating the array of crystal horses and knights with drawn swords.

Laurel's friends closed around them in a tight circle with the Mare on the left and Gort and the shimmering stallion flanking them on the right. They presented an unbreakable united front to those who would oppose them.

Gwynn ap Nudd regarded them for a moment and answered, "If I must. I hate to break a bargain."

Music swelled and colors flowed as the crystal army shifted at his words. With a loud crack, like thunder, or the mighty crashing of fighting stags, a large figure stepped out of the flowing colors. He was huge and powerful with strong thick legs and large hands. His eyes were the brown of woodland streams, tangled in his hair were leaves bearing both the green of spring and the gold and red of autumn, the hair on his arms as rough as bark. Most astounding and majestic were the antlers rising from his brow. They glowed in the light of the cave and leant him even more size, as if he needed it.

"Cernunnos," the Lady greeted him, "come to weigh in on this issue?"

"It would seem you are in need of a mediator," he answered her, his voice deep and bell-like.

"It appears to me you have lost Gwynn ap Nudd," Cernunnos intoned. "You can't keep the bargain by taking more than was bargained for in the beginning. In this case a Daughter of Eve. You can't take a Son of Adam and an immortal instead. Neither is the object of the bargain," he smiled at Anna, "willing to go along with it. Which I admit is most unusual; mortals usually jump at a second chance at life."

Gwynn ap Nudd deflated and resignation crossed his face. "Oh, fine then. Let the Daughter of Eve renege on her bargain," he said crossly.

"Yet she does not renege," Cernunnos reminded him. "She was willing to pay the price of her bargain."

"Well, Daughter of Eve, what shall I do with you?" Cernunnos regarded her with kindly eyes. "It seems you have gathered an army without even asking."

Laurel trembled at the depth and wisdom in his eyes. She saw the circle of the wheel; the harvest and the death, which comes with winter so the spring can be reborn. The endless cycle of the stars and the sun and moon, the tides and the magic and the mystery lying hidden even in a winter field.

"Do what you want, as long as Mom is okay."

Her mother's fingers tightened on her shoulder. "I will not trade my daughter's life for mine. It is Laurel who must be allowed to return to the world of the living."

Cernunnos looked across at the Lady and smiled. "I leave it your good judgment." He bowed to Her, his antlers dipping low. "I will meet with you again soon," he promised her. "Farewell, Children of the Sky, we too shall meet again, though not soon I think."

Laurel smiled at him, watched entranced as he took a step sideways and disappeared with a swirl of music and the far off belling of stag. When she looked for Gwynn ap Nudd, he was gone as well.

The Lady came forward and smiled at them. "Such love as this is written in the tales and myths. You have both chosen Death selflessly to spare the other with no hidden reservations or conditions."

The Lady stepped closer still and laid her hands one on Laurel's head and one on her mom's. The Lady's voice deepened and expanded to fill the whole chamber, indeed the whole universe.

"Because you have chosen Death freely, so I will grant you Life."

Power surged through her; the cavern rang with skirls of music and colors danced and swooped around them. Somewhere the stag was belling and she saw in her mind's eye the lines of light glow and pulse brighter. The light blinded her, and the Lady was gone. She sagged against her mom.

Laurel's mom seemed to waver with the light. "I have to go, baby girl."

"But the Lady said you'd be okay now," Laurel's voice quavered as she tried not to cry.

"I will be," her mom assured her. "I have to go back to my own body now and get better so we can bring you home. I've been here too long as it is."

There was a shining silver cord attached to her mom; it wound up through the chamber and out the ceiling. Her mom looked up at it and smiled.

"All I have to do is follow it home. I'm so proud of you, sweetie. I will see you soon." Her mom vanished—there one minute and gone the next.

The Crystal Mare moved under Laurel's hand, and she realized her left hand was still entwined in her mane.

"Time to journey back." The words chimed.

"Will I see you again?"

"Oh, yes, my dear. Look for me in your pony's eyes and on the star paths."

Laurel spoke to all the crystal horses and knights who championed her.

"I don't know how to thank you for what you did. I'm honored by you."

"We will see you home safely. Farewell, Laurel, we will meet again," they answered as one.

The next thing she saw was the wise eyes of the Seal Stone and felt his blessing on her as she passed out of the Tor. In a blink of an eye, she was sitting against the Men an Tol in the World of the Sky feeling more tired than she could ever remember feeling. Aisling and Coll were sprawled in the grass beside her. It was still night, and the moon was just past the zenith.

We can't have been gone very long at all. It only seemed like forever. She looked over at Coll and Aisling as they both struggled into upright positions.

"Did we dream it?" Laurel asked them. "Do you remember going into the hill and the crystal horses and Gwynn ap Nudd? Was it real?"

Because if it was real, her mom was going to be okay. Away across the ocean her mom was waking up and was going to be okay.

"Yeah," Coll said, "your mom was there and the creepy guy and the big guy with the antlers."

"And the piskies," Aisling's voice rang with wonder. "I met piskies and knockers and all kinds of magics. They're my friends now. I can meet them here or at any of the Stones."

“My mom is going to be okay. I can’t wait for my dad to call and tell me. Gort,” Laurel called. “Where do you think Gort is?” she asked looking all around the Stone. “Did we lose him somehow?”

“Bloody Hell,” Coll swore. “You don’t think he stayed there do you, what with him always talking about his knights and his bloody crystal caves and King Arthur? I should never have got him started with all that.”

“Oh, no,” Aisling cried. . “He would have stayed if he couldn’t bring the crystal horse with him. I think the horse promised Gort he could be his knight or something. That’s what the little people told me.”

“Bother and damn!” Laurel exclaimed, borrowing a phrase she heard Sarie use when she was frustrated. “How do we get him back now?”

She searched the sky and the Men an Tol with her eyes. There were no crystal knights to guide them and no horses anywhere, crystal or otherwise.

Entwined in the fingers of her left hand was a bunch of long hairs. Except they weren’t ordinary hairs—these glimmered and shone like spun glass. “Or crystal,” Laurel whispered the thought out loud. Wound around her fingers were crystal hairs from the Mare’s mane. She gathered them and braided them together into a talisman she could carry with her. The colors blazed in the moonlight before fading to become ordinary black horse hair.

“Look for me in your pony’s eyes.” The Mare’s voice sounded softly. Laurel tucked the hairs safely in the pocket of her jeans. She raised her eyes to look at Coll and Aisling.

“What do we do now?” Aisling asked in a small voice.

“I don’t know,” Coll said hopelessly.

“Should we head back to Sarie’s, or wait for, I don’t know, the moon to set or something?”

“He can’t just be *gone,*” Aisling’s voice raised on the last word, and tears streamed down her cheeks.

“This wasn’t part of the bargain,” Laurel shouted at the sky. “Gwynn ap Nudd, you answer me right now!”

“Bloody Hell,” Coll yelled at her. “Watch who you call down on us.”

She glared at him, tears starting in her own eyes. "Gort wasn't part of my bargain at all."

"Maybe he made a bargain of his own with someone and didn't tell us," Coll said.

"Maybe he did," Aisling agreed. "GogMagog was the realization of all Gort's dreams. Maybe he would rather stay there with him instead of coming back with us."

"But what happens here?" Laurel wondered. "Do people just forget he existed?"

"I'll never forget him," Aisling said firmly. "If he never comes back, every year on this night, I'll come here to the Men an Tol and remember him."

"Me, too," Coll vowed.

"I'll never forget him. Let's wait here for sunrise. A few more hours can't hurt." *And maybe Gort will show up,* she finished silently.

All three of them huddled together against the Men an Tol, sharing some tea from the flask they left in the grass with their packs. Without speaking, they watched the stars move across the sky and the moonlight fade toward the dawn. By the time the darkness heralding the beginning of dawn arrived, they were all fast asleep like a tangle of puppies.

Laurel woke to the sound of a pony tearing grass beside her; sleepily she reached out thinking it was Lamorna. She came wide awake, as she remembered the events of the night before. Her eyes snapped open, and she looked in astonishment at a horse she didn't know. Startled, she tried to jump up and see who was here, but Coll and Aisling were all entwined with her limbs so all she did was wake them up, too.

"Bout time you woke up, my beauties." A familiar voice rang across the moor.

Laurel scrambled to her feet along with Coll and Aisling. Aisling got there first and hugged Gort, who was leaning on the Men an Tol.

"Where were you?" Aisling demanded. "Do you know how worried we were?"

"Who's the horse?" Coll wanted to know. The horse regarded Coll with a steady gaze. "When and how did you get back here?" Laurel questioned.

"Isn't that a story, just?" Gort crowed. "Wait till you hear! The seal guardian asked me to bring this back to you." Gort handed Laurel Vear Du's talisman which she took and shoved in her pocket.

Voices carried on the morning breeze: Sarie, Emily, and Aisling's parents were making their way along the track to the Men an Tol.

"Laurel," Sarie's voice carried across the gorse. "Your dad called late last night and we had to wait til this morning to get out here and check on you. I've wonderful news. It looks like your mom is going to be okay, she started to respond to the new treatment."

"We did it; we did it!"

Laurel wrapped her arms through the hole in the Men an Tol and hugged it and kissed the top of the sun warm stone.

"Thank you," she whispered. "Thank you."

The End

Appendix

Gramma Bella's Letters

August 12, 1964
Dearest Sarie,
The trip has been awful. It stormed the whole way across the Atlantic, or at least it felt that way. I miss you and Cornwall so much. I'm afraid to ask, but I must. Have you been to Seal Rock, have you seen him? I never knew that missing someone could hurt so much. I arrived in Halifax, Nova Scotia four days ago and am now on a train headed west. I will post this letter from Toronto, when we arrive there later today.

I am well but seem to have picked up a bit of a flu as my stomach has been queasy of late. No matter, I'm sure it will be right as rain in no time. I will write with an address as soon as I reach Alberta. I hope the man that Da has chosen for me is kind and hopefully not too old. I will be in touch as soon as I can.

Love,
Bella

September 3, 1964
Dearest Sarie,
I am looking out the window of the train at miles and miles of wheat fields. They call them the Great Plains. It is hard to fathom how very large they are; the wheat goes on forever and ever. We left Winnipeg, Manitoba this morning, and since we have been traveling for hours past endless vistas of wheat, just land and sky. Occasionally, at small towns, there are high thin buildings that the conductor told me are for storing grain to wait for the train to come and take it to market. The prairies are kind of like the moors at home.

I know I just wrote to you a few days ago, but I miss you so much and writing to you helps me feel closer to home. I miss the sea; it is very dry here. The heat shimmers over the fields, and even the wind is dry and hot. I think there is a stop in Regina this afternoon. Regina is in a province they call Saskatchewan. Such strange sounding names to my ears! If you see him, tell him I miss him, please. Please take good care of Ebon; you know how she likes bread crusts with sugar. I miss her, too. I hope there will be a horse for me to ride once I reach this ranch in Alberta. It is near some place called Pincher Creek. I will write soon with a return address.

Love,
Bella

October 31, 1964

Dearest Sarie,

Sorry I have been so long out of touch. I have been here almost a month now. Strange how it seems both longer and shorter than that! D'Arcy, the man Da picked for me, met me at the train station and brought me here to this ranch. He raises cattle and some grain.

We were married a week ago yesterday. It is not how I imagined my wedding would be.

Sorry, about the blotches on the paper, I am just so sad. My husband is as kind as he can be to me, but he does not understand how I can be so homesick when there are so many things to keep me busy. I cook and bake for my husband and his ranch hands, a score of them, all told. And I do laundry for my husband and his foreman. The other hands take care of their own. They measure the land in "sections" here. A section has four quarters; each quarter is one hundred sixty acres. My husband owns thirty sections. The size is beyond my comprehension. Miles and miles of prairie and no hope of ever seeing the sea again.

I have some news that is good and bad at the same time. I am with child! My husband is very happy; however, I have not told him that I am three months gone in my confinement. This baby has a Cornish father. If you are out at Seal Rock and see him, please tell him I carry part of him with me. I think my husband suspects the child is not his, but as long as I hold up my end of the bargain and keep house for him and let others believe the child is his, he will not cast me out. Oh, if only he would cast me out! I could go home to Penzance. I must go now as I need to start the bread for supper.

I have written the return address on the outside of the envelope. Please write soon.

As always,

Bella

May 7, 1965

Dearest Sarie,

Thank you so much for going out to Seal Rock and looking for him. Maybe if you try again at the fullness of the moon, we will have better luck. I had the baby yesterday. He has black hair like his father and fortunately, like my husband. I have named him Colton Douglas. Colton after my husband's father and Douglas after the baby's father. In Gaelic it means black or dark water, quite fitting I think. My husband seems quite happy to have a little son to teach ranching to and is putting about the story that first babies are often early. One of the young neighbor girls has come to help me with the baby and cook and clean for the men until I am up and about. I am dreadfully tired still. I will write more in a few days. I wonder if my son will be like his father. Ask Vear what he thinks if you find him.

Love,
Bella

July 10, 1965

Dearest Sarie,

I just received your post today. I feel so out of touch with you, it takes so long for the mail to go between us. I am glad that Ebon is doing well at your place. You said you had talked to Vear Du, how is he? Does he miss me? Is he happy about our baby? What a silly question to ask when there is no chance of Vear every seeing his son. I am enclosing a picture of Colton, could you please leave it for Vear in his cave by Seal Rock? If you put it inside his can of pipe tobacco, he will find it next time he is there. I must try harder to forget and live for today instead of dreaming of the past and what could have been. I have Colton to live for now, otherwise I think I would just fade away with longing to be home. D'Arcy is kind to me, but I don't love him, and I don't see how he could expect me to. He was Da's choice not mine. I could run away with Colton and try to come home, but I am too afraid and weak of spirit. And to be most practical, what can Vear Du offer me and Colton? He is what he is, and I knew that from the start. Love has a way of making us blind to what we don't want to see. Even knowing what I do now, I don't regret a second of the time I had with Vear. I will write again when I am more cheerful and can fill the page with happy thoughts.

Love,

Bella

May 15, 1966

Dearest Sarie,

It hardly seems possible that Colton is a year old now. We had a lovely party for his birthday. D'Arcy bought me a new dress and bonnet for the occasion. Colton took his first steps the other day. He is growing up to be quite the little man. So far no sign that he has his father's unique ability, which is probably a good thing, as there is no water here except in the sloughs for the cattle and the small creek that runs near the house. Thank you for leaving Colton's picture for Vear Du. I still miss him but not as painfully as before. They say time heals all wounds; I pray fervently that this is so. I have had no word from Da since I got here. I did send a letter and a picture of his grandson, but he has not found it in his heart to answer me. I hope he is well. How are you faring, Sarie? Has that young man from Paul been around to see you lately? His name was Simon, was it not? I wish only good things for you and wish we could be closer and have our babies play together while we gossip and sip our tea. Sometimes when the wind is howling around the eaves of the house at night, I think I can hear the ocean pounding on the cliffs out by Land's End. I try not to think too hard about that, or it makes me cry. I hear Colton getting up from his nap, so I will close. Please write soon.

As Ever,
Bella

June 21, 1985

Dearest Sarie,

It seems so hard to believe that my little Colton is getting married! I feel like it was only yesterday he was tagging along at my knee and learning to ride his first pony. Now I see a young man before me. He has Vear Du's dark eyes, and his hair falls over his face like a horse's forelock. Just like Vear. Colton's bride is lovely girl, and I think they shall do very well together. I wish you could come for the wedding. It has been so many years since we have been together, but I understand why you can't. I will send you lots of pictures and describe it so you can imagine that you are here. I have a beautiful cornflower blue dress and hat for the wedding and a wonderful lavender one for the gift opening the day after the wedding. I am so proud of Colton and the young man he has become. I am also glad he was able to choose his bride for love and not convenience. D'Arcy has been very good to me, and although I do love him, it is not that great romantic love of my life that you and I used to dream about when we picnicked on the moors with our ponies. Colton's bride has picked soft pink and ivory roses for her bouquet and also for the tables. They are getting married on our back lawn under an arbor of ivy and roses. D'arcy's mother will play the wedding march. Colton looks so handsome in his suit and best black hat that I think my heart will burst with love and pride. Sometimes it seems like my childhood in Cornwall is all a lovely dream that happened to someone else. But I have only to look into Colton's eyes to know that it was true, and I did not dream it. I will write soon and send photos.

Love,

Bella

December 15, 1995

Dearest Sarie,

I have a granddaughter! Colton and Anna have named her Laurel, so she has the names of two sacred trees. Laurel Rowan. She is perfect in every way, and she has her father's eyes and her mother's hair. D'Arcy dotes on her. As you know D'Arcy is much older than I, and his health is not good. Colton will be taking over the management of the ranch, but we will wait until after D'Arcy is gone. It would break D'arcy's heart to leave this house, and it is the least I can do to grant him this small comfort. There is a beautiful little house behind the main house where I have my wonderful garden. I will move there once D'Arcy has passed on. Colton and Anna will have the main house, and I hope they fill it with children! I will be the wildly eccentric Gramma Bella and bake cookies and goodies for my grandchildren and their friends. I have enclosed a photo of Laurel; it was taken just a few hours after she was born. Just think soon I can look for a pony for her. Anna says I am rushing things, but it takes a long time to find a good pony. Maybe, I can find the time and money to come and visit you. It has been far too long, and I still miss the moors of Cornwall after all these years. I know I can never go back to the way things were when we were young, but maybe we can make new beginnings in our old age.

I will write again soon. With more photos! It was so nice to speak to you on the telephone last week. Just like old times.

Love,
Bella

September 29, 2000

Dearest Sarie,

Well, the worst thing that I could imagine has happened. Colton found out that D'Arcy was not his biological father. He found an old journal of mine that I kept in the first few years of my marriage. I was so lonely and sad, and I used the journal to help keep me sane. Colton was livid with me for keeping such a secret from him; even worse, he was horrified when he realized who and what his biological father was. Anna tried to calm him and cool his rage. If anything, Anna seems more ready to believe the truth about Vear Du than my son is. There has always been something slightly fey about Anna; maybe that is why Colton chose her without realizing it.

Colton has told me he wants me off the ranch. D'Arcy left it to Colton in his will but failed to include any stipulations about my residency for the rest of my life. I have no recourse legally, though I am sure D'Arcy never figured on Colton being so angry. In some ways, I can't say as I blame him, but what purpose would it have served to tell him the truth? There was never a chance Vear Du could be a father to Colton, and D'Arcy loved him like he was his own. I am packing as I write this. I have five days to leave this little house. Colton has taken Anna and Laurel to Waterton Lakes National Park for the week. I don't know what they plan to tell Laurel about why I have just packed up and left. I hope they are kind in what they tell her. I will miss Laurel most of all, I think. She is such a joy to me. I am moving to a small village called Bragg Creek; the address is on the envelope. I will write or call you once I have a new phone number. I thought the anguish of leaving Vear Du was the worst thing I could ever experience, but I was wrong. My heart feels as though it will burst from my chest with the immensity of the pain. I have thought about coming home to Penzance, but somehow I just can't make myself leave the same country where my son and his family are. Da is gone now, and even if I could find Vear Du, what would he do with me, a mortal woman to care for?

Perhaps in time I will feel different, just now it is all too new and raw. I know you understand Sarie. Thank you so much for your unwavering friendship and support all my life. It seems that we will be just two single old women until the end of our days. If Colton or Anna should contact you, they know that I kept in touch all these years, please let me know. Colton has sworn never to speak or lay eyes on me again, and I believe he is serious. Anna may feel differently, but she would never go against Colton's wishes out of respect for his feelings. Anna is devoted to Colton and to Laurel, and I would never wish to be the cause of any conflict. I will write again when I am settled.

Love Always,
Bella

June 20, 2001
General Delivery,
Bragg Creek, Alberta

Dearest Sarie,

Well, I am all settled into my little cabin in the trees. The creek runs through my property at the back, and I can hear it rushing along as I lay in bed at night. Early in the morning when it is quiet, I wake up and imagine that the sound of the water is the tide coming against the shingle by Vear Du's cave. I never told you before, but he comes to me in my dreams, and we talk the night away. When I am gardening or standing by Elbow Falls with the water resonating through the stone under my feet, I often feel his arm about me and his strength by my side. Like a waking dream, I know he is actually with me at these times. You were always more practical than me, and I know you are probably shaking your head at this minute as you read this. Maybe you are right, maybe it is just a trick of my mind, taking my longings and forgotten memories and forging them together. But my heart tells me, I am right in believing Vear Du can come to me here by these majestic mountains. There is magic here, strong and clear. Not the same as the magic I knew in Cornwall but magic all the same. All enchantments and magic and Light comes from the same source to comfort and guide us if we just reach out our hand. I miss Laurel more than I imagined I would, which is saying a great deal. My heart hopes Colton will have a change of mind about banishing me from his family's life, but my intellect tells me it is not very likely to happen. I have been thinking about accepting your kind offer to come and stay with you for a while. I would love to see the house in Penzance again. Do the new people look after the front garden like Da did? Something is holding me back, I'm not sure what, but I will trust my instincts and see where this new path I am on leads me.

Love Always,
Bella

March 4, 2008

Dearest Sarie,

I have the most sad news. Anna has cancer and is not doing well. She has convinced Colton it would be best for Laurel to have a change of scenery. Colton is spending all his time at the hospital, and Laurel is left with the neighbors. Colton cannot bring himself to let me look after her. Now I need to ask you a huge favor. Can

Laurel come and stay with you in Cornwall? Colton has agreed, through Anna, that it would be good for Laurel and all right with him. I used to tell Laurel stories about Penzance and the Penwith Peninsula when she was little and draw pictures of the old stones and the moors and cliffs. In the contact I had recently with Anna, she gave me a drawing Laurel did recently. It was of Roche Rock Castle; it was very good, and it made me homesick for Cornwall. Please give me a ring when you get this, so we can see if we can make it work. Laurel loves horses, and Anna says she is quite self-sufficient. Laurel does not know I am alive. Apparently Colton let her believe I am dead. I guess it was easier than explaining the real reason I had to leave. I would be eternally grateful to you Sarie if you could find it in your generous heart to help me out with this favor. Anna is hoping also that Colton will finally soften and relent enough to let me help Anna through this ordeal. I will have more details in a few days, please feel free to contact Anna directly if you wish. Do you still have the old phone number where you used to reach me? If not, I can give it to you when you call me here. My new number is 403-555-1457. I know I am a coward for not ringing you directly about this. I tell myself it is so I don't put you on the spot and expect an answer right away without giving you a chance to think on it. But I know it's just I hope so much this will work out, and this will insulate me a little bit from the disappointment if the plans don't work out.

Gratefully and love always,
Bella

Nancy M Bell is a proud Albertan and lives near Balzac, Alberta with her husband and various critters. She is a member of The Writers Union of Canada and the Writers Guild of Alberta. Nancy has numerous writing credits to her name, and her work has been published in various magazines. Laurel's Quest is her first book with Books We Love, it will be followed by A Step Beyond and December Storm.

She has also had her work recognized and honoured with various awards, and most recently, a silver medal in the Creative Writing category of the Alberta 55 Plus Summer Games in 2013. Nancy has presented at the Surrey International Writers Conference in 2012 and 2013, and at the Writers Guild of Alberta Conference in 2014. She has publishing credits in poetry, fiction and non-fiction.

Please visit her webpage http://www.nancymbell.ca
You can find her on Facebook at http://facebook.com/NancyMBell
Follow on twitter: @emilypikkasso

Manufactured by Amazon.ca
Bolton, ON

27687878R00146